MY TRUE LOVE GAVE TO ME

MY TRUE LOVE GAVE TO ME

Twelve Holiday Stories

Edited and with a Story by
STEPHANIE PERKINS

ST. MARTIN'S GRIFFIN ⚞ NEW YORK

MY TRUE LOVE GAVE TO ME. Copyright © 2014 by Stephanie Perkins. All rights reserved. Printed in the United States of America. For information, address St. Martin's Press, 175 Fifth Avenue, New York, N.Y. 10010.

"MIDNIGHTS." Copyright © 2014 by Rainbow Rowell. "THE LADY AND THE FOX." Copyright © 2014 by Kelly Link. "ANGELS IN THE SNOW." Copyright © 2014 by Matt de la Peña. "POLARIS IS WHERE YOU'LL FIND ME." Copyright © 2014 by Jenny Han. "IT'S A YULETIDE MIRACLE, CHARLIE BROWN." Copyright © 2014 by Stephanie Perkins. "YOUR TEMPORARY SANTA." Copyright © 2014 by David Levithan. "KRAMPUSLAUF." Copyright © 2014 by Holly Black. "WHAT THE HELL HAVE YOU DONE, SOPHIE ROTH?" Copyright © 2014 by Gayle Forman Inc. "BEER BUCKETS AND BABY JESUS." Copyright © 2014 by Myra McEntire. "WELCOME TO CHRISTMAS, CA." Copyright © 2014 by Kiersten Brazier. "STAR OF BETHLEHEM." Copyright © 2014 by Ally Carter. "THE GIRL WHO WOKE THE DREAMER." Copyright © 2014 by Laini Taylor.

www.stmartins.com

Designed by Anna Gorovoy

Interior illustrations by Jim Tierney

The Library of Congress Cataloging-in-Publication Data is available upon request.

ISBN 978-1-250-05930-7 (hardcover)
ISBN 978-1-4668-6389-7 (e-book)

St. Martin's Griffin books may be purchased for educational, business, or promotional use. For information on bulk purchase, please contact Macmillan Corporate and Premium Sales Department at 1-800-221-7945, extension 5442, or write specialmarkets@macmillan.com.

First Edition: October 2014

10 9 8 7 6 5 4 3 2 1

FOR JARROD, BEST FRIEND AND TRUE LOVE

CONTENTS

ACKNOWLEDGMENTS

This book was birthed over crème brûlée lattes in Charleston, South Carolina, with my dear friend, and fellow secret Hallmark Christmas movies enthusiast, Myra McEntire.

Thank you to Kate Schafer Testerman for making it happen. Thank you to Sara Goodman for understanding it *completely*. Thank you to Alicia Adkins, Angela Craft, Stephanie Davis, Olga Grlic, Bridget Hartzler, and Jeanne-Marie Hudson for additional help and support. Thank you to Jim Tierney for the perfect illustrations. And thank you, especially, to the authors for trusting me and for being crazy, incredible, talented, and kindhearted: Ally, David, Gayle, Holly, Jenny, Kelly, Kiersten, Laini, Matt, Myra, and Rainbow.

Thank you to my family. Always.

And thank you to Jarrod Perkins. Always + always x always.

MY TRUE LOVE GAVE TO ME

Midnights

Rainbow Rowell

Dec. 31, 2014, almost midnight

It was cold out on the patio, under the deck. Frigid. Dark.

Dark because Mags was outside at midnight, and dark because she was in the shadows.

This was the last place anyone would look for her—anyone, and especially Noel. She'd miss all the excitement.

Thank God. Mags should have thought of this years ago.

She leaned back against Alicia's house and started eating the Chex mix she'd brought out with her. (Alicia's mom made the best Chex mix.) Mags could hear the music playing inside, and then she couldn't—and that was a good sign. It meant that the countdown was starting.

"*Ten!*" she heard someone shout.

"Nine!" more people joined in.

"Eight!"

Mags was going to miss the whole thing.

Perfect.

Dec. 31, 2011, almost midnight

Are there nuts in that?" the boy asked.

Mags paused, holding a cracker piled with pesto and cream cheese in front of her mouth. "I think there are pine nuts . . ." she said, crossing her eyes to look at it.

"Are pine nuts tree nuts?"

"I have no idea," Mags said. "I don't think pine nuts grow on pine trees, do they?"

The boy shrugged. He had shaggy brown hair and wide-open blue eyes. He was wearing a Pokémon T-shirt.

"I'm not much of a tree-nut expert," Mags said.

"Me neither," he said. "You'd think I would be—if I accidentally eat one, it could kill me. If there were something out there that could kill you, wouldn't you try to be an expert on it?"

"I don't know. . . ." Mags shoved the cracker in her mouth and started chewing. "I don't know very much about cancer. Or car accidents."

"Yeah . . ." the boy said, looking sadly at the buffet table. He was skinny. And pale. "But tree nuts specifically have it out for me, for me *personally*. They're more like assassins than, like, possible dangers."

"Damn," Mags said, "what'd you ever do to tree nuts?"

The boy laughed. "Ate them, I guess."

The music, which had been really loud, stopped. "It's almost midnight!" somebody shouted.

They both looked around. Mags's friend Alicia, from homeroom, was standing on the couch. It was Alicia's party—the first New Year's Eve party that Mags, at fifteen, had ever been invited to.

"Nine!" Alicia yelled.

"Eight!" There were a few dozen people in the basement, and they were all shouting now.

"Seven!"

"I'm Noel," the boy said, holding out his hand.

Mags brushed all the pesto and traces of nuts off her hand and shook his. "Mags."

"Four!"

"Three!"

"It's nice to meet you, Mags."

"You, too, Noel. Congratulations on evading the tree nuts for another year."

"They almost had me with that pesto dip."

"Yeah." She nodded. "It was a close call."

Dec. 31, 2012, almost midnight

Noel fell against the wall and slid down next to Mags, then bumped his shoulder against hers. He blew a paper party horn in her direction. "Hey."

"Hey." She smiled at him. He was wearing a plaid jacket, and his white shirt was open at the collar. Noel was pale and flushed easily. Right now he was pink from the top of his forehead to the second button of his shirt. "You're a dancing machine," she said.

"I like to dance, Mags."

"I know you do."

"And I only get so many opportunities."

She raised an eyebrow.

"I like to dance *in public,*" Noel said. "With other people. It's a communal experience."

"I kept your tie safe," she said, and held out a red silk necktie. He'd been dancing on the coffee table when he threw it at her.

"Thank you," he said, taking it and slinging it around his neck. "That was a good catch—but I was actually trying to lure you out onto the dance floor."

"That was a coffee table, Noel."

"There was room for two, Margaret."

Mags wrinkled her nose, considering. "I don't think there was."

"There's always room for you with me, on every coffee table," he said. "Because you are my best friend."

"Pony is your best friend."

Noel ran his fingers through his hair. It was sweaty and curly and fell past his ears. "Pony is also my best friend. And also Frankie. And Connor."

"And your mom," Mags said.

Noel turned his grin on her. "But especially you. It's our anniversary. I can't believe you wouldn't dance with me on our anniversary."

"I don't know what you're talking about," she said. (She knew exactly what he was talking about.)

"It happened right there." Noel pointed at the buffet table where Alicia's mom always laid out snacks. "I was having an allergic reaction, and you saved my life. You stuck an epinephrine pen into my heart."

"I ate some pesto," Mags said.

"Heroically," Noel agreed.

She sat up suddenly. "You didn't eat any of the chicken salad tonight, did you? There were almonds."

"Still saving my life," he said.

"*Did* you?"

"No. But I had some fruit cocktail. I think there were strawberries in it—my mouth is all tingly."

Mags squinted at him. "Are you okay?"

Noel looked okay. He looked flushed. And sweaty. He looked like his teeth were too wide for his mouth, and his mouth was too wide for his face.

"I'm fine," he said. "I'll tell you if my tongue gets puffy."

"Keep your lewd allergic reactions to yourself," she said.

Noel wiggled his eyebrows. "You should see what happens when I eat shellfish."

Mags rolled her eyes and tried not to laugh. After a second, she looked over at him again. "Wait, what happens when you eat shellfish?"

He waved his hand in front of his chest, halfheartedly. "I get a rash."

She frowned. "*How* are you still alive?"

"Through the efforts of everyday heroes like yourself."

"Don't eat the pink salad, either," she said. "It's shrimp."

Noel flicked his red tie around her neck and smiled at her. Which was different than a grin. "Thanks."

"Thank *you*," she said, pulling the ends of the tie even and looking down at them. "It matches my sweater." Mags was wearing a giant sweater dress, some sort of Scandinavian design with a million colors.

"Everything matches your sweater," he said. "You look like a Christmas-themed Easter egg."

"I feel like a really colorful Muppet," she said. "One of the fuzzy ones."

"I like it," Noel said. "It's a feast for the senses."

She couldn't tell if he was making fun of her, so she changed the subject. "Where did Pony go?"

"Over there." Noel pointed across the room. "He wanted to get in position to be standing casually near Simini when midnight strikes."

"So he can kiss her?"

"Indeed," Noel said. "On the mouth, if all goes to plan."

"That's so gross," Mags said, fiddling with the ends of Noel's tie.

"Kissing?"

"No . . . kissing is fine." She felt herself blushing. Fortunately she wasn't as pale as Noel; it wouldn't be painted all over her face and throat. "What's gross is using New Year's Eve as an excuse to kiss someone who might want not want to kiss you. Using it as a trick."

"Maybe Simini *does* want to kiss Pony."

"Or maybe it'll be really awkward," Mags said. "And she'll do it anyway because she feels like she has to."

"He's not going to maul her," Noel said. "He'll do the eye contact thing."

"What eye contact thing?"

Noel swung his head around and made eye contact with Mags. He raised his eyebrows hopefully; his eyes went all soft and possible. It was definitely a face that said, *Hey. Is it okay if I kiss you?*

"Oh," Mags said. "That's really good."

Noel snapped out of it—and made a face that said, *Well, duh.* "Of course it's good. I've kissed girls before."

"*Have* you?" Mags asked. She knew that Noel talked to girls. But she'd never heard of him having a girlfriend. And she *would* have heard of it—she was one of Noel's four to five best friends.

"Pfft," he said. "Three girls. Eight different occasions. I think I know how to make eye contact."

That was significantly more kissing than Mags had managed in her sixteen years.

She glanced over at Pony again. He was standing near the television, studying his phone. Simini was a few feet away, talking to her friends.

"Still," Mags said, "it feels like cheating."

"How is it cheating?" Noel asked, following her eyes. "Neither of them is in a relationship."

"Not that kind of cheating," Mags said. "More like . . . skipping ahead. If you like someone, you should have to make an effort. You should have to get to know the person—you should have to *work* for that first kiss."

"Pony and Simini already know each other."

"Right," she agreed, "and they've never gone out. Has Simini ever even *indicated* that she's interested?"

"Sometimes people need help," Noel said. "I mean—look at Pony."

Mags did. He was wearing black jeans and a black T-shirt. He had a half-grown-out mohawk now, but he'd had a ponytail back in middle school, so everyone still called him that. Pony was usually loud and funny, and sometimes loud and obnoxious. He was always drawing on his arm with ink pens.

"That guy has no idea how to tell a girl he likes her," Noel said. "None at all. . . . Now, look at Simini."

Mags did. Simini was small and soft, and so shy that coming out of her shell wasn't even on the menu. If you wanted to talk to Simini, you had to climb inside her shell with her.

"Not everyone has our social graces," Noel said, sighing, and leaning into Mags's space to gesture toward Pony and Simini. "Not everyone knows how to reach out for the things they want. Maybe midnight is exactly what these two need to get rolling—would you begrudge them that?"

Mags turned to Noel. His face was just over her shoulder. He smelled warm. And like some sort of Walgreens body spray. "You're being melodramatic," she said.

"Life-or-death situations bring it out in me."

"Like coffee table dancing?"

"No, the strawberries," he said, sticking out his tongue and trying to talk around it. "Duth it look puffy?"

Mags was trying to get a good look at Noel's tongue when the music dropped out.

"It's almost midnight!" Alicia shouted, standing near the television. The countdown was starting in Times Square. Mags saw Pony look up from his phone and inch toward Simini.

"Nine!" the room shouted.

"Eight!"

"Your tongue looks fine," Mags said, turning back to Noel.

He pulled his tongue back in his mouth and smiled.

Mags raised her eyebrows. She hardly realized she was doing it. "Happy anniversary, Noel."

Noel's eyes went soft. At least, she thought they did. "Happy anniversary, Mags."

"Four!"

And then Natalie ran over, slid down the wall next to Noel, and grabbed his shoulder.

Natalie was friends with both of them, but she wasn't a *best* friend. She had caramel-brown hair, and she always wore flannel shirts that gapped over her breasts. "Happy New Year!" she shouted at them.

"Not yet," Mags said.

"One!" everyone else yelled.

"Happy New Year," Noel said to Natalie.

Then Natalie leaned toward him, and he leaned toward her, and they kissed.

Dec. 31, 2013, almost midnight

oel was standing on the arm of the couch with his hands out to Mags.

Mags was walking past him, shaking her head.

"Come on!" he shouted over the music.

She shook her head *and* rolled her eyes.

"It's our last chance to dance together!" he said. "It's our senior year!"

"We have months left to dance," Mags said, stopping at the food table to get a mini quiche.

Noel walked down the couch, stepped onto the coffee table, then stretched one long leg out as far as he could to make it onto the love seat next to Mags.

"They're playing our song," he said.

"They're playing 'Baby Got Back,'" Mags said.

Noel grinned.

"Just for that," she said, "I'm never dancing with you."

"You never dance with me anyway," he said.

"I do everything else with you," Mags whined. It was true. She studied with Noel. She ate lunch with Noel. She picked Noel up on the way to school. "I even go with you to get a haircut."

He touched the back of his hair. It was brown and thick, and fell in loose curls down to his collar. "Mags, when you don't go, they cut it too short."

"I'm not complaining," she said. "I'm just sitting this round out."

"What're you eating?" he asked.

Mags looked down at the tray. "Some kind of quiche, I think."

"Can I eat it?"

She popped another one in her mouth and mushed it around. It didn't taste like tree nuts or strawberries or kiwi fruit or shellfish. "I think so," she said. She held up a quiche, and Noel leaned over and ate it out of her fingers. Standing on the love seat, he was seven-and-a-half feet tall. He was wearing a ridiculous white suit. Three pieces. Where did somebody even find a three-piece white suit?

"S'good," he said. "Thanks." He reached for Mags's Coke, and she let him have it—then he jerked it away from his mouth and cocked his head. "Margaret. They're playing our song."

Mags listened. "Is this that Ke$ha song?"

"Dance with me. It's our anniversary."

"I don't like dancing with a bunch of people."

"But that's the best way to dance! Dancing is a communal experience!"

"For you," Mags said, pushing his thigh. He wavered, but didn't fall. "We're not the same person."

"I know," Noel said with a sigh. "*You* can eat tree nuts. Eat one of those brownies for me—let me watch."

Mags looked at the buffet and pointed to a plate of pecan brownies. "These?"

"Yeah," Noel said.

She picked up a brownie and took a bite. Crumbs fell on her flowered dress, and she brushed them off.

"Is it good?" he asked.

"Really good," she said. "Really dense. Moist." She took another bite.

"So unfair," Noel said, holding on to the back of the love seat and leaning farther over. "Let me see."

Mags opened her mouth and stuck out her tongue.

"Unfair," he said. "That looks delicious."

She closed her mouth and nodded.

"Finish your delicious brownie and dance with me," he said.

"The whole world is dancing with you," Mags said. "Leave me alone."

She grabbed another quiche and another brownie, then put Noel behind her.

There weren't that many places to sit in Alicia's basement; that's why Mags usually ended up on the floor. (And maybe why Noel usually ended up on the coffee table.) Pony had claimed the beanbag by the bar in the corner, and Simini was sitting on his lap. Simini smiled at Mags, and Mags smiled back and waved.

There wasn't any booze in the bar. Alicia's parents put it away whenever she had a party. All the barstools were taken, so Mags got a hand from somebody and sat up on the bar itself.

She watched Noel dance. (With Natalie. And then with Alicia and Connor. And then by himself, with his arms over his head.)

She watched everybody dance.

They had all their parties in this basement. After football games and after dances. Two years ago, Mags hadn't really known anybody in this room, except for Alicia. Now everybody here was either a best friend, or a friend, or someone she knew well enough to stay away from . . .

Or Noel.

Mags finished her brownie and watched Noel jump around.

Noel was her very best friend—even if she wasn't his. Noel was her *person*.

He was the first person she talked to in the morning, and the last person she texted at night. Not intentionally or methodically. That's just the way it was between them. If she didn't tell Noel about something, it was almost like it didn't happen.

They'd been tight ever since they ended up in journalism class together, the second semester of sophomore year. (*That's* when they should celebrate their friendiversary—not on New Year's Eve.) And then they signed up for photography and tennis together.

They were so tight, Mags went with Noel to prom last year, even though he already had a date.

"*Obviously, you're coming with us,*" Noel said.

"*Is that okay with Amy?*"

"*Amy knows we're a package deal. She probably wouldn't even like me if I wasn't standing right next to you.*"

(Noel and Amy never went out again after prom. They weren't together long enough to break up.)

Mags was thinking about getting another brownie when someone suddenly turned off the music, and someone else flickered the lights. Alicia ran by the bar, shouting, "It's almost midnight!"

"Ten!" Pony called out a few seconds later.

Mags glanced around the room until she found Noel again— standing on the couch. He was already looking at her. He stepped onto the coffee table in Mags's direction and grinned, wolfishly. All of Noel's grins were a little bit wolfish: he had way too many teeth. Mags took a breath that shook on the way out. (Noel was her *person*.)

"Eight!" the room shouted.

Noel beckoned her with his hand.

Mags raised an eyebrow.

He waved at her again and made a face that said, *Come on, Mags.*

"Four!"

Then Frankie stepped onto the coffee table with Noel and slung an arm around his shoulders.

"Three!"

Noel turned to Frankie and grinned.

"Two!"

Frankie raised her eyebrows.

"One!"

Frankie leaned up into Noel. And Noel leaned down into Frankie. And they kissed.

Dec. 31, 2014, about nine p.m.

Mags hadn't seen Noel yet this winter break. His family went to Walt Disney World for Christmas.

It's 80 degrees, he texted her, *and I've been wearing mouse ears for 72 hours straight.*

Mags hadn't seen Noel since August, when she went over to his house early one morning to say good-bye before his dad drove him to Notre Dame.

Noel didn't come home for Thanksgiving; plane tickets were too expensive.

She'd seen photos he posted of other people online. (People from his residence hall. People at parties. Girls.) And she and Noel had texted. They'd texted a lot. But Mags hadn't seen him since August—she hadn't heard his voice since then.

Honestly, she couldn't remember it. She couldn't remember ever thinking about Noel's voice before. Whether it was deep and rumbled. Or high and smooth. She couldn't remember what Noel sounded like—or what he looked like, not in motion. She could only see his face in the dozens of photos she still had saved on her phone.

You're going to Alicia's, yeah? he'd texted her yesterday. He was in an airport, on his way home.

Where else would I go? Mags texted back.

Cool.

Mags got to Alicia's early and helped her clean out the basement, then helped Alicia's mom frost the brownies. Alicia was home from college in South Dakota; she had a tattoo on her back now of a meadowlark.

Mags didn't have any new tattoos. She hadn't changed at all. She hadn't even left Omaha—she got a scholarship to study industrial design at one of the schools in town. A full scholarship. It would have been stupid for Mags to leave.

Nobody showed up for the party on time, but everybody showed up. "Is Noel coming?" Alicia asked, when the doorbell had stopped ringing.

How would I know? Mags wanted to say. But she did know. "Yeah, he's coming," she said. "He'll be here." She'd gotten a little chocolate on the sleeve of her dress. She tried to scrape it off with her fingernail.

Mags had changed three times before she settled on this dress.

She was going to wear a dress that Noel had always liked, gray with deep red peonies—but she didn't want him to think that she hadn't had a single original thought since the last time she saw him.

So she'd changed. Then changed again. And ended up in this one, a cream-colored lace shift that she'd never worn before, with baroque-patterned pink and gold tights.

She stood in front of her bedroom mirror, staring at herself. At her dark brown hair. Her thick eyebrows and blunt chin. She tried to see herself the way Noel would see her, for the first time since August. Then she tried to pretend she didn't care.

Then she left.

She got halfway to her car, then ran back up to her room to put on the earrings Noel had given her last year for her eighteenth birthday—angel wings.

Mags was talking to Pony when Noel finally arrived. Pony was in school in Iowa, studying engineering. He'd grown his hair back out into a ponytail, and Simini was tugging on it just because it made her happy. She was studying art in Utah, but she was probably going to transfer to Iowa. Or Pony was going to move to Utah. Or they were going to meet in the middle. "What's in the middle?" Pony said. "Nebraska? Shit, honey, maybe we should move home."

Mags felt it when Noel walked in. (He came in through the back door, and a bunch of cold air came in with him.)

She looked up over Pony's shoulder and saw Noel, and Noel saw her—and he strode straight through the basement, over the love seat and up onto the coffee table and over the couch and through Pony and Simini, and wrapped his arms around Mags, swinging her in a circle.

"Mags!" Noel said.

"Noel," Mags whispered.

Noel hugged Pony and Simini, too. And Frankie and Alicia and Connor. And everybody. Noel was a hugger.

Then he came back to Mags and pinned her against the wall, crowding her as much as hugging her. "Oh, God, Mags," he said. "Never leave me."

"I never left you," she said to his chest. "I never go anywhere."

"Never let me leave you," he said to the top of her head.

"When do you go back to Notre Dame?" she asked.

"Sunday."

Noel was wearing wine-colored pants (softer than jeans, rougher than velvet), a blue-on-blue striped T-shirt, and a gray jacket with the collar turned up.

He was as pale as ever.

His eyes were as wide and as blue.

But his hair was cut short: buzzed over his ears and up the back, with long brown curls spilling out over his forehead. Mags brought her hand up to the back of his head. It felt like something was missing.

"You should have come with me, Margaret," he said. "The young woman who attacked me couldn't stop herself."

"No," she said, rubbing Noel's scalp. "It looks good. It suits you."

Everything was the same, and everything was different.

Same people. Same music. Same couches.

But they'd all grown apart for four months, and in wildly different directions.

Frankie brought beer and hid it under the couch, and Natalie was drunk when she got there. Connor brought his new college boyfriend, and everyone hated him—and Alicia kept trying to pull Connor aside to tell him so. The basement seemed more crowded than usual, and there wasn't as much dancing. . . .

There was about as much dancing as there would be at a normal party—at somebody else's party. *Their* parties used to be *different*. They used to be twenty-five people in a basement who knew each other so well, they never had to hold back.

Noel didn't dance tonight. He stuck with Pony and Simini and Frankie. He stuck by Mags's side, like he was glued there.

She was so glad that she and Noel hadn't stopped texting—that she still knew what he woke up worried about. Everybody else's inside jokes were seven months old, but Noel and Mags hadn't missed a beat.

Noel took a beer when Frankie offered him one. But when Mags rolled her eyes, he handed it to Pony.

"Is it weird being in Omaha?" Simini asked her. "Now that everybody's left?"

"It's like walking through the mall after it closes," Mags said. "I miss you guys so much."

Noel startled. "Hey," he said to Mags, pulling on her sleeve.

"What?"

"Come here, come here—come with me."

He was pulling her away from their friends, out of the basement, up the stairs. When they got to the first floor, he said, "Too far, can't hear the music."

"What?"

They went down the stairs again and stopped midway, and Noel switched places with her, so she was standing on the higher step. "Dance with me, Mags, they're playing our song."

Mags tipped her head. "'A Thousand Years'?"

"It's our actual song," he said. "Dance with me."

"How is this our song?" she asked.

"It was playing when we met," Noel said.

"When?"

"When we met," he said, rolling his hand, like he was hurrying her along.

"When we met *here*?"

"Yes. When we met. Downstairs. Sophomore year. And you saved my life."

"I never saved your life, Noel."

"Why do you always ruin this story?"

"You remember the song that was playing when we met?"

"I always remember the song that's playing," he said. "All the time."

That was true, he did. All Mags could think to say now was, "What?"

Noel groaned.

"I don't like to dance," she said.

"You don't like to dance *in front of people,*" he said.

"That's true."

"Just a minute." Noel sighed and ran downstairs. "Don't go anywhere," he shouted up to her.

"I never go anywhere!" she shouted back.

She heard the song start over.

Then Noel was running back up the stairs. He stood on the step below her and held up his hands. "Please."

Mags sighed and lifted up her hands. She wasn't sure what to do with them . . .

Noel took one of her hands in his and put her other hand on his shoulder, curling his arm around her waist. "Jesus Christ," he said, "was that so hard?"

"I don't know why this is so important to you," she said. "Dancing."

"I don't know why it's so important to you," he said. "Not to dance with me."

She was a little bit taller than him like this. They were swaying.

Alicia's mom came down the stairs. "Hey, Mags. Hey, Noel—how's Notre Dame?"

Noel pulled Mags closer to let Mrs. Porter squeeze by. "Good," he said.

"You guys really fell asleep against Michigan."

"I'm not actually on the football team," Noel said.

"That's no excuse," Mrs. Porter said.

Noel didn't loosen his grip after Alicia's mom was past them. His arm was all the way around Mags's waist now, and their stomachs and chests were pressed together.

They'd touched a lot, over the years, as friends. Noel liked to touch. Noel hugged. And tickled and pulled hair. Noel pulled people into his lap. He apparently kissed anyone who raised their eyebrows at him on New Year's Eve. . . .

But Noel had never held Mags like this.

Mags had never felt his belt buckle in her hip. She'd never tasted his breath.

Mrs. Porter came back up the stairs, and Noel held Mags even tighter.

"A Thousand Years" began again.

"Did you tell somebody to start it over?" Mags asked.

"I put it on repeat," he said. "They'll stop it when they notice."

"Was this on the *Twilight* sound track?"

"Dance with me, Mags."

"I am," she said.

"I know," he said. "Don't stop."

"Okay." Mags had been holding herself rigid, so that she'd still be standing upright, even if Noel let go. She stopped that now. She relaxed into his grip and let her arm slide over his shoulder. She touched the back of his hair again because she wanted to—because it was still missing.

"You don't like it," he said.

"I do like it," she said. "It's different."

"You're different."

Mags made a face that said, *You're crazy.*

"You are," Noel said.

"I'm exactly the same," she said. "I'm the only one who's the same."

"You're the most different."

"How?"

"I don't know," he said. "It's like we all left, and you let go—and *you're* the one who drifted away."

"That's bananas," Mags said. "I talk to you every day."

"It's not enough," he said. "I've never seen this dress before."

"You don't like my dress?"

"No." Noel shook his head. She wasn't used to seeing him like this. Agitated. "I like it. It's pretty. But it's different. You're different. I feel like I can't get close enough to you." He pushed his forehead into hers.

She pushed back. "We're pretty close, Noel."

He sighed, frustrated, and it filled her nose and mouth. "Why don't you have a boyfriend?"

Mags frowned. "Maybe I do."

He looked devastated and pulled his head back. "You wouldn't tell me something like that?"

"No," she said, "no—Noel, of course, I would. I'd tell you. I just don't know what you want me to say. I don't know why I don't have a boy-friend."

"It's going to get worse," he said. "You're going to keep changing."

"Well, so are you," she said.

"I never change."

Mags laughed. "You're a kaleidoscope. You change every time I look away."

"Don't you hate that?" he asked.

Mags shook her head. Her nose rubbed against his. "I love it."

They'd stopped swaying.

"Are we still dancing?" she asked.

"We're still dancing. Don't get any big ideas, Margaret." He let go of her hand and wrapped that arm around her, too. "Don't go anywhere."

"I never go anywhere," Mags whispered.

He shook his head like she was a liar. "You're my *best* friend," he said.

"You have lots of best friends," she said.

"No," Noel said. "Just you."

Mags held on to his neck with both arms. She pushed on his forehead. He smelled like skin.

"I can't get close enough," Noel said.

Somebody realized that the song was on repeat and skipped to the next one.

Somebody else realized that Mags and Noel were gone. Natalie came looking for Noel. "Noel! Come dance with me! They're playing our song!"

It was that Ke$ha song.

Noel pulled away from Mags. He grinned at her sheepishly. Like he'd been silly on the stairway, but she'd forgive him, wouldn't she? And there was a party downstairs, they should be at the party, right?

Noel went downstairs, and Mags followed.

The party had changed while they were gone: Everybody seemed a little bit younger again. They'd kicked off their shoes and were jumping on couches. They were singing all the words to the songs they always sang all the words to.

Noel took off his jacket and threw it to Mags. She caught it because she had good hands.

Noel looked good.

Long and pale. In dark red jeans that no one else would wear. In a T-shirt that would have hung on him last year.

He looked so good.

And she loved him so much.

And Mags couldn't do it again.

She couldn't stand across the room and watch Noel kiss someone else. Not tonight. She couldn't watch somebody else get the kiss she'd been working so hard for, since the moment they'd met.

So, a few minutes before midnight, Mags scooped up a handful of Chex mix and acted like she was going into the hall. Like maybe she was going to the bathroom. Or maybe she was going to check the filter on the furnace.

Then she slipped out the back door. No one would think to look for her outside in the snow.

It was cold, but Mags still had Noel's jacket, so she put it on. She leaned against the foundation of Alicia's house and ate Alicia's mom's Chex mix—Mrs. Porter made the best Chex mix—and listened to the music.

Then the music stopped, and the counting started.

And it was *good* that Mags was out here, because it would hurt too much to be in there. It always hurt too much, and this year, it might kill her.

"*Seven!*"

"*Six!*"

"Mags?" someone called.

It was Noel. She recognized his voice.

"Margaret?"

"*Four!*"

"Here," Mags said. Then, a little louder, "Here!" Because she was his best friend, and avoiding him was one thing, but hiding from him was another.

"*Two!*"

"Mags . . ."

She could see Noel then, in a shaft of moonlight breaking through the slats of the deck above her. His eyes had gone all soft, and he was raising his eyebrows.

"*One!*"

Mags nodded, and pushed with her shoulders away from the house, then Noel pushed her right back—pinning her as much as he was hugging her as much as he was crowding her against the wall.

He kissed her hard.

Mags hooked both arms around the back of his head, pressing their faces together, their chins and open mouths.

Noel held on to both of her shoulders.

After a few minutes—maybe more than a few minutes, after awhile—they both seemed to trust the other not to go.

They eased up.

Mags petted Noel's curls, pushing them out of his face. Noel pinned her to the wall from his hips to his shoulders, kissing her to the rhythm of whatever song was playing inside now.

When he pulled away, she was going to tell him that she loved him; when he pulled away, she was going to tell him not to let go. "Don't," Mags said, when Noel finally lifted his head.

"Mags," he whispered. "My lips are going numb."

"Then don't kiss," she said. "But don't go."

"No . . ." Noel pushed away from her, and her whole front went cold. "My lips are going numb—were you eating strawberries?"

"Oh, God," she said. "Chex mix."

"Chex mix?"

"Cashews," she said. "And probably other tree nuts."

"Ah," Noel said.

Mags was already dragging him away from the wall. "Do you have something with you?"

"Benadryl," he said. "In my car. But it makes me sleepy. I'm probably fine."

"Where are your keys?"

"In my pocket," he said, pointing at her, at his jacket. His tongue sounded thick.

Mags found the keys and kept pulling him. His car was parked on the street, and the Benadryl was in the glove compartment. Mags watched Noel take it, then stood with her arms folded, waiting for whatever came next.

"Can you breathe?" she asked.

"I can breathe."

"What usually happens?"

He grinned. "This has never happened before."

"You know what I mean."

"My mouth tingles. My tongue and lips swell up. I get hives. Do you want to check me for hives?" Wolfish.

"Then what?" she asked.

"Then nothing," he said. "Then I take Benadryl. I have an EpiPen, but I've never had to use it."

"I'm going to check you for hives," she said.

He grinned again and held out his arms. She looked at them. She lifted up his striped T-shirt. . . . He was pale. And covered in goose bumps. And there were freckles she'd never known about on his chest.

"I don't think you have hives," she said.

"I can feel the Benadryl working already." He dropped his arms and put them around her.

"Don't kiss me again," Mags said.

"Immediately," Noel said. "I won't kiss you again immediately."

She leaned into him, her temple on his chin, and closed her eyes.

"I knew you'd save my life," he said.

"I wouldn't have had to save it if I didn't almost kill you."

"Don't give yourself too much credit. It's the tree nuts who are trying to kill me."

She nodded.

They were both quiet for a few minutes.

"Noel?"

"Yeah?"

She had to ask him this—she had to make herself ask it: "Are you just being melodramatic?"

"Mags, I promise. I wouldn't fake an allergic response."

"No," she said. "With the kiss."

"There was more than one kiss. . . ."

"With all of them," she said. "Were you just—embellishing?"

Mags braced for him to say something silly.

"No," Noel said. Then, "Were you just humoring me?

"God. No," she said. "Did it feel like I was humoring you?"

Noel shook his head, rubbing his chin into her temple.

"What are we doing?" Mags asked.

"I don't know. . . ." he said eventually. "I know things have to change, but . . . I can't lose you. I don't think I get another one like you."

"I'm not going anywhere, Noel."

"You *are,*" he said, squeezing her. "And it's okay. Just . . . I need you to take me with you."

Mags didn't know what to say to that.

It was cold. Noel was shivering. She should give him his jacket.

"Mags?"

"Yeah?"

"What do *you* need?"

Mags swallowed.

In the three years she and Noel had been friends, she'd spent a lot of time pretending she didn't need anything more than what he was already giving her. She'd told herself there was a difference between wanting something and needing it. . . .

"I need you to be my person," Mags said. "I need to see you. And hear you. I need you to stay alive. And I need you to stop kissing other people just because they're standing next to you when the ball drops."

Noel laughed.

"I also need you not to laugh at me," she said.

He pulled his face back and looked at her. "No, you don't."

She kissed his chin without opening her mouth.

"You can have all those things," he said carefully. "You can have me, Mags, if you want me."

"I've always wanted you," she said, mortified by the extent to which it was true.

Noel leaned in to kiss her, and she dropped her forehead against his lips.

They were quiet.

And it was cold.

"Happy anniversary, Mags."

"Happy New Year, Noel."

The LADY and the FOX

KELLY LINK

Someone is in the garden.

"Daniel," Miranda says. "It's Santa Claus. He's looking in the window."

"No, it's not," Daniel says. He doesn't look. "We've already had the presents. Besides. No such thing as Santa."

They are together under the tree, the celebrated Honeywell Christmas tree. They are both eleven years old. There's just enough space up against the trunk to sit cross-legged. Daniel is running the train set around the tree forwards, then backwards, then forwards again. Miranda is admiring her best present, a pair of gold-handled scissors shaped like a crane. The beak is the blade. *Snip, snip,* she slices brittle needles one by one off the branch above her. A smell of pine. A small green needle rain.

It must be very cold outside in the garden. The window shines with frost. It's long past bedtime. If it isn't Santa Claus, it could be a burglar come to steal someone's jewels. Or an axe murderer.

Or else, of course, it's one of Daniel's hundreds of uncles or cousins. Because there isn't a beard, and the face in the window isn't a jolly face. Even partially obscured by darkness and frost, it has that Honeywell look to it. The room is full of adult Honeywells talking about the things that Honeywells always talk about, which is to say everything, horses and houses and God and grouting, tanning salons and—of course—theater. Always theater. Honeywells like to talk. When Honeywells have no lines to speak, they improvise. All the world's a stage.

Rare to see a Honeywell in isolation. They come bunched like bananas. Not single spies, but in battalions. And as much as Miranda admires the red-gold Honeywell hair, the exaggerated, expressive Honeywell good looks, the Honeywell repertoire of jokes and confidences, poetry and nonsense, sometimes she needs an escape. Honeywells want you to talk, too. They ask questions until your mouth gets dry from answering.

Daniel is exceptionally restful for a Honeywell. He doesn't care if you are there or not.

Miranda wriggles out from under the tree, through the press of leggy Honeywells in black tie and party dresses: apocalyptically orange taffeta, slithering, clingy satins in canary and violet, foamy white silk already spotted with wine.

She is patted on the head, winked at. Someone in cloth of gold says, "Poor little lamb."

"Baaaah humbug," Miranda blurts, beats on. Her own dress is green, fine-wale corduroy. Empire waist. Pinching at the armpits. Miranda's interest in these things is half professional. Her mother, Joannie (resident the last six months in a Phuket jail, will be there for many years to come), was Elspeth Honeywell's dresser and confidante.

Daniel is Elspeth's son. Miranda is Elspeth's goddaughter.

There are two men languorously kissing in the kitchen. Leaning against the sink, where one of the new Honeywell kittens licks sauce out of a gravy boat. A girl—only a few years older than Miranda lays soiled and tattered Tarot cards out on the farmhouse table. Empty wine bottles tilt like cannons; a butcher knife sheathed in a demolished Christmas cake. Warmth seeps from the stove: just inside the Aga's warming drawer, Miranda can see the other kittens, asleep in a crusted pan.

Miranda picks up a bag of party trash, lipstick-blotted napkins, throwaway champagne glasses, greasy fragments of pastry, hauls it out through the kitchen door. Mama cat slips inside as Miranda goes out.

Snow is falling. Big, sticky clumps that melt on her hair, her cheeks. Snow on Christmas. None in Phuket, of course. She wonders what they give you to eat on Christmas Day in a Thai prison. Her mother always makes the Christmas cake. Miranda helps roll out the marzipan in sheets. Her ballet flats skid on the grass.

She ties the bag, leaves it against the steps. And here is the man in the garden, still standing before the window, looking in.

He must hear Miranda. Surely he hears her. Her feet upon the frozen grass. But he doesn't turn around.

Even seen from the back, he is recognizably a Honeywell. Lanky, yellow-haired; perfectly still, he is somehow *perfectly* still, perfectly posed to catch the eye. Unnaturally natural. The snow that is making Miranda's nose run, her cheeks blotchy with cold, rests unmelted upon the bright Honeywell hair, the shoulders of the surprising coat.

Typical Honeywell behavior, Miranda thinks. A lovers' quarrel, or else he's taken offense at something someone said, and is now going to sulk himself handsomely to death in the cold. Her mother has been quite clear about how to behave when a Honeywell is being dramatic when drama isn't required. Firmness is the key.

At this last thought of her mother, Miranda has some dramatic feelings of her own. She focuses on the coat, sends the feelings away. It is *quite* a coat. A costume? Pilfered from some production. Eighteenth century. Beautifully cut. Not a frock coat. A *justacorps*. Rose damask. Embroidered all over with white silk thread, poppies and roses, and there, where it flares out over the hips, a staghorn beetle on a green leaf. She has come nearer and nearer, cannot stop herself from reaching out to touch the beetle.

She almost expects her hand to pass right through. (Surely there are ghosts at Honeywell Hall.) But it doesn't. The coat is real. Miranda pinches the damask between her fingers. Says, "Whatever it is that happened, it isn't worth freezing to death over. You shouldn't be out here. You should come inside."

The Honeywell in the *justacorps* turns around then. "I am exactly where I am supposed to be," he says. "Which is here. Doing precisely what I am supposed to be doing. Which does not include having conversations with little girls. Go away, little girl."

Little girl she may be, but Miranda is well armored already against the Honeywell arsenal of tantrums, tempests, ups, downs, charm, strange.

Above the wide right pocket of the *justacorps* is a fox stitched in red and gold, its foreleg caught in a trap.

"I'm Miranda," she says. And then, because she's picked up a Honeywell trick or two herself, she says, "My mother's in jail."

The Honeywell looks almost sympathetic for the briefest of moments, then shrugs. Theatrically, of course. Sticks his hands in his pockets. "What's that got to do with me?"

"Everyone's got problems, that's all," Miranda says. "I'm here because Elspeth feels sorry for me. I hate when people feel sorry for me. And I don't feel sorry for you. I don't know you. I just don't think it's very smart, standing out here because you're in a mood. But maybe you aren't very smart. My mother says good-looking people often don't bother. What's your name?"

"If I tell you, will you go away?" the Honeywell says.

"Yes," Miranda says. She can go in the kitchen and play with the kittens. Do the dishes and be useful. Have her fortune told. Sit under the tree again with Daniel until it's well past time to go to sleep. Tomorrow she'll be sent away home on a bus. By next year Elspeth will have most likely forgotten she has a goddaughter.

"I'm Fenny," the Honeywell says. "Now go away. I have things to not do, and not a lot of time to not do them in."

"Well," Miranda says. She pats Fenny on the broad cuff of the sleeve of his lovely coat. She wonders what the lining is. How cold he must be. How stupid he is, standing out here when he is welcome inside. "Merry Christmas. Good night."

She reaches out one last time, touches the embroidered fox, its leg caught in the trap. Stem stitch and seed stitch and herringbone. "It's very fine work, truly," she says. "But I hope he gets free."

"He was stupid to get caught," Fenny says, "you peculiar and annoying child." He is already turning back to the window. What does he see through it? When Miranda is finally back inside the drawing room where tipsy Honeywells are all roaring out inappropriate lyrics to carols, pulling Christmas crackers, putting on paper crowns, she looks through the window. The snow has stopped. No one is there.

But Elspeth Honeywell, as it happens, remembers Miranda the next year and the year and the year after that. There are presents for Miranda under the magnificent tree. A ticket to a London musical that she never sees. A makeup kit when she is thirteen.

The year she is fourteen, Daniel gives her a chess set and a box of assorted skeins of silk thread. Under her black tights, Miranda wears a red braided leather anklet that came in an envelope, no letter, from Phuket. The kittens are all grown up and pretend not to know her.

The year she is twelve, she looks for the mysterious Fenny. He isn't there. When she asks, no one knows who she means.

The year she is thirteen, she has champagne for the first time.

The Christmas she is fourteen, she feels quite grown up. The man in the *justacorps* was a dream, or some story she made up for herself in order to feel interesting. At fourteen she's outgrown fairytales, Santa Claus, ghost stories. When Daniel points out that they are standing under the mistletoe, she kisses him once on each cheek. And then sticks her tongue in his ear.

It snows again the Christmas she is fifteen. Snow is predicted, snow falls. Something about the chance of snow makes her think of him again. The man in the snowy garden. There is no man in the garden, of course; there never was. But there is Honeywell Hall, which is enough—and seemingly endless heaps of Honeywell adults behaving as if they were children again.

It's exhausting, almost Olympic, the amount of fun Honeywells seem to require. She can't decide if it's awful or if it's wonderful.

Late in the afternoon the Honeywells are playing charades. No fun, playing with people who do this professionally. Miranda stands at the window, watching the snow fall, looking for something. Birds. A fox. A man in the garden.

A Honeywell shouts, "Good god, no! Cleopatra came rolled up in a carpet, not in the Sunday supplement!"

Daniel is up in his room, talking to his father on Skype.

Miranda moves from window to window, pretending she is not looking for anything in particular. Far down the grounds, she sees something out of place. Someone. She's out the door in a flash.

"Going for a walk!" she yells while the door is swinging closed. In case anyone cares.

She finds the man navigating along the top of the old perimeter wall, stepping stone to stone. Fenny. He knocks a stick against each stone as he goes.

"You," he says. "I wondered if I'd see you again."

"Miranda," she says. "I bet you forgot."

"No," he says. "I didn't. Want to come up?"

He holds out his hand. She hesitates, and he says, "Suit yourself."

"I can get up by myself," she says, and does. She's in front of him now. Walks backwards so that she can keep an eye on him.

"You're not a Honeywell," he says.

"No," she says. "You are."

"Yes," he says. "Sort of."

She stops then, so that he has to stop, too. It isn't like they could keep on going anyway. There's a gap in the wall just behind her.

"I remember when they built this wall," he says.

She's probably misheard him. Or else he's teasing her. She says, "You must be very old."

"Older than you anyway," he says. He sits down on the wall, so she sits down, too. Honeywell Hall is in front of them. There's a copse of woods behind. Snow falls lazily, a bit of wind swirling it, tossing it up again.

"Why do you always wear that coat?" Miranda says. She fidgets a little. Her bum is getting cold. "You shouldn't sit on a dirty wall. It's too nice." She touches the embroidered beetle, the fox.

"Someone very . . . special gave it to me," he says. "I wear it always because it is her wish that I do so." The way he says it makes Miranda shiver just a little.

"Right," she says. "Like my anklet. My mother sent it to me. She's in prison. She'll never get out. She'll be there until she dies."

"Like the fox," he says.

"Like your fox," Miranda says. She's horrified to find that her eyes are watering. Is she crying? It isn't even a real fox. She doesn't want to look at the man in the coat, *Fenny,* to see if he's noticed, so she jumps down off the wall and begins to walk back toward the house.

When she's halfway to the Hall, the drifting snow stops. She looks back; no one sits on the wall.

The snow stops and starts, on and off all day long. When dinner is finished, Honeywells groaning, clutching their bellies, Elspeth has something for Miranda.

Elspeth says, wagging the present between two fingers like it's a special treat, Miranda some stray puppy, "Someone left it on the doorstep for you, Miranda. I wonder who."

The wrapping is a sheet of plain white stationery, tied with a bit of green thread. Her name in a scratchy hand. *Miranda.* Inside is a scrap of rose damask, the embroidered fox, snarling; the mangled leg, the bloodied trap.

"Let me see, sweet," Elspeth says, and takes the rose damask from her. "What a strange present! A joke?"

"I don't know," Miranda says. "Maybe."

It's eight o'clock. Honeywell Hall, up on its hill, must shine like a torch. Miranda puts on her coat and walks around the house three times. The snow has all melted. Daniel intercepts her on the final circuit. He's pimply, knobbly at present, and his nose is too big for his face. She loves him dearly, just like she loves Elspeth. They are always kind to her. "Here," he says, handing her the bit of damask. "Secret Santa? Secret admirer? Secret code?"

"Oh, you know," Miranda says. "Long story. Saving it for my memoirs."

"Meanwhile back in there everyone's pretending it's 1970 and they're all sweet sixteen again. Playing Sardines and drinking. It'll be orgies in all the cupboards, dramatic confessions and attempted murders in the pantry, under the stairs, in the beds and under them all night long. So I took this and snuck out." Daniel shows her the bottle of Strongbow in his coat pocket. "Let's go and sit in the Tiger. You can tell me all about school and the agony aunt, I'll tell you which Tory MP Elspeth's been seeing on the sly. Then you can sell the story to *The Sun*."

"And use the proceeds to buy us a cold-water flat in Wolverhampton. We'll live the life," Miranda says.

They drink the cider and eat a half-melted Mars bar. They talk and Miranda wonders if Daniel will try to kiss her. If she should try to kiss Daniel. But he doesn't, she doesn't—they don't—and she falls asleep on the mouse-eaten upholstery of the preposterous carcass of the Sunbeam Tiger, her head on Daniel's shoulder, the trapped fox crumpled in her fist.

Christmas after, Elspeth is in all the papers. The Tory MP's husband is divorcing her. Elspeth is a correspondent in the divorce. Meanwhile she has a new thing with a footballer twenty years her junior. It's the best kind of Christmas story. Journalists everywhere. Elspeth, in the Sunbeam Tiger, picks up Miranda at the station in a wide-brimmed black hat, black jumpsuit, black sunglasses, triumphantly disgraced. In her element.

Miranda's aunt almost didn't let her come this year. But then, if Miranda had stayed, they would have both been miserable. Her aunt has a new boyfriend. Almost as awful as she is. Someone should tell the tabloids.

"Lovely dress," Elspeth says, kissing her on the cheek. "You make it?"

Miranda is particularly pleased with the hem. "It's all right."

"I want one just like it," Elspeth says. "In red. Lower the neckline, raise the hem a bit. You could go into business. Ever think of it?"

"I'm only sixteen," Miranda says. "There's plenty of room for improvement."

"Alexander McQueen! Left school when he was sixteen," Elspeth says. "Went off to apprentice on Savile Row. Used to sew human hair into his linings. A kind of spell, I suppose. I have one of his manta dresses somewhere in the Hall. And your mother, she was barely older than you are now. Hanging around backstage, stitching sequins and crystals on tulle."

"Where's Daniel?" Miranda says. She and her mother have been corresponding. Miranda is saving up money. She hasn't told her aunt yet, but next summer Miranda's going to Thailand.

"Back at the house. In a mood. Listening to my old records. The Smiths."

Miranda looks over, studies Elspeth's face. "That girl broke up with him, didn't she?"

"If you mean the one with the ferrets and the unfortunate ankles," Elspeth says, "yes. What's her name. It's a mystery. Not her name, the breakup. He grows three inches in two months, his skin clears up, honestly, Miranda, he's even better looking than I expected he'd turn out. Heart of gold, that boy, a good brain, too. I can't think what she was thinking."

"Preemptive strike, perhaps," Miranda says.

"I wouldn't know about the breakup except for accidentally overhearing a conversation. *Somewhat* accidentally," Elspeth says. "Well, that and the Smiths. He doesn't talk to me about his love life."

"Do you *want* him to talk to you about his love life?"

"No," Elspeth says. "Yes. Maybe? Probably not. Anyway, how about you, Miranda? Do you have one of those, yet? A love life?"

"I don't even have ferrets," Miranda says.

On Christmas Eve, while all the visiting Honeywells and cousins and wives and boyfriends and girlfriends and their accountants are out caroling in the village, Elspeth takes Miranda and Daniel aside. She gives them each a joint.

"It's not as if I don't know you've been raiding my supply, *Daniel*,"

Elspeth says. "At least this way, I know what you're up to. If you're going to break the law, you might as well learn to break it responsibly. Under adult supervision."

Daniel rolls his eyes, looks at Miranda. Whatever he sees in her face makes him snort. It's annoying but true: he really has become quite spectacular looking. Well, it was inevitable. Apparently they drown all the ugly Honeywells at birth.

"It's okay, Mi*randy*," he says. "I'll have yours if you don't want it."

Miranda sticks the joint in her bra. "Thanks, but I'll hang on to it."

"Anyway I'm sure the two of you have lots of catching up to do," Elspeth says. "I'm off to the pub to kiss the barmaids and make the journos cry."

When she's out the door, Daniel says, "She's matchmaking, isn't she?"

Miranda says, "Or else it's reverse psychology?"

Their eyes meet. *Courage, Miranda.* Daniel tilts his head, looks gleeful.

"In which case, I should do this," he says. He leans forward, puts his hand on Miranda's chin, tilts it up. "We should do this."

He kisses her. His lips are soft and dry. Miranda sucks on the bottom one experimentally. She arranges her arms around his neck, and his hands go down, cup her bum. He opens his mouth and does things with his tongue until she opens her mouth, too. He seems to know how this goes; he and the girl with the ferrets probably did this a lot.

Miranda wonders if the ferrets were in the cage at the time, or out. How unsettling is it, she wonders, to fool around with ferrets watching you? Their beady button eyes.

She can feel Daniel's erection. Oh, God. How embarrassing. She pushes him away. "Sorry," she groans. "Sorry! Yeah, no, I don't think we should be doing this. Any of this!"

"Probably not," Daniel says. "Probably definitely not. It's weird, right?"

"It's weird," Miranda says.

"But perhaps it wouldn't be so weird if we smoked a joint first," Daniel says. His hair is messy. Apparently she did that.

"Or," Miranda says, "maybe we could just smoke a joint. And, you know, not complicate things."

Halfway through the joint, Daniel says, "It wouldn't have to complicate everything." His head is in her lap. She's curling pieces of his hair around her finger.

"Yes, it would," Miranda says. "It *really, really* would."

Later on she says, "I wish it would snow. That would be nice. If it snowed. I thought that's why you lot came here at Christmas. The whole white Christmas thing."

"Awful stuff," Daniel says. "Cold. Slippy. Makes you feel like you're supposed to be singing or something. In a movie."

"Or in a snow globe."

"Stuck," Miranda says. "Trapped."

"Stuck," Daniel says.

They're lying, tangled together, on a sofa across from the Christmas tree. Occasionally Miranda has to remove Daniel's hand from somewhere it shouldn't be. She doesn't think he's doing it intentionally. She kisses him behind the ear now and then. "That's nice," he says. Pats her bum. She wriggles out from under his hand. Kisses him again. There's a movie on television, lots of explosions. Zombies. Cameron Diaz unloading groceries in a cottage, all by herself.

No, that's another movie entirely, Miranda thinks. Apparently she's been asleep. Daniel is still sleeping. Why does he have to be so irritatingly good-looking, even in his sleep? Miranda hates to think what she looks like asleep. No wonder the ferret girl dumped him.

Elspeth must have come back from the pub, because there's a heap of blankets over the both of them.

Outside, it's snowing.

Miranda puts her hand in the pocket of her dress, feels the piece of damask she has had there all day long. It's a big pocket. Plenty of room for all kinds of things. Miranda doesn't want to be one of those designers who only makes pretty things. She wants them to be useful, too. And provoking. She takes the prettiest blanket from the sofa for herself, distributes the other blankets over Daniel so that all of him is covered.

She goes by a mirror, stops to smooth her hair down, collect it into a ponytail. Wraps the blanket around herself like a shawl, goes out into the snow.

He's there, under the hawthorn tree. She shivers, tells herself it's because of the cold. There isn't much snow on the ground yet. She tells herself she hasn't been asleep too long. He hasn't been waiting long.

He wears the same coat. His face is the same. He isn't as old as she thought he was, that first time. Only a few years older than she. Than Daniel. He hasn't aged. She has. Where is he, when he isn't here?

"Are you a ghost?" she says.

"No," he says. "I'm not a ghost."

"Then you're a real person? A Honeywell?"

"Fenwick Septimus Honeywell." He bows. It looks better than it should, probably because of the coat. People don't really do that sort of thing anymore. No one has names like that. How old is he?

"You only come when it snows," she says.

"I am only allowed to come when it's snowing," he says. "And only on Christmas Day."

"Right," she says. "Okay, no. No, I don't understand. Allowed by whom?"

He shrugs. Doesn't answer. Maybe it isn't allowed.

"You gave me something," Miranda says.

He nods again. She puts out her hand, touches the place on the *justacorps* where he tore away the fox. So he could give it to her.

"Oh," Miranda said. "The poor old thing. You didn't even use scissors, did you? Let me fix it."

She takes the piece of damask out of her pocket, along with her sewing kit, the one she always keeps with her. She's had exactly the right thread in there for over a year. Just in case.

She shows him the damask. A few months ago she unpicked all of the fox's leg, all of the trap. The drops of blood. The tail and snarling head. Then she reworked the embroidery to her own design, mimicking as closely as possible the feel of the original. Now the fox is free, tongue lolling, tail aloft, running along the pink plane of the damask. Pink cotton backing, a piece she cut from an old nightgown.

He takes it from her, turns it over in his hand. "You did this?"

"You gave me a present last year. This is my present for you," she says. "I'll sew it back in. It will be a little untidy, but at least you won't have a hole in your lovely coat."

He says, "I told her I tore it on a branch. It's fine just as it is."

"It isn't fine," she says. "Let me fix it, please."

He smiles. It's a real smile, maybe even a flirtatious smile. He and Daniel could be brothers. They're that much alike. So why did she stop Daniel from kissing her? Why does she have to bite her tongue, sometimes, when Daniel is being kind to her? At Honeywell Hall, she is only as real as Elspeth and Daniel allow her to be. This isn't her real life.

It's ridiculous, of course. Real is real. Daniel is real. Miranda is real when she isn't here. Whatever Fenwick Septimus Honeywell is, Miranda's fairly sure it's complicated.

"*Please*," she says.

"As you wish it, Miranda," Fenny says. She helps him out of the coat. Her hand touches his, and she pushes down the inexplicable desire to clutch at it. As if one of them were falling.

"Come inside the Hall," she says. "Just while I'm working on this. I should do it inside. Better light. You could meet Daniel. Or Elspeth. I could wake her up. I bet Elspeth knows how to deal with this sort of thing." Whatever this sort of thing is. "Theater people seem like they know how to deal with things like this. Come inside with me."

"I can't," he says regretfully.

Of course. It's against the rules.

"Okay," Miranda says, adjusting. "Then we'll both stay out here. I'll stay with you. You can tell me all about yourself. Unless that's against the rules too." She busies herself with pins. He lifts her hand away, holds it.

"Inside out, if you please," he says. "The fox on the inside."

He has lovely hands. No calluses on his fingertips. Manicured nails. Definitely not real. His thumb smooths over her knuckles. Miranda says, a little breathless, "Inside out. So she won't notice someone's repaired it?" Whoever *she* is.

"She'll notice," he says. "But this way she won't see that the fox is free."

"Okay. That's sensible. I guess." Miranda lets go of his hand. "Here. We can sit on this."

She spreads out the blanket. Sits down. Remembers she has a Mars bar in her pocket. She passes that to him. "Sit."

He examines the Mars bar. Unwraps it.

"Oh, no," she says. "More rules? You're not allowed to eat?"

"I don't know," he says. "I've never been given anything before. When I came. No one has ever talked to me."

"So you show up when it snows, creep around for a while, looking in at the windows. Then you go back wherever when the snow stops."

Fenny nods. He looks almost abashed.

"What fun!" Miranda says. "Wait, no, I mean how creepy!" She has the piece of embroidery how she wants it, is tacking it into place with running stitches, so the fox is hidden.

If it stops snowing, will he just disappear? Will the coat stay? Something tells her that all of this is very against the rules. Does he want to come back? And what does she mean by *back,* anyway? Back here, to Honeywell Hall? Or back to wherever it is that he is when he isn't here? Why doesn't he get older?

Elspeth says it's a laugh, getting older. But oh, Miranda knows, Elspeth doesn't mean it.

"It's good," Fenny says, sounding surprised. The Mars bar is gone. He's licking his fingers.

"I could go back in the house," Miranda says. "I could make you a cheese sandwich. There's Christmas cake for tomorrow."

"No," he says. "Stay."

"Okay," she says. "I'll stay. Here. That's the best I can do in this light. My hands are getting too cold."

He takes the coat from her. Nods. Then puts it around her shoulders. Pulls her back against his chest. All of that damask: it's heavy. There's snow inside and out.

Fenny is surprisingly solid for someone who mostly isn't here. She wonders if she is surprising to him, too.

His mouth is just above the top of her head, blowing little hot circles against her hair. She's very, very cold. Ridiculous to be out here in the snow with this ridiculous person with his list of ridiculous rules.

She'll catch her death of cold.

Cautiously, as if he's waiting for her to stop him, he puts his arms around her waist. He sighs. Warm breath in her hair. Miranda is suddenly so very afraid that it will stop snowing. They haven't talked about anything. They haven't even kissed. She knows, every part of her knows, that she wants to kiss him. That he wants to kiss her. All of her skin prickles with longing. Her insides fizz.

She puts her sewing kit back into her pocket, discovers the joint Elspeth gave her, Daniel's lighter. "I bet you haven't ever tried this, either," she says. She twists in his arms. "You smoke it. Here." She taps at his lips with the joint, sticks it between his lips when they part. Flicks the lighter until it catches, and then she's lunging at him, kissing him, and he's kissing her back. The second time tonight that she's kissed a boy, the first two boys she's ever kissed, and both of them Honeywells.

And oh, it was lovely kissing Daniel, but this is something better than lovely. All they do is kiss, she doesn't know how long they kiss, at first Fenny tastes of chocolate, and she doesn't know what happens to the joint. Or to the lighter. They kiss until Miranda's lips are numb and the *justacorps* has come entirely off of her, and she's in Fenny's lap and she has one hand in Fenny's hair and one hand digging into Fenny's waist, and all she wants to do is keep on kissing Fenny forever and ever. Until he pulls away.

They're both breathing hard. His cheeks are red. His mouth is redder. Miranda wonders if she looks as crazed as he looks.

"You're shivering," he says.

"Of course I'm shivering! It's freezing out here! And you won't come inside. Because," Miranda says, panting, shivering, all of her vibrating with cold and with *want, want, want,* "it's against the rules!"

Fenny nods. Looks at her lips, licks his own. Jerks back, though, when Miranda tries to kiss him again. She's tempted to pick up a handful of wet snow and smush it into his Honeywell face.

"Fine, fine! You stay right here. Don't move. Not even a inch, understand? I'll get the keys to the Tiger," she says. "Unless it's against the rules to sit in old cars."

"All of this is against the rules," Fenny says. But he nods. Maybe, she thinks, she can get him in the car and just drive away with him. Maybe that would work.

"I *mean* it," Miranda says. "Don't you *dare* go anywhere."

He nods. She kisses him, punishingly, lingeringly, desperately, then takes off in a run for the kitchen. Her fingers are so cold she can't get the door open at first. She grabs her coat, the keys to the Tiger, and then, on impulse, cuts off a hunk of the inviolate Christmas cake. Well, if Elspeth says anything, she'll tell her the whole story.

Then she's out the door again. Says the worst words she knows when she sees that the snow has stopped. There is the snow-blotted blanket, the joint, and the Mars-bar wrapper.

She leaves the Christmas cake on the window ledge. Maybe the birds will eat it.

Daniel is still asleep on the couch. She wakes him up. "Merry Christmas," she says. "Good morning." She gives him his present. She's made him a shirt. Egyptian cotton, gray-blue to match his eyes. But of course it won't fit. He's already outgrown it.

Daniel catches her under the mistletoe when it's past time for bed, Christmas night and no one wants to go to sleep yet, everyone tipsy and loose and picking fights about things they don't care about. For the sheer pleasure of picking fights. He kisses Miranda. She lets him.

It's sort of a present for Elspeth, Miranda rationalizes. It's sort of because she knows it's ridiculous, not kissing Daniel, just because she wants to be kissing someone else instead. Especially when the person she wants to be kissing isn't really a real person at all. At least not most of the time.

Besides, he's wearing the shirt Miranda made for him, even though it doesn't fit.

In the morning, Daniel is too hungover to drive her down to the village to catch the bus. Elspeth takes her instead. Elspeth is wearing a vintage suit, puce gabardine, trimmed with sable, something Miranda itches to take apart, just to see how it's made. What a tiny waist she has.

Elspeth says, "You know he's in love with you."

"He's not," Miranda says. "He loves me, but he's not in love with me. I love him, but I'm not in love with him."

"If you say so," Elspeth says. Her tone is cool. "Although I can't help being curious how you've come to know so much about love, Miranda, at your tender age."

Miranda flushes.

"You know you can talk to me," Elspeth says. "You can talk to me whenever you want to. Whenever you need to. Darling Miranda. There's a boy, isn't there? Not Daniel. Poor Daniel."

"There's nobody," Miranda says. "Really. There's nobody. It's nothing. I'm just a bit sad because I have to go home again. It was such a lovely Christmas."

"Such lovely snow!" Elspeth says. "Too bad it never lasts."

Daniel comes to visit in the spring. Two months after Christmas. Miranda isn't expecting him. He shows up at the door with a bouquet of roses. Miranda's aunt's eyebrows go almost up to her hairline. "I'll make tea," she says, and scurries off. "And we'll need a vase for those."

Miranda takes the roses from Daniel. Says, "Daniel! What are you doing here?"

"You've been avoiding me," Daniel says.

"Avoiding you? We don't live in the same place," Miranda says. "I wasn't even sure you knew where I lived." She can hardly stand to have him here, standing in the spotless foyer of her aunt's semidetached bungalow.

"You know what I mean, Miranda. You're never online," he says. "And when you are, you never want to chat. You never text me back. Aren't you going to invite me in?"

"No," she says. Grabs her bag.

"Don't bother with the tea, Aunt Dora," she says loudly, "We're going out."

She yanks at Daniel's hand, extracts him violently from her life, her *real* life. If only.

She speed walks him past the tract houses with their small, white-stone frontages, all the way to the dreary, dingy, Midlands-typical High Street. Daniel trailing behind her. It's a long walk, and she has no idea what to say to him. He doesn't seem to know what to say, either.

Her dress is experimental, nothing she's ever intended to wear out. She hasn't yet brushed her hair today. It's the weekend. She was planning to stay in and study. How dare he show up.

There's a teashop where the scones and the sandwiches are particularly foul. She takes him there, and they sit down. Order.

"I should have let you know I was coming," Daniel says.

"Yes," Miranda says. "Then I could have told you not to."

He tries to take her hand. "Mirandy," he says. "I think about you all the time. About us. I think about us."

"Don't," she says. "Stop!"

"I can't," he says. "I like you. Very much. Don't you like me?"

It's a horrible conversation. Like stepping on a baby mouse. A baby mouse who happens to be your friend. It doesn't help that Miranda knows how unfair she's being. She shouldn't be angry that he's come here. He doesn't know how she feels about this place. Just a few more months and she'll be gone from here forever. It will never have existed.

They are both practically on the verge of tears by the time the scones come. Daniel takes one bite and then spits it out onto the plate.

"It's not that bad," she snaps. Dares him to complain.

"Yes it is," he says. "It really truly is that bad." He takes a sip of his tea. "And the milk has gone off, too."

He seems so astonished at this that she can't help it. She bursts out laughing. This astonishes him, too. And just like that, they aren't fighting anymore. They spend the rest of the day feeding ducks at the frozen pond, going in and out of horror movies, action movies, cartoons—all the movies except the romantic comedies, because why rub salt in the wound?—at the cinema. He doesn't try to hold her hand. She tries not to imagine that it is snowing outside, that it is Fenny sitting in the flickering darkness here beside her. Imagining this is against the rules.

Miranda finishes out the term. Packs up what she wants to take with her, boxes up the rest. Sells her sewing machine. Leaves a note for her aunt. Never mind what's in it.

She knows she should be more grateful. Her aunt has kept her fed, kept her clothed, given her bed and board. Never hit her. Never, really, been unkind. But Miranda is so very, very tired of being grateful to people.

She is sticky, smelly, and punch-drunk with jetlag when her flight arrives in Phuket. Stays the night in a hostel and then sets off. She's read about how this is supposed to go. What you can bring, how long you can stay, how you should behave. All the rules.

But, in the end, she doesn't see Joannie. It isn't allowed. It isn't clear why. Is her mother there? They tell her yes. Is she still alive? Yes. Can Miranda see her? No. Not possible today. Come back.

Miranda comes back three times. Each time she is sent away. The consul can't help. On her second visit, she speaks to a young woman named Dinda, who comes and spends time with the prisoners when they are in the infirmary. Dinda says that she's sat with Joannie two or three times. That Miranda's mother never says much. It's been over six months since her mother wrote to either Elspeth or to Miranda.

The third time she is sent away, Miranda buys a plane ticket to Japan. She spends the next four months there, teaching English in Kyoto. Going to museums. Looking at kimonos at the flea markets at the temples.

She sends postcards to Elspeth, to Daniel. To her mother. She even sends one to her aunt. And two days before Christmas, Miranda flies home.

On the plane, she falls asleep and dreams that it's snowing. She's with Joannie in a cell in the prison in Phuket. Her mother tells Miranda

that she loves her. She tells her that her sentence has been com-
muted. She tells her that if Miranda's good and follows the rules very
carefully, she'll be home by Christmas.

She has a plan this year. The plan is that it will snow on Christmas.
Never mind what the forecast says. It will snow. She will find Fenny.
And she won't leave his side. Never mind what the rules say.

Daniel is going to St. Andrews next year. His girlfriend's name is
Lillian. Elspeth is on her best behavior. Miranda is, too. She tells various Honeywells amusing stories about her students, the deer at the
temples, and the girl who played the flute for them.

Elspeth is getting *old*. She's still the most beautiful woman Miranda
has ever seen, but she's in her sixties now. Any day she'll be given a
knighthood and never be scandalous again.

Lillian is a nice person. She tells Miranda that she likes Miranda's
dress. She flirts with the most decrepit of the Honeywells, helps set
the table. Daniel watches everything that she does as if all of it is brand
new, as if Lillian has invented compliments, flirting, as if there were no
such thing as water glasses and table linens before Lillian discovered
them. Oh newfound land.

Despite all this, Miranda thinks she could be fond of Lillian. She's
smart. Likes maths. Actually, truly, *really* seems to like Miranda's
dress, which, let's admit it, is meant as an act of war. Miranda is not
into pretty at the moment. She's into armor, weaponry, abrasiveness,
discomfort—hers and other peoples'. The dress is leather, punk,
studded with spikes, buckles, metal cuffs, chain looped round and
around. Whenever she sits down, she has to be careful not to gash,
impale, or skewer the furniture. Hugging is completely out of the
question.

Lillian wants a tour, so after dinner and the first round of cocktails,
Miranda and Daniel take her all through Honeywell Hall, the parts that
are kept up and the parts that are falling into shadow. They end up in

one of the attics, digging through Elspeth's trunks of costumes. They make Lillian try on cheesecloth dresses, hand-beaded fairy wings, ancient, cakey stage makeup. Take selfies. Daniel reads old mail from fans, pulls out old photos of Elspeth and Joannie, backstage. Here's Joannie perched on a giant urn. Joannie, her mouth full of pins. Joannie, at a first-night party, drunk and laughing and young. It should hurt to look at these pictures. Shouldn't it?

"Do you think it will snow?" Lillian says. "I want snow for Christmas."

Daniel says, "Snowed last Christmas. Shouldn't expect that it will, this year. Too warm."

Not even trying to sound casual about it, Miranda says, "It's going to snow. It has to snow. And if it doesn't snow, then we're going to do something about it. We'll make it snow."

She feels quite gratified when Lillian looks at her as if Miranda is insane, possibly dangerous. Well, the dress should have told her that.

"My present this year," Miranda says, "is going to be snow. Call me the Snow Queen. Come and see."

Her suitcases—her special equipment—barely fit into the Tiger. Elspeth didn't say a word, just raised an eyebrow. Most of it is still in the carriage house.

Daniel is game when she explains. Lillian is either game, or pretending to be. There are long, gauzy swathes of white cloth to weave through tree branches, to tack down to the ground. There are long strings of glass and crystal and silver ornaments. Handcut lace snowflakes caught in netting. The pièce de résistance is the Snowboy Stage Whisper Fake Snow Machine with its fifty-foot extending hose reel. Miranda's got bags and bags of fake snow. Over an hour's worth of the best quality fake snow money can buy, according to the guy who rented her the Snowboy.

It's nearly midnight by the time they have everything arranged to Miranda's satisfaction. She goes inside and turns on the Hall's floodlights, then turns on the snow machine. A fine, glittering snow begins. Lillian kisses Daniel lingeringly. A fine romance.

Elspeth has been observing the whole time from the kitchen stair.

She puts a hand over her cocktail. Fake snow dusts her fair hair, streaks it white.

All of the Honeywells who haven't gone to bed yet, which is most of them, *ooh* and *ah*. The youngest Honeywells, the ones who weren't even born when Miranda first came to Honeywell Hall, break into a spontaneous round of applause. Miranda feels quite powerful. Santa Claus exists after all.

All of the Honeywells eventually retreat back into the house to drink and gossip and admire Miranda's special effects from within. It may not be properly cold tonight, but it's cold enough. Time for hot chocolate, hot toddies, hot baths, hot water bottles and bed.

She's not sure, of course, that this will work. If this is playing by the rules. But isn't she owed something by now? A bit of luck?

And she is. At first, not daring to hope, she thinks that Daniel has come from the Hall to fetch her in. But it isn't Daniel.

Fenny, in that old *justacorps,* Miranda's stitching around the piece above his pocket, walks out from under the hawthorn tree.

"It worked," Miranda says. She hugs herself, which is a mistake. All those spikes. "Ow. Oh."

"I shouldn't be here, should I?" Fenny says. "You've done something." Miranda looks closely at his face. How young he looks. Barely older than she. How long has he been this young?

Fake snow is falling on their heads. "We have about an hour," Miranda says. "Not much time."

He comes to her then, takes her in his arms. "Be careful," she says. "I'm all spikes."

"A ridiculous dress," he says into her hair. "Though comely. Is this what people wear in this age?"

"Says the man wearing a *justacorps,*" she says. They're almost the same height this year. He's shorter than Daniel now, she realizes. Then they're kissing, she and Fenny are kissing, and she isn't thinking about Daniel at all.

They kiss, and Fenny presses himself against her, armored with spikes though Miranda is. He holds her, hands just above her waist, tight enough that she thinks she will have bruises in the shape of his fingers.

"Come in the Hall with me," Miranda says, in between kisses. "Come with me."

Fenny bites her lower lip. Then licks it. "Can't," he says.

"Because of the rules." Now he's nibbling her ear. She whimpers. Tugs him away by the hair. "Hateful rules."

"Could I stay with you, I vow I would. I would stay and grow old with you, Miranda. Or as long as you wanted me to stay."

"Stay with me," she says. Her dress must be goring into him. His stomach, his thighs. They'll both be black and blue tomorrow.

He doesn't say anything. Kisses her over and over. Distracting her, she knows. The front of her dress fastens with a simple clasp. Underneath she's wearing an old T-shirt. Leggings. She guides his hands.

"If you can't stay with me," she says, as Fenny opens the clasp, "then I'll stay with you."

His hands are on her rib cage as she speaks. Simple enough to draw him inside the armature of the dress, to reach behind his back, pull the belt of heavy chain around them both. Fasten it. The key is in the Hall. In the attic, where she left it.

"Miranda," Fenny says, when he realizes. "What have you done?"

"A crucial component of any relationship is the capacity to surprise the one you love. I read that somewhere. A magazine. You're going to love women's magazines. Oh, and the Internet. Well, parts of it anyway. I won't let you go," Miranda says. The dress is a snug fit for two people. She can feel every breath he takes. "If you go, then I'll go, too. Wherever it is that you go."

"It doesn't work that way," he says. "There are rules."

"There are always ways to get around the rules," Miranda says. "That was in another magazine." She knows that she's babbling. A coping mechanism. There are articles about that, too. Why can't she stop thinking about women's magazines? Some byproduct of realizing that you're in love? "Fifteen Ways to Know He Loves You

Back." Number eight. He doesn't object when you chain yourself to him after using fake snow in a magic spell to lure him into your arms.

The fake snow is colder and wetter and heavier than she'd thought it would be. Much more like real snow. Fenny has been muttering something against her neck. Either *I love you* or else *What the hell were you thinking, Miranda?*

It's both. He's saying both. It's fake snow and *real*. Real snow mingling with the fake. Her fake magic and real magic. Coming down heavier and heavier until all the world is white. The air, colder and colder and colder still.

"Something's happening, Fenny," she says. "It's snowing. Really snowing."

It's as if he's turned to stone in her arms. She can feel him stop breathing. But his heart is racing. "Let me go," he says. "Please let me go."

"I can't," Miranda says. "I don't have the key."

"You can." A voice like a bell, clear and sweet.

And here is the one Miranda has been waiting for. Fenny's *she*. The one who catches foxes in traps. Never lets them go. The one who makes the rules.

It's silly, perhaps, to be reminded in this moment of Elspeth, but that's who Miranda thinks of when she looks up and sees the Lady who approaches, more Honeywell than any Honeywell Miranda has ever met. The presence, the *puissance* that Elspeth commands, just for a little while when Elspeth takes the stage, is a game. Elspeth plays at the thing. Here is the substance. Power is something granted willingly to Elspeth by her audience. Fenny's Lady has it always. What a burden. Never to be able to put it down.

Can the Lady see what Miranda is thinking? Her gaze takes in all. Fenny keeps his head bowed. But his hands are in Miranda's hands. He is in her keeping, and she will not let him go.

"I have no key," Miranda says. "And he does not want to go with you."

"He did once," the Lady says. She wears armor, too, all made of ice. What a thing it would be, to dress this Lady. To serve her. She could go with Fenny, if the Lady let her.

Down inside the dress where the Lady cannot see, Fenny pinches the soft web between Miranda's thumb and first finger. The pain brings her back to herself. She sees that he is watching her. He says nothing, only looks until Miranda finds herself again in his eyes.

"I went with you willingly," Fenny agrees. But he doesn't look at the Lady. He only looks at Miranda.

"But you would leave me now? Only speak it and I will let you go at once."

Fenny says nothing. A rule, Miranda thinks. There is a rule here.

"He can't say it," she says. "Because you won't let him. So let me say it for him. He will stay here. Haven't you kept him from his home for long enough?"

"His home is with me. Let him go," the Lady says. "Or you will be sorry." She reaches out a long hand and touches the chain around Miranda's dress. It splinters beneath her featherlight touch. Miranda feels it give.

"Let him go and I will give you your heart's desire," the Lady says. She is so close that Miranda can feel the Lady's breath frosting her cheek. And then Miranda isn't holding Fenny. She's holding Daniel. Miranda and Daniel are married. They love each other so much. Honeywell Hall is her home. It always has been. Their children under the tree, Elspeth white-haired and lovely at the head of the table, wearing a dress from Miranda's couture label.

Only it isn't Elspeth at all, is it? It's the Lady. Miranda almost lets go of Daniel. Fenny! But he holds her hands and she wraps her hands around his waist, tighter than before.

"Be careful, girl," the Lady says. "He bites."

Miranda is holding a fox. Scrabbling, snapping, carrion breath at her face. Miranda holds fast.

Then: Fenny again. Trembling against her.

"It's okay," Miranda says. "I've got you."

But it isn't Fenny after all. It's her mother. They're together in a small, dirty cell. Joannie says, "It's okay, Miranda. I'm here. It's okay. You can let go. I'm here. Let go and we can go home."

"No," Miranda says, suddenly boiling with rage. "No, you're not here. And I can't do anything about that. But I can do something about this." And she holds on to her mother until her mother is Fenny again, and the Lady is looking at Miranda and Fenny as if they are a speck of filth beneath her slippered foot.

"Very well then," the Lady says. She smiles, the way you would smile at a speck of filth. "Keep him then. For a while. But know that he will never again know the joy that I taught him. With me he could not be but happy. I made him so. You will bring him grief and death. You have dragged him into a world where he knows nothing. Has nothing. He will look at you and think of what he lost."

"We all lose," says an acerbic voice. "We all love and we all lose and we go on loving just the same."

"Elspeth?" Miranda says. But she thinks, it's a trap. Just another trap. She squeezes Fenny so hard around his middle that he gasps.

Elspeth looks at Fenny. She says, "I saw you once, I think. Outside the window. I thought you were a shadow or a ghost."

Fenny says, "I remember. Though you had hardly come into your beauty then."

"Such talk! You are going to be wasted on my Miranda, I'm afraid," Elspeth says. "As for you, my lady, I think you'll find you've been bested. Go and find another toy. We here are not your meat."

The Lady curtseys. Looks one last time at Elspeth, Miranda. Fenny. This time he looks back. What does he see? Does any part of him move to follow her? His hand finds Miranda's hand again.

Then the Lady is gone and the snow thins and blows away to nothing at all.

Elspeth blows out a breath. "Well," she says. "You're a stubborn girl, a good-hearted girl, Miranda, and brighter than your poor mother. But if I'd known what you were about, we would have had a word or two. Stage magic is well and good, but better to steer clear of the real kind."

"Better for Miranda," Fenny says. "But she has won me free with her brave trick."

"And now I suppose we'll have to figure out what to do with you," Elspeth says. "You'll be needing something more practical than that coat."

"Come on," Miranda says. She is still holding on to Fenny's hand. Perhaps she's holding on too tightly, but he doesn't seem to care. He's holding on just as tightly.

So she says, "Let's go in."

angels in the snow

matt de la peña

I didn't tell anyone how dire shit had become.

Yeah, maybe my old man could slip a few bucks in an envelope, mail it to my Brooklyn apartment (where it might get carried off by a pack of gangster rats), but he had his own worries. He
was saving up for my little sis's summer camp. And our dog, Peanut—
probably the most flea-bitten, bucktoothed crossbreed you could
ever imagine—had just required an emergency dental extraction. I
know, right? The dog with the busted grill has dental needs. Okay.
But according to my sis, the procedure cost over three hundred
bones, and they had to put my old man on some kind of payment
plan.

It's fine.

I'd just go hungry this holiday season.

Nothing to see here.

"Mijo," he told me over the phone on my first full day of cat sitting. "Everything is good up at your college?"

I stuck Mike's acoustic guitar back on its stand. "It's all good, Pop."

"That's good," he said.

This word *good,* I thought. How many times did he and I throw that shit around these days? My old man because he didn't trust his English, me because I didn't want him to think I was showing off.

"Next year we'll get you a ticket so you could fly home for Christmas," he said. "And me, you, and Sofe will be together as a family. How we belong."

"Sounds good, Pop."

He didn't know it yet, but by next Christmas I planned to be living near home again, in southeast San Diego, taking classes at the local community college. Everyone seemed to think I had it made out here in New York—and on paper maybe I did. Full academic scholarship to NYU. Professors that blew my mind every time I sat in one of their lecture halls. But to understand why I planned to drop out after my freshman year you'd have to read the e-mails my sis had been sending. Some nights my pop—the toughest man I've ever known—cried himself to sleep. She could hear him through her bedroom wall. He wouldn't eat dinner unless my sis physically dragged him to the table and sat him down in front of a plate of food. Point is, back home real-life shit was happening. Genuine mourning. And here I was, clear across the country, having the time of my life.

It would be impossible to describe the weight of that guilt.

There was a long, awkward pause between me and my old man—we'd yet to master the art of talking on the phone—before he cleared his throat and told me: "Okay, *mijo.* You will be safe from that storm. The news says it's very, very bad."

"I will, Pop," I said. "Tell Sofe to stay away from dudes."

We said our good-byes and hung up.

I slipped my cell back in my pocket and went to Mike's cupboards for the two hundredth time. One multigrain hot dog bun and a few stray packets of catsup. That was it. The stainless steel fridge wasn't any better. An unopened dark chocolate bar, a half-full bag of baby carrots, two plain yogurts, and a bottle of high-end vodka. How could such a beautiful apartment contain so little food? My stomach grumbled as I stared at the beautiful yogurt cartons. But I had to conserve. It was still three days before Christmas, and I wouldn't see a dime until the day after that.

My manager at the campus bookstore, Mike, and his wife, Janice, were paying me to cat sit at their brand-new apartment—which was about three hundred times nicer than the broken-down room I rented in Bushwick—but Mike forgot to hit the ATM before he left and asked if he could pay me when they got back from Florida.

No problem, I lied.

To make matters worse, a few hours after they left, a record-setting blizzard sucker punched New York City, blanketing Mike's Park Slope neighborhood in thirteen inches of angry-ass snow. Translation: even if I wanted to dust off the survival skills I'd picked up back home (how to mug somebody), I couldn't. Everyone was waiting shit out in the warmth of their cozy apartments.

I closed the fridge and went into the living room and stared out the front window, next to the cat—Olive, I think Mike said her name was. My empty stomach clenched and twisted and slowly let go, then clenched again. The few remaining cars parked along the street were buried under snow, and it was *still* falling. The trees that framed my view all sagged under the weight of the stuff.

I turned to Mike's cat, said, "I promise not to eat you."

She looked at me, unimpressed, then hopped down onto the hardwood and sauntered off toward the kitchen, where a heaping bowl of salmon-flavored dry food awaited her.

Faulty Plumbing

I was a quarter of the way through one of Mike's precious yogurts when there was a knock at the door. I froze, my spoon halfway between my mouth and the plastic carton. Who could *that* be? You could only enter the building if you got buzzed in, and Mike told me I was the only one in the entire seven-story complex who hadn't traveled anywhere for Christmas.

More knocking.

Louder this time.

I stashed the yogurt back in the fridge, went to the door, and looked through the peephole. A pretty white girl was standing on the other side—long sandy-blond hair and porcelain skin and light brown eyes. I was still getting used to being around people like this. The kind you see in movies and commercials and sitcoms. Back home everyone you passed on the street was just regular-old Mexican, like me.

I undid the chain and pulled open the door and tried to play it cool. "Can I help you?"

"Oh," she said with a look of disappointment. "You're not Mike."

"Yeah, we work together at—"

"And you're *definitely* not Janice." She looked past me, into the apartment.

"Mike's my boss," I said a little too quickly—definitely *not* cool. "I'm cat sitting while he and Janice are in Florida visiting friends. He totally knows I'm here." My heart picked up its pace. I didn't need this sitcom girl thinking she'd stumbled into an active crime scene. I pointed into the apartment, but Mike's cat—my lone alibi—was nowhere to be found. "I'd be happy to pass along a message. They'll be back the day after Christmas."

"Do you know anything about pipes?" she asked.

"Pipes?"

"Pipes." She paused, waiting for a look of recognition from me that never came. "Like, sinks and showers and . . . you know, pipes."

"Oh, *plumbing.*" I didn't know the first thing about plumbing, but that didn't stop me from nodding. When it comes to attractive females my policy has always been to nod first and ask questions later. "Sure. Why, what seems to be the problem?"

The cat strolled out from its hiding place and rubbed itself against my leg. "Awww," the girl cooed, kneeling down to scratch behind its ear. "She likes you."

Mental note: Give Mike's cat extra food before bed. It's impossible to look like a criminal when there's a well-groomed calico rubbing against your calf.

"Yeah, we've really hit it off these last twenty-four hours," I said. "I'm already dreading our good-byes."

"You're a little cutie, aren't you?" she said in that strange voice girls reserve for animals and small children. I watched her scratch down by the cat's tail. She was wearing an old, beat-up sweatshirt, ripped jeans, and Ugg boots, but I could still tell she came from money. This gave her a certain power over me that I was nowhere near schooled enough to understand.

She stood back up, and when our eyes met this time, my stomach growled so loudly I had to cover it up by faking a small coughing fit.

"You okay?" she asked.

I straightened up, nodding. "Yeah. Wow. Excuse me."

"Anyway," she said. "I have a little situation upstairs. When I try and turn on the water in the shower, nothing comes out. Like, not even a drizzle. Do you know about stuff like that?"

"A little bit." *Lies!* "Need me to take a look?"

"Would you?"

"Lemme grab the keys." I darted back into Mike's living room trying to call back all the times I'd seen my old man go at the plumbing underneath the kitchen sink with his trusted wrench. I could still picture him lying on his back, halfway in the cabinet, twisting and turning things in a chorus of clanging metal.

Why hadn't I paid more attention?

Fake Espinoza

Her place smelled like tomato sauce and garlic bread and Parmesan cheese. As she led me through the kitchen, into the long hall, my mouth started watering its ass off. Maybe I was better off staying in Mike's pad, where I'd been able to convince myself that the entire borough of Brooklyn was participating in a Christmas fast.

"I'm Haley, by the way."

"Shy," I told her.

She glanced at me, still walking. "Like, S-H-Y?"

"Exactly." I'd been through this exchange dozens of times since landing in New York. Which I found strange. Nobody back home even thought twice about my name.

Haley shrugged and we shook hands awkwardly on the move, and then she stopped in front of the bathroom door and motioned me inside. "This is it. It's the same thing with my roommate's shower, too."

Her bathroom smelled of perfumed soaps, and there was a framed poster of a couple kissing in front of the Eiffel Tower. Her sink was covered with makeup and eyelash curlers and this fancy circular vanity mirror that made my face look three times its normal size. There were pastel-colored towels in two sizes stacked neatly beside the black polka-dot shower curtain, which Haley swept aside. She turned both valves all the way on, but nothing came out. "See?" she said.

"Interesting," I told her, staring at the faucet and rubbing my chin. I turned on the Hot valve again, then the Cold. They didn't work for me, either. Then I ducked my head under the bath spout and stared up into the matchbook-sized hole, pretending to be studying God knows what.

I knew my old man was proud of me in certain ways. When NYU called from across the country offering to pay my entire tuition—as well as a monthly stipend for living expenses—he even threw a party to celebrate. My aunties, uncles, a few cousins, and my girl at the time, Jessica, all came over with home-cooked dishes and booze, and just before we sat down to eat, Pops held up his can of Tecate to say a few words (in English out of respect for Jessica). "I never believe this was possible," he said, looking around our small living room. "A college boy is an Espinoza. But it happens. Congratulations to my son, Shy!" Everybody clinked glasses and drank and patted me on the back and told me they always knew I would do something special.

But at the same time, all of us were aware that I'd failed to learn the one thing that defined Espinoza men: the ability to work with one's hands. Pops had tried to show me how to change the oil in his truck, how to strip shingles off an angled roof and lay hot tar, how to rewire a dead outlet, but it didn't take long for him to realize I was a lost cause. My one talent in life? Filling in those little bubbles on Scantron sheets. That was it. Honest to God, I had a gift for those damn bubbles.

"I wonder if it has something to do with this weather," Haley said, as I continued turning the valves back and forth. "Like, maybe the pipes froze."

"I was just thinking that." I looked up at her. "It would explain the lack of water pressure." I had no idea what I was going to say next until I said it.

"Great," she said, sarcastically. "My shower doesn't work, and the super's upstate until after the holidays. I guess I'll be growing some holiday dreadlocks."

"Seems weird the pipes would freeze in a brand-new building," I said.

"Right? And why does the toilet still flush?" Haley pushed down the silver handle to prove it, and we both watched the water swirl and suck down the bowl in a gurgling crescendo before slowly rising again. "Maybe they're on different lines or something?"

"They're definitely on different lines," I said, because it sounded pretty logical. Plus, I would hate to think my shitter was connected to the faucet I used to brush my teeth.

"The kitchen sink works," Haley said, "but not this one." She turned those two valves as well and nothing came out. She shook her head. "I should be back home in Portland right now, standing under a scalding-hot shower. But like an idiot I waited until the last minute to book my ticket. And then, you know, they canceled all those flights."

"You're welcome to use Mike's shower," I said.

Haley looked at me for a few long seconds, like she was thinking. "That's sweet, but I'll be all right. Isn't it supposed to be good for your skin to occasionally skip showers?"

"I've heard about that." But I knew the real reason. I didn't strike her as the trustworthy type. I was wearing ripped jeans and an ancient-looking T-shirt. I had my home area code tattooed clumsily onto my knuckles on both hands.

Don't ask.

I was only fifteen and tequila was involved.

"Something about the natural oils or whatever." She shrugged. "Anyway."

I turned back to Haley, who was obviously waiting for me to leave now that I'd proven useless. "Well, I should probably get back downstairs to feed the cat. Sorry I couldn't help."

"No worries." She led me out of the bathroom and back through the hall and kitchen, where my empty stomach sounded like the Fourth of July.

She held open the front door.

"Happy holidays," I told her.

"You too." She smiled. "And I appreciate you coming up here to take a look."

As I walked toward the elevator, I listened for the click of Haley's door behind me. When I finally heard it, I felt crushingly alone.

How to Pass a Night

I finished the plain yogurt for dinner along with half a hot dog bun, then I broke into Mike's vodka. I sipped a few glasses over ice while strumming the guitar in the bathroom—my favorite place to play because of the acoustics. Mike's guitar was about six thousand times better than mine. It was like playing a stick of butter. Basic open chords came alive inside the tiled walls, especially after I flipped off the lights.

Once the vodka kicked in, I even sang a few of the tiny songs I'd been making up since high school—melancholy tunes about females and back home and losing my mom. Tunes made out of minor chords, where my pedestrian voice was no more than a whisper.

This was where music had always existed for me.

Inside a dark bathroom.

Alone.

The feeling it gave me was an odd combination of weightless self-pity and excitement. I understood my life was meaningless, and this knowledge freed me up to accomplish absolutely anything.

Anyway, I passed most of the night this way.

The cat came into the bathroom a few times to check me out. And whenever I'd hear Haley's subtle footfalls—her place was directly above Mike's—I would stop singing and strum more softly.

Around midnight, I put away the guitar and pulled out the book I was reading and moved into the living room, and it wasn't long until I found the cat curled up next to my feet. I guess we were becoming actual friends. Something like that. I leaned over to read the charm hanging from her collar: Olive.

Mike had told me her name when he showed me how to do the food and change the litter, but this felt like our true introduction.

I scratched behind Olive's ear the way Haley had and listened to the ceiling, but it had gone quiet up there.

Long-Distance Relationships

L ate the next afternoon, there was another knock at the door. I turned away from the window, where Olive and I had been sitting together, staring at the perpetually falling snow. I kicked the blanket off my feet and went to the door and looked through the peephole. Haley again. This time she'd brought with her a towel, a change of clothes, and a bathroom bag. I opened the door, saying, "You changed your mind."

She peered into the living room. "Your TV's not on."

"Uh . . . yeah." I looked over my shoulder, at Mike's dormant big screen. "I mean, no. Wait, why?"

"What do you *do* in here all day?"

"I cat sit."

Haley rolled her eyes. "Most cat sitters can manage to watch TV at the same time." She switched her bathroom bag from one arm to the other, adding: "Not sure you're aware of this, but we're kind of snowed in right now, which is the perfect excuse to stream Netflix. I watched an entire season of *Downton Abbey* yesterday."

"Is that the one about those rich British people?"

"I'm pretty sure your TV feed didn't go the way of my shower pipes," Haley said, ignoring my question.

I pointed to her bathroom bag. "I see you reconsidered the Christmas dreads."

She let out a dramatic sigh. "I thought about it last night. And I'm going to take you up on your offer."

I sensed a *but* coming.

"But here's my thing. . . ." Haley glanced around Mike's apartment. "Interesting," she said, distracted. "It's the exact same layout as my place, but at the same time it looks totally different." She turned back to me. "In order for me to feel comfortable taking a shower down here, we have to both share something about ourselves first. Then I'll feel like I know you better. And it won't be so weird."

"Seriously, Haley. I'll stay way on this side of the apartment. I promise."

"That's not the point."

I glanced into the kitchen where Olive had gone back to housing her wet food. My empty stomach was beyond the cramping stage now, which made me wonder if I'd started digesting muscle. I stepped aside, motioning for Haley to come in.

She walked over to Mike's L-shaped couch and sat down.

I sat, too. "So, what kind of stuff are we supposed to say?"

"Anything," she said. "It could be about your childhood. Or about where you're from. Or why you're wearing a beanie indoors. Seriously, anything."

I pulled off my beanie and opened my mouth to ask a follow-up question, but she cut me off. "On second thought, maybe you should put that back on."

"Why?" I stood up to look in the mirror mounted on the wall behind the couch. My hair was a rats' nest of thick, brown waves. It was the longest I'd ever had it. I put the beanie back on, saying: "I guess I kind of need a haircut."

"You think?"

Sweet, another thing I couldn't afford.

Back home my auntie Cecilia always cut it for free.

"Okay, I'll start." Haley paused for a few seconds, looking around, then said, "Long-distance relationships are all about patience. And my boyfriend, Justin, is probably the most patient man alive."

"How so?" I took the bait, even though I knew what she was doing. This was Haley's way of establishing that she was in a relationship, which she believed would lessen the risk of me trying to sneak into the shower with her while she was busy rinsing out her Awapuhi.

"Like I said yesterday," Haley answered. "I was supposed to book my own ticket home. But I procrastinated. So Justin's back in Portland right now, hanging out at home, when we were supposed to be heading to a B&B in Seaside. Our parents are friends, and they said as long as we were back by Christmas day. . . . Anyway, instead of getting mad at me, which is what I would've done, all Justin wants to talk about is my frozen pipes. He actually feels bad for me, can you believe it? That's some serious patience."

"Wow," I said, playing along. "He sounds . . . patient."

"Okay, now you."

I sat there for an uncomfortable amount of time, trying to think of something interesting to say. I couldn't talk about a distant girlfriend the way I wanted to—which would *definitely* make Haley feel more comfortable about the shower situation.

"It doesn't have to be some big profound thing," she told me. "It can be simple."

"Got it," I said, still brainstorming. Then it came to me. "My little sister, who's probably my best friend in the world, turns seventeen on Christmas day. This is the first birthday of hers I'll have ever missed." Sofe wasn't technically my best friend, and she didn't technically turn seventeen until the week *after* Christmas, but the point was to show Haley I was a solid brother, which would hopefully increase her trust in me.

"Ah, that's sad. Why didn't you go home?"

No money! "Because I promised Mike I'd cat sit."

Haley frowned. "I'm sure he'd have understood. It's Christmas. *And* your sister's birthday."

"I have a lot of homework and stuff, too," I lied.

"Ah, I figured you were a student," Haley said. "What school?"

"NYU."

She nodded. "Isn't your semester over?"

I pulled my beanie tighter over my forehead and shifted positions on the couch. "Actually, it's for *next* semester." I pointed at the novel I'd been reading. "This one lit class I'm taking has a grip of reading. I'm trying to, like, get ahead, you know?" It was true that a class I'd signed up for had a large reading list, but the book on the couch had nothing to do with school. And I was a fast reader.

"What year are you?" Haley asked.

"Freshman. You?"

"I'm a sophomore at Columbia."

"Nice, a college veteran," I said.

Haley forced a laugh. "Please. I have no idea what I'm even going to major in."

I glanced at my book again.

There was another awkward silence at that point, and after a few seconds Haley stood up and said, "See?"

I stood up, too. "See what?"

"Now we know a little about each other. Which means it's less weird for me to take a shower at your place."

"Well, technically," I pointed out, "it's not *my* place."

"It's yours through the holidays, right?"

"I guess so." I watched Haley disappear into the hall, and a few seconds later I heard the bathroom door in the master bedroom close. I looked around the apartment, trying to imagine it as my place. The designer couch. The expensive-looking leather chair. The massive flat-screen mounted on the wall. The fancy-looking paintings.

What would my old man say if he saw me standing here right now?

He'd think I was cat sitting in a museum.

I read the entire time Haley was in Mike's bathroom—which was a shockingly long time. When she finally walked back into the living room, her hair was wet and I could tell she was wearing fresh makeup. She looked beautiful.

I sat down my book and got up, saying, "Everything go okay in there?"

"It was quite lovely. Thanks." She waited for me to open the front door. When I did, she looked me dead in the eye and said, "Thank you, Shy."

I got a weird, unbalanced feeling hearing her say my name, and I told her, "My shower's your shower, Haley." But that sounded kind of sexual so I quickly added: "I mean, you can bathe in my place anytime." But that was creepy, too. "I mean—"

"I know what you mean," she said, saving me from myself. "I appreciate it."

She gave me a nice smile and left Mike's apartment.

When I closed the door, I found Olive looking up at me, accusatorily.

"What?" I asked.

She meowed.

"Look," I told her, "you're gonna have to start speaking English around here."

She stuck out her front paws, stretched her multicolored back, and crept away.

Angels in the Snow

Haley was back early the next morning with her bathroom bag, a change of clothes, and a fresh towel. "I don't mean to keep interrupting . . . whatever it is you do down here," she said, "but I kind of had an accident in the kitchen." She held out the front of her gray Columbia sweatshirt. There was a large catsup stain between the *m* and the *b*.

I motioned for her to come inside. "You can just leave your stuff in there if you want."

She forced a laugh. "Yeah, I don't think so. That would be taking it *way* too far. Besides, how do I know you're not the kind of person who snoops through people's things?"

"I don't even shower in there. I use the one in the spare bedroom."

"That's what they all say." She looked down at her catsup stain again. "I know technically this is more of a laundry issue, but I *feel* dirty."

"Like I said, you can shower down here whenever you want."

She set her stuff on the dining room table and reached down to pet the cat. "You're a friendly one, aren't you girl? Oh, yes, you are."

"Her name's Olive," I said.

Haley looked up at me. "We're on a first-name basis now, I see."

I shrugged. For some reason I wasn't feeling like my usual laid-back self. I think the hunger was making me irritable. But at the same time, I was happy to be talking to Haley again. Being hungry is bad news. Being hungry and alone? That's when people start Googling info about suicide hotlines.

She stood up and put her hands on her hips, like she was waiting for something. That unbalanced feeling I got whenever we made eye contact was no longer confined to my stomach. It had moved up into my chest.

"What?" I said.

"You go first this time," she said.

"We're doing that getting-to-know-you thing again?"

"Yep," Haley said. "Every time I come down here, we have to share one new thing. Those are the rules. And ideally it should be something highly personal. The last thing you shared was kind of boring—no offense to your sister." She glanced over my shoulder, into Mike and Janice's kitchen. "What are you doing for meals? It never smells like you've cooked anything, and I usually hear the takeout guys when they're coming up the steps."

"Oh, Mike left a stocked fridge for me," I lied. "The cupboards are all full, too. They made this big grocery-store run to the new Whole Foods before they left and said I should eat as much as I can."

"Nice," Haley said. "But I'm guessing you don't actually cook."

I shook my head. "I mostly make sandwiches. And cereal. Easy stuff like that." My stomach cramped so aggressively at the thought of these mythical meals I winced in pain.

"You're welcome to eat with me. It's just as easy to cook for two as it is for one."

For reasons I didn't fully understand, Haley's offer made me want to cry.

I broke eye contact and kneeled down to pet Olive. I was so hungry now I constantly felt lightheaded. My arms and legs felt like Styrofoam. I'd finished off the hot dog bun and baby carrots and the yogurts the night before. When I awoke in the morning, I had half of the chocolate bar. I still felt hungry, though, and drank glass after glass of tap water thinking it would fill me up. It didn't work.

"Well?" Haley said. "Do you want to come up and have dinner tonight? I was thinking of making vegetable lasagna, my mom's special holiday recipe."

My mouth started watering.

Real food.

"I can't," I told her.

"What do you mean you can't?"

I didn't know how to answer this truthfully. Maybe it was stupid pride—the one thing I *had* picked up from the rest of the Espinoza men. Or maybe it was a fear of being found out. I constantly felt like an imposter among the other students at NYU. When were they going to figure out I didn't belong here, that some lady in admissions had made a mistake, had offered a scholarship to the wrong guy? I probably spent as much time trying to hide my ghetto as I did on homework.

"I'm supposed to talk to my family back home," I said.

"Then come up after."

"No, like my *whole* family," I told her. "Since I won't be there on Christmas. But I totally appreciate the offer."

She just stared at me for a few long seconds. "You're weird."

I guess she had that part right.

"Anyway." Haley grabbed her stuff off the table. "You go first this time."

I still felt oddly emotional, which wasn't like me. In fact, I hadn't cried for over a year, since my mom's funeral.

Maybe that's what I could tell her, I thought. How when I saw my mom lying in the casket, my dumb ass broke down . . . in front of *everyone*. How I started shouting about the world being a fucked-up piece-of-shit place that I was done with, too. How a few relatives tried to get me to calm down, but all I did was turn my wrath on them. "Who you talking to?" I shouted in my uncle Guillermo's face. "You don't know shit about me!" When he reached for my arm I smacked his hand away. I could tell Haley about *that*. How tears were streaming down

my face, even though my expression never changed, not even a little. And I kept shouting, "I don't give a fuck about anything! You
hear me?"

I didn't stop crying until my dad came over and slapped me across
the face. Right there, in front of everyone. At the foot of my mom's
casket. Slapped me like I was some punk five-year-old.

And as I walked out of the funeral home that day I made myself a
promise.

I would never cry again.

For as long as I lived.

No matter what happened or who got sick and died.

"Hel-lo." Haley waved her hands in front of my face. "Earth to Shy."

I took a deep breath and let it out slow. Instead of telling her about
my dead mom, I told her about the first time I saw snow.

Two years ago, our family drove to the mountains outside of San
Diego and stayed at a campsite, in a family-sized tent my uncle loaned
us. My parents promised me and my little sis we'd see snow, but the
first three days there was nothing. It was just cold. And windy. We
spent the majority of our time inside the tent, playing stupid games
like Uno and Loteria and Mexican dominos. But when we woke up on
the morning on the fourth day, it happened. Thick beautiful snowflakes were falling from the sky. And it had accumulated on the ground
all around us. I told Haley how while my dad and sis took turns going
down this little hill near our campsite on a cheap plastic sled, me and
my mom lay on our backs and did snow angels just outside our tent.
Like a couple of giggling kindergartners. And when we got up to check
them out, it looked like our angels were holding hands.

Haley smiled. "You're getting better at this."

I shrugged, still picturing the life I used to have.

"Isn't it funny how one day you'll be hoping for something, like
snow, and the next day you'll be hoping it goes away?" Haley motioned
toward Mike's big windows, where the snow was still coming down.

We watched it for a while, then Haley told me about the time she
first became aware of race. She didn't know why, but last night, the
memory came to her out of nowhere. Maybe because of something
she was watching on TV. Anyway, she was a little girl living in a

wealthy suburb outside of Portland. And for her sixth birthday, her parents took her into the city to see a musical. They made a big thing of it, got dressed up and everything, hopped in her dad's Mercedes and made the drive. Haley said she remembered driving by this one McDonald's, in a sketchy part of the city, where she saw a group of black women dressed strangely, wearing tons of makeup—they were prostitutes, though she was too young to understand that. Haley was in the backseat, in her fancy white dress, staring at these women, because she'd never seen anything like it. Her dad stopped at a light right in front of them, and while he waited for it to change, Haley stared and stared, until one of the women turned and met eyes with her. But Haley still couldn't look away. She was transfixed. After a few seconds, the woman wobbled right up to Haley's window, in her sparkly high heels, and pointed a finger in Haley's face. "Wha'chu staring at, white girl? You trying to steal my story?"

"I don't know why I just told you that," Haley said. "I don't think I've shared that with anyone before. Not even my closest girlfriends."

We both stood there awkwardly for a few seconds. It was like we'd ripped open our chests and revealed our beating hearts. And how do you transition back to small talk after that?

Finally Haley cleared her throat and said she was going to clean up. She seemed embarrassed. I went over to the couch and tried to read my book, but all I could think about was Haley's story. Did she tell me that because I was part Mexican? Because she thought I was from a bad neighborhood? Or maybe it had nothing to do with me. We were just two people alone in a building, during a blizzard. As soon as the skies cleared, maybe this strange little dream we seemed to be sharing would slip away from us forever.

I read the same paragraph about sixty straight times, but I still had no idea what I was reading. And then Haley walked back into the living room, her hair wet, makeup freshly applied. She looked more beautiful than ever. "God, I love being clean," she said.

"Me, too." I pulled my weak body off the couch.

"When you get in there today," she said, "maybe try and do something with that hair?"

I pulled off my beanie. "You mean this?"

She took a few steps toward me and rustled my hair a little, which caught me off guard. "At least you don't have to worry about going bald," she said.

I pulled my beanie back on.

"Anyway, if you change your mind about dinner just come up. Doesn't matter what time."

"Cool." I opened the door for her.

Haley did the "eye contact" thing, which led to the "unbalanced" thing. "Because I don't see how a call home can take all night. But whatever." She gave a little wave and left.

It wasn't until a few hours later that I discovered Haley had left her towel and bathroom bag in Mike's master bathroom.

Breaking Point

I didn't go up to Haley's for dinner that night.

Didn't call home, either.

I ate the rest of Mike's chocolate bar and drank a plastic cup full of vodka and played music in the bathroom, and then I did something kind of weird, I guess. I fell asleep in the bathtub. I don't even know why. It's not like I passed out or anything. I just didn't feel like going to the living room. Or the spare bedroom. So I lay Mike's guitar on the bathroom floor and climbed into the tub and slid down so that I could rest my head against the lip of it, and I closed my eyes and thought about my life.

Back home I had known exactly who I was, but out here, in New York, I didn't have a clue. Everything seemed to be spinning out of control. And I was brutally hungry now. It felt like someone was wringing my insides out like a washcloth.

All I wanted to do was have one of those deep talks me and my mom used to have.

But I couldn't.

When I woke up, I had a slight hangover and Olive was sitting on the toilet, staring at me, and I had this intense feeling of shame. Because of the cat. Seriously. I didn't want her to see me this way. Sleeping in a bathtub. You know how they say animals can sense emotional shit way beyond what humans are capable of? I wondered what Olive was sensing about me as she sat there staring.

Or maybe I didn't want to know.

Just as I was climbing out of the tub, I heard Haley knocking again. I pulled on my beanie and rushed to the front door. Before I opened it, though, I had a moment of panic. My clothes. I was wearing the same jeans and shirt she'd seen me in the day before. But it's not like I could pretend I wasn't home.

I swung open the door, saying: "I'm the one who got catsup all over myself today. I had to change back into my clothes from yesterday."

Haley was standing there with more than a change of clothes this time. She had a plate of muffins, too. "I baked these this morning," she said, ignoring my catsup lie, "and I need them out of my house so I don't, like, eat every single one in the next fifteen minutes."

"Thanks," I said, feeling another strange surge of emotion.

Instead of handing me the plate, she pushed past me and went into the kitchen. "They're banana nut, by the way. I'll stick them in the fridge so Olive doesn't—"

"No, wait!" I shouted.

But it was too late.

Haley froze, staring into Mike's empty fridge. It took a while before she turned around, wearing a confused expression. "There's nothing in here."

My heart sank.

She stuck the plate of muffins on the shelf and closed the fridge and turned her attention toward the empty cupboards. I didn't even try to stop her this time, just watched her open and close all the doors. "Why'd you lie to me?" she asked in a hurt voice.

I tried to laugh it off. "Lie to you? I didn't lie."

"You said Mike and Janice left you groceries."

"They did," I said, trying to maintain my smile. "I just . . . went through them already. Pretty stupid, right? It's not even Christmas until tomorrow. Guess I'll go pick a few things up at the corner bodega."

Haley went to the trash can by the sink and lifted the lid. "There's nothing in the trash, Shy."

I leaned against the wall and didn't say anything.

"I'm gonna take a shower." She pointed toward the fridge. "And then we're gonna talk."

"About what?"

"Everything," Haley answered. "In the meantime, eat the muffins." Then she turned and headed off toward the master bathroom.

Soon as I heard the door click shut behind her, I went to the fridge and stared at the plate of muffins. I peeled back the cellophane she'd used to cover them and took one out and smelled it. They were still warm. Saliva pooled around my tongue. My nutrient-starved brain felt swollen and slow.

I needed to eat.

Badly.

But I couldn't.

Not with Haley still in the apartment. She couldn't know how hungry I was. Because if she did, she'd know how different our lives were. And she'd probably stop coming down here to use the shower.

I put the muffin back and closed the fridge and went to the couch and pretended to read. When Haley came out of the bathroom this time—hair damp, face freshly made up—she went directly into the kitchen and opened the fridge.

"What's wrong with you?" she said on her way back into Mike's living room. "Seriously, Shy."

"*Nothing's* wrong with me," I answered in an even tone.

She stared at me for several long seconds. Then she threw her hands in the air and let herself out the front door.

Once I was sure she wasn't going to come barging back in, I flung open the fridge door and took out the plate of muffins and sat on the floor and shoved the entire first one into my mouth, and I chewed and chewed and chewed, while at the same time grabbing the next one, getting ready to shove that one into my mouth, too.

And I began to sob.

I don't even know why.

But it was the first time I'd felt tears on my cheeks since the day of my mom's funeral. And they felt surprisingly good. They felt alive.

Mostly because they reminded me of my mom, I think. And because it felt so amazing to fill my stomach.

I stayed there on the floor like that for a long, long time.

Eating and crying.

Crying and eating.

Trying not to think about anything but Haley's muffins.

What Would It Be Like?

Maybe I'm more like my old man than I realize.

Remember how I said my sis has to sometimes drag him to the dinner table? That's pretty much what Haley had to do for me tonight.

She came down at around seven, but she wasn't looking to use the shower. She grabbed me by the wrist, without saying a word, and led me out of Mike's place, onto the elevator, then into her amazing-smelling apartment where she sat me at her dining room table. "Stay," she said, like I was some kind of German shepherd. Then she marched into her kitchen and pulled open her oven door.

I sat there, looking at my hands and thinking about back home.

Christmas Eve is always better than Christmas for us Espinozas. All the cousins and aunties and uncles show up at my grandma's, and the whole place smells like tortillas and chile colorado, and Auntie Cecilia brings in heaping plates of sweet tamales, and my uncle Guillermo sneaks us hits off the Patrón bottle he always dresses up in Christmas wrapping paper ("A little present for my own self, *esé!*"). In the living room, all the men tell stories about work, while the women in the kitchen tell stories about the men. And the whole apartment is filled with nonstop laughter, even when one of the little ones knocks something over, a glass frame or crystal figurine, we all just laugh and laugh and laugh, even Grandma as she sweeps the glass shards into her ancient metal dust pan.

Home, man.

I missed that shit so much.

I missed *them.*

"There's no way I'm going to let you starve down there on Christmas Eve," Haley said, walking back into the dining room with a plate full of food. She set it down in front of me.

"I wasn't starving," I said, staring at her beautiful dinner.

She lowered her eyes at me. "Yes, you were, Shy."

"Okay, maybe a little."

Why was she doing all of this for me? I wondered. Because I'd loaned her Mike's shower? If that was it, she was definitely getting the raw end of the deal. All I'd had to do is let her in the front door. Judging by what was on my plate, she'd busted her ass in the kitchen. She'd grilled some sort of white fish and made roasted potatoes and sourdough bread and these broccoli pieces with long stems I always forget the name of.

"You want a Pinot Gris or a Chardonnay?" she shouted from the kitchen.

"Are you talking about wine?" I called back.

She came out with a second plate of food and set it down across from me. "Of course I'm talking about wine. What else would I be talking about?"

"When it comes to that stuff," I told her, squirming in my chair, "you're gonna have to dumb it down a little. All I know is red or white."

She stood there, staring at me. "Well, they're *both* white. White goes with fish."

"So, that settles it then," I said. "We'll go with the white."

"I know, but—oh, forget it." She went back into the kitchen and came back with a bottle of wine and poured our glasses full. "Cheers," she said, holding up her glass.

"*Salud,*" I said, the way my old man always does.

We clinked glasses.

After the half dozen muffins I'd wolfed down for breakfast—that's right, I ate every last one of those bastards—I was no longer desperate. But my entire body came alive when I started putting down Haley's perfectly grilled fish. This was *real* food. With *real* nutritional value. I felt like I was turning from a floppy, stuffed bear into an actual human being.

The wine wasn't hurting, either, and Haley was quick to refill our glasses.

"Oh, and don't think you're getting off the hook," she said.

"What do you mean?"

"The truth game," she said. "Just because I didn't take a shower tonight doesn't mean we're not sharing."

"This dinner's amazing," I said, pointing at my half-empty plate.

"It's just baked cod." Haley paused for a few seconds before adding: "But thank you. I need to be better at taking compliments."

"You go first this time." I stabbed another piece of long-stemmed broccoli. I don't know why, but I was excited to hear what Haley had to share. Maybe I was kind of getting into her corny game.

"Okay." Haley took a sip of wine and then just sat there, holding her glass, like she was thinking. "Sometimes I worry. About myself, I mean. I don't have a . . . 'thing.' I got good grades all through high school, right? Strike that. I got *very* good grades. I was valedictorian. And I scored high on the SATs. And I had all the extracurriculars my counselor said I should have for my college applications. I volunteered at a mental health clinic during sophomore year, but I only did it because I knew it would look good. Messed up, right?"

It was at that moment that I realized how truly beautiful Haley was. She had a perfect complexion and high cheekbones and there were these cute little freckles surrounding her nose. But I don't just mean physically. A lot of girls look good to me—I have what you might call a flexible aesthetic. But there was something about Haley that went beyond looks. Like how she had these dimples whenever she grinned. And when she said something self-effacing, she'd shrug her shoulders a little and tilt her head and glance at her feet. And sometimes when her light brown eyes locked on to my dark brown ones, it was like she was reaching a hand all the way into my chest, like she was digging around in there for the most honest thing she could find. It made me want to quit hiding, even though I'd be taking the chance of her not liking what she discovered.

"The problem is," Haley went on, "I never understood *why* I was doing anything—other than I knew it was expected." She refilled both our glasses again. "And I'm not even saying my parents pushed me. Or my counselors at school. It was *me*. I wanted to excel. But every decision I made through high school was based on how I thought it might make me look on paper. I never once stopped to think about what I actually *liked* to do. That's kind of sad, don't you think?"

"More like honest." Usually, I liked to keep quiet. I liked to listen. But the wine was just reaching my head, and I felt oddly comfortable, so I let myself talk. "Here's a question," I told her. "Would you rather be great at something you like, or just okay at something you love?"

"Jesus, I don't know," Haley said. "That's hard. What about you? Sounds like this is coming from a personal place."

I stuck my silverware on my empty plate and leaned back with my wineglass. I felt like I was in a movie or something. One about rich British people, like the show Haley had mentioned before. Talking all deep in a beautiful New York apartment. Swirling damn wine in an actual wineglass. The only other time I'd had wine, me and Jessica drank it out of shot glasses, because that's all we could find at her stepdad's place. "The one thing I know I love," I said, "besides my family, is music. Guitar. But I also know I'm not that good at it."

"You play down there sometimes, don't you?"

"Me? No way, not at Mike's. I'm talking about at my own place." *Stop lying!* "Okay, maybe I mess around a little. Not for real, though."

"I knew it," Haley said. "At first I thought it was the radio, which must mean you're pretty good."

I shook my head, embarrassed. "Anyways, let's just move on."

Haley laughed. "Looks like I'm not the only one who could be better at taking compliments."

After a short stretch of silence, one that didn't even feel that awkward, I said, "I guess I don't really know what I want to do, either. Sometimes I feel like a shook-up bottle of soda. Like, I have all this passion that wants to explode, but I don't know where to aim it yet. Is that kind of what you mean?"

"Exactly. And sometimes I get worried I'll *never* know where to aim it." Haley emptied the rest of the wine bottle into our glasses, but there were only a few drops left so she got up and opened the second one.

We talked for hours after dinner. When the second bottle of wine was gone, I raced downstairs to grab Mike's bottle of vodka. When I came back, Haley fixed us vodka cranberries and we sat on the couch in the living room and we talked and talked and talked. Haley told me what it was like growing up in Oregon. I told her about life near the Mexican border. Haley described what she'd be doing back home right now—dinner at a fancy restaurant with her mom, dad, and little sister, followed by each of them opening one gift by the fire—and I told her about Christmas Eve at my grandma's.

By midnight I was officially drunk, and as much as I liked talking to Haley, I also wondered what it would be like to kiss Haley, so I started down a very different road. "Hey, Haley," I said.

"Hey, Shy."

"Maybe it's my turn to make up the rules."

"Uh-oh." Haley looked away from me, sensing where I was going. "This isn't my game anymore, though. This is just two people talking. Please tell me you know the difference."

"I know," I said. "But I just maybe . . . sort of . . ."

"What?"

"I wonder how it would feel to, like, you know, hold your hand. That's all." I set down my wineglass and faced her. "Like if we were on an actual date."

Haley forced a laugh. "We wouldn't be on an actual date, though. Because I have a boyfriend back home, *remember*?"

"Oh, shit," I said. "The patient guy. I almost forgot about him."

It was true. I'd gotten so caught up in the moment I completely forgot about the world outside of the apartment complex. I picked up my wineglass again, sipped a little more vodka cranberry.

That's when Haley did something that surprised me. She set down her glass, then took my glass out of my hand and set *it* down, too. "But it's not like you're talking about getting married, right? You're talking about holding hands. Hypothetically."

I swallowed hard. "To test the feel."

"Which I suppose is pretty harmless in the grand scheme of things."

"Though, I'll be honest." I touched Haley's bare ankle. "A small part of me might also be talking about marrying you."

She slapped my hand away. "See, this is why I never should've taken a shower down there. Showers can lead to hand-holding, which can lead to. . . . People are better off growing Christmas dreads."

Haley smoothed her pretty hair behind her ears and reached for my hand.

I could barely breathe.

It was everything I wanted, but at the same time, it was scary as shit, too. Because I knew myself. I felt the "unbalanced thing" to the point that I couldn't even think straight. Haley's eyes locked inside mine. Her hand in my hand, which was making my whole arm tingle, my whole body.

"It's a pretty good fit," I managed to say.

She made it so our fingers were linked and, for a few long seconds, we just looked at each other. I glanced at her lips before forcing myself back to her eyes. Her face grew more serious, and she cleared her throat softly. "I have to admit something. It's kind of bad."

"Uh-oh," I said, nervous she was going to pull the plug.

"I didn't really procrastinate. I bought my plane ticket home *weeks* ago."

In my drunken state it took me a few seconds to realize what she was saying. She'd *chosen* not to go home. Which meant she was avoiding something. Possibly some*one*. My heart pounded against the inside of my chest.

"I just never went to the airport," she said.

"Why?"

"Because I'm a coward." She scooted a little closer to me on the couch. "Do you think less of me now?"

"Why would I?" I said.

She shrugged. "What are you thinking, then?"

I swallowed and stared at my drink for a couple seconds. When I looked back up at her I said, "I'm thinking about what it would be like to kiss your cheek."

Haley breathed deeply and squeezed my hand. "Maybe you should find out."

But when I leaned in, aiming for just inside her left ear, she turned suddenly and I ended up kissing her on the lips instead.

It was just a peck and then I pulled back and looked at her. Both our eyes locking on each other's and our chests going in and out and in and out. Without thinking, I took her face in my hands, gently as I could, and I kissed her again. Longer this time. Not a peck, but the real kind. And she kissed me back.

She shoved me onto my back, still kissing me, her hands gripping wildly at my hair, mine slowly moving down her warm body. "What are we doing?" she breathed into my ear.

"I don't even know," I said, and then we were kissing again.

I got lost in it. Her lips. Her touch. Me and Haley. She'd made me dinner, and now we were together on her couch. It didn't seem possible. And for a few seconds, my amazement pulled me out of my body. I found myself hovering up near the ceiling, watching everything unfold in awe. But then I forced myself to focus on her lips again, and the feel of my hands on her stomach, and I rematerialized.

It was all so . . . alive.

I felt like I was breathing the world into my lungs.

In a few minutes, I flipped her onto *her* back and pinned *her* arms. And I pulled away and just stared at her, both of us breathing, wanting more.

"What is it?" she said.

"I wonder more things," I told her.

She closed her eyes and slowly opened them. "I know you do, but . . ."

"Like how it would feel to *be* with you."

When she didn't answer, I lowered my face toward hers and we kissed some more, but this time I felt this surge of energy so powerful my mind slipped away completely, and I reached up and undid her blouse, one button at a time, and then I reached around her back and undid her bra clasp.

That's when she stopped me.

She turned her head and spun out of my grip and immediately started re-clasping her bra and buttoning her blouse.

"Oh, shit." I watched her, my stomach flooding with nervous butterflies. "Shit, I went too far, didn't I?" When she didn't answer right away, I said, "Haley?"

She stood up and covered her face with her hands for a few seconds.

When she removed them, her expression was worried. "What am I *doing*?"

"It was totally my fault," I said.

She started to pick up our still half-full wineglasses, then she put them back down and went to the door and pulled it open. "I'm going to have to ask you to leave, Shy. I'm sorry."

"I apologize, Haley. I got carried away—"

"Just, please," she said, cutting me off.

And she wouldn't look at me. That was maybe the worst part of all. If she'd have just looked at me, then she'd know how sincerely apologetic I was, and everything would be okay. But she never did.

"Okay." I moved through the door, into the hall. I hit the elevator button and stared at my shoes, listening to her door click closed behind me.

Christmas Day

Haley didn't come down for a shower on Christmas morning. I waited around in the living room on the couch next to Olive, listening for her knock, but it never came.

I stared at the text of my novel, but really I was analyzing the night before, from every possible angle. It always came down to the same thing: me. I knew she had a boyfriend. Yeah, maybe the fact that she didn't fly home meant they were on the rocks or whatever, but still. I'd taken it too far.

Why'd I have to be that guy?

The one who always wanted more?

I didn't call home until noon because of the three-hour time difference. I talked to my dad a little, but mostly I talked to my sis. Merry Christmas, we both told each other. She described all the food she was making, and how Pops was driving to Chula Vista to pick up Grandma, who had promised to bring a big stack of tortillas. Then they were going to drive up to the cemetery with flowers. "It won't be the same without you," my sis told me.

"Yeah."

"No, I'm serious, it'll be the first time I've ever gone there without you." She paused. "You better not be spending today alone, Shy. Because that would just be sad."

"Oh, hell no. A few friends are coming over and we're baking a ham and shit. It's gonna be legit." I switched the phone from one ear to the other. "I still wish I was with you guys, though."

"By the way, Peanut's tooth is better. We can tell 'cause he's constantly hounding us for food again. Which *you* started."

I smiled, remembering how I used to sneak Peanut my dinner scraps on the sly.

We talked a little more, about my old man, who she claimed was doing better, too, and then I told her I had to go get ready for my friends. We said our good-byes, but before she could hang up I said, "Oh, and Sofe?"

"Yeah?"

"Stay away from dudes."

I showered with the door open and put on the best shirt I'd packed for cat sitting, and I even put some of Mike's gel in my hair, trying to tame my crop. Then I sat with the cat and read my book, though secretly I was still listening for a knock.

Snow-Covered Stoop

I woke up from a nap to the sound of Olive scratching at the front door.

"Where *you* trying to go?" I said, climbing off the couch.

Then I saw it.

A small card on the ground, just inside the door. My name written in neat, girl handwriting. I picked it up and looked through the peephole. Nobody there.

I tore open the envelope. A skinny Santa was on the front of the card, waving from behind the wheel of a hybrid convertible. The handwritten note inside said: "Leftover lasagna from the night you stood me up. Heat in microwave for two or three minutes. Also, Merry Christmas."

I opened the door and found a large plate covered in tinfoil. *She didn't hate me!* The second I reached down for it, though, Olive squirted out into the hall.

"Hey, man!" I set down the plate and lunged for her, but she took off up the stairs. The door slammed behind me as I took the stairs, two at a time, to Haley's floor. Olive was nowhere to be found.

Great, I thought. My one damn job.

I hurried to the highest floor and searched the landing and looked out the window at the snow-covered fire escape, then I ran all the way back down to the ground floor and checked the front vestibule, where the mailboxes were. There was no sign of Olive anywhere.

After another fifteen minutes of unsuccessful searching, I found myself standing on Haley's welcome mat, knuckles hovering in front of her door. She'd obviously left me a plate of food, as opposed to inviting me over, because she didn't want to see me. And asking for help had never been my strong suit.

Still.

I knocked.

She opened the door right away, wearing a look of concern. "What's wrong? I heard you go up and down the stairs like fifteen times."

"Olive made a run for it. I can't find her anywhere. Mike and Janice are gonna *kill* me."

Haley grabbed her keys. "I'm sure she's here somewhere. Come on."

We went back to the top floor and looked in every corner. Haley even opened the window to the fire escape and stuck out her head. Nothing. Olive wasn't in the elevator, either. Or the trash chute. Or the bike room. We scoured every floor, all the way down to the ground, but on the way back up Haley grabbed me by the wrist and pointed.

"You gotta be shittin' me," I said.

There was Olive, sitting right beside the tinfoil-covered plate, licking her right paw. She didn't even protest when Haley scooped her up into her arms. I keyed open Mike's door, and Haley set down Olive, and we both watched her saunter over to her bowl of dry food, not a care in the world.

"Scared me to death," I said.

"You tried to cat sit and watch TV at the same time, didn't you?"

I gave her a sarcastic laugh. "Seriously, though. Thanks. I don't know what I would've done."

"No worries." Haley's hair was wet, which confused me. And her eyes looked puffy. She reached down for the plate of lasagna. "Even if it *was* just a big ploy to get me back down here." She handed me the plate.

"And thanks for this." I stood there holding it, staring at the floor. "About last night, Haley. I'm really, really sorry—"

"I know you're probably starving," she said, cutting me off. "But is it absolutely crucial for you to eat right this second?"

"Now?" I said. "Not really. Why?"

"Put on your heaviest coat and rain boots and meet me downstairs in five."

The clouds had finally cleared, and the sun was low in the sky. The outside air was crisp. I could see my breath as I followed Haley up the buried sidewalk. We were moving slowly because a thick layer of snow blanketed everything. "I seriously love being the first one to walk in it," she said, crunching into a sea of untouched white.

"Same with me." All I had on was a pair of shell-top Adidas, and my socks were already soaked. My Padres sweatshirt was way too thin. I had to bury my hands deep inside my pockets to keep them warm. But trekking through fresh snow in Brooklyn was pretty cool. Usually it turned into a nasty brown slush within minutes of falling.

When we got up to 7th Avenue, we looked up and down the empty street. "Tonight we have it all to ourselves," Haley said.

"Where we going anyway?"

"Prospect Park. I have a feeling it's gorgeous up there right now."

All the shops and restaurants were closed, their graffitied storefront gates lowered and bolted shut. Trash bags were still piled high, buried under mountains of snow. The plowers had yet to come through so you couldn't tell where the sidewalks ended and the street began. Not that there were any cars on the move. Or pedestrians, for that matter. Haley was right, we were the only two people out braving the post-blizzard conditions.

Halfway up the next block, we heard music coming from the open window of somebody's brownstone. A corny Christmas song that didn't even seem that corny. "Wanna stop and listen for a minute?" Haley asked. "It'll feel more like Christmas."

"Sure." I brushed off two spots at the bottom of the stoop, and we sat down. It felt strange being so close to her. I thought about bringing up last night again, to try and clear the air, but the timing didn't seem quite right. So I kept quiet, both of us listening to the music and thinking our own thoughts. The sun had ducked behind a row of brownstones to the west of us, and the wind had picked up slightly, but for some reason I no longer felt as cold.

Haley bumped her knee against mine. "I have to admit something to you."

"One last round of the getting-to-know-you game?"

She grinned a little and shook her head. "No, we're done with that." She picked at a loose string near the pocket of her coat. "So, you remember when you came up to check out my shower?"

I nodded.

"Well, a funny thing happened that night after you left. It miraculously started running again."

"Wait," I said, slow on the uptake. "But you still came down to use Mike's—"

"Oops."

It dawned on me what she was saying. She'd used the shower as an excuse to . . . keep coming down to see me. "So, your pipes aren't frozen anymore?"

"I don't know if they ever were." She reached into her hood and pulled out a few strands of her damp blond hair. "I had just finished showering when you knocked on my door. My mom would kill me if she knew I was sitting out here with wet hair."

We heard little-kid laughter in the apartment with the music, and we both looked up. But you couldn't see anything. It sounded like a boy.

"Oh, and one other thing," Haley said. "I called home earlier today. And I officially stopped being a coward."

"What do you mean?"

"I told Justin what I told you last night. That I had a ticket to come home, but I couldn't bring myself to get on the plane."

I decided it wasn't my place to say anything. So I just listened. And nodded.

"And I'll tell you something," she said. "That wasn't fun at all. We spent half the day crying to each other on the phone." She stopped picking at the loose thread and stuck her hands in her coat pockets. "But breaking it off was the right thing to do."

"It's hard," I said.

"Tell me about it."

It felt wrong to be excited in the wake of some other dude's misfortune. But excitement was exactly what I felt. Because if Haley was no longer taken . . .

Maybe . . .

We were getting up to leave when a new song started playing. "Here Comes Santa Claus." Me and Haley looked at each other and cracked up, and we both sat back down. And through my laughter, I imagined the boy in the apartment above us, sitting near the radio with his little sis and his mom and dad. I wished I could tell him to remember every single thing about today. Not just whatever presents he got but his family, too. His mom. Because one day he'd be far away from home, sitting on a snow-covered stoop with a girl he might like, laughing, and he'd want to picture how they all used to be.

POLARIS IS WHERE YOU'LL FIND ME

JENNY HAN

lves. Elves in motion are otherworldly. They are long and lovely and lean; when they dance they are whirling dervishes that sparkle and gleam like sun shining on snow. I should know. I've been watching them my whole life.

The decorations committee has gone all out for the Snow Ball this year. Which I suppose they do every year, but this year feels especially tinseled. Twinkle lights cover every inch of the Great Hall, so many that we don't even need overhead lighting. There's a huge spruce in the center that goes all the way to the ceiling, and from its branches hang wooden carvings of every elf who's ever lived at the North Pole. Just the elves, though.

Around the perimeter of the Great Hall, there are lots of smaller Christmas trees close to eight feet tall, all themed. There's a paper-crane tree from Japan, a Dutch tree with dangling wooden shoes painted in all different kinds of colors, a Day of the Dead tree from Mexico, which is covered in tiny sugar skulls. There's a 1950s tree, which might be my favorite. It has a purple-and-pink poodle skirt around the base.

All the teen elves have paired off for the Snow Ball. It's the most romantic night of the season. The last hurrah before things really kick into gear with the holidays. It's like prom for elves. Not that I myself have ever been to a prom, but I imagine this is what it must be like.

Boys and girls all dressed up, dancing.

Tonight Elinor is wearing a white dress with silver spangles. Under the lights, her hair looks white too. So does Flynn's.

The dress I'm wearing is made of the same cranberry red fabric as Papa's suit. We match. A pre-Christmas gift. My first year at the North Pole, my dress had puffy sleeves and a lacy white pinafore. This year my dress has a scoop neck and cap sleeves and a full skirt. It came with a white fur muff as well. It's a doll's dress, not a fifteen-year-old girl's.

Oh, Papa. Can't he see that I'm growing up?

Everyone at the North Pole knows the story of how Santa found me. Fifteen Christmases ago, he was delivering presents to an apartment complex in Seoul, South Korea. He loves the big apartment complexes because he can zip from floor to floor and be done in a jiffy. When he returned to his sleigh, there I was in a basket with a note that said, 내 딸을 부탁해, which means, *Please take care of my daughter.* Santa didn't know what to do. Every time he put me down, I cried, and he still had all of Asia to get to. So he took me along. He said I slept the whole way. Santa had every intention of bringing me back to Korea before morning, but by the end of night, he just couldn't. I grabbed hold of his pinky and wouldn't let go. And so here I live, at the North Pole, a place no human girl has ever lived before.

I'm standing with my back pushed up against the wall, and my tights itch, and I'm wishing someone, *anyone,* would ask me to dance. Even out of pity. That would be fine. I catch Flynn's eye while he's spinning Elinor around. She looks good in his arms. She looks right. If it were me dancing with him, I would only come up to his chest. I wouldn't be able to dance cheek to cheek.

I hang by the refreshment tables. They are my safe zone. For the first twelve days of December, dessert is themed. It's a tradition, one of many. On the first day of Christmas, a partridge in a pear tree. This year, they did chocolate partridges stuffed with chestnut cream and drizzled with a tart pear syrup.

The chocolate partridge reminds me of the wooden bird in my coat pocket.

When I was eight, a robin got stuck in the Great Hall. It flew in an open window, and it couldn't figure out how to fly back out. It kept flying up to the ceiling. I tried to shepherd the bird out the door with a Quidditch broom—the number-one requested present with six-to-eight-year-olds that year, though I think kids were hoping it would actually fly. None of us could figure out how to help the bird. But then Flynn climbed up on the banister, and the robin flew right up to him. He caught the bird and carried it outside, cradled in the palms of his hands, and the robin flew away. For days it was all anyone could talk about.

So for Christmas that year, I gave Flynn a bird I carved out of wood. I tried to do a robin, but I just couldn't capture its likeness. So instead I did a chickadee with a glass eye, carved out of pine. I was nervous to give it to him.

Because the thing to understand about elves is that they aren't usually into presents. They make things, they create, they labor, but they don't like to receive. It's not in their nature.

There was a good chance he wouldn't accept it, but when he opened up the box, he stared at the chickadee for a long time. I watched as he held it in his hand, turning it over, feeling its weight. Was it good enough? I'd practiced other birds as well, but this was the only one I thought worthy enough of my friend. And then he said, "No one ever gave me a gift before."

I let out the breath I was holding. "So you'll keep it?"

"I'll keep it."

I've given him a bird every Christmas ever since. This year, I finally got the robin right. Black walnut, painted holly-berry red.

I'm pouring myself another cup of raspberry-ginger punch when I hear Elinor say, "It's sad that Natty didn't have anyone to come to the ball with. I doubt she's ever even met a human boy before."

"Yes, she has," Flynn says. "That guy Lars, remember?"

Their backs are to me. They don't know I'm standing in earshot. I could still slip away without them knowing.

Then Elinor says, "Oh, Flynn. It's so obvious she made that up to make you jealous. She's always had a crush on you."

My vision goes blurry, and I drop my cup of punch. Red liquid streams all over the refreshments table and some splashes on my dress. *How could she say that?* Never mind the fact that she's right, I do have a crush on Flynn. Always have.

"She didn't make it up," he says, and his voice rings out loud and clear like a bell. "I checked it out. The databases haven't been completely updated so I looked in Santa's actual logs. There really was a boy named Lars."

"You're just saying that to be kind," Elinor says. "We all know Natty tells stories."

My cheeks burn hot. I *used* to tell stories. For attention. Like the time I told everyone I got lost in a blizzard and Rudolph the Red-Nosed Reindeer came and rescued me. But I don't tell stories anymore. Aren't people allowed to change?

I clear my throat before I can stop myself. They whirl around in one motion, as if it were choreographed. Elinor has the grace to look ashamed. She's worried I'll tell Santa. I won't. I'm not a little baby tattletale anymore. I can handle myself. My heart pumps so hard in my chest, I worry that everyone can hear it. So I speak loudly. "I don't 'tell stories,' Elinor. And I *wasn't* lying about Lars."

Two years ago, because I begged and pleaded, because it was my Christmas wish, Santa took me out with him on Christmas Eve.

Most things about the night are a blur, as most magical things are. But when I close my eyes and try hard to remember, I remember dogs that yapped and dogs that barked, the smells of other people's houses, the thrill of being somewhere I wasn't supposed to be. Christmas trees and Christmas cookies and Christmas stockings. Christmas everything. Mostly I took pleasure in watching Papa work, because *he* took so much pleasure in it. The way he arranged the presents just so. He really does know the name of every girl and boy. He'd adopt all the lost little girls and boys if he could. I just got lucky. Sometimes I think about my mother, my real mother, and I wonder if she knew whom she was giving me to. I like to think so.

Papa and I visited a house—it was small and blue with white shutters—by the sea. I remember the smell of salt and the sound of the water. While Papa got to work, I set off looking for the cookies. So far my favorites were peanut M&M's ones at an apartment in Charleston, South Carolina, and a close second were fancy raspberry macarons in Paris.

I found a blue-and-white china plate with cookies dusted in powdered sugar. I bit into one. It was hard nougaty pecan. I was licking sugar dust off my fingers when I heard him. It was a teenaged boy, thirteen or fourteen, standing at the foot of the stairs, staring right at me. He had hair the color of lemon candy, a translucent yellow. *"Jävlar!"* he whisper-shouted.

The way he said it, it definitely sounded like a curse word.

"My father says cussing is a terrible habit," I told him, furtively wiping my hands on my coat.

The boy just stared at me, round-eyed.

"Oh, sorry. You probably don't speak any English, huh? Where are we again? Sweden?" I cleared my throat. *"God jul."* That means Merry Christmas. I can say Merry Christmas in every language. The elves can *speak* every language, but I'm only human.

"Are you and your dad robbers?" he asked me.

I gasped. So he did speak English! "Excuse me, but my father *gives* people gifts, he doesn't steal them. He's *Santa*." The boy just kept staring at me, so I clarified. "Claus. Santa Claus. Saint Nick? Père Noël?" Oh, right, we were in Sweden. *"Tomte? Nisse?"*

He just looked more confused. "Santa Claus is Asian?"

"I'm adopted," I explained. "He's not my biological dad."

The boy backed up on the staircase. "If you guys don't get out of here right now I'm gonna call the *polisen.* Police, understand?"

The police? Eeks. Weakly I called out, "Papa . . ."

From the living room he called back, "Almost done in here, Natty! Pack a few cookies for me and we'll hop back in the sleigh."

"The sleigh," the boy repeated.

"Oh, um, a sleigh is like a sled. Or . . . a wagon? It's how Santa travels."

He glared. "I know what a sleigh is."

"It's parked in the snow," I said. "Go look if you don't believe me."

He ran over to the window and looked outside. He turned back around with saucer eyes and sank down onto the floor. He closed his eyes and whispered, "This isn't real. I'm dreaming."

I pinched his arm so hard he yelped. "See? You're not dreaming."

He rubbed his arm. "That's not proof of anything."

That's when I noticed it—the bundle of mistletoe hanging above our heads. I thought, *here's my chance.* And so I grabbed him and kissed him, and he tasted like Swedish Christmas candy.

Then I heard a throat clearing and a *ho ho ho,* and we sprang apart. The boy's eyes just about fell out of his head when he saw Santa in all his cranberry-velvet glory. "Time to go, Natty," Papa said.

"You really are real," the boy whispered.

"That's right, and I know when you've been naughty or nice," Papa joked, but it was awkward, of course.

Papa whisked me away, and the boy ran to the window and called out, "My name is Lars! What's yours?"

I screamed back, "Natalie!"

When I think back on it, I realize it was the first time I ever got to introduce myself. I'd known everyone at the North Pole since I was a baby, and they all called me Natty, because that was what Santa called me. It was my first time being Natalie.

We're all still standing near the refreshment tables when my papa comes bounding into the party, waving and ho-ho-hoing. The elves go wild. Elves don't normally give in to big displays of emotion, but they make an exception where Santa is concerned. He's a rock star to them. "Happy December First!" Papa calls out.

"Happy December First," everyone shouts back.

"You've all been working so hard, and I'm just so darn proud of you. It's going to be a real push to finish in time but we're going to get it done, just like we do every year. Have a great time tonight! And tomorrow it's game on!" Everyone claps and Papa looks around the crowd. "Where's my Natty? Natty, come up here and say something to the troops."

It's the last thing I want, but the elves pull me forward and deposit me next to Papa, who puts his arm around me and looks at me the way he always looks at me, doting and proud. I wipe at the stains forming on the front of my dress. It's a good thing my dress is the same color as the punch.

Papa beams at me. "Say something, Natty."

What am I supposed to say? I'm just the boss's daughter. "Um, merry Christmas," I say, and everyone claps out of courtesy.

Papa signals to the elf band, who launch into a rousing rendition of "Last Christmas," my dad's favorite Christmas song. The elves all think it's Elvis's version of "Santa Claus Is Coming to Town," but I know the truth. Papa loves Wham!

"Dance with your dear old dad, Natty," he says, taking my hand in his. He leads me in a foxtrot, and I do my best to keep up. I can feel all the elves watching us, feeling sorry for me that I'm here dancing with my dad and not an actual date. "I bet your dance card's been full all night. Natty, tell me what you want for Christmas."

I cannot say the thing I want, because it's the one thing he can't give me, and that would break his heart. "I haven't really thought about it," I lie.

Papa gives me a knowing look and pats me on the shoulder before he twirls me. You'd think I'd know better than to lie to Santa Claus. "Dearest one, if you believe, I think you will get exactly what you want."

I want to believe. I want so badly to believe.

There are two kinds of children. The kind who believe and the kind who don't. Every year, it seems there are fewer in the world who do. Papa says it's not an easy thing to ask a child to believe in what they can't see; he says it's its own magic. He says that if you have that magic inside you, you should protect it all your life and never let it go, because once it's gone, it's gone forever.

After the song is over, Papa wishes everyone a good night and goes back to his office. I want to follow him and fall asleep by the fireplace watching him go over his Naughty or Nice lists. But I don't go, I stay in the Great Hall and sway to music and watch everyone else dance. Sondrine glides up beside me and says she likes my dress, which I know she doesn't, but I say thank you anyway because she's only trying to be kind. At least I'm not standing alone. Sondrine tells me about a dancing-elf video game they cooked up in the gaming department, complete with nonslip dance pad. At first it was a joke, but then they all got really into it, and now it looks like it might end up under a few kids' Christmas trees.

But then Roan, a puppeteer elf, asks Sondrine to dance, and she skips off with him, smiling from pointy ear to pointy ear. When I was little, I used to tape my ears to try to get them to point. I was unsuccessful.

Elinor and Flynn are dancing again.

At lunch in the workshop last week, Elinor asked me, "Who are you going to the Snow Ball with, Natty?"

There was a long silence. And then I said, "No one."

"Oh," she said, and there was so much pity in that one little word I couldn't stand it.

I swallowed a bite of mooseloaf and then I said, "I thought about flying in this boy I know who lives in Sweden, but—"

"Who do you know that lives in Sweden?" she asked.

When I told her the story of yellow-haired Lars and the Swedish candy, her eyes got that squinched look they get when she doesn't believe you. "Hmm," she kept saying.

"So why is this the first we're hearing about him?" Elinor ran her fingers through her silvery hair. "It sounds like you two had a strong connection."

I bit my lip. "We did have a strong connection. But we—we lost touch. I don't even have his address anymore." I never had his address. We were never in touch.

"I think you should find this boy, Natty. See if it's meant to be." Then she called out, "Flynn? Would you please look up the address of a Swedish boy named Lars? Aged fifteen to seventeen." He didn't answer, so she called out his name again. "Flynn?"

"What?" he said at last.

Sweet as spun sugar, she said, "We need you to look up a boy named Lars from Sweden. Natty, did you say what he asked for? We can cross-reference his Christmas wish with Swedish boys with blond hair named Lars."

Flynn took off his headphones and pointed at the countdown clock on the wall. Twenty-five days till Christmas Eve. "You guys should get back to work if you want to hit your numbers today."

"Don't be such a Scrooge," she said, and she went over to the computers, and nudged Flynn over, bending over the keyboard. Her silken hair grazed his cheek. "Okay, so I have the year, a first name, hair color, toy, country of origin. Natty, you said he lived by the sea?"

I nodded.

She typed some more. "Hmm. I don't see anything."

"Maybe it wasn't Sweden. Maybe it was Norway. Or Finland. It could have been Finland!" I could hear the note of desperation in my voice, and they heard it too, and it was unseemly.

Elinor straightened up. "I should get back to the BB gun station. Ever since they started showing *A Christmas Story* on TV all day, it's all kids are asking for."

When she was gone, Flynn said to me with a grin. "You made that story up, didn't you?"

"I didn't make it up," I said. "I was telling the truth! And you're supposed to be my friend, which means you're supposed to believe me."

"I am your friend, Natty. And as your friend, I'm telling you, you shouldn't make up stories anyone can easily disprove."

"I'm not! There really *is* a boy named Lars! I don't know why he's not in the database, but there has to be an explanation." I let out a big sigh. "And I wish everyone would stop calling me Natty. My name is Natalie."

"Sorry. You're not a Natalie to me. It sounds so . . . grown up."

"Well, I'm not a little girl anymore," I said, putting my head down on the table.

"Whatever you say," Flynn said.

I sat there with my head on the desk, watching him work. He gets a very intense look about him when he works. Silver head bent over a toy, eyes narrowed in concentration. When he's working, he doesn't like to be disturbed. No elves do.

To his back, I asked, "Who . . . who are you taking to the Snow Ball, Flynn?" I held my breath. *Don't say Elinor. Anyone but Elinor.*

He hesitated. And then, without turning around, he said, "Elinor," and I could feel something in me wither.

"Why?"

"Because I always go with Elinor."

"Oh. Right. Of course you do."

If I had outright asked and not only hinted, would he have said yes? Would he have changed course? Or would it have been the same as it is every year?

Flynn, the handsomest of all the boy elves. And me, at the Snow Ball. I've got a good imagination, but even I have trouble picturing it.

We were both quiet. Too quiet. I had to speak, because if I didn't, I would cry, and that wouldn't do.

I got up and stood behind Flynn, and I tried to stand up tall, as tall as an elf. Shoulders back, chin up. Up, up so tears don't fall. Up so high that I was looking at the ceiling and not straight ahead. I cleared my throat, and my voice came out thick like molasses. "I think you should go really dramatic in the bathroom. Gold faucets and black tiles. Also I think that the staircase you designed is sort of dated."

"I've already told you, this is a mid-century modern dollhouse." Flynn was annoyed but he was also relieved, I could tell. He was relieved I wasn't pressing the issue. The issue of him and her.

I leaned in closer, as close as Elinor stood next to him. I could smell his hair; it smelled faintly of pine. "And I'm telling you, this house needs a more feminine touch. It's looking too sterile."

Another thing elves hate—to be criticized. "Can you please just let me work?" he asked.

"Not until you say you believe me about Lars."

"I'm not going to say I believe something when I don't." Flynn finally turned his head to look at me. "I have a job, Natty. I mean, Natalie. We all do. Christmas Eve is—"

"I know. Twenty-five days away."

Flynn nodded, satisfied that I got it, that we were on the same page, both of us understanding how great is the magnitude of twenty-five days away. He swiveled back around to his computer.

"Are you saying we all have jobs to do here but me?" I demanded.

Flynn turned back around. He looked perplexed when he said, "No, that's not what I'm saying—"

"My father says that my contributions to the cowgirl outfits were inspired. He—he said that it was the single most requested outfit for girls ages five to seven, so don't you dare try to minimize what I do. And just so you know, I wasn't lying about Lars. He really does exist, and he really was my first kiss. I don't care if it's in the database or not."

I turned on my heel and left before he could say another word. I knew what I'd done. I picked a fight with my only friend because I was mad. Mad that Flynn picked Elinor. Mad that it wasn't me.

I'm the foolish one for being surprised. There's no such thing as elves and humans dating. It's just elves and elves. They marry, they have elf children, and the North Pole keeps spinning and children keep getting their toys and everyone is happy. It's the way it's always been. Nothing ever changes here.

A few years from now, I can see it. Her in a silvery wedding gown made to match her hair, a wreath of ivy at the crown of her head, him, tall and slim, together in front of the marriage tree every North Pole elf has ever married in front of. Of course he will love her. Of course he will marry her. Who else would he love? Not me, obviously. I'm not an elf. I'm not like them.

I stepped outside of the Great Hall for a breath of fresh air, but then I just kept walking.

The air smells like peppermint all the time now. The candy-cane factory is just next door, and the confectionery elves are working round the clock.

It's snowing, of course. There's always snow on the ground here. It makes everything look diamond dusted. The thing about snow is, it's very quiet. The air is hushed. It's like church.

It's reverential.

It's dark, but it's always dark this time of year. We won't have sunshine for weeks. The elves don't mind it, because it's their natural habitat, but my papa worries I'll get seasonal affective disorder, so in our house there are light-therapy boxes everywhere.

The sound of my boots crunching along the ground is the only sound I hear besides the sound of my heartbeat as I walk along the path from the Great Hall to our house. And then through the silence I hear Flynn call my name. "Natty, wait!"

I freeze. When I turn around he's already caught up with me, and he's just standing there, not wearing a coat. The cold doesn't really bother the elves. I eye him warily. "Are you here to give me a lecture on holiday cheer and a joyful spirit?"

"No. I just wanted to make sure you're okay."

"Oh." And then I draw up all my courage, and I just ask, because I have to know. "Why does it have to be her?"

"It's only a Snow Ball, Natty." But it isn't. He knows it, and I know it.

Flynn looks up at the sky, at the North Star above us. Polaris, it's called. A fixed point, more accurate than any compass. You always know where you are when you look up at it. Home. "The north celestial pole is shifting, did you know that? It's because of the gravitational forces of the sun and moon. Polaris won't always be what it is now." I'm about to reply when he asks me, "Do you ever think about the future, Natalie?"

It thrills me to hear him say my name. So much so that I don't answer so he'll say it again.

"Natalie?"

"I've only ever thought about the future in days till Christmas," I tell him. No more than three hundred sixty-four days ahead. It never occurred to me that anybody thought differently. Especially not elves. But I guess Flynn *is* different, and I guess I've always known that. It's why we are friends. It's why he knew I wasn't okay, why he followed me out here to check. Whatever we are, we'll always be friends.

I'm thinking maybe now is the right time to give him the robin. I feel around for it in my pocket. And then he says, "You don't really belong here."

His words hit me like a snowball to the face. They sting, but they land true. The robin slips through my fingers and deep into my pocket.

Flynn is still talking. "Sometimes I wonder how different things would be if you weren't here. Sometimes I think maybe *I'd* be different."

I frown. "What do you mean?"

"I don't know. Like . . . maybe if you weren't here, maybe I wouldn't wonder about what the world is like beyond the North Pole."

I wave him off. "Flynn, it's not that great. I saw the world two Christmas Eves ago and I'm telling you, what we have here is better than anything out there. There's eggnog every day! And candy cane hot chocolate, and those marshmallow cakes with the little red dots."

"I'm pretty sure they have all that stuff, too. You'll see. You're going to go away someday," he says, and it sounds like a premonition. "You'll stop believing."

Tears spring to my eyes. "Not me. I'll never stop. Never ever ever."

Stubbornly, he shakes his head. "One day you will, and you'll forget all about us."

"Stop saying that!"

"It's all right. It's what you're supposed to do."

I don't like the sad look on his face; it weighs on me in a way that is unfamiliar and strange. We've never talked like this before. I don't like the way it makes me feel—too real. Lightning quick, I pull the robin out of my pocket and hand it to him. "Here," I say. "Merry Christmas."

He holds the bird up to the moonlight and examines it. "It's your best work," he says, and from an elf, there's no higher compliment. "It's beautiful."

"Thank you."

Faster than I can blink, as fast as only an elf can be, he touches my cheek with his fingertips, whisper soft and cool. He tucks my hair behind my ear. And then, a sharp intake of breath, my own. Is this really happening?

I lean in closer, I close my eyes, and I purse my lips. And nothing.

I open my eyes. "Um . . . were you going to kiss me?"

"I—I can't."

"Why not?"

He hesitates and then he says, "I don't want anyone to get hurt."

"You won't hurt me," I quickly say.

Flynn shakes his head.

I can see that he means to stand firm. The answer is no. So I say it, my whammy, my ace in the hole, the one thing an elf cannot refuse. "It's my Christmas wish, Flynn."

He opens and closes his mouth. He tries not to smile. "How is it that you always find a way to get what you want?" Before I can reply he says, "Don't answer that. Just—close your eyes."

Dutifully, I do.

"And Natalie?"

"Yes?"

"You aren't the one I'm worried about getting hurt."

Before I even have time to think, he tips my chin up, and he brushes his lips against mine. Flynn's lips aren't cool the way I imagined; they are warm. He is warm. He's warm but why is he shivering? When I open my eyes again to ask him, he's already backed away from me. "I have something for you, too," he says.

I hold out my gloved hand, and he drops a piece of paper inside, and then he's gone. Leaving me to wonder if I imagined the whole thing. Living where I live, it can sometimes be hard to tell the difference between magic and make believe.

I open the piece of paper.

Lars Lindstrom
10 Osby

IT'S A YULETIDE MIRACLE, CHARLIE BROWN

Stephanie Perkins

Marigold loved this Christmas tree lot. It was brighter—and maybe even *warmer*—than her mother's apartment, for one thing. Fires crackled inside metal drums. Strings of bare bulbs crisscrossed overhead. And, beside the entrance, there was a giant plastic snowman that glowed electric orange. Its pipe gave off real puffs of smoke.

She loved the husky green scent of the Fraser firs and the *crinkle crunch* of their shavings underfoot. She loved the flannel-shirted men, hefting the trees on top of station wagons and sedans, tying them down with twine pulled straight from their pockets. She loved the makeshift wooden shack with its noisy old cash register. The shack's walls were bedecked with swags and wreaths, and its rooftop dripped with clear-berried mistletoe like icicles. And she especially loved the search for the perfect tree.

Too tall, too short, too fat, too skinny. Just right.

Marigold Moon Ling's family had been coming here for years, for as long as she could remember. But this year, Marigold had been coming here alone. Frequently. For an entire month. Because how do you ask a complete stranger for a completely strange favor? She'd been wrestling this question since Black Friday, and she had yet to discover a suitable answer. Now she was out of time. The solstice was tomorrow, so Marigold had to act tonight.

Marigold was here . . . for a boy.

God. That sounded bad, even in her head.

But she wasn't here because she *liked* him, this boy who sold Christmas trees, she was here because she *needed* something from him.

Yes, he was cute. That had to be acknowledged. There was no getting around it, the boy was an attractive male specimen. He simply wasn't her usual type. He was . . . *brawny*. Lugging around trees all day gave one a certain amount of defined musculature. Marigold liked guys who were interested in artsier, more *indoor* activities. Reading the complete works of Kurt Vonnegut. Maintaining a respected webcomic. Playing the stand-up bass. Hell, even playing video games. These were activities that tended to lead to bodies that were pudgy or scrawny, so these were the bodies that Marigold tended to like.

However, this Christmas Tree Lot Boy possessed something that the other boys all lacked. Something she needed that only he could provide.

She needed his voice.

The first time she heard it, she was cutting through the parking lot that lay between her apartment and the bus stop. Every holiday season, Drummond Family Trees ("Family Owned and Operated Since 1964") took up residence in the northeastern corner of the lot, which belonged to an Ingles grocery store. It was the most popular tree-buying destination in Asheville. Lots were everywhere in the mountains of North Carolina—this was Christmas-tree-farm country, after all—so to distinguish themselves, the Drummonds offered friendliness and tradition and atmosphere. And free organic hot apple cider.

Asheville loved anything organic. It was that type of town.

The boy's voice had stopped Marigold cold. He was unloading slim, straitjacketed trees from the back of a truck and shouting instructions at another employee. Marigold crouched behind a parked minivan and peered over its hood like a bad spy. She was shocked at his youth. He looked to be about her age, but the voice issuing from him was spectacularly age-inappropriate. Deep, confident, and sardonic. It seemed far too powerful for his body. Its cadence was weary and dismissive, yet somehow a remarkable amount of warmth and humor underlay the whole thing.

It was a good voice. A *cool* voice.

And it was the exact missing piece to her current project.

Marigold made comedic animated short films. She'd been making them for herself, for fun, since middle school, so by the time she launched an official YouTube channel last year—her senior year of high school—she had the practice and talent to catch the attention of thousands of subscribers. She was currently trying to catch the attention of one of the many animation studios down in Atlanta.

She did most of the voices herself, getting additional help from her friends (last year) or her coworkers at her mother's restaurant (this year). But this film . . . it was important. It would be her mother's winter solstice present, *and* her ride out of town. Marigold was cracking. She didn't know how much longer she could live here.

She needed this boy's help, and she needed it now.

It was an unusually blustery night. Marigold searched between the trees—free organic hot apple cider clutched between her hands, she was not immune to its lure—and strained her ears over the sounds of laughing children and roaring chain saws. Under any other context, this combination would be alarming. Here, it was positively merry. Or it would've been, had her stomach not already been churning with horror-movie-like dread.

"Can I help you with anything?"

There. In the far corner. Marigold couldn't hear the customer's reply, but the boy's follow-up said enough. "No problem. Just flag any of us down when you're ready."

She barreled toward his voice, knowing that the only way this would happen would be to place herself before him with as much speed as possible, so they'd be forced to interact. Cowardly, yes. But it was the truth. She hurried through a row of seven-footers, recently cut and plump with healthy needles. The boy rounded the corner first.

She almost smacked into his chest.

The boy startled. And then he saw her face, and he startled again. "You've been here before."

Now it was Marigold's turn to be surprised.

"That hair." He nodded at the thick, stylish braid that she wore like a headband. The rest of her coal-black hair was pinned up, too. "I'd recognize it anywhere."

It was true that it was her signature look. A sexy twenty-something with an eyebrow scar had once told her it looked cute. She *felt* cute in it. She did not feel so cute in this moment. She felt like someone who was about to upchuck.

"You know," he said over her silence, "most people only have to buy a tree once."

"I live over there." Marigold pointed at the apartment complex next door. "And I catch the bus over there." She pointed at the street beside the grocery store.

"Ah. Then I won't stand in your way." Though he didn't move.

"I'm not going to the bus stop."

"So . . . you *are* buying a tree?" He looked at her as if she were somehow askew. But at least he didn't seem frustrated. His brown eyes and brown hair were as warm as chestnuts. He was even larger up close, his arms and chest even broader. He was wearing a red plaid flannel shirt with the sleeves rolled up, the uniform of Drummond Family Trees. Was he a Drummond or a seasonal hire?

It wasn't that Marigold didn't want a tree. She did. She really, really did. But her mother was saving for a new house, and she was saving for an apartment of her own in Atlanta. Her brain scanned for another way around this situation. She needed time to suss him out— and time to show him that she was a totally normal human being— before asking him the scary question. Unfortunately, a tree seemed to be her only option.

"Yes," she said. "Well, *maybe.*" Better to qualify that now. "I was wondering if you guys had any . . . you know. Charlie Browns?"

The moment she asked it, she felt sheepish and ashamed. And then further ashamed for *feeling* ashamed. But the boy broke into an unexpected grin. He took off, and Marigold hurried after him. He led her to a gathering of pint-size trees near the register. They came up to her kneecaps.

"They're so . . . short." It was hard not to sound disappointed.

"I'm sorry," he said. "But did you or did you not ask me for the *Peanuts* special?"

A thrill went through her, hearing his voice again at such a close range. Superior and aloof, but definitely with that paradoxical underpinning of friendly amusement. It probably allowed him to get away with saying all sorts of rude things.

Marigold could play this game.

"Charlie Brown's tree was pathetic," she said, "but it was almost as tall as he was."

"Yeah. And he was short."

Marigold couldn't help cracking a smile. "How about something taller . . . but with a large, unsightly, unsalable hole? Do you have anything like that?"

The boy's eyes twinkled. "All of our trees are salable."

"Surely you have at least *one* ugly tree."

He spread out his arms. "Do you see any ugly trees?"

"No. That's why I'm asking you where they are."

The boy grinned—a slow, foxlike grin—and Marigold sensed that he was pleased to be verbally caught. "Yeah. Okay. Maybe we have something over here. *Maybe.*"

He strode back into the trees and led her down the row beside the chain-link fence. They stopped before a tree that was shorter than him but taller than her. Exactly in between. "This one's been sitting on the lot for a few days. It has a sizable hole down here"—he picked it up and turned it, so its backside now faced forward—"and then this other one up here. But you could put them against a wall—"

"Like you guys did?"

He gave her another mischievous smile. "And it would still look full to anyone inside your home."

A boisterous, chatty family wandered the row beside them—a mother, a father, and a young girl. The girl pointed at the tallest tree on the lot. It towered above everything else, a twenty-footer, at least. "Can we get *that* one?" she asked.

Her parents laughed. "We'd need a much bigger living room," her mom said.

"Do people *own* living rooms that big?"

"Some people," her dad said.

"When I grow up, I'm gonna have one that big, so I can buy the tallest tree here every year."

The words pierced through the air to stab Marigold in the heart. Memories of her own childhood here—of that exact same proclamation to her father—flooded her system. Last year had been the first year that her family hadn't purchased a tree. Melancholia blossomed into longing as Marigold realized . . . *she wanted one.* Desperately. She touched the tall Charlie Brown, letting her fingers fan down its boughs.

"I *do* like it. . . ." She turned over the paper card attached to the tree and winced.

"Oh, that's the old price," the boy said. "I could knock off ten bucks."

It still cost way more than her mother would be happy for her to spend. "I'd take it for half price," she said.

"For a tree this size? You're crazy."

"You said it's been sitting here, unwanted, for several days."

"I said a *few* days. Not several."

She stared at him.

"Fine. I'll knock off fifteen."

"Half price." And when he looked exasperated, she added, "Listen, that's all I *can* give you."

The boy considered this. Considered *her*. The intensity of his gaze made it a struggle to keep her eyes on his, but she refused to relent. She had the distinct feeling that she was about to get the discount.

"Deal," he finally grumbled. But with a sense of enjoyment.

"Thank you," Marigold said, meaning it, as he hefted away her tree.

"I'll freshen the trunk while you pay." And then he called out, "Mom! Fifty percent off this orange tag!"

So he *was* a Drummond.

His mother—a woman with a cheerful face that, regrettably, somewhat resembled a russet potato—sat inside the wooden shack. She looked up from a paperback romance, eyebrows raised high. "Ah," she said, at Marigold's approach. "It all makes sense again."

"Sorry?" Marigold said. A chain saw sputtered to life nearby.

The woman winked. "It's rare to get a discount outta my son."

It took her a moment—Marigold was distracted by that pressing question she had yet to ask—but as the woman's meaning sunk in, the heat rose in Marigold's cheeks.

"Our customers usually leave with *more* tree than anticipated." The woman's voice was pleasant but normal, though rural in a way that her son's was not.

"Oh, I wasn't even going to buy a tree," Marigold said quickly. "So this is definitely still more."

The woman smiled. "Is that so?"

"He's a good salesman." Marigold wasn't sure why she felt compelled to protect the boy's reputation with his mother. Maybe because she was about to ask him a favor. She paid for the tree in cash, eager to escape this conversation while dreading the one that still lay ahead. Her stomach squirmed as if it were filled with tentacles.

She glanced at her phone. It was almost eight o'clock.

The chain saw stopped, and a moment later, the boy headed toward her with the tree nestled in his arms. She was going to have to ask him. She was going to have to ask him right—

"Which one is your car?" he asked.

Shit.

They realized it at the same time.

"You don't have a car," he said.

"No."

"You walked here."

"Yes."

They stared at each other for a moment.

"It's okay," Marigold said. How could she have forgotten that she'd have to get the stupid tree *home*? "I can carry it."

"That's ridiculous."

"No, it's okay. *That's* my place. Right there." Marigold pointed at the only black window in the neighboring apartment complex. All of the others featured prominently displayed trees or menorahs. Every balcony had strings of lights wrapped around their railings or large illuminated candy canes or plug-in signs blinking *Merry Christmas*.

"That's yours?" he asked. "The dark one on top?"

"Yep."

"I've been staring at that apartment for weeks. It's a real downer."

"You should see the inside," Marigold joked. Because *no one* saw the inside of her apartment.

"I guess I'll have to."

"What?" Marigold was alarmed. "Why?"

"You wouldn't even make it halfway. This tree is heavy. Unwieldy." To demonstrate, he shifted the tree in his grip and grunted. The whole tree shook. But Marigold was enthralled by the way he said the word *unwieldy*. A fantasy flashed through her mind in which he dictated an endless list of juicy-sounding words.

Innocuous. Sousaphone. Crepuscular.

Marigold snapped back into the present. She hated feeling helpless, but she did need this boy's help—and now she needed it in *two* ways. She dug her arms between the branches and grabbed the trunk, wrestling it toward herself. Hoping he'd wrestle it back. "It's okay," she said. "I've got it."

"Let go."

"Seriously, I'm stronger than I look."

"Let!" He tugged it, hard. "Go!"

Marigold let go. She pretended to look put out.

"Sorry," he said, after a moment. He actually did look sorry. "But it'll go faster without you dragging it down."

Marigold kept her hands surrendered in the air. "If you say so."

"I'm a lot taller than you. The balance, it'd be uneven," he explained. She shrugged as he called out to his mother, "I'll be back in fifteen!"

His mother's eyes narrowed with suspicion. "You're taking your break?"

"I'm helping a customer."

"You're taking your break?" she asked again.

He sighed. "Yeah, Mom."

Marigold trotted behind him as he struggled out of the lot. She felt like an idiot. She also felt a strong surge of guilt. "You shouldn't be doing this."

"You're right. I shouldn't."

There was a gust of freezing wind, and Marigold pushed up her knitted scarf with one hand and held down her woolen skirt with the other. She was glad she was wearing her thickest tights. "Thank you," she said. "I really appreciate it."

The boy grunted.

But it was a nice enough grunt, so she asked, "What's your name?"

"North."

"Huh." This was surprising. "So . . . your mom's a hippie, too. I wouldn't have guessed it."

"Why?" He stopped to look at her, and needles showered to the pavement. "What's your name?"

"Marigold. Marigold Moon."

North smiled. "That's very Asheville."

"Born and raised."

"My parents aren't hippies," he said, resuming walking. "I'm North as in the North Pole. Unfortunately. My brother is Nicholas, and my sister is Noelle."

"Wow. God. That's . . ."

"About a hundred times worse than your name."

"I was going to say *devoted*. Festively devoted."

He laugh-snorted.

Marigold smiled, pleased to have earned a laugh. "So where's the family farm?"

"Sugar Cove." He glanced back at her, and she shrugged. "Near Spruce Pine?"

"Ah, okay," she said. "Got it." That made sense. There were tons of tree farms up there, just north of the city.

"You know how small Spruce Pine is?" he asked.

"It's barely recognized by GPS."

"Well, it's Shanghai compared to Sugar Cove."

Once again, Marigold was startled out of their conversation by his word choice. Her mother's parents were immigrants from Shanghai. He couldn't know that, but was this his way of saying that he guessed she was Chinese? Most non-Asian-Americans were terrible guessers. They'd say Japanese, Korean, or Vietnamese before Chinese. As if they were afraid "Chinese" was a stereotype, and they'd get in trouble for suggesting it. As if China weren't the most populous country in the world.

But Marigold didn't have time to dwell. He'd *finally* given her an entrance. "You don't talk like you're from the boonies," she said.

"You mean I don't talk like my mother."

She flinched. She'd walked right into that one. "I'm sorry."

His voice flattened. "I used to. It took a concentrated effort to stop."

They crossed into her apartment complex, and she re-pointed out her building. North groaned. "Right," he said. "Of course it's the one in the back."

"So why'd you stop?" she asked, nudging a return to topic.

"Because city folk keep a-callin' it 'the boonies' and makin' assumptions about mah intelligence."

This was not going well.

North thunked down the tree at the bottom of her stairs. He let out a singular, exhausted breath. "You. Help." He leaned the tree on its side. "Take that end."

She lunged forward to grab ahold of its top half. With their significant differences in height and strength, it took several uncomfortable steps to get their rhythm down. "*Of course* you live in the back building," he said. "*Of course* you live on the top floor."

"*Of course* you're going to make me"—Marigold grunted—"regret your help forever."

They navigated awkwardly around the small U-shaped landing between the first and second floors. "Can't you move a little faster?" he asked.

"Can't you be a little nicer?"

He laughed. "Seriously, you're like a sea cucumber. Which I assume are slow, because they're named after a vegetable. Which don't move at all."

They reached the second floor, and Marigold almost dropped her end. North kept moving. "Sorry," she said, scuttling to keep up. "It's hard to get a good grip."

"It's a tree. Trees have great grip. Their whole body is made for gripping."

"Well, maybe I could get a decent grip if you weren't pulling so hard."

"Well, maybe I wouldn't have to pull so hard if you could carry your fair share of the weight."

"That doesn't even make sense." Marigold slammed her elbow against the railing on the next stairway landing. *"Ow."*

North shot forward, wrenching the tree completely from her hands. "AHHHHH!" He yelled like a gladiator as he ran full throttle up the last flight of stairs. He dropped the tree on the third floor, and it skidded forward several feet.

"What the hell was that?" Marigold shouted.

North grinned. "Went a lot faster, didn't it?"

"You nearly took off my fingers."

"Looks like I didn't need your help after all. Because you weren't any. Help, that is. You weren't any help."

"I didn't even want a tree." Marigold glared at him. Forget it, enough. The voice work was out. "You talked me into this. This is your fault."

"Then next time, pick someplace else to loiter."

She heaved the tree into a standing position and shuffled it toward her door. "I wasn't *loitering.*"

"What's going on out here?" a sandpapery voice called from below.

Marigold cringed. "Sorry, Ms. Agrippa!"

"I knew it was you! I knew you were up to something!"

North raised one eyebrow.

Marigold leaned the tree against the wall beside her door, shaking her head. "I'm just bringing home a Christmas tree, Ms. Agrippa. Sorry for shouting."

"You're not putting it on your balcony, are you? I don't want it dropping down needles onto mine. I don't want to have to clean up your filthy mess."

Both of North's eyebrows rose.

Marigold dug through her purse for her key. "It's going inside, Ms. Agrippa. Like all normal Christmas trees," she added under her breath. The door below slammed shut.

"She's a peach," North said.

Marigold was done with this whole irritating escapade. Finished. The end. "Well, thank you. I appreciate you carrying this home for me, but I've got it from here." She opened her door and turned on the light. "Good night."

But North wasn't looking at her. He stared past her with widened eyes. "And how, exactly, do you plan on carrying a tree into *that*?"

Furniture and bags and boxes were stacked to the ceiling. Literally *to the ceiling*. Even with the overhead fixtures turned on, the apartment was still dark. The towering, shadowy objects blocked most of the light. And there was only one pathway through it, straight ahead, barely wider than a person.

"You're a hoarder." North's voice was amazed and incredulous.

"I'm not a hoarder. And neither is my mom."

"Then what's with all the hoarding, hoarder?"

Marigold's chest tightened like a Victorian corset. "It's a temporary situation. We're . . . between houses."

"Why isn't this stuff in storage?"

"Because storage costs money, and we're saving it for the new house."

North didn't have a comeback for that one. An abashed expression crossed his face, but it disappeared quickly. Purposefully. Maybe he understood. "So . . . where am I supposed to put the tree?"

"I told you. I've got it from here."

"Clearly you don't. It can't even fit through there." He gestured at the narrow pathway. "And where's your end game? Where do you plan on putting it?"

Marigold was overwhelmed by a familiar sense of fear and humiliation. How could she have let him up here? How could she have spent money on something that they'd have to throw out next week? Something that couldn't even fit into their apartment? Her mother would be furious. Marigold's heart raced. "I—I don't know. I was going to put it in front of the sliding-glass door. Like all the others in the building."

North craned his neck across the threshold. "The balcony door? The one straight ahead? The one *behind* that china cabinet?"

"Yeah. Maybe?"

"You're insane. Why would you buy a Christmas tree?"

"Because you're extremely persuasive!"

North whipped around to stare at her. For a moment, his expression was unreadable. And then . . . he smiled. It was warm—unexpectedly warm—and it made Marigold feel the teensiest bit calmer.

"So what are you gonna do?" he asked.

"I guess . . . shift some of this around?" Her expression was as doubtful as her question. After all, she and her mother hadn't touched anything since they'd moved in.

North took a tentative step inside the apartment. As he scratched the back of his head, Marigold's chest sunk. She shouldn't be embarrassed—*They had a reason for this, damn it. This was all temporary, damn it*—but she was.

"This is madness," he said. "There's no way it's safe."

"We've been here for a year, and nothing has fallen on us yet."

"You've lived in this pit of death for *a year*?" He slunk into its depths. The pathway led to the most basic and primal living areas—kitchen, bathroom, bedrooms. "I'm sorry, I can't let you bring my tree in here," he called out from around the corner. "It would die before Christmas. And that's only five days away."

"Doesn't matter. *My* tree only has to live until tomorrow."

"What's tomorrow? The day the demolition crew arrives?"

"It's Yule. The winter solstice."

North's head popped out from behind a wobbly stack of dining room chairs. "Are you a witch?"

Marigold burst into a surprised laugh.

"Wiccan, I mean? A Wiccan witch?" he asked.

"No."

"Pagan? Some kind of . . . neopagan?"

Marigold shook her head.

"A druid? I don't know, who celebrates the solstice?"

"Anyone can celebrate it." She followed him farther inside. "It's an astronomical phenomenon. *Science.* The winter solstice is the shortest day of the year."

"So you and your mother are . . . scientists."

Marigold grinned. "No. My mom's definitely a pagan."

"And here I am, asking again: why, exactly, did you buy a Christmas tree?"

"Because I *like* them. My dad"—Marigold stopped herself before continuing uneasily—"He celebrated Christmas. My mom didn't, but she agreed to make them a part of our tradition, because they're nice. And nature-y. And, besides, the Christians probably wouldn't even have them if it weren't for the pagans who celebrated Yule. Evergreens were *their* thing first."

She expected him to call her out on being so defensive—Marigold was always getting defensive—but the lines in his forehead softened. "And where's your dad now?" he asked.

Dead. He was expecting her to say *dead.*

"In Charlotte," she said.

"Oh." North looked relieved, but only momentarily. "Divorce?"

"They were never married."

"Siblings?"

"I'm an only child."

"And where's your mom?"

Marigold had thought she'd made this clear. "She lives here, of course."

"I meant, where is she *now*?"

She felt embarrassed again, which was followed quickly by frustration. "Work. She works a night shift." But as soon as the words left her mouth, Marigold was horrified. She'd just told a *stranger* that they were *alone.* How could she be so stupid?

But North only seemed irritated. "So there's no one here to help us. Fantastic."

"Excuse me?"

He slid out a turquoise Moroccan end table from the top of a furniture tower as carefully as if he were playing a game of Jenga. "You'll have to back up now."

Marigold's frustration was growing at a colossal rate. "Sorry?"

"This can all be reorganized, but I'll need a lot more space to work. Everything in these front rooms"—North gestured his head from side to side—"needs to be moved out there." He jerked his head toward the outside hall. "You're in my way." And then he pushed forward, backing her out of her own apartment with her own Moroccan end table.

Marigold was gobsmacked. "What are you *doing*?"

"Helping you." He set down the table beside her Christmas tree. "Obviously."

"Don't you have to get back to work?"

"I do. Which is why you're going to keep doing this while I'm gone. One item at a time, okay?" He nodded, answering his own question. "Okay. I'll be back when my shift is over."

Marigold didn't understand how he'd talked her into this. For the last two hours, she'd been carrying dusty chairs and dirty cardboard boxes and trash bags filled with linens and laundry baskets filled with tchotchkes into the outside hallway. Ms. Agrippa had yelled at her three times.

What would her mother say when she came home—in the earliest hours of the morning—and found that their *entire apartment* had been rearranged? And that Marigold had let a *stranger* help her do it? That it was his *suggestion*?

Though . . . this wasn't true. Not entirely.

Marigold did sort of know why she'd let him talk her into this, and it wasn't just because she thought, for sure, that *now* she could ask for his help with the voice work. North's company had been the most entertaining she'd had in ages, since her friends had left for college last autumn. With North, she didn't know what would happen next. And for the last several months, Marigold had known *exactly* what would happen next. A broken, depressed mother and an endless schedule of work, alleviated only by the silent company of her computer—and the world and people contained within it.

North was real. North was *flesh.*

And now her own flesh was covered with a thin glaze of sweat. Great.

It was just after ten o'clock, and she was paper-toweling her armpits, when she heard his heavy footsteps coming up the stairs. She hastily threw away the paper towel and greeted him at the door.

"Happy solstice." North handed her a tree stand.

"We *do* have one of these. Somewhere," she added.

"I believe you. I think you have one of everything in here. But I'm not betting on our chances of finding it."

Marigold wasn't sure if she was amused or annoyed.

North barged past her and into the apartment. "Thank you, North," he said.

Annoyed. Her jaw clenched. "Thank you, North."

"You're welcome, Marigold." He glanced around the room appreciatively. "Wow. You got more cleared out than I thought you would."

"Like I told you earlier: I'm stronger than I look."

"It's brighter in here, too."

Marigold couldn't refute that, but . . . everything still had to come back inside. She wished she could throw it all away instead. "You seriously think we can fit all of that back in here? And with enough room for the tree?"

"You sound doubtful. Why do you sound doubtful? I have yet to do a single dubious thing in your presence."

Dubious. That was another good word. Not only did she like *how* he spoke, but she liked *what* he spoke. "You've done a few dubious things," she said.

"Name one."

"Helping out *me,* someone you don't even know, in such an extreme manner? That's textbook dubious."

"I'd like to argue that"—he grinned—"but I can't."

"Why *are* you helping me?"

His eyes returned to her apartment, scanning its square footage, measuring its nooks and crannies. "Because I have superior organizational skills. I sense how things can fit together. I'm, like, a human Tetris. It's my superpower. It's my duty to help you."

Marigold crossed her arms. "Your superpower."

"Everyone has at least one. Unfortunately, most people have dumb ones like always being the first to spot a four-leaf clover. Or always being able to guess a person's weight to the exact pound."

Marigold wondered if that were true. It was nice to think that she might have a superpower, even a dumb one, hidden inside of her. What might it be?

"Okay." North pushed her back into the real world. "While I move the rest of this furniture"—she hadn't been able to move the bigger items—"you'll need to vacuum and dust. It's like eight cats live here. Do you have eight cats?"

"I have eighteen."

"Ah. But you do have a vacuum cleaner?"

Marigold lifted her chin. "Yes, of course." Though, admittedly, they hadn't been able to use it here.

"Will Ms. Agrippa be angry to hear you vacuuming at this hour?"

"Very."

North's eyes glinted. "Perfect."

Marigold vacuumed, fended off her neighbor, and dusted the newly emptied areas of her apartment while North hauled around the furniture. She hadn't wanted to admit that they didn't have dust rags— well, they *did,* but God only knew where they were packed—so she used washcloths from one of the trash bags. They were the decorative washcloths that they used to save for company.

The apartment had two bedrooms, one bathroom, a kitchen, a dining room, and a living room. When the front rooms were clear, North explained their next move. They were standing in the center of the small dining room. Marigold had never stood on this particular patch of carpeting before.

"We're gonna turn this room—since it's divided from the others— into your storage space. We should be able to fit almost everything in here, including the stuff from your bedrooms, and we'll stack the rest alongside that wall." He pointed toward the longest wall in the living room.

Marigold frowned.

"It's all about how it's packed and stacked," he said. "What I saw when I arrived was a complete mismanagement of space."

She understood his logic, but after how she'd been living for the last year, she still couldn't imagine anything different. Or, she had to acknowledge, maybe she wasn't *allowing* herself to imagine it. Maybe that would only lead to disappointment.

"The movers did that," she said. "They're the ones who put everything up here."

"But *you* left it."

Marigold was too ashamed to answer his unasked question. *Why?* She wasn't even sure she understood the full answer. Thankfully, North was already walking through the apartment again. "We'll need the biggest, flattest pieces first," he said.

"Like the china cabinet?"

"Exactly."

They carried it together, stiffly and clunkily, but the instant it was in its new place, Marigold felt . . . lighter. The sliding-glass door was free and clear. She could see outside—the tree lot, the grocery store, the December sky. The crescent moon. She could step onto her balcony, if she wanted. If it weren't so cold and windy.

And now there was a place for the tree.

"What's next?" It was hard to downplay her excitement. "The bookcases?"

North shook his head. "That's an *empty* china cabinet. Wasted real estate."

"Oh." Marigold hesitated. The cabinet usually held a mixture of hand-thrown pottery crafted by her mother's friends and heirloom china that her grandparents had actually brought here *from* China. But she had no idea where these items were currently located. "I'm not sure where we packed the nice dishes," she admitted.

"We don't need the nice dishes. We just need to fill it."

North pointed out the correctly sized boxes and bags, and they used them to pack the interior. They moved on quickly, removing the large farmhouse table from her mother's bedroom and resting it on its side across from the china cabinet. Into this arrangement, they inserted the bookcases—stacking their shelves with still-packed boxes of books—and two overstuffed living room chairs. A porch swing, two rocking chairs, four patio chairs, a lawn mower, and half of the regular dining room chairs were further tucked in with expert precision.

The way North stacked everything—some things upside down, some things on their sides—*was* Tetris-like. Blocky. Stable. Every piece of furniture was padded with linens and towels, and every remaining crevice was jammed with knickknacks and small appliances. Everything was dusted before it was slid into place. North only vetoed a handful of items—a lamp, a table, a rug, and a few others. Those were set aside.

The air was cleaner. Emptier. As more space was created, Marigold became more aware of her breath, became aware that she *could* breathe. Her lungs felt hungry.

"What about the couch?" she asked. "It's still in my bedroom."

North mopped his forehead with his shirtsleeve. He was sweating. "It's going in the living room so you can use it."

The thought—that incredibly simple thought—felt peculiar.

"You guys need something to sit on beside your beds. Somewhere to relax when you come home from work." He unbuttoned his red-plaid flannel shirt. "Something to sit on while you admire my tree."

Holy mother of Earth. Marigold was thankful she was already flushed from exertion. She tried to remain focused, but the sight of North undressing was monumentally distracting. "You keep calling it *your* tree."

He grinned. "I grew it, didn't I?"

"I bought it, didn't I?"

"And I'm very glad you did." North tossed aside the flannel shirt. He was now wearing a black T-shirt . . . with an NPR logo on it.

Marigold was doubly tongue-tied.

She knew, on some level, that North must like her. Guys just didn't *do* things like this if they *didn't* like you. But this was the first out-loud acknowledgment that maybe he was here for something more than utilizing his superhuman organizational skills.

It was thrilling.

And then . . . there was the T-shirt. National Public Radio seemed like something a boy who liked *indoor* activities would be interested in. Maybe they had more in common than she thought they did, more than a mutual appreciation for verbal sparring.

But the fact that Marigold hadn't immediately given him a smart-ass retort took North's own smartassery down a notch. He looked unsure of himself, like maybe he'd misread the situation. Maybe she wasn't interested in him.

Oh, Marigold was interested.

Marigold was *definitely* interested.

She gave him a cocky smile. "NPR, huh?"

Her expression made him straighten his shoulders, and Marigold couldn't help but notice—really, really notice—the shape of his upper body. The fact that it *had* a shape. But as her question sunk in, he grew embarrassed. He turned around to shove a shoebox filled with nuts and bolts into one of the last remaining crevices.

"I got it during their last pledge drive," he said, meaning the T-shirt.

"Mm-hm," Marigold said.

"I like keeping up with the news. I like learning things."

"My *mom* listens to NPR."

His back was still turned. "So I should have asked this earlier, but are there any boxes of Christmas"—he shook his head—"*Yule* decorations that we should be looking for?"

He was changing the subject instead of playing along. Interesting. Until now, he hadn't seemed like someone who could resist a comeback.

"Or are solstice trees bare?" he continued drily. "The way nature made them?"

There was the North she knew. But . . . she didn't know him, did she? Marigold was suddenly struck by how badly she *wanted* to know him.

She moved toward him. "We decorate ours."

North turned around, not realizing how close she was standing behind him. He didn't step backward, and his confidence didn't waver. "So you're saying there's a box."

His voice was so deep that it rattled through her. "Yeah. There are two."

North smiled. "Care to describe these boxes?"

"One is for an old Fisher-Price castle. The other is for a Fisher-Price Tudor house."

"I don't think I've seen those yet." His voice had gotten even deeper, somehow. Even—okay, she could admit it—*sexier.* Deep and sexy . . . about Fisher-Price boxes.

She turned away from him, smiling to herself. "Can I get you something to drink? Water? Coffee? Tea?"

He seemed amused by her amusement. Even if he didn't understand it. "Yeah. Coffee, thanks."

The kitchen was a wreck, but—unlike how the rest of the apartment had been—it contained more room to maneuver around in. As Marigold brewed the coffee, North grabbed a round patio table and two dining room chairs, and he made a cozy new dining area in one corner of the living room. Marigold usually ate standing up or at her desk. She couldn't remember the last time she and her mother had eaten together.

North appeared behind her, pointing at her coffee-making device. "What's that?"

"A French press."

"Fancy."

She shrugged. "My mom doesn't believe in electric coffeemakers."

"At least she believes in coffee."

Marigold laughed as she removed two mugs (handmade, her mother also believed in supporting local artists) from the cabinet. "How do you take yours?"

"Black," he said.

"Figures. A hearty lumberjack like yourself."

North snorted.

Marigold grinned. "I take mine black, too."

He leaned over the island in the kitchen, leaned his tall body toward hers. "And here I had you figured for an herbal-tea kind of girl."

"Right." Marigold rolled her eyes. She handed him his coffee. "Because of the restaurant."

"Because of the *solstice*. And your *name*. And this *pottery*." He held up the mug. "What's the restaurant?"

She'd forgotten that she hadn't told him. It seemed like he should already know. Marigold sat down at the patio table, and North sat across from her. "My mom owns a late-night vegan comfort-food restaurant downtown," she said in one breath. "Yes, I know. It's very Asheville."

"Henrietta's? Is your mom *Henrietta*?"

Marigold's eyebrows shot up in surprise.

North shrugged. "There aren't many late-night restaurants—and there aren't *any* in Sugar Cove—so I've wound up there after a ton of movies and shows. Everyone knows your mom," he added. "Or, at least, her reputation. Helping out the homeless and all. It's pretty cool."

Marigold had expected him to tease her. Instead, she felt a lump in her throat. It had been awhile since she'd heard anyone speak well of Henrietta. Her mother's employees were as sick of the sadness and anger as Marigold was. But her mother had built her reputation on feeding everyone well, regardless of how much money they had in their pockets. Included on her menu was a simple beans-and-rice dish that customers paid for on a sliding scale. Those who paid *more* than the dish was worth, their money went toward those who had little or none. People were surprisingly good at paying it forward.

"Thank you." Marigold could barely speak the words.

"Are you a vegan?"

"Not even a vegetarian. But," she admitted, "I eat mainly vegan by default. I'm not allowed to have meat in the house, so I *used* to eat it in the school cafeteria."

"School-lunch meat. That's desperation."

Marigold smiled. "You have no idea."

"So . . . you aren't a student anymore?"

"Not since I graduated high school. You?"

"Same," North said. "How old are you?"

"Nineteen. You?"

"Same."

They smiled at each other, shyly. Pleased. The moment grew bigger and bigger, until it was *too* big. North shifted in his seat. "I was a vegetarian for a few months. I had to go back to eating meat, because I needed that level of protein and energy for the farm work. But the moment I'm out of here, I'm gonna try it again."

"You aren't interested in the family business?"

"No way. You?"

Marigold shook her head. "The restaurant gene did *not* pass on to me. My grandparents also own a restaurant," she explained. "Down in Atlanta."

"That's cool. My grandparents started our tree farm."

"Family owned and operated since 1964," she said, quoting their sign.

Something flashed inside North's eyes. As if he were feeling the same thing she'd felt when he'd spoken highly of her mother. Pride, maybe relief. "That's right," he said.

"So why don't you want to be a farmer, North Drummond?"

"Just not in me." He sipped his coffee. "Like you and restaurant-ing, I suppose."

But there was something in his tone that he couldn't quite hide. Something that was more distressed than indifferent.

"So," she asked again. "Why don't you want to be a farmer, North Drummond?"

He smiled grimly. "It's true that I'm not interested in it. But Nick— my older brother who was *supposed* to inherit the farm—it turned out that he didn't want it, either. About two years ago, he left in the middle of the night. Packed up everything he owned and moved to Virginia to live with his girlfriend. Now they breed designer dogs. Puggles and Labradoodles."

Marigold was struck by the excessive bitterness in his pronunciation of these words. "But . . . wasn't he getting out, like you want to do?"

"My dad had just been diagnosed with Parkinson's."

"Shit. Oh, *shit*. I'm sorry."

North stared at his coffee mug. "It's getting harder for him to work, and my parents have been relying on me more and more. They want me to take over the farm, but my sister is the one who actually wants it. My parents are good people, but . . . they're kind of old-fashioned. There was a big fight last summer. Now Noelle's gone, too."

Marigold wished she could reach through the table to hug him. She understood everything—the love, the shame, the needing to stay until things were okay again.

"I've been trying to convince her to come back—and trying to convince my parents to give *her* the farm—so that I can leave."

"Why can't you just leave anyway? Like your brother and sister did?"

"The farm barely turns a profit as it is. My parents would go broke without me."

Marigold swallowed. She'd made the same decision. She had also put her future on hold. "I—I'm staying home to help out, too."

North looked up. His hardness, his edge, dissolved. "Does this have something to do with your father?"

"It has everything to do with my father."

"And the reason why you've been living like this?"

Now Marigold was the one staring at her coffee. "You know those stories about women who didn't know that their husbands had secret, second families?"

"Yeah."

Marigold shrugged.

There was a beat. "Are you serious? You can't be serious."

"In Charlotte. A wife and two daughters."

North looked appropriately shocked.

"They weren't happy to hear about our existence either," Marigold said. "And now he's living there. With them. Making amends. To them. Maybe starting a third and fourth secret family, I don't know. We found out just before Christmas, last year."

North shook his head. "I didn't know things like that happened in real life."

Marigold hadn't known either.

"So why didn't you get to keep your house?" he asked.

"Because my mom and I . . . *we* were the second family."

North's eyes widened with understanding.

"He married the other woman before he ever met my mom. We were his exotic, wild-child, hippie side project." Marigold spat this like poison. "So now his wife, his legal wife, is taking all the money in lawsuits. He had to sell our house, and we had to move."

"I'm sorry. I don't even know what to say."

She pushed away her mug. "We're gonna find a new house this spring."

"And . . . you'll stay here in Asheville? Helping your mom?"

Marigold had almost forgotten why she'd approached North in the first place. Almost. She'd decided that even if he couldn't do it—or, more likely, even if she never asked him to do it—having another person to talk to was enough. *Tonight* was enough.

"It's hard, you know?" she said. "I love this town. I love its art deco architecture and its never-ending music festivals. Its overly friendly locals. But . . . there's no future for me here. No career. When my mom's settled, I'm moving to Atlanta."

North frowned. "To work with your grandparents?"

"No." But her smile returned, because he'd remembered. "Animation."

She scooted forward with a new eagerness and told him about the studios that were only three-and-a-half hours away. How the market in Atlanta had been growing for years—how the major television networks were all creating shows down there. She told him about her YouTube channel, her success, her aspirations. Marigold told him everything. Everything except the crucial role that she'd wanted him to play in this.

North leaned in. "Do you want to go to college for that? For animation?"

"I want to work. I'm *ready* to work." Marigold paused. "Do you want to go to college?"

"Yeah. I do . . ." But he trailed off, embarrassed.

Marigold leaned in. Mirroring him.

His words came out in a rush as he gestured at his T-shirt. "I know it's a dying art and all that, but I want to study broadcasting. I want to work in radio."

An alarm sounded, full blast, inside Marigold's head.

"Someone once told me I had a good voice for radio," he continued. "I've never been able to get it out of my head. And I *love* radio. And podcasts. I listen to *This American Life* and *WTF* and *Radiolab* all day long, obsessively, while I work."

"You *do* have a good voice. You have an *amazing* voice."

North looked taken aback by her level of enthusiasm, but it was too late to stop.

"I have a confession," she said. And the rest of her story poured out, the one that revealed that this whole night had been about the sound of his voice.

North was frozen.

"—and I've clearly freaked you out, and I'm totally mortified, and now I'm going to stop talking," she said. *And now I'm going to die.*

There was a long and painful silence. And then North's features slid back into their usual state of composure. "First of all," he said, as smoothly and sardonically as anything he'd said yet, "I'm flattered that you came looking for *me* and not a tree. This shows excellent taste on your behalf."

The corners of Marigold's mouth twitched. "I came looking for your *voice.*"

"Second of all, I can't believe it took you an *entire month*—not to mention, me *physically entering your apartment*—for you to ask me that question. Which, by the way, you still haven't formed into an actual query, so I couldn't possibly give you my reply until you do."

Marigold sat back and crossed her arms.

North grinned. "Obviously, I don't have anything else to do tonight. So I can sit here as long as it takes."

"North," she said through gritted teeth. "Would you please consider lending me your voice for my new video?"

"That depends." He placed his hands behind his head. "How much does it pay?"

Marigold's heart staggered. She couldn't believe it, but she'd never even *thought* about paying him. Her friends and coworkers had always done it for free. But of course she should pay him. *Of course.*

"Marigold," he said, after she'd been silent for twenty seconds. "I'm kidding."

"What?"

"I'm kidding. Of course I'll do it. It sounds awesome."

"I could pay you in food," she said quickly. "From Henrietta's."

North stared at her. "You know what's the strangest thing about tonight? Tonight, being an astoundingly strange night?"

"What's that?"

"That you still don't realize I'm willing to do anything, *anything*"— he gestured in a full circle around them—"to stay in your company. You don't need to pay me."

Marigold's heart was in her throat. It'd been over a year since she'd been in a situation like this with a boy. A *handsome* boy. Suddenly, she couldn't think straight.

North nudged one of her boots with one of his.

Her boot—her *foot*—tingled.

A pounding on the door startled her out of her trance. "Keep it down in there! Some of us are trying to sleep!"

"Jesus," North said. "She doesn't stop."

"Never." Marigold got up and trudged to the door.

"I mean, this is the quietest we've been since I arrived."

"She does this even when my mom and I are asleep. *She'll* wake *us* up." Marigold opened the door and plastered on a fake smile. "Ms. Agrippa. How can I help you?"

"It's midnight. I can't sleep with this racket—" Ms. Agrippa cut herself off. "Oh my lord! You've been robbed!"

"No!" Marigold took a step forward.

Ms. Agrippa bolted back—one shaking hand on her chest, the other pointing at North. "That man! There's a strange man in your apartment!"

"That's my friend." Marigold steadied her voice. "He works at the tree lot next door. You saw him up here earlier? He's been helping me clean. Doesn't it look nice?"

"Do you need me to phone the police?" Ms. Agrippa hissed. "Are you in danger?"

"Really and truly, everything's fine. That's North. He's my *friend*."
North waved.

Ms. Agrippa's expression changed. "Does your mother know he's here?"

"Of course she does," Marigold said firmly. Better to lie about that one. "Good night, Ms. Agrippa."

"Will he be leaving soon? You've been so *loud* tonight—"

"Yes, Ms. Agrippa. We're sorry to have disturbed you."

Marigold wanted to slam the door shut, but she waited. Stared down her neighbor. It had gotten chillier outside, brisker. It felt . . . almost like snow weather. At last, Ms. Agrippa relented and headed down the stairwell. Marigold exhaled.

"Hello, friend," North said, right behind her ear.

Marigold startled.

And then she chanced it—she bumped his chest with her shoulder, lightly. North looked delighted. "Is that . . ." He sniffed the air. "Snow. It smells like snow."

"I was thinking the same thing."

It didn't snow often here, but when it did, most of it happened after New Year's. They'd only had one brief snowfall, back in November. The flakes didn't even stick.

"I love snow."

They said it at the same time. They glanced at each other and smiled.

"I *hope* it snows," Marigold said.

"I've always felt lucky to live someplace where snow is rare, you know? It's the rareness that makes it so special."

"That could be said about a lot of things."

"True." North stared at her. His smile widened.

Marigold felt it, too. The rareness, the *specialness,* of North. Of this night. She wished it could last forever.

"Oh, no." The wonderful thought had triggered a nerve-wracking one. She pushed North inside. "My mom! If it snows, she'll close the restaurant early."

They glanced at the lingering items in the hallway—and the tree—and hurried back to work. As fast as they could, faster than

Marigold would have thought possible, everything was stacked flat against the living room's longest wall.

Only the tree remained.

North hefted it inside—a groom carrying his bride across the threshold—and placed it proudly before the sliding-glass door. As he adjusted it in its stand, Marigold vacuumed away the fallen needles. She did another quick sweep of the bedrooms while he rearranged the last of the furniture—the couch, a coffee table, the Moroccan end table, a glass lamp—into an agreeable living space.

She was almost done when she spotted them in a newly cleared corner of her own bedroom. The Fisher-Price boxes.

Marigold carried them into the living room as if they were sacred.

"Look," she said.

North turned on the lamp, and Marigold's heart jolted. The area he'd created—everything on top of her favorite floral tufted rug—looked warm and snug and inviting. He'd even found the rainbow afghan that they used to wrap around themselves while watching television. He'd draped it over the back of the couch.

It looked perfect there. Everything looked perfect.

"It's not much . . ." he said.

"No. It *is*." This was, perhaps, the greatest gift she'd ever received. Her eyes welled with tears. "Thank you."

North smiled. "Come on. Let's decorate your tree."

Marigold laughed, dabbing at her eyes with her sweater sleeve. "Oh, so it's my tree now? I've earned it?"

He pretended to look shocked, as if it had been a slip of the tongue. Marigold laughed again. She felt happy—the kind of happy that reached every part of her body—as she opened the first box. It was filled with neatly bound strings of white and blue lights.

North peered over her shoulder. "Ha! Go figure."

"What?"

It was as if she'd caught him doing something wrong. He looked uneasy, but he answered with the truth. "I was surprised by how carefully these strands were put away. Christmas lights are usually this big, tangled mess. But this—*this*—is the tidiest thing in your entire apartment."

128 ★ STEPHANIE PERKINS

"When we put those away two years ago," Marigold said, "our lives were a lot different."

North removed a string of pale blue lights and began to unwind them. "You can tell a lot about a person by looking at the state of their surroundings."

"If that's true," she mused, "then my life is looking significantly better."

"But does it *feel* any better?"

Marigold met his gaze. She smiled. "Without a doubt."

They strung the tree with lights. Tons of lights. Marigold wanted to use *all* the lights, and when they were done, it shone like a beacon— marvelous and sparkling and bright.

North opened the second box and removed a pinecone on a white ribbon. He raised an eyebrow.

"You won't find any Santas or angels in there," Marigold said. "This is a *scientific* household, remember?"

He laughed.

Each ornament was bundled in tissue paper. They gently un- wrapped them one by one—red cardinals and spotted deer and black bears. Suns and moons and stars. Apples and pears and roses. And snowflakes. Lots and lots of silver snowflakes.

"Did you know," North said, as he hung a feathery blue jay, "that real trees are better for the environment than fake ones? A lot of people think the fake ones are better, because you have to throw out the real ones every year, but real trees produce oxygen and provide wildlife habitats while they grow, and then, when they're done, they can be ground into mulch to fertilize the earth. While the plastic ones just . . . rot in landfills. They can take *hundreds* of years to decompose."

Marigold waited until he was done with his rant. "Yeah," she said. "I know."

"Oh." North stilled. A tiny skunk swayed on his index finger.

But she understood why he'd felt the need to tell her. She nudged his arm. "I'm glad you work for the good guys, North."

"I *am* the good guys," he said, trying to regain some swagger.

As the final ornaments bedecked the tree, Marigold glanced out the sliding-glass door. Tiny snowflakes were swirling and pirouetting down from the sky.

Marigold paled. "Did you know it was snowing?"

"It must have just started."

"You have to go. My mom will be shutting down the restaurant now. She'll be home soon."

She scrambled, shoving the tissue paper back into the boxes. She felt him staring at her, wanting to know something—something *she* wanted to know, too—but they were out of time. He tucked away the boxes as she rushed into the kitchen. She pulled out a foil-covered serving dish from on top of the refrigerator and ran back to the tree. She shoved the dish at North's chest. "Take these home, please. As a thank-you."

His face was illuminated in blue and white light. "What are they?"

"Cookies. Vegan gingerbread ladies. It's all we have, but they're really good, I promise. You'd never know they didn't have butter in them."

"Gingerbread ladies?"

Marigold shrugged. "My mom isn't really into men right now."

"That's understandable," North said. "The last one was pretty bad."

"The worst."

"And . . . how do you feel about them?" he asked carefully. "Are you okay?"

She was surprised at how much the truth—the simple, obvious truth—hurt to speak out loud. "I've been better," she finally said.

North stared at her. The lights of the tree glimmered in his warm brown eyes. "I'm so sorry, Marigold."

Her heart thumped harder.

North took the serving dish. "Would it . . . would it be okay if I called you sometime? I mean, if you're still interested in the voice work, I'd be happy to help. I could stop by after a shift. I'll need to bring this back, anyway." He lifted the dish in an uncharacteristically awkward gesture.

North could have kissed her. He could have done it, he could have swooped in, but he was being respectful. It made her want to devour him whole. Or *be* devoured whole. She grabbed the serving dish, shoved it aside, and placed one hand on each side of his face. She pulled him down into her.

She kissed him.

He kissed her back.

Their mouths opened, and he tasted clean and healthy and *new*. He pulled her closer. Her fingers slid down the nape of his neck. Down to his chest. He lifted her up, and her legs locked around his waist, and it felt like the most natural thing in the world. As if they had rediscovered something essential that they didn't realize they'd lost. They kissed deeper. They kissed like this, her body wrapped around his, for minutes.

When she finally slid back down to the ground, both of their knees were shaking.

"I've been wanting to do that all night," North said.

His voice, so close to her ears, resonated inside of her. It filled her. "I've been wanting to do that all month."

"I want to do that for the *rest* of the month." North kissed above her lips, below her lips. "And after."

"And after," she agreed, as their mouths slipped over each other again.

"Okay, okay." She laughed, a minute later. "You *have* to go. *Now*."

They kissed some more.

"Ahhhhhhh," he shouted as he pulled away. "Okay! Now!"

North's hair was scruffled and wild. Marigold's braid was halfway unpinned. They were laughing again. Dizzy with discovery—the wonder and thrill of connection. She tossed him his flannel shirt. "Don't forget this."

He threw it on over his T-shirt. "So what do you think your mom will say when she comes home and sees all of this?"

"Honestly?" Marigold shook her head as she repinned her hair. "She'll be pissed. But then . . . I think she'll be glad. Maybe even happy."

"I hope so."

"Here, give me your phone." Marigold tugged hers out of a pocket and tossed it to him. He did the same. They added each other's numbers. "Text me when you get home, okay? Let me know you got home safely."

North smiled. "I will."

They kissed again beside the front door.

"I'm working tomorrow night," he said, between kisses.

"Thank God."

"I know. I've never been so happy to work for my parents."

They laughed.

"Until tomorrow, Marigold Moon." And he kissed her one last time.

Marigold peeked through the sugary frost that was growing, shimmering, on her balcony door. She watched North cross into the lot next door. His entire figure looked perfect from here, like something she ached to scoop up and cradle in her hands. As he climbed into the seat of his truck, he glanced up at her window.

He smiled when he saw *her* figure. He waved.

Her heart leapt as she waved back. She watched his truck until it disappeared. The tree lot's lights were off and its fires were out. Through the dull glow of the grocery store, she could see that the evergreens were coated in a fine white dusting. Everything outside was cold and empty and dark.

There was a rattling of keys at her door.

Marigold turned around. Everything inside was warm and cozy and bright. She had needed North's help to create her mother's present, but *this* was the gift—a beautiful apartment. And a beautiful tree.

The doorknob turned.

"Mom," Marigold said. "Welcome home."

YOUR *temporary* SANTA

DAVID LEVITHAN

It's hard not to feel just a little bit fat when your boyfriend asks
you to be Santa Claus.

"But I'm Jewish," I protest. "It would be one thing if you were
asking me to be Jesus—he, at least, was a member of my tribe, and
looks good in a Speedo. Plus, Santa requires you to be jolly, whereas
Jesus only requires you to be born."

"I'm serious," Connor says. It is rare enough for him to be serious
with me that he has to point it out. "This might be the last Christmas
where Riley believes in Santa. And if I try to be Santa, she'll know. It
has to be you. I don't have anyone else."

"What about Lana?" I ask, referring to the older of his younger
sisters.

He shakes his head. "There's no way. There's just no way."

This does not surprise me. Lana's demeanor is more claws out than Claus on. She is only twelve, and I am scared of her.

"Pweeeeeeeeeeeeeease," Connor cajoles.

I tell him I can't believe he's resorting to his cute voice. As if I'm more likely to make a fool of myself if he's making a fool of himself.

"The suit won't even need to be altered!" he promises.

This is, of course, what I am afraid of.

Christmas Eve for me has always been about my family figuring out which movies we're going to see the next day. (The way we deliberate, I think it's easier to choose a Pope.) Once that's done, we retreat to our separate corners to do our separate things.

Nobody in my family is particularly religious, but there's still no way I'm letting them see me leave the house in a Santa costume. Instead I sneak out a little before midnight and attempt to change in the backseat of my car. Because it is a two-door Accord, this requires some maneuvering on my part. Any casual passerby looking into the window would think I was either strangling Santa or making out with him. The pants and my jeans don't get along, so I have to strip down to my boxers, then become Santa below the belt. I had thought it would feel like pajamas, but instead it's like I'm wearing a discarded curtain.

And that's not even taking into account the white fur. It occurs to me now to wonder where, exactly, this fur is supposed to have come from, if Santa spends so much time at the North Pole. Perhaps it's him, not global warming, that's dooming the polar bears. It's a thought. Not much of one, but it's all I can muster at this hour, in the backseat of this car.

As I'm strapping on my belly and putting on my coat, Connor is meant to be asleep, safe in his dreams. He offered to stay up, but I thought that would be too risky—if we got caught, not only would we be in trouble, but the gig would be up with Riley. Lana and his mother are supposed to be asleep, too—I don't think they have any idea I'm coming, and only have a vague idea of who I am in the first place. It's Riley who's supposed to be awake—if not right at this moment, then when I appear in her living room. This is all for her six-year-old eyes to take in. I wouldn't be doing it otherwise.

I also have a gift of my own to deliver—a wrapped box for Connor, which I am trying desperately not to smash as I grasp in the dark for my boots and my beard. It's the first Christmas since we started dating, and I spent way too much time thinking about what to get him. He says presents aren't important, but I think they are—not because of how much they cost, but for the opportunity they provide to say *I understand you.* Plus, there was the risk factor: When I ordered the present three weeks ago, there was always the slim chance we wouldn't make it to Christmas. But that hasn't happened. We've made it.

Once I'm dressed, I find it near impossible to slide into the front seat with any ease. I must manipulate both the seat and the steering wheel in order to lever my Santatude into the driver's seat. Suddenly, I understand the appeal of an open sled.

I have only been to Connor's house a few times, and most of those were before we started dating. His mother mostly knows me as one of a group of friends, a body on the couch or a face over a bowl of chips, because Connor and I were very much part of a six before we decided to become a two. Every now and then, Riley would visit our adolescent playground, steal some of our snacks, flirt with whoever would pay attention to her. Lana, meanwhile, would stay in her room and blast her music loud enough to haunt any sound we were trying to make.

I feel strange pulling up the driveway in a Santa suit, so I park at the curb, in front of the house next door. I can only imagine what I must look like as I step out of the car—the street is eerily quiet, its own midnight mass. Instead of feeling like a roly-poly emissary of cheer and good will, I picture myself as the killer from a Z-grade horror movie—*Santa's Slay Ride!*—about to wreak havoc on some upstanding citizens and a few underintelligent, underdressed youth. Then I realize I've left Connor's key in my jeans, so I have to go back and fetch it—making myself look like an *incompetent* serial killer.

Plus, the beard itches.

———

Even though we're Jewish, my parents insisted at first that Santa did, in fact, exist. He just never came to our house. The way they presented it, it was a time-management issue.

"He can only go to so many houses in one night," they told me. "So he skips over the boys and girls who already had eight days of Hanukkah. But you can wave to him as he flies past, if you want."

This meant that at a young age I would stay up late on Christmas Eve to wave to Santa before he visited our neighbors' house. These neighbors, who had a boy my age, were the real reason I wasn't told the truth about Santa—my parents assumed that I would share my myth-busting knowledge the minute I learned it, which was not an incorrect assumption. I had already ruined the Easter bunny for most of my friends—while a fat man flying around the world to give presents seemed rational to me, the idea of a bunny handing out eggs just seemed stupid.

In the end, it was the neighbor boy who gave me the information I needed to expose the truth. Our conversation went something like this:

Him: "Santa's other name is Saint Nick."

Me: "Saint Nick Claus?"

Him: "No. Just Saint Nick. For Saint Nicholas."

Me: "But aren't all saints dead? Like, if Santa Claus is a saint, doesn't that mean he's *dead*?"

I could see the truth hitting him. Then he burst into tears.

I have been given very explicit instructions, as if this is some one-man production of *Ocean's Eleven*. The presents have already been placed under the tree, and the stockings have already been stuffed, and I am supposed to undo this to some degree, then jostle Riley's doorframe so she wakes up, sneaks out, and sees me put everything in place. I have made Connor assure me at least a half dozen times that his mom doesn't keep a firearm under her bed. He swears that she does not, and that she will be so tranq'd up that I could ride a full coterie of reindeer through her bedroom and she still wouldn't wake up. I fear this has implications for fire safety, but keep that fear to myself.

I want Connor to be awake. I want him to be with me in his house. It's strange to tiptoe through the kitchen without him. It's strange to be hearing the shelter silence of the hallway without having his breathing there as well. I know his presence would ruin the charade, but I want him whispering from the wings, my own yuletide Cyrano.

Instead I have pictures of him watching over me, pictures of him and his sisters, with an occasional cameo by their mom. A photographic growth chart as I get closer to the living room. I am waiting for one of the photos to start laughing at me—the left leg of my pants keeps getting caught beneath my boot. I fear a rip at any time.

The room is lit by the tree, and the tree is lit by strings of colored lights. There's a star at the top, and I think that, yes, this is how it's supposed to be—the point of a Christmas tree is to look like all the other Christmas trees, but still be a little bit your own. There aren't as many presents underneath as I imagined there would be—I have to remind myself that we aren't dealing with Von Trapps here—there are only four people in this house. And there's only one day of Christmas, not eight.

I feel somewhat ridiculous moving the presents to the base of the fireplace—but if I'm going to fake this, I'm going to have to fake it authentically, and make it look like the chimney was my entryway, despite my—Santa's—girth. I keep my stirrings to a sub-mouse level, because the last thing I want is Riley waking up and seeing Santa pulling her presents from under the tree, which would totally bedevil our plans. When the right number of gifts have been safely stationed, I add my present for Connor into the mix—I haven't told him I'm going to leave it, and I like the idea of surprising him.

I am not usually up this late without a computer open in front of me. The heat in the room draws up into my armpits to remind me all over again of what I'm wearing. I decide not to take things out of the stockings, because I'm worried I won't remember how to put everything back in the right place.

Now I have to go jostle Riley's door and alert her to my presence. I have no idea what I'm supposed to do if she doesn't come out of her room. Am I supposed to go in and get her? Waking up to Santa leaning over your bed would probably be traumatizing. The last thing I want is for her to scream. The last thing I want is to have to explain any of this to her mother.

At least her door is easy to identity—Connor may be the gay one, but Riley's cornered the market on the Disney princesses. I wish I'd brought a bell to jingle, or a reindeer to make the appropriate hoof-roof sounds. Knocking seems wrong. From the door, Elsa gives me an icy stare, and Ariel looks at me like I'm drowning. Even perky Belle's smile seems to say, *The only thing worse than being Santa is being a half-assed Santa. Do your job, Jewboy.*

Quietly, I lean into Belle so that my beard is brushing her cheek. Then, louder with each syllable, I release a "ho . . . Ho . . . HO!" I hear a rustling on the other side of the door—Riley's clearly been waiting for this moment. Treading with the authority of a man a couple hundred pounds larger than me, I move back to the living room.

When I'm out of the hall, a doorway squeaks open. Pint-size footsteps patter behind me, trying to be silent but not quite managing it.

I have to ask myself: *What would Santa do?* I head to where I stashed the presents, and start returning them to their place under the tree. This seems a little menial for Santa—surely, there are elves to do this kind of thing? But I suppose since he travels solo, this is part of the gig. I think about whistling a tune, but "Santa Claus Is Coming to Town" seems too egotistical, and "Jingle Bells" makes me think of . . .

"Excuse me," a small voice interrupts.

I look down, and there's Riley in a nightgown that makes me think of Wendy from *Peter Pan*. Only it's Tinkerbell who's wearing it. Riley is a sleepy-eyed wisp of a girl at this hour. But her voice is wide awake.

Connor had told me she wouldn't interrupt. He'd sworn she'd see me and run back to bed, pleased to have her Christmas wishes confirmed.

"Yes, little girl," I say. I am very conscious that this makes me sound like the Big Bad Wolf, so I cheer it up about halfway through, which makes me sound like the Big Bad Wolf after three Red Bulls.

"Are you real?"

"Of course I'm real! I'm right here!"

This logic seems to satisfy her . . . momentarily.

"But who are you?" she asks.

Who do you want me to be? I almost ask back. But I know the answer. And it isn't me. And it isn't Santa Claus.

I am grateful for the dimness of the room, and the tenacity of my beard. I am grateful that I remembered to change out of my sneakers. And I am scared that I am going to fuck this up for her anyway. If I don't answer well, I am going to give her the amazing gracelessness of the hour she first disbelieved.

And at the same time . . . I can't bring myself to say *I am Santa Claus.* Because I know I am not Santa Claus. And I know I am not a good enough liar to make her believe it.

So I say, jolly as a jelly donut, "You know who I am. I came all the way from the North Pole to be with you tonight."

Her eyes widen. And in that moment, in that momentary loss of logic to wonder, I see the family resemblance. I see Connor and the way he is never too cool to show that something is special to him—whether it's his glee as we're watching *Harold and Maude,* or his beaming when a favorite song comes on the radio, or the simple smile he gets when I walk into the room and he's been waiting for me. There is no cynicism there. It's as if he hasn't even heard of the concept of cynicism. Which allows me to retreat from it, from time to time.

Now here's Riley, at that age where the delicate shell of childhood is starting to show its cracks. I know all of the department store questions I could be asking her—*Have you been a good girl this year? What would you like Santa to bring you?* But that's not what I want to say.

"Don't stop believing," I tell her.

She looks at me quizzically. "Like the song?"

I chortle out a "ho ho ho!" and then say, "Yes. *Exactly* like the song."

I am bending over so I can look her in the eye as I say this. Before I can rise up, she reaches out for my beard. I flinch, expecting the yank, the unmasking. But instead she reaches past it to pat me on the shoulder.

"You're doing a very good job," she says.

I have no idea if she's talking to me or to Santa. In order for the former to continue to do a good job, I have to act as if it's the latter.

"*Ho ho ho!* Thank you, Riley!"

She's happily surprised. "You know my name!"

"Of course! How else would I know which presents to bring?"

This statement pleases her. She nods and takes a step back.

I smile.

She smiles.

I smile some more. Shuffle a little.

She smiles back. Doesn't move.

I wonder if it would be rude for Santa to glance at his watch.

She keeps looking at me.

"So . . . um . . . I'm not supposed to deliver the presents while you're in the room. It's against the Santa rules."

"But you're the only Santa. Don't you make rules?"

I shake my head. "Nope. It's passed down from Santa to Santa."

"And who was the Santa before you?"

I think for a second before I say, "My mom."

She giggles at that.

I smile.

She smiles.

She will not leave the room.

I imagine Connor watching us, thoroughly amused.

You're so bad at good-byes, he whispers in my ear. Which is true. There is an average of about forty-seven minutes between the time we first type "goodnight" and the moment we actually stop sending our words back and forth.

"The reindeer need me," I say. "Other kids need me. This is actually near the start of my route."

I know that six-year-olds are rarely moved by an appeal to the greater good. But Riley seems to get it. She backs up a little. Thinks about it.

Then, before I can prepare myself, she runs in for a hug. Her head snuggles against the pillow of my stomach. Her arms link behind my legs. There's no way she can't tell the pillow is a pillow. There's no way she can avoid how baggy the pants are around my legs. But that's not what she's thinking about. Right now, all she's thinking about is holding on. I feel it in the way she puts all of her six-year-old strength into it.

She wants me to be real.

"Merry Christmas, Riley," Santa says. "Merry, merry Christmas."

She pulls away, looks up at me, and says, with complete earnestness, "I'm gonna go to sleep now."

"Sweet dreams," Santa wishes her. Then I add another "Ho ho ho!" for good measure.

She returns to her room with the same careful footsteps as before. She wants to keep the secret from the rest of the house.

I watch her go, and wait until I hear the determined close of her door. Then I start to move the presents back under the tree. Within a minute, though, there's another noise. It sounds like . . . clapping.

"Bravo, Santa," a sarcastic voice says. "That must make you feel awesome, fooling little girls like that."

Lana is in the doorway that leads to the kitchen. She's got on a nightshirt and sweatpants, but doesn't look like she's slept yet tonight—she's vampiric even on a full night's sleep, so it's hard to tell for sure.

"Hi, Lana," I say quietly. I don't want Riley to hear us.

"Hi, *Santa*." She steps into the room and looks me over. I am not used to such scrutiny from a twelve-year-old. "I have no idea what sexual favors my brother promised you to do this, but really? You look like a dumbfuck asshat."

"It's wonderful to see you, too!" I chirp, and continue to put the presents back under the tree.

"What, no 'ho ho ho' for me? Is it because I've been a bad girl this year? It seems so entirely fair that an old white guy would get to judge that. Haven't you at least brought me my lump of coal?"

"*Shhh.* She'll hear you."

"And that would be a bad thing why? I know Connor is a big fan of maintaining illusions, but I think that's bullshit. I can't *believe* he gave you that costume. He had no right to do that."

I have not been dating Connor long enough to yell at his sister. I know this. Which is why I don't answer her, don't look at her. The presents are almost all under the tree by now. Then I can go.

"What . . . reindeer got your tongue?" Lana taunts. "Oh, I see how it is. Indulge Riley in whatever delusion you want. But you don't have to pay attention to me. None of you do."

"Lana, really. Keep your voice down, please."

"*Please!* Santa, you're so *polite.*" She's coming closer now. "No wonder Connor likes you."

Normally, it would make me really happy to hear that Connor likes me. But she says it like it's an accusation.

"You know who always did this, right?" she goes on. "You know whose suit that is? You know that for years I was just as stupid as Riley, thinking that it was Santa, thinking that it would always be this way. But now I'm guessing Connor was the stupidest, if he thought he could just dress you up and make it like he wasn't abandoned like the rest of us."

I move the last present back into place.

"What? Aren't you going to defend him? Aren't you going to tell me that it makes sense? I'm dying to hear how you can justify being here. How you pretend this is normal when everything has completely fallen apart."

I look at her in the eye for the first time. But the way she's looking at me is so unfriendly that I have to look away.

"I'm here because he asked me to," I say. "That's all."

"Awwww," she says, as if I were a kitten video. "You're in *wuv.*"

And this time I can't stand it. This time I have to say something. So I look her in the eye again, and this time, unwavering, say, "Yes. I am. In love."

For a second she is silent. For a second, I think this has placated her. For a second, I think she'll understand. But her recovery is so smooth it doesn't even seem like she's recovering.

"I hate you," she says.

Now I'm the one who's stunned.

"Why?" I ask.

"Because you can't have him. You can't just start dating him and then have him. You can't be this to him. You're not important enough to be this."

My natural inclination is to say I'm sorry. To apologize for being here. To apologize for tricking her sister into believing for one last year.

But I'm not really sorry, I find. So instead I say, "You're so angry."

"Duh! I think I have reason to be."

"But not with me."

As soon as I say it, I realize it's the wrong thing to say. Because it's not about me at all.

"It's not because you're gay," Lana says. "You know that, right? I'd be just as pissed if you were a girl."

It's a strange concession to get.

"So what do you want for Christmas, little girl?" I resume in my Santa voice.

I figure she'll give me shit for the *little girl* part. But instead she says, "I want it to not be you in that suit."

I nod. I go back to my own voice. "I get that. But you've got to tell me something Santa can actually give you."

"It's not like you brought any presents."

"I brought one."

"For Riley? Oh, for Connor."

"I hope you understand why I didn't bring one for you."

"Why?"

"Because you're always so goddamn fucking mean to me."

She laughs out in surprise, then says, "Fair enough."

We stand in silence for a moment. Then we both hear it.

A door opening. We stay silent.

Small footsteps.

"Shit," Lana whispers.

Riley reappears, and only seems a little bothered to see that Lana's with me.

"Are you getting him cookies?" the younger sister asks of the older. "I was going to sleep, but I remembered I didn't give him any cookies."

And the older sister, without missing a beat, replies, "I'll go get them."

She leaves for the kitchen. Riley, unable to help herself, stares at the presents under the tree. I remember doing the same thing with the presents around the menorah—trying to calculate which ones were for me, and what could be inside. My mother would often wrap things in boxes larger than they needed, just to throw me off.

"Where do you go next?" Riley asks me.

"Nebraska," I reply.

She nods.

Lana comes out of the kitchen with some Pepperidge Farm cookies thrown on a plate and a glass of milk.

"Here you go," she says.

I take a cookie. It's a little stale.

"Best cookie I've had all night!" I proclaim for Riley's benefit.

I can see Lana wants to cry bullshit. But she keeps it to herself.

"Well, then," she says, "I guess it's time for you to go."

"To Nebraska!" Riley chimes in.

The weird thing is, I want to stay. Now that we've gotten here, now that at least one of them knows who I really am, I want to remain a part of this. I want Lana to offer to wake Connor up. I want the four of us to eat cookies until sunrise.

"C'mon," Lana interrupts my thoughts. "Nebraska is waiting."

"You're so right," I say, moving toward the door.

"Not that way!" Lana gestures to the chimney. "This is the only way up to the roof."

I can feel Riley's eyes on me. Although I'm sure there is one somewhere, I can't think of a rational explanation for me to use the door.

So I head over to the fireplace. It looks like it's never been used. I lean in and see the chimney isn't very wide. I lean back out and make eye contact with Riley.

"Off you go to bed!" I cry.

Riley starts to wave. Lana mostly smirks.

"Safe travels," she says.

I don't know what else to do. I crawl into the fireplace. Then I pull myself up into the chimney and count to two hundred—which is roughly the number of cobwebs I'm surrounded by. For one scary moment, I think my stomach is going to keep me wedged inside, but there is a little room to maneuver—thankfully Santa hasn't been having cookies at all the stops. There is dust on my tongue, dust in my eyes. Surely, there are better ways to enter and exit a house? Why doesn't Santa just park the goddamn sleigh in the driveway like a normal guest?

I hear Lana wish Riley good night. I hear both doors close. Quietly,

I pull myself out of the chimney and shake as much dust as possible from my suit, causing a hoarder's snowfall on the carpet. Let Lana explain that one.

My work here is done, I think. But the thought feels hollow. I know I can't leave without seeing him. That wasn't the plan, but none of this was really the plan. I can't be in his house without letting him know I was here. It will all be unfinished, otherwise.

The house has retreated into its nighttime breathing of whirs and clicks and groans. I step carefully for a moment, then stop: There is no way that Riley will have fallen asleep by now, and the path to Connor's door leads right past hers. So I stand still, and realize how rarely I ever stand still. I have to quell any desire to be participant, and recline into the shape of a total observer. My phone is back in the car, the weapon with which I usually kill time. Unarmed, I look around. The Christmas-lit room appears lonely in its pausing; something is missing, and I am not that something. There are books on the shelves, but I cannot read what they are. They are a row of shapes leaning. On one shelf, the books are guarded by pairs of small figurines. Salt and pepper shakers. Somebody's collection.

I let the minutes pass, but by thinking about them, I make them pass slowly. This is not my house, and I am caught in the knowledge that it never will be. I half expect Lana to come back out, to tell me to go home. *Why are you still here?* she'd ask, and the only answer I could give would be her brother's name.

I know he wanted me here, but why did it have to be like this? I want him to introduce me as his boyfriend. I want to be sitting at the dinner table, making jokes with Riley that Lana can't help but laugh at too. I want them to see me holding his hand. I want to be holding his hand. I want him to love me when I'm naughty and when I'm nice. I want. I want. I want.

I am worried about being in love, because it involves asking so much. I am worried that my life will never fit into his. That I will never know him. That he will never know me. That we get to hear the stories, but never get to hear the full truth.

"Enough," I say to myself. I need to say it out loud, because I need to really hear it.

I listen for Riley. I listen for Lana. I hope they're not listening for Santa, or for me.

I make it down the hall. I make it past their doors. Connor's room is in sight.

It's only when I am standing in front of it, only when I am about to let myself inside, that I sense there's someone else in the hall with me. I turn around and see her standing in her doorway—Connor's mother. Her eyes are nearly closed, her hair limp. She's wearing a Tennessee Williams nightgown that makes me feel sad and awkward to see it. It hangs lifeless on her body, worn too often, too long. I should not be seeing her like this, the deep dark haze of it.

I want to be as much of a ghost to her as she is to me. But there can be no hiding. I am about to explain. I am about to tell her the whole thing. But she stops me by speaking first.

"Where have you been?" she asks.

I suddenly feel I could never explain enough. I could never give the right answer.

"I'm not here," I say.

She nods, understanding this. I think there will be more, but there isn't any more. She turns back to her room and closes the door behind her.

I know I should not have seen this. Even if she forgets, I will know. And for a moment, I find myself feeling sorry for Santa. I can only imagine what he sees in his trespasses. But, of course, those would all be people he doesn't really know. I have to imagine it's less sad with strangers.

I am not going to tell Connor any of this. I am just going to say hello and say good night. I sneak into his room and close the door with as little sound as possible. I want him to have been awake the whole time, wishing me well. I want him to greet me the moment the coast is clear. But all that welcomes me is the sound of his sleeping. There is enough light coming in from the window that the room is a blue-dark shadow. I can see him there in his bed. I can see the rise and fall of his breathing. His phone is on the ground, fallen from his hand. I know it was there in case I needed him.

I have never seen him sleeping before. I have never seen him like this, enfolded in an unthreatening somewhere else. My heart is drawn, almost involuntarily, toward him. I see him asleep and feel I could love him for a very long time.

But here I am, standing outside of it. Even as I love him, I feel self-conscious. I am the interruption. I am the piece that's not a dream. I am here because I climbed through the chimney instead of knocking on the door.

I take off my hat and unstick my beard. I take off my boots and move them aside. I unfasten my stomach and let it fall to the floor. I pull the red curtain from around my body, pull it over my head. I shed the pants, feel the cold air on my legs. I do this all quietly. It's only as I am folding Santa's clothes into a safe red square that I hear Connor say my name.

It should be enough as I step over to him and see the welcome in his eyes. It should be enough to see his hair pointing in all different directions, and the fact that there are cowboys on his pajama pants and he is telling me he can't believe he fell asleep. It should be enough that he is beckoning me now—it should be enough to join him in the bed, blanket pulled aside. It should be enough to feel his hand on my shoulder, his lips lightly on my lips. But something is not right. I still feel that, in some way, I should not be here.

"I'm an imposter," I whisper.

"Yes," he whispers back. "But you're the right imposter."

Without my Santa suit, I am shivering. Without my Santa suit, I am just me, and I am in his house after midnight on Christmas Day. Without my Santa suit, I am real, and I want this to be reality. I want this to be the way things are, or at least how they will be.

Connor feels me shiver. Without a word, he wraps the blanket around us. Our home within his home. Our world within this world.

Outside, there may be reindeer that fly across the moon. Outside, there may be questions with the wrong answers and lies that are better to tell. Outside, it may be cold. But I am here. I am here, and he is here, and everything I need to know is that I will hold him and he will hold me until I am warm again, until I know I belong.

HOLLY
BLACK

KRAMPUSLAUF

airmont's second annual *Krampuslauf* felt a little bit like a
parade and a lot like a zombie crawl, except instead of the
undead, we were dressed up like Saint Nick's creepy buddy,
the Krampus. Fairmont wasn't a place where we'd usually spend the
afternoon. It was full of overpriced boutiques, overpriced coffee, and
Mossley Academy, which was full of overpriced assholes.

Everything wrong with Fairmont was exemplified in the *Krampuslauf*. It was for charity and came with free hot chocolate. They
had turned the whole thing into something *completely against* the
true spirit of *Krampusnacht,* which ought to be about scaring the living shit out of people, running around with torches and whips, screaming in the faces of crying children so they'd be good for goodness
sake. Not hot chocolate. Not charity. The Fairmont *Krampuslauf* was
exactly the kind of thing that rich people like Roth did. They took

something awesome and sanitized it until it became something go-dawful.

Despite how Roth thought all Penny's friends were ignorant, scum-sucking dirtbags because we went to an overcrowded public high school, I was smart enough to research Krampus. He's an interesting guy, the son of Hel in Norse mythology. Older than the devil, too, so if they seem alike, it's because the devil bit Krampus's style. I bet Roth doesn't know any of that. I bet Roth just likes him because he looks cool.

I had hoped Penny would realize me and her and definitely Wren didn't belong, and then we could go home or maybe do some holiday shopping at the good mall, since we'd driven all the way over. But, of course, Penny didn't. She craned her neck, looking for Roth and his *other* girlfriend, the one who was rich and went to Mossley Academy and who Penny didn't want to believe actually existed.

"This is a perfect chance to find out," she'd said when she'd explained to me about the flyer she'd seen in Roth's room, with the date circled in Sharpie. "We'll be in disguise."

That part was fun. We made horns out of papier-mâché—ripping up old newspapers and mixing them with flour and water. The resulting gluey slop had stuck in our hair, clumped on our clothes, and made six sweet-looking horns.

Penny's were the sharp, spiky kind that stuck up from the forehead. Wren's were the curved kind that formed part of a spiral, like a ram. And mine were the kind that shot straight back over my head. We painted them silver, tipped with red, and raided our closets for demonic clothes. I found my grandmother's weird old shaggy fur cape. Wren has some crazy spiked shoes that don't have heels and look like hooves. And Penny has a red thrift-store Venetian mask with a long, phallic nose to keep Roth from recognizing her. I thought we looked pretty damn festive.

When I was a kid, I didn't understand that Santa's elves weren't the kind from storybooks. I thought his toy shop was staffed with fauns and boggarts, sprites and trolls, goblins and pixies. Before Mom left, when I made lists to give to Santa, they were always full of magical things. I wanted a cloak that could make me fly. I wanted a tiny doll, no bigger than my finger and as perfectly jointed as a living person. After Mom left, I wanted crystal balls with which to scrye my mother and magical chalk that could draw me a doorway to her, and a magical potion I could make her drink that would make her care about us.

Finally, someone explained to me that Santa's elves weren't those kind of elves and the list was just so Dad and Grandma didn't have to think too hard about what to buy for me. After that, I started putting normal stuff on it, like skinny jeans and new sneakers.

We lined up in front of a desk where a nice lady let us write down our names. I could tell she wasn't really impressed with our costumes.

"Season's beatings!" yelled one guy in a green fur suit, with horns crafted out of red Solo cups and painted black. He wore colored contacts that turned his eyes yellow and saluted us with hot chocolate swishing back and forth in a massive earthenware goblet.

Maybe some of these folks knew how to scare people after all.

Wren and Penelope and I all got numbers that the registration lady called "race bibs" that we were supposed to safety pin to our clothes. Once we managed that, we waded into the fray.

"There he is," Penny said, pointing over to the chocolate line.

Roth was standing in a group of prep school Krampuses. Three girls in short tight red satin skirts with plastic horns from the costume store, big glittery fake lashes, and high heels. Two boys with Krampus masks pushed up onto their heads so they could drink from the white Styrofoam cups.

They looked clean and mint-in-box, the way rich kids somehow managed. Like the blond girl Roth had his arm around. My hair is blond, too, but that's because I bleach it with stuff from the beauty supply store. Her hair grew from her head bright as spun white gold.

"That's his girlfriend?" Wren frowned. "You could totally take her."

"I'm not going to *fight* some girl from Mossley." Penny's curly black hair was a gorgeous nimbus around her face, and the carnival mask made her dangerous looking, but her black-lipsticked mouth trembled like she was about to cry. "She doesn't even know about me. She probably thinks she's his real girlfriend."

She probably *was* his real girlfriend. The one he told his parents about. The one he took to dances and out for pizza and to places that weren't the backseat of his car or Penelope's bedroom. Penny had clearly not wanted to believe the girl existed, somehow convincing herself that we were dressing up and coming all this way to prove an unprovable negative.

Wren shrugged. "I'm just saying."

Wren had been more or less raised by her grandparents, on whose fold-out couch she slept. They taught her to skin squirrels, knee guys hard enough to rupture their testicles, and roll cigarettes as tight as ones in the store. She had no patience with the rest of us.

"Let's go get hot chocolate," I told them. My job was to be the negotiator and sometimes the tie-breaker, an ambassador to both their nations. In return, they didn't call me crazy when I dreamed up stuff like papier-mâché horns, so even though I sometimes wanted to quit that job, I never would.

"No," Penny said, with a little sob. "I don't want him to see us. What if he recognizes me?"

Wren grabbed her arm. "Then either he'll introduce you to his friends or he'll stand there awkwardly until his friends introduce themselves to us. Either way, he's busted. This is what you came for."

Penny wilted, even though she'd come up with this plan herself. That's why Wren and I were along—to force her to go through with her own scheme.

As we waded through the crowd toward Roth, a guy passed me. He was wearing an amazing outfit, the best I'd seen. He had on fur leggings, tight to his calves, tapering to the most amazing hooves, so good that they didn't look like a costume. A black Utilikilt covered his waist, so the transition between fur and flesh was hidden, and despite the cold, his very fine chest was bare. He had big beautiful horns like those of a springbok rising up from his head. They were so real that I figured they were either resin molds or actual horns that he'd managed to attach to some kind of hidden hairband. His tanned skin was smeared with the deep gold of old mirrors, and his eyes were lined with black kohl.

"You look awesome," I called to him, because he really did. If all Krampuses looked like him, naughtiness would rule.

He turned and gave me a mischievous, toe-curling smile. It was like he'd stepped out of a different, better story than the kind I knew—not the one that Roth was in, born to be a rich jerk and to reap the rewards of never rising above that. Not the kind Penny and Wren and I were in, either, where we had to be *realistic* all the time, whatever that meant. No, the boy with the goat legs seemed to distort reality a little in absolutely fantastic ways.

Wren had to drag me away. I grinned on as Penny and I were hauled to the hot-chocolate line.

"You guys are the worst," Penny said in a muffled voice.

"You mean the best," Wren told her, and then elbowed me in the side.

"Hey," I yelled to Roth, waving. I wasn't sure if that was what I was supposed to do to avoid getting elbowed again, but I figured Wren would be happy with any forward momentum.

Penny gave me an evil look, which looked extra evil from behind her mask.

For a moment, Roth seemed confused, then he realized how he knew me and I saw the beginnings of panic. After months of watching Penny suffer because of him, it was satisfying. "I don't think I know y—" he started.

"Hi," Wren said to the blond girl, interrupting him. "You must be Roth's girlfriend. He's told us so much about you. *So much.* Don't worry—all good stuff."

The girl smiled, which was pretty damning. None of the other kids looked at all surprised, like of course Roth would tell a bunch of people about how cool his girl was. Roth began turning a tomato red, shut his mouth and ground his teeth.

I knew Penelope was considering escaping—we were at a *run,* after all, so if she just ran, it wouldn't look crazy or anything. I hoped Wren had a good grip on her.

"We're having an *absolutely brutal* New Year's party," Wren continued, and this was why you shouldn't bring Wren to things if you didn't want chaos. She loved chaos above all other things. "You should all come. Roth knows how hard we go. I guarantee you'd have a good time. Right, Roth?"

Roth stammered something affirmative. He knew he couldn't afford to piss us off. *Call us scum-sucking dirtbags now,* I thought. *Double-dog dare you.*

There was just one problem. We hadn't been planning on having a New Year's party. The last party I remember one of us having involved birthday cake, candles, and a Slip 'n Slide.

The blonde looked intrigued, though. We were townies and, to her, that meant we had drugs and booze and enough space to party without getting in trouble. The first one was silly, because, sure, we *could* get drugs. Anyone could, if they had the cash and the hookup. But at Mossley, dealers stopped by and *delivered* drugs straight to their door.

She was right about the other two, though. We had booze, because we had older siblings and cousins who would buy it for us, and liquor cabinets in our houses that our parents never bothered to lock, and because, compared to drugs, booze was dirt cheap.

And we had freedom. We could stay out all night for the price of a sloppy lie. No one was concerned about where we were for hours at a time and sometimes a lot longer than that. Theoretically, all of the Mossley students went home for winter break, but most of them drifted back the first week of January. After all, they spent most of the year here. Who did they know at home?

"Okay, yeah," the girl said, looking from her friends to Roth, to me and Penny and Wren and smiling her oblivious smile. "That sounds like fun."

My dad was fond of bringing home stuff he thought was still usable. Slightly moldering books from the local college, damaged sports equipment and used furniture he spotted leaning against dumpsters. He was responsible for the book that confused me about the faeries— and also got me to leave milk curdling in the sun outside Grandma's trailer in the hopes of attracting a brownie to clean my room—and there was another book with devil stories.

The devil stories were a lot like the faerie stories. The devil was always a trickster, always seemed up for a good time, and was usually defeated in the end. In the stories where he prevailed and dragged a soul down to hell, the person usually deserved it.

He punished the naughty and rewarded the nice. Just like someone else who wore a lot of red. Scramble the letters in S-A-N-T-A and you get S-A-T-A-N.

It turned out Roth's girlfriend's name was Silke, which seemed completely improbable, but apparently was the kind of Nordic name that went with naturally ice-blond hair and swimming-pool blue eyes.

Wren plugged her number into my cell. Roth watched Penny like she was a dangerous animal who might suddenly bite him. I wished she would. Behind her mask, Penny was probably red-nosed and blotchy from crying, but from the outside at least, she looked like an avenging devil. Roth was right to be afraid.

Then Wren gave an address for this New Year's party. My dead grandmother's not-as-yet-sold trailer.

"Wren—" I said, trying to inject myself into the process. But Wren kept talking until it became too late to stop her. Which was, I reminded myself, the problem with Wren's brand of chaos. She was always making the trouble the rest of us had to wriggle out of.

I had no idea what she was thinking. How would this help Penny?

I couldn't picture anyone from Mossley at a trailer park, no less Roth and his friends. I was sure that was part of what Wren thought would be awesome about it, imagining Silke's distress as she wobbled around the pickup trucks and plastic reindeer in her high heels, Roth on her arm. And Grandma's trailer wasn't a bad spot for a party, per se. I could volunteer to clear it out, a job that my dad had been avoiding. It might be fun to have a party.

But not a party with Roth and the kids from Mossley. Not a party that we couldn't even pretend was cool, because they'd be there reminding us that it sucked.

I glared at her.

Wren's grin only got wider.

"You can invite him, too," she turned and pointed. When I pivoted, I realized she was talking about the hot Krampus boy I'd called to earlier, who was behind us in line, close enough to have heard her. My cheeks scorched, and I probably looked as ridiculous and sputtering as Roth had. The bare-chested, gold-streaked Krampus tipped his head toward us, in acknowledgment of being noticed.

"Want to come to a New Year's party?" I called to him, in an act of uncharacteristic daring. It was only November fifth—officially *Krampusnacht*—so it was remotely possible he hadn't firmed up plans.

"It would be my pleasure," he said in a voice that shivered down my spine, a voice that seemed to come from a reality that had gotten a little bent.

"Bring all your friends," Penny said with a vengeful smile in my direction, as though messing with Roth at the *Krampuslauf* was our fault and not her idea. As though maybe there was something wrong with the hot Krampus boy bringing his friends to a party in a trailer park. As though I had something to be ashamed of.

A few minutes later, we got our steaming Styrofoam cups of marshmallow-strewn chocolate and started the *Krampuslauf,* loping along for a half mile as Penny cursed out us, cursed out Roth, and cursed out love. Then we ditched and headed for the good mall.

It wasn't like I didn't understand about crappy boyfriends. I'd had one too. His name was Nicandro, and he'd been way too old for me. After we broke up, I was so messed up that instead of dating anyone else, I made up a boyfriend with an equally extravagant name.

Joachim.

I wrote his name on my notebooks in Sharpie, like he was a real person. So yeah, I understood how Penny could pretend that Roth loved her. After all, I'd pretended a whole person into being.

I figured the New Year's party wouldn't turn into a real thing, but I was wrong. The more time passed, the more the idea came alive in my mind. Even though it had started to goad Roth, and maybe even get Silke and him to come, it became more than that.

Although it was definitely still that, too.

"No, they're coming," Pen said, lying on my floor, scrolling through the messages on her phone. "Roth swears. And he said that he was sorry about not introducing me to Silke, but he'd just been so surprised to see us. We probably should have told him we were going."

"So she's not his girlfriend?" Somehow the toad had convinced her not to dump him yet again.

Penny sighed, long-sufferingly. "Kind of. I mean, I guess he never said we were exclusive."

"He said *you* were his *girlfriend*," Wren said. She sat in front of the pieces of cracked mirror I'd glued to the wall and ran her fingers over her half-shaved head, checking for too-long pieces.

"Not his *only* girlfriend." She answered this too quickly, like maybe she was parroting back excuses Roth had given her. "Anyway, he promises that he's going to drop her after the holidays. Before New Year's Eve. He just doesn't want her to be sad when they go home. Their parents know one another."

Wren snorted. "Whatever. He's a liar. So about the party . . ."

No one we knew had the kind of fancy New Year's parties I was imagining. Not like the kind in black-and-white movies. The kind where people wore long, glittering silver gowns and drank champagne out of coupe glasses and kissed one another at midnight. The kind I was determined to somehow throw, despite our limited resources and even more limited experience.

"Probably someone has those," Penelope said when I explained my vision.

"Roth's parents," Wren said. "State senators. Movie stars. People who get cars for Christmas. People who spend Christmas at ski chalets. Not us. You can't have one of those parties in a trailer."

"Sure I can," I said, gripped by compulsion. Sometimes I felt like I was waiting for my life to begin and more than anything, in that moment, I wanted to force some kind of beginning. I wanted things to be different than usual. I wanted to bend reality. "Sort of. We all dress up. And we make, like, canapés instead of onion dip."

Wren started to laugh. "Canapés? What the hell are those?"

"Finger food," I said. "Crackers with stuff on them. If you want us to use my dead grandmother's place to throw a party, it has to be the kind where we wear a gown and drink out of real glasses. No plastic cups or bags of chips or ripped T-shirts. It has to be nice. Otherwise, I'm out."

They agreed, which I later realized meant that I not only needed to finagle the keys to the trailer, but that I had to actually throw a party worthy of all my big talking. When I volunteered to clean out Grandma's trailer, Dad looked at me like he could see exactly what I was planning, but he gave me permission all the same.

"She had a lot of junk," he said, from his chair in front of the television. A crime show was playing, and he had a big cup of tea balanced on his stomach.

"Some of it was nice," said my stepmother, Anne. She was sitting on the couch, our pit bull, Lady, resting her box of a head on Anne's lap. "Don't throw out anything nice, okay? We could have a garage sale."

"You're not going to have a garage sale," Dad snapped at her. "It's all just going to rot in our basement."

Lady blinked, roused from her nap. She let out a gentle wuff of concern.

"We could get the good stuff appraised," Anne said. She and Dad had been together too long for her to pay attention to his moods. "Sell it online."

"Oh, yeah, and who is going to pack up those boxes?" He threw up his hands, making the tea slosh in his cup. "Who is going to take them to the post office? It won't be you!"

And just like that, my party was forgotten. I escaped with the keys and no particular instructions. I went over to the trailer, sat on Grandma's worn velveteen sofa, and schemed. My grandmother had been the kind of lady who loved to drink and smoke and tell stories about being a nurse and the wild times she got up to before she married my grandfather. I hoped that if her spirit watched over the place, she'd be glad to be watching over a party.

My dad always said that I was a good kid with a great imagination, but also that I was a little bit of a space cadet. Anne told him he couldn't say stuff like that to me. That it wasn't good for my self-esteem.

When he first married her, I wasn't sure how things would be, but she was sweet and normal and not at all like my real mom, who'd been fond of flying into rages and throwing things and who was off somewhere in New Mexico, committing credit card fraud. Our first Christmas together, Anne sewed me a tiny doll with jointed cloth limbs and thin embroidery floss for hair. I guess Dad had told her about my old Christmas lists.

I didn't let her know, but I'd teared up when I saw the doll. I was too old for it, but I didn't care. I carried her around in my purse, until she got so sticky with Jolly Ranchers and marked up by pens that I had to retire her to a bookshelf in my room. For a few months after that Christmas, I pretended Anne was my real mother.

I guess that's what gave me the idea of pretending about Joachim.

No matter where I looked, there were things piled neatly upon piles of other things, deceptively tidy until I started dismantling them. Shoeboxes stacked under the bed. A closet crammed full of clothes. A dresser so full the drawers didn't open. A glass-fronted cabinet piled with two sets of dishes and seemingly endless glassware. The ironware bowl she would let me put milk in for the faeries, which she called by the Sicilian name, *donas de fuera*. The glass terrarium arranged with succulents, marbles, and a few of my old *Star Wars* figures. The Santa Claus plate for cookies. Dozens of hand towels and napkins and bath towels. Boxes of jewelry, boxes of holiday decorations, unlit themed candles from decades back, and dozens upon dozens of ceramic figurines.

It was a treasure trove.

I found cookbooks from the sixties and seventies with pictures of people in front of trays of crackers or pots of fondue. I found champagne coupes, shot glasses, aperitif glasses, and highballs. I found long sparkly dresses in silver and pink and gold, with shoes to match. I found rhinestone necklaces and even a half-full bottle of Scotch.

Wren came over with her friend Ahmet, and we worked on hauling out stuff we didn't need for the party. I kept all the old photos for Dad, the sets of china and some of the jewelry for Anne, and some of the clothes for me. We took the big wooden cabinet down to a consignment shop and managed to trade it for more glassware, including a little ice bucket. We threw out loads of slips, towels, and greeting cards.

Then I started to really plan.

We needed food.

We needed booze.

We needed music.

We needed décor.

And we needed guests.

We pooled our Christmas cash, and I borrowed Dad's Costco card. We bought a whole wheel of Brie, a block of cheddar, a bunch of grapes, and tiny, individual quiches that cooked in the oven. We also got chips, crackers, hummus, and salsa, and fancy glass bottles of Coke. It wasn't exactly my dream of canapés, but I figured that once it was all arranged on trays surrounded by grapes, it would look pretty nice.

Then we arranged for the drinks. Penelope had a cousin we could pay extra to get booze for us. I would make a big vodka punch in Grandma's punchbowl, and then hopefully we could pool our funds and get some bottles of Korbel, a few more of André, and a case of supercheap beer. I know that over at Mossley, they probably guzzled capital-C champagne, the kind that comes from the Champagne region of France. But no matter how classy I wanted our party to be or how much I read about fancy things, I knew Korbel was stretching the limits of my budget.

It would have to do.

Ahmet agreed to make a playlist on his phone and had the stuff to run it through Grandma's ancient sound system. We texted our crew from school. Wren even asked a guy she liked from the local coffee shop if he'd come. He said he had another party to go to, but he'd try to stop by, and ever since she'd been trying to play like the possibility wasn't on her mind a lot.

For décor, I fished through all the Christmas decorations and picked out the strings of fairy lights. Wren, Penny, and I hung them from the ceiling of the trailer and from the trees outside. We stuck candles in silver snowflake candleholders, covered the furniture in white sheets, and polished trays until they gleamed.

It took a week and a half of work to get the place shipshape. Some nights I would stay overnight at the trailer, stretched out on the scratchy sheets of Grandma's bed, a brightly woven afghan over my feet. I thought that maybe I'd dream of her, but instead I dreamed of the gold-smeared Krampus. In my dreams, he flayed off all my skin with his whips, and underneath I was made from pressed glass, like one of Grandma's pretty trays. Then the glass cracked and fell, sharp shards of ice melting in the torch fire, and my real self was underneath, a self no one had ever seen before.

You created me, he said, eyes bright and hot as coals. *But once you create a thing, you can't always control it.*

I was raw and trembling in front of him. I opened my mouth to speak, to beg for him not to hurt me or maybe to hurt me more, I wasn't sure which—and then woke, sweat cooling on my skin.

After that, I tried not to sleep so much. After all, there was lots of work to do.

The night before New Year's Eve, I moved on to fixing up the outside of the trailer. I arranged some lawn chairs around an outdoor table and lit some more candles to make a smoking parlor. I hung silver Christmas-tree ball ornaments from the trees with fishing wire. Then, finally, I took a step back and looked around. It was beautiful. Glimmering. Magical.

One of the other things my dad had brought back from dumpster-diving was occultist Aleister Crowley's book, *Magick.* I remember his definition of magic vividly: "the Science and Art of causing Change to occur in conformity with will."

I'd willed this into being. For a moment, I felt like a magician.

Then my vision shifted, and I saw the place as Roth and Silke were going to see it, as the boy in gold with the beautiful, no-doubt-expensive costume would see it. A sad, ramshackle trailer hung with a bunch of cheap lights.

"They're not really coming," I said. "You know that, right?"

"What?" Wren sat in the open doorway, trying to fit into a pair of narrow silver shoes that she'd borrowed from Penelope. She never wore heels.

"The Mossley kids. Roth. Silke. Why would he let his friends come when he knows having two girlfriends at the same party is a recipe for disaster? He wouldn't. And why would Silke come to a trailer park? What if no one else comes, either? What if it's just us at this party?"

"Then we get loaded," Wren said. "Really, really, really loaded."

I sighed, slumping in a lawn chair. "And eat all those little quiches by ourselves. And cry."

Wren and I had been friends for years, since we'd met at the muddy pond the town called a swimming hole. She was trying to drown a boy she liked and got in trouble with his mother. Penny and I rescued her by lying and saying the boy had started it. Which pretty much set a precedent. One of us would get in boy trouble, and the other two had to bail her out.

Even though Penny and I had known each other longer, Wren was the one who knew my dumbest secret. After Wren found out about my fake boyfriend, I'd had to have a fake breakup with fake texts and everything so Penny didn't guess. If they'd both known, we would all have had to talk about it.

It was too bad. My fake boyfriend was the best boyfriend I'd never had.

Joachim was a name I'd found on a website that I'd stumbled across when I was looking up the meaning of my own name. It stuck in my head until it came blurting out of my mouth as a boy I really liked, a boy who never existed. After that, I just embroidered the lie. I made up details about his life, about how we met online and how we had plans for him to come up that summer. I sent myself long e-mails full of things we would do in the future, nicknames for one another and lines copied from favorite movies and books and then showed off those e-mails like they were real. I made him into the one person who truly understood me—and weirdly, sometimes he seemed to understand me better than I understood myself.

With my fingers, he wrote that all I needed was to believe that the world wasn't one way. That it was big enough to contain a lot of different stories in it, big enough to be unpredictable. But I wasn't sure how to believe him. I knew it was only me talking.

After I'd been found out and "broke up" with Joachim, I cried into my pillow for so long that my face was swollen and puffy at school the next day. Penny snuck out during lunch and came back with a mocha Frappuccino of sympathy. Wren, knowing that both the breakup and the boyfriend were fake, spent the day marveling and being creeped out by my acting prowess.

A couple of nights later, when I couldn't sleep, I went outside and sat on the stairs in front of my house. Looking up at the glow of streetlights buzzing with moths and feeling the shiver of the wind, I wished that the stars or Santa's elves or Satan himself would bring me someone like Joachim—or at least give me some kind of sign that the world was big enough and unpredictable enough to contain someone like him—then I'd be as good or bad as I needed to be to deserve it.

"Let's text Silke," Wren said, pulling out her phone. A few minutes later she was grinning.

"What?"

"You were totally right. He told his friends the party was off. But I told her that Roth was a piece of shit who was cheating on her and that she should come anyway. I told her we could prove it."

"You didn't," I said.

"She cursed me out, too." She raised both her eyebrows. "But if she comes, we give her details."

I groaned. "Penny will never forgive us—"

Wren cut me off. "If we want Pen to dump Roth, we're going to have to prove to Pen that he's a rat. Now we just have to prove it to Silke, too."

"There's nothing we can do about the way she feels. We're her friends. Our job is to roll our eyes and stand by her, right?"

"Well, *I* have a plan," Wren said, looking at me like I was a little slow. "I figured we'd get Roth really drunk and confess to being a douchenozzle, and if that didn't work, I thought we'd trap him in the bathroom until he told the truth."

I wanted to take the phone out of her hand and see what she'd told Silke and what she'd said back. "That's a terrible plan. That may be literally the worst plan you've ever had."

Wren shrugged. "I just think he would admit stuff eventually, that's all. Although I guess eventually someone else would want to pee."

Wren seemed to just know things about people. Often those things turned out to be true. But I wasn't so sure about her intuition this time.

"Anyway," she said, standing up and wobbling in the borrowed heels. "It doesn't matter if he doesn't come. We need a new plan and that plan should be to get Silke and Pen to compare notes so they see he's been running a game on them."

In that moment, I wished I could take back the whole party. It had been a ton of work, I was broke, and now I was pretty sure it would be a catastrophe. But all I could do was go home, collapse on my bed, and promise myself that I was never, ever, ever volunteering to throw a party ever again, no matter how much I wished I was the kind of person who ate crudités and canapés.

Dad was right. I needed less imagination.

The next day, I crawled out, took a super-hot shower, and got ready for the party. I had borrowed a dress out of Grandma's closet—a floor-length cocktail number in a shimmery silver-black semi-sheer fabric with billowy sleeves, heavy cuffs, and a peekaboo front.

I put on my Converse underneath it, since I still had a lot to do. I tried to pin up my hair, using a YouTube tutorial, but I rushed my way through, and it came out looking not quite right. My smoky eyes looked awesome, though, and I did that lipstick thing where you layer powder and pigment so the stuff is supposed to never come off.

After that, I told my dad I was spending the night at Penelope's and headed out to buy ice to stick in the bathtub to cool the Cokes and beer and bottles of champagne, cut-up carrots, and make boozy punch.

"Call if you need a ride. Annie and I will be up until the ball drops," Dad called after me, putting down a bowl of food for Lady, who was dancing around the kitchen in an eager circle.

Nothing got done on time. Even though Ahmet had plugged his phone into the stereo perfectly the last time, it took him an hour to make it happen on New Year's—and that was after he was three hours late. Penelope's cousin showed up without the booze, wanting me to make a list of what we needed all over again after demanding an extra twenty bucks for the errand. Wren came by in sweatpants, ready to work, but then needed to take a super long break to get ready—a break that involved Penny doing her hair in Grandma's bathroom, so that neither of them helped me for the better part of two hours. After he was done setting up the electronics, Ahmet settled himself on the couch, eating all the crackers and cheese, making me paranoid that we would run out of crackers before the party even started (there was no way that we would ever run out of cheese). By the time the first guests showed up, I was nearly in tears. I greeted Sandy, Jen, and Xavier, pointed to the food, and then walked straight to Grandma's bedroom in the back, kicking the door closed behind me and throwing myself down on her bed.

It still smelled like her: faded rose perfume, medicine, and dust, as though she'd been drying out and crumbling away instead of dying of cancer. Ahmet's playlist pounded through the walls, urging me to go back to the party.

I didn't go anywhere.

A knock sounded on the door. When I didn't say anything, Penny came in, carrying two glasses of champagne. She was wearing a gold sequin tube dress. Her eyes were magnificent with golden lashes, golden powder, and liquid golden shadow.

"Hey," I said, shoving myself up so that my head was resting against the headboard. "Just taking a break."

She sat down on the edge of the bed, holding out a coupe glass. "I put vodka in it. It wakes up the champagne."

I took a deep swig. The bubbles stung my tongue deliciously. The vodka cut through the cheap sweetness of the André. I didn't know if the champagne had woken up, but it woke *me* up. For the first time that day, I had a giddy feeling of anticipation. The feeling you were supposed to have when you went to a party. The feeling that as the night went on, reality might grow more malleable, like taffy, until anything could happen and everything might change.

"Thanks," I said.

"I think our goal should be for you to fall in love tonight," Penny said, taking a dainty sip from her own glass. "I am going to find someone for you to fall in love with."

"Shouldn't I get to pick?" I asked her.

"Fate picks," she told me. "Cruel fate. But don't be like me. Don't settle for less. Don't lower your standards."

"What do you mean?" I levered up off the bed, draining the glass.

"Nothing," Penny said. "New year, new me. I'm over it. I'm over him."

"Yeah, right." I smiled because we'd heard that before. We heard it regularly, in fact.

"New year, new me." She drained her glass too. "You know you made this place awesome, right? This is the first classy New Year's party I've ever been to. You actually did it. So get up and enjoy."

I got up. More people had arrived, all dressed to the nines and bringing offerings—homemade Skittles vodka in bright colors, a mysterious chocolate pie baked with hash, peach-flavored champagne, pink champagne, and a half-full bottle of bourbon. Girls wore fancy dresses, guys had on shirts that buttoned, a few even with bow ties. Oscar had his pink mohawk teased up and wore pink shoes to match. Marc had on a leather vest over a crisp white shirt that looked like it might even have been ironed. In the candlelight, everything shimmered.

Wren was sucking face with the guy from the coffee shop in the kitchen area. Apparently he decided to forsake his other plans.

Everyone seemed to be having a good time and, if I squinted my eyes a little, it was all as beautiful as I'd imagined. I went over to the bar table and refilled my glass with more vodka and champagne, a smile pulling up the corners of my face.

A few more people from school came in, laughing. They'd brought prosecco and sparkly party hats. Everything started blurring together and being awesome. Penny told a filthy story about one of her cousins. Marc's boyfriend told us about going out with a guy who had "insurance salesman" on his online dating profile, but turned out to be a preacher; the preacher tried to make a joke out of it, too, claiming that he sold religion and that was a lot like selling insurance. I told a story about how one Christmas Eve my aunt got so drunk that she peed the bed—my bed, with me in it. Everyone screamed in horror.

We played several rounds of "I Never" and when someone said, "I never wanted to make out with anyone at this party," lots of people had to take shots.

By the time Silke arrived, I'd decided none of the Mossley kids were coming and felt relieved. Then the door opened and she stepped through, shivering in a short silvery dress, looking completely confused to find herself in a trailer. Behind her was Roth. He had three people with him, two guys and a pissed-off looking girl. Everyone but the girl looked drunk.

"You call this a party?" Roth slurred, eyes bright and hair messy. His cheeks were pinked by the cold and manic cheer.

"Who the hell are you?" Marc demanded, crossing the floor. Marc was a big guy with long hair, the fuzzy beginnings of a beard, and a soft, deep voice. Once, after I'd twisted my ankle at a mutual friend's house, he'd carried me home in his arms like he was a superhero.

Punching rich kids was a bad idea, but I kind of hoped he'd do it anyway.

"It's okay," Penny said, grabbing his arm. "We invited them."

I looked around for Wren, but she'd snuck off to the back room with her barista. "Have a drink," I said, but I couldn't make myself sound like I meant it.

"I don't think so." Roth turned toward me, his words slurring a little. "Are you the one who's been texting lies to my girlfriend?"

"Lies?" I snorted. Penny appeared to be frozen in place, like she already knew how this would go, like she already knew she wasn't going to be able to pretend anymore. She stumbled back, sitting down hard on one of the arms of Grandma's sagging couch. She didn't even seem angry with us, although she must have guessed one of us had sent the texts.

Conversations had stopped around the small room. Outside, a siren howled. Music still thrummed through the speakers of Grandma's stereo, not loud enough.

"Are you the one he was sleeping with?" Silke asked, and I noticed her eyes were bright and red-rimmed, like she'd been crying. Then she looked past me to Penny. The moment she saw her, I think she knew. "Or was it—"

"What if I was?" I asked, interrupting, because it wasn't fair for Penny to have to confront Silke seconds after Roth broke her heart. "You know he cheated, even if he says he didn't. What you don't know is that you're the one he cheated with. You're the other woman."

Silke turned to Roth, shaking her head. "She was your *girlfriend*?"

"No! Are you crazy? I *told you*. I brought you here to see how pathetic they were. To understand that they're lying. Maybe they want money. I don't know. They're trailer trash in a real, actual, *literal* trailer park. Nailing one of these girls would be worse than slumming. It would be like swimming through a sewer. I'd never get the smell out."

His friends guffawed at that. A dude-bro Greek chorus.

No one else so much as cracked a smile. Oscar cracked his knuckles instead.

Silke looked uncomfortable.

I took my phone out of my pocket. I wasn't as good at this as Wren would have been, but with the liquor singing through my veins, I knew I had to do something. "I have a picture of Roth here—"

"No you don't." Roth grabbed for the phone. "Give me that."

I didn't actually have a picture of him and Penny together, but Roth didn't know that. He lunged. I turned away from him, tossing my phone toward the couch as Roth twisted my wrist hard enough to make me yell.

And then everything happened at once. Wren burst out of the back in her underwear. Marc tried to get between me and Roth. One of Roth's friends tried to get in Marc's way. Oscar hit somebody. I was on the floor and guys were punching one another and Wren was smashing a lamp over someone's head and everyone was screaming.

That's when Roth kicked the table with the punch bowl on it. The leg cracked, and the punch bowl went over, spilling a fizzing frozen strawberry and booze tide onto all the food, soaking the cheese and crackers, splashing into the hummus and onion dip, ruining the quiches. Ruining everything.

I full-on screamed. Way louder than when he bent my arm. I screamed so loud that Marc let Roth go. Bloody-nosed, Roth turned and saw my horrified face. I don't think it was until that moment that he realized how much destroying the party would hurt me. His smile was smug and hideous.

I wanted to claw his eyes out. I wanted to hide in the back room. I wanted to go outside and sit in the cold until I was frozen all the way through. I wanted to do all those contradictory things so intensely that I did absolutely nothing at all. I just stood there, my eyes filling with tears as Roth's smile grew into a laugh.

Then the door opened again, letting in a cold breeze that guttered the candles.

It was the beautiful Krampus boy with the goat legs and the gold paint. He must have misunderstood about dressing up for the party, because he was in a variation on his costume at the *Krampuslauf*. He'd paired his goat legs with a green brocade jacket stitched with silver thread and matching knee breeches with tiny silver buttons along the cuffs. Two friends were with him, both in costume. One, a girl in a white dress with a single sleeve stitched with glittering crystals. The other, a boy with waist-length blond hair. He wore pointed-eared prosthetics and a black wool Edwardian suit.

Roth and his friends looked thrown by their arrival, but they weren't standing there with tears in their eyes and a wrecked table of food.

"We brought gifts," the boy with the hooves said, and the blond reached into his coat and brought out a bottle of clear liquor. He removed the cork with his teeth. "Mine is holiday cheer."

"Are you guys for real?" one of the Mossley kids said.

Roth snorted, still spoiling for a fight. Silke stepped back, into the

kitchen of the trailer. A few of our friends were rearranging themselves in case Roth and the Mossley boys wanted to throw a few more
punches. I was trying to edge my way to where I'd left my grandmother's broom. If Roth tried anything else, I'd crack it over his skull.

"I brought a gift, too," said the girl, and drew a curved knife out of
her bodice. She took two steps. Before the rest of us even reacted, she
had it pressed against Roth's throat. His eyes went wide. I was pretty
sure no one had ever had a knife on him before, especially not a girl.
"I understand this boy was causing some trouble."

"Are you robbing us?" the dark-haired Mossley girl asked. "Seriously? In those outfits?"

The boy with the goat legs laughed.

The blond boy with the elf ears looked from me to Penelope to
Silke and then to Roth. "What ought his fate be?"

I let go of the broom and took a step toward Roth and the girl in
white. "Don't hurt him. I get the impulse, but he'll sue."

"Who *are* you?" Penny asked, awed.

"Joachim," the Krampus boy said. "And my companions, Griselda
and Isidore."

Wren's eyebrows went so high it was like they were trying to climb
off her face. "I thought he was . . ."

Penny looked at me. "*That's* Joachim?"

But of course, he wasn't. He couldn't be. Joachim wasn't anyone.
He didn't exist.

"So what would you have me do with him?" Griselda asked. "I'd
like my gift to be well received."

Silke stepped out of the kitchen, moving as though drawn against
her better judgment. "I want him punished." At that, Silke turned to
Penny. "Don't you?"

Penelope walked up to Roth. His eyes widened the closer she got.
And in that moment, I could see her dilemma. She could save him
and indebt him to her. She could prove that she was better than his
other girlfriend—better than *him*. But he might leave her anyway—
and then she'd feel like an even bigger fool.

But she'd still be a better person.

"I don't want him hurt," Penny said, looking over at me. She hesitated. "But I do want him punished. You're dressed up like a Krampus, right? So punish him like one."

Christmas is supposed to be this time when everyone is nice to one another and forgives one another and all that, but the true meaning of Christmas is *presents*. And in the real world, Santa's not fair. Rich kids get everything and poor kids get secondhand crap their parents bust their asses to afford. It costs money just to sit on Santa's lap.

But Krampus, he brings justice. If you're bad, you get served up a big plate of steaming hot coals. You get whipped with birch rods until you bleed. You get put in shackles and fished out of pools of ink with pitchforks. That's the spirit of Krampus. It might look like it's all hipsters and charity, but underneath it's justice, and I get the appeal.

"Easily done," Griselda said. "Boy, you've been an ass—and so, until you're forgiven by these two ladies, that's exactly what seeming you'll take."

Her lips went to his cheek, pressing a kiss to his skin as her blade kept him in place. As she withdrew, he began to change. Gray whiskers sprouted over his face. His neck elongated and nose flared. He was changing shape. His head was becoming the head of an animal.

I'd wished for magic, for reality to bend, but watching this, I wondered if it was possible for reality to bend so far it broke.

Roth's two friends looked at one another, then at us and at Griselda, like they were trying to figure out who dosed them. We were all watching in gluttonous wonderment.

Roth brayed from his donkey head as Griselda put away her knife. He stumbled toward his friends. They screamed and ran for the door of the trailer. Silke edged closer to Penny, who looked as freaked out as I felt.

Joachim threw an arm over Roth's neck, eyes dancing with mirth. "Oh, come now, it's not so bad. You have very fine fur and a magnificent nose—a much better nose than your last one. And I'd wager you'll like your fate betimes."

Oscar reached out wonderingly to touch one of Roth's twitching ears. Roth shied back, and Oscar snorted with amazed laughter. "That is some Harry Potter shit."

"This cannot be happening," Wren said, laughing, still in her bra and panties, one hand on her hip, looking like she'd stepped out of a forties pinup postcard. "It's just too good."

But it was happening. And we were drunk enough to go along with it. Even with the implications of Roth having an ass head buzzing in the back of my mind, like how if magic was real, then Joachim's goat legs were probably not part of any costume, and when I'd left out milk for the faeries, I probably should have made sure to wash the bowl every time, I was focused on propping up the broken table. I couldn't stand around freaking out forever. Some people helped me mop the spilled punch. I rinsed off the cheese and scraped off the top layer of hummus. It turned out I still had some chips left in the bags out in the kitchen, so I refilled the bowls. Most bottles of booze hadn't gotten broken. Some of the food couldn't be salvaged, but in the face of magic being real and magical creatures in attendance, I was ready to declare the party a success anyway.

Isidore poured shots from his bottle into aperitif glasses set up on Grandma's kitchen counter. The liquor tasted like thyme and caraway seeds and burned all the way down my throat. Griselda taught us a drinking song. We screamed the words as we danced around the room, spinning madly and jumping on the furniture.

Someone found an apple for Roth to eat.

Near midnight, we turned the television to MTV, where they showed the ball dropping in Times Square. We counted down with everyone else.

Ten. Nine. Eight. Seven. Six. Five. Four. Three. Two. One.

We went crazy shrieking and blowing paper horns and kissing one another. People yelled out the lyrics to "Auld Lang Syne," Isidore singing lines I didn't know. *We two have run about the slopes and picked the daisies fine. And we'll take a cup of kindness yet, for auld lang syne.* And then I found myself in the hall, kissing Joachim, a boy I barely knew, a boy with a pretend name and who might be a demon or a faerie or a disturbing hallucination.

My head was swimming. My hands were tangled in his hair, and I pushed him against the wall. His breath caught as I tugged his mouth to mine. I had no idea what I was doing.

Then Ahmet changed playlists to some louder, madder, midnight stuff, and we were dancing again. We danced and drank, drank and danced until the mix ran out and Ahmet fell asleep under the table, his arm thrown over Griselda.

At five in the morning, I found myself bundled up in a moth-eaten fur coat from Grandma's closet, slumped in a chair at the plastic table as the sun began to burn the frozen horizon. I had a coupe glass full of cinnamon schnapps the color of Rudolf's nose.

Joachim was smoking a cigarette of meadow grass and comfrey. He'd found a bottle of bubble solution and held up the wand, exhaling smoke into each delicate shimmering globe, grinning up at them as they got carried up into the dawn.

He was the kind of beautiful that got under your skin. Before, my crushes had been on normal-looking boys—pudgy boys and bean-pole skinny ones, boys with bad haircuts and boys with shadowy mustaches they were trying to grow, boys with crooked teeth and spotty skin. No one would probably believe me, but Joachim's ridiculous hotness made me uncomfortable. He was like a painting you wanted to burn so you could finally stop staring at it. Copper gold hair and copper gold eyes. Looping curls. He looked like something you were allowed to look at, but never touch.

I remembered the warm slide of his lips.

"Why *Joachim*?" I asked him.

He looked over at me, a little bit drunk and clearly baffled. It made me happy to know that whatever he was, however he looked, he still could get wasted on New Year's.

"The name," I said.

He laughed, throwing his head back and glancing up at the stars. "You bargained with the universe, remember?"

The words sent a shiver down my spine. I didn't even remember exactly what I'd said or promised, but I knew I'd done it. "And the universe heard me?"

"Nah." Above his head, a bubble burst, releasing a supernova of smoke before it was blown shapeless by the wind. "But I did. Lots of things hear when you make rash offers like that."

"So you want—?" I was rigid with alarm, trying to think through the fog of alcohol.

He shook his head, throwing me an easy smile. "Not a thing. I just remembered the name when I saw you at the *Krampuslauf.* We don't have names, not like you do. Isidore and Griselda have been called many things before and will be called many things again. Names, they just don't stick to us. But I like Joachim, and I knew you liked it as well."

I tried to imagine a name sliding off of me, as though not quite attached. It felt wrong, like losing one's shadow. I'd always been Hanna, and I couldn't imagine not being her. "Why were you even at that thing?"

"The *Krampuslauf*?" He had a rich throaty laugh. "I wanted to be among people without any disguise. It's a great prank, don't you think?"

"Oh, yeah. Absolutely." I took a swig from my cup. It tasted like someone had melted those cinnamon hearts into a thick syrup. I wondered who'd brought it. I wondered why I'd decided to drink it and then took another swig.

"I owe you a gift," he said, into the silence. "Griselda brought something and Isidore brought something. Now it's my turn. Only name your desire, and I will do my best to give you its pale approximation."

That made me laugh. "I'm glad you came. And turning Roth into a donkey was way more than enough."

"My people are often beseeched for favors, but seldom invited to share in feasts," he spoke with a sly humor, as though he was talking formally half in jest—but only half. "Let me give you a gift for being made so much welcome."

"Okay," I said, relenting, looking back at the trailer. Faint music had started up inside, and I could see people moving around. They'd gotten a second wind. Soon someone would come outside and drag us back into the dregs of the after-after-party. Soon after that, I'd collapse in Grandma's bed along with as many people as would fit. Soon it would be morning and for all I knew, Joachim and Griselda and Isidore would be gone at first light, like dew burned up in the sun. "Okay. What I want is to never forget there's magic in the world. I get to keep my memories of tonight. I get to keep them always."

His smile went crooked. Leaning over, he mashed his cigarette in

Grandma's heavy glass ashtray and pressed his lips to my forehead. He smelled like burning grass.

"I promise," he whispered, mouth hot against my skin.

And, although I was, admittedly, not even a little bit sober, that was the moment I decided that since magic was real, since I conjured up Joachim by the sheer power of wanting him to happen, since I'd made this party out of two hundred bucks and sheer determination, then maybe I was wrong about the things I thought I couldn't have, that weren't for me. Maybe it was okay to imagine greater things. Maybe it was all for me, if I wanted it.

With dawn of the new year on the horizon, I resolved to exert my will on the world.

What the hell have you done, Sophie Roth?

Gayle Forman

In the fifteen weeks since starting her freshman year at the University of Bumfuckville, Sophie had counted at least a dozen *What the Hell Have You Done, Sophie Roth?* moments. The first was when Sophie's mother dropped her off at the dorms, which were covered in brick and ivy, just like the catalog promised. The rental car's engine had not yet stopped ticking when Sophie understood that the *idea* of a college in the country, in the *middle* of the country—*pastoral* was how'd she'd been describing it to friends back in Brooklyn—wasn't so much pastoral as it was foreign, as if she'd decided to enroll at the University of Beirut. Attendant sinking feelings in the stomach soon followed the revelation that really shouldn't have been a revelation—it was so obvious. It *had* been obvious to all her friends, who were perplexed by her choice to go here, and to her mother, who wasn't.

As she and her mother hauled her suitcases into the dorm, Sophie didn't dare let her feelings show. It would only make her mother feel guilty. The University of Bumfuckville being *pastoral* wasn't the real reason Sophie had enrolled.

The second *What the Hell Have You Done, Sophie Roth?* moment had come later that weekend when she'd met her roommates. Nice girls, pretty girls, welcoming girls, but that first night together—beer and pizza with crusts thick as the length of Sophie's thumb—Sophie had had to say *I'm kidding* at least a half dozen times, a trend that continued well into the term until Sophie finally realized that sarcasm was like a separate dialect, one not universally understood. "You're so big city," one of the Kaitlynns (there were three on her hall) would say. Sophie was never quite sure if this was an insult.

Sophie had imagined *she* would be the mysterious one on campus—she was from the big city, after all—but it was the girls from the small Midwestern towns who had dreamed of going to college here all their lives, whose parents had gone here, who were inscrutable.

The guys were no better. Strapping and big-toothed specimens, with names like Kyle and Connor. At the start of term, one such guy had asked Sophie out on what she'd thought was a date, but what had turned out to be a group outing to play ultimate Frisbee. Sophie had been grouchy about it, but then to her surprise had gotten into the game, catching a scoring pass, talking smack against the other team. On the walk back to the dorms, Kyle/Connor had said, "You're really competitive, aren't you?" Sophie had no doubt as to whether *that* was an insult.

That was *What the Hell Have You Done, Sophie Roth?* moment number four—or maybe it was five. There'd been several with the boys here. She was starting to lose count. She'd long since lost hope.

She had no one to blame for tonight's *What the Hell Have You Done* moment except herself. Finals had ended two days ago and most of the students had decamped for winter break. Flight prices back to

New York halved if Sophie left the following week, so she had to stick around and twiddle thumbs. Earlier that day, Sophie had been selling her books back to the bookstore—getting a pittance in return, because two editions were about to be updated, the clerk explained, causing Sophie to get into an argument with the poor sap about why all textbooks should be digital and updated automatically, only it wasn't really an argument because the clerk wanted nothing to do with the debate. On the way out she'd seen a flier for caroling on the quad that night. And for some reason, she'd thought: *This seems like a good idea.*

Sophie wondered when was she going to learn that lots of things *seem* like a good idea but a small amount of analysis might uncover that such seemingly good ideas are, in fact, intrinsically faulty. Take communism. Seemed like a good idea: Everyone shares, no one goes hungry. But maybe give it a good think and you'd come away understanding for it to work you'd need an inhuman capacity for cooperation, or a much more human capacity for totalitarianism. Anyways, she'd heard Luba describe breadlines and bugged phones and Siberian gulags enough to know which way *that* went.

A caroling concert? She really should've known better. The entire point of a caroling concert was to join in. First of all, Sophie was Jewish. It was bad enough that she'd basically skipped Hanukkah this year, but to spend the last night of the Jewish holiday serenading the birth of Jesus. . . . Just. No. And even if they were to throw in "I Have a Little Dreidel" (they wouldn't; dreidels were as foreign to Bumfuckville as moon rocks) Sophie wouldn't sing. Not in public. Not here.

In her defense, she did like Christmas carols, not the horrible dirges sung over mall speakers, but people singing in pretty harmonies. Sophie remembered when she first heard carolers, wandering the streets outside her apartment in Brooklyn. They had harmonized so beautifully, Sophie had asked her grandmother if those were angels singing. "No, darling," Luba had replied, "just gentiles."

There was nothing *wrong* with the singing tonight. It was fine. But not remotely magical or angelic. And everyone seemed to be wearing

Christmas sweaters. Like with appliques of Rudolph or Santa on them. One girl even had a sweater with a tree that actually *lit up*. If Sophie had gone to NYU, such sweaters would've been worn ironically. But here, they weren't. Everything was so godddamned sincere.

Including the carols. Not that she expected ironic Christmas carols—*Jingle bells, Batman smells, Robin laid an egg*. . . . Wasn't that how they sang it in elementary school? But there was so much eye-shining and heart as they *pa-rum-pum-pum-pummed* about Little Drummer Boys. Plus the sweaters. She couldn't take it anymore.

"Oh, the Ned Flanders of it all," she muttered to herself. Which was something she'd been doing a lot lately. When she admitted this to Zora, her friend had warned that it was a certain step on the road to Crazy Cat Lady-ism. Sophie had laughed but when she thought of her mother, alone in the apartment with only her sculptures, and now Luba's cats, for company, it didn't seem quite so funny.

"Yo, you just say something about Ned Flanders?"

Caught Cat-Ladying out loud? Oy. Sophie felt as though she'd been spotted streaking the quad naked. She pretended she had not heard the question.

"You did. You said, 'the Ned Flanders something something.'"

She turned around. Standing about three feet away was one of the Black Guys on Campus. Sophie hated herself for thinking of him like that—she'd grown up on the Bed-Stuy side of Clinton Hill, after all—but here, it was hard not to. There seemed to be like twenty black students at the entire college, a lot of them scholarship students like her. She knew this because she'd met quite a few at that Dean's Reception for Excellence the first week of school. She'd been flattered by the invite until she walked in and was given a handout with still-open work-study slots and understood that it was a get-together for all the scholarship students. She'd hid out in a corner, eavesdropping on a bunch of guys from the basketball team (basketball was huge here, she'd been surprised to learn) comparing notes about some of the sillier comments they'd gotten in their first week. Sophie had been dying to chime in with some choice examples of her own, but stopped herself. Though she may have felt like a minority here, she was still white.

She tried to remember if this guy had been at the reception. He was looking at her like he might know her. "I didn't say it so much as mutter it," she said, or, rather, muttered.

He laughed. A big, open-chested laugh, and for a second Sophie felt the tiny thrill of landing a successful joke, but it was followed by doubt because people here didn't get her humor. When she made people laugh, she suspected it was after she'd left the room. Which annoyed the shit out of her. Back home, people at least had the decency to laugh in your face.

This caroling thing was a supremely bad idea. She turned to walk away.

She felt a hand, a huge hand, on her shoulder. "Sorry. I'm not messing with you. For real. Just I was thinking the same thing."

She turned around. "You were thinking about Ned Flanders?"

She waited for him to say "Diddly-oh," or some such. It would be exactly what the Kyles or Connors would say. Then they'd ask her major. But he just smiled, a slow oozy grin, too hot for this cold night. "Yeah. Ned Flanders," he said. "Among others." He made it sound risqué, the *among others,* and Sophie felt herself flush.

He stuck out a hand, sheathed in a fingerless glove. "Russell," he said.

She looked at him, or rather up at him. He was very tall, a whole foot taller than Sophie, at least, and Sophie was five feet five. Tall enough to play basketball. Maybe he *was* on scholarship, same as her. The thought was as reassuring as his grip, which was firm, not crushing; he wasn't one of those guys who had to break your hand to prove just how much they treated you as equals.

"Sophie," she said.

"So, Sophie." He opened his arms wide. "What brings you here?"

It felt like a variation of the *What's your major?* query, the implication really being, What are *you* doing *here*? Sophie hated being asked her major. (She didn't have one; she was a first-term freshman for Christ's sake. Not everyone had their lives figured out by the time they exited the womb.)

As for what was she doing here . . . A year ago, she hadn't even heard of this place. Her high school guidance counselor suggested it, apparently knowing the ins and outs of obscure colleges with ridiculous endowments. When the school made a financial aid offer so generous, so above and beyond anywhere else, Sophie simply couldn't turn it down. Before she'd had time to think about what it would mean—all this pastoralia, et cetera—she had enrolled. Now she found herself checking off days in the calendar, awaiting her parole. (And yes, she knew she was being hyperbolic and dramatic and it was a free fifty-grand-a-year education and she should be grateful, but no matter how many times she told herself that, it didn't erase how unhappy she was.)

"I believe in the value of a liberal arts education," Sophie said now. It was her standard response to the annoying question she'd grown accustomed to, along with iceberg lettuce in the salad bar and cheese served on top of things that wouldn't seem worthy of dairy.

Russell laughed: "I meant *here,* at the Ned Flanders-ist Christmas Caroling Concert of All Time."

There was something about the way he said it, as if he and Sophie were on the same side. It loosened something in her.

"I'm doing anthropological research," she said.

"An ethnography of sorts?"

"Yeah," Sophie said. "I'm particularly interested in the sweaters. The symbolism of the light-up ones."

Sophie paused a beat, waiting for the blank expression and the *really?* she would've gotten off a Kyle or a Connor. To which Sophie would've had to say, *no not really, just kidding* and the conversation would've fizzled.

But Russell was nodding along, stroking his chin in exaggerated professorial motions. "I believe those represent a mating ritual."

"A mating ritual?"

"Yes. You see the male lights up in order to attract the attention of the female so that procreation may ensue."

"Like fireflies?" Sophie asked.

"And anglerfish," Russell said.

"Here's a question: are the sweaters mating, or the people in them?" Sophie asked.

When Russell grinned, he no longer looked professorial. "Couldn't tell you, Sophie," he said. "But both prospects scare the shit out of me."

Sophie laughed. Not fake-laughed or polite-laughed, but her real laugh, with the almost snort at the end. It had been awhile.

"You wouldn't find it so funny if you knew the rest of the ritual," Russell warned, a hand over his mouth, all conspiratorial.

"I'm almost afraid to ask." Sophie tilted her head up to listen. She was flirting a bit, something else she hadn't done in a while.

"'Rudolph the Red-Nosed Reindeer' is like a trigger. As soon as they hear it, all those sweaters . . ." He shakes his head. "Just trust me. You don't wanna see it."

"What? Is it like a sweater orgy?"

"Think about it. The lighting up of Rudolph's nose, all red and pulsating, it's a symbol for—"

"I get it," Sophie interrupted, waving away the image. But she was still laughing "You've put a lot of thought into this."

"Scary, ain't it?"

Sophie wasn't sure if he was referring to the amount of thought he'd put into it or the vision of all these nice, clean, singing people having an orgy. But when, a few moments later, the carolers chimed in with the opening notes and words, "Rudolph the red-nosed reindeer, had a very shiny nose . . ." Sophie and Russell looked at each other, and, as if by some mutual agreement, took off running.

The problem was, there was nowhere to go. The campus *was* pastoral, surrounded by farms and woodlands. There was a small commercial strip but places tended to shutter early, even when school was in session.

They were standing in front of the student union, which was open, but going inside felt like admitting defeat, and after the last few months—or maybe the last few minutes—Sophie couldn't bear it.

But then Russell said, "I'm parked just over there." He flashed the key remote and a car with Texas plates chirped and lit up.

"I'm not going to wind up at the bottom of some limestone quarry, am I?" Sophie asked, almost as a formality, to prove that she, a tough New Yorker, wasn't just naïvely getting into the car with him. But then she worried that he'd take the question differently, because he was black. And then she chastised herself for obsessing about this. Zora was black. She never acted this way around her. Then again, Zora wasn't a guy.

But he just grinned again and undid the top two buttons of his coat to reveal his sweater underneath. Heather gray and plain. "No Rudolph, no light-ups. You're safe."

Once in the car, Russell flipped the ignition and started driving. He seemed to have a destination in mind, which was a welcome change. Her few outings with the Kyles and Connors had been group affairs with everyone chiming in, *What do you want to do? I don't know; what do you want to do?* It made Sophie want to do precisely nothing.

The car was plush, leather interior, that new-car smell.

"Nice car," she commented.

"Thanks," he said. "Hand-me-down."

"Really? My hand-me-downs are usually more of the winter-coat-slash-ice-skating variety. And yachts. Everyone gives me their castoff yachts. It's really a pain."

Russell laughed. "Yeah. I hate it when that happens."

On the dash were the controls for butt warmers. Sophie loved butt warmers. Loved anything that made her warm. She'd been surprised by how cold it was here, a chill that never left her bones. She'd stand under the shower for twenty minutes and still be cold. She missed her bathtub.

"Shall we fire up the butt warmers?" Sophie asked.

"We can fire up anything you want," Russell said, which made the need for butt warmers immediately redundant. Russell switched them on and Sophie grew the toastiest she'd been since winter had descended, as if on a schedule, the day before Halloween.

"How about some tunes?" he asked.

"Sure," Sophie said.

He turned on the stereo. "You spin."

Sophie looked around for an iPhone or a dock or something. Russell glimpsed her and said: "It's voice activated. Just call out a song."

"Ohh, magic," Sophie said. Except then she realized that she wouldn't have the luxury of browsing Russell's collection to see what he had. Sophie had the musical taste of a fifty-year-old woman, in other words, her mother's musical taste. But that was embarrassing. What did normal people like? Zora was into this indie folky music that put Sophie to sleep. Maybe Kanye. Or was that too presumptuous? Lorde? Didn't everyone like Lorde?

"It's not a test," Russell said. "Just tell it your favorite song."

"'You Can't Always Get What You Want,'" Sophie blurted.

She started to explain that it was the Rolling Stones but Russell was already asking the magic car to play track nine of *Let It Bleed*. A few seconds later, the opening chorus of choirboys singing (sounding much better than tonight's carolers, Sophie thought) filled the car, followed by Mick Jagger's beautifully ruined voice.

They drove, and let Mick Jagger croon them over the dark country roads. Sophie loved this song, and mouthed the words, but resisted the urge to sing out loud. One of the *What the Hell Have You Done, Sophie Roth?* moments had involved an ill-advised rendition of "To Sir, with Love" on the karaoke machine in the common room. "Maybe not the best choice if you're tone-deaf," one of the girls had said. She'd been trying to be helpful, but none of Sophie's NYC friends—some of whom had attended the performing arts high school—had ever seen fit to make such a comment.

Sophie wasn't sure where they were going. It was rural out here; they just seemed to be driving, but that was okay. Driving and listening to the Stones definitely qualified as the best date she'd had here so far. (Not that this was a date. Was this a date?)

After about twenty minutes, Russell pulled off the highway. In the middle of an otherwise empty stretch of road, all lit up like a beacon, was a diner. Not just a diner, but an old-school, aluminum-sided diner. It looked like a giant Airstream trailer.

"What *is* this place?" Sophie asked as they crunched over the gravel parking lot. It was so completely unexpected, like being handed a beautifully wrapped gift for no special reason.

"This," Russell said, "is the best pie in the state."

"But where did it come from?" Sophie heard the question. It was the diner equivalent of *What are* you *doing here?* But the only diner-type places she'd seen around campus had been chains: Applebee's and Fridays and the like.

"Oz," Russell said.

That seemed exactly right. Oz, like it had been blown in on a twister, or like it was in Technicolor after everything these past few months had been in black and white. Maybe when people asked Sophie where she was from—in that overly solicitous but also mildly suspicious tone that suggested that wherever it was, they were glad they weren't from there—she should stop saying Brooklyn (so big city) and start saying Oz.

Oz was packed. They found the last remaining booth. A waitress in jeans and a T-shirt with a Saint Bernard in an elf hat on it plopped a couple of menus on the table. "Merry Kiss-My-Ass," she crooned in a smoke-scarred voice.

"Right back at you, Lorraine," Russell said. "What's good tonight?"

"Why you always ask me that?"

"I like the way you talk pie."

"Oh, stop it."

"Also, I have a guest."

Lorraine glanced at Sophie. "So you do." She cleared her throat. "We got some specials: banana cream. Reese's peanut butter pie, sweet potato. Plus, the cherry's good. Fruit's frozen but the cherries were grown only two miles from here."

Russell looked to Sophie. "Well?"

"Do you have apple?" she asked.

Lorraine looked at Russell. *"Really?"*

"Hey, I didn't know."

"Didn't know what?" Sophie asked but nobody answered her.

"Two apples then," Lorraine said. "You want 'em à la mode or with cheese?"

Sophie winced. Pie with cheese. Why not add some gravy while you're at it?

Russell registered the look. "You ever had apple pie with cheese?"

Sophie shook her head.

"But you know it's no good?"

"Yep," Sophie said.

"Without ever having tried it?"

"Well, I've never had apple pie with toenail clippings either, but I'm pretty sure where I stand on that."

Russell smiled. Lorraine tapped her pencil against the pad.

"We'll take one of each," he told Lorraine. He turned to Sophie. "You might be tempted."

"Don't bet on it," Sophie said.

"I always go for the long shot."

He was teasing her, Sophie could tell, but she wasn't entirely sure he was teasing her about pie.

"That all?" Lorraine asked.

"Almost," Russell said. He looked right at Sophie, as if they were in cahoots. "Coffee. Right?"

"Obviously."

"Two coffees, please."

After Lorraine left, Sophie looked around. It was an interesting mix of people; farmers in Carhartt, but also people who looked at home in a city, even though the nearest city was more than a hundred miles away. How had they all found out about this place?

"Is this place on Yelp?" Sophie asked.

"Don't think it has a name, let alone a Yelp listing," he said.

"How'd you find it?"

"You knock three times on the fourth red barn on your left and someone whispers you directions."

"Very underground," Sophie said.

"Yep," Russell said. "Only for the cool kids." He gestured to an elderly couple behind them. "The ultimate insiders."

She laughed at that. Not that she'd ever been an insider, but never less so than in the last three months. "I miss diners."

"They've got good diners in New York," Russell said.

"They do. There's this one me and my mom sometimes go to for upside-down dinner, which is—"

"Breakfast for dinner," Russell interrupted. "Big fan of the upside-down dinner."

"Me, too. Wait, how'd you know I was from New York?"

Russell didn't answer. Or let his oozy grin do the answering.

"Oh, I see. It's obvious. Because I'm so big city."

"Big city?"

"That's what they tell me here all the time. Only they don't mean it as any kind of geographical designation. It's more of an all-purpose commentary on how strange they think I am. You watch foreign films and are sarcastic, therefore so big city."

Russell thought about it a minute. "You eat spicy food, therefore so big city."

"You read the *New York Times* and not for an assignment, totally big city."

"You listen to jazz, whoa, big city."

"You wear black, definitely big city."

"You *are* black, definitely big city. Only then they call you *urban*."

Sophie laughed. "Sometimes *I* think big city is code for Jewish, even if people here don't realize it because they've never met a Jew before."

"Seriously?"

Seriously. When Sophie first got here, she'd been asked about what kind of church she went to. She'd explained that Jews went to temple (not that *she* did; her family wasn't that kind of Jewish). She'd been incredulous that people did not know this, but a lot of people didn't. Her mother had packed her a small menorah for Hanukkah, but it had remained stuffed in the far reaches of her closet. Sophie couldn't bear the number of explanations that lighting the candles would require.

Sophie was wondering how much of this to tell to Russell, but he was now looking at his phone and then he was waving Lorraine over, and for a small second Sophie feared she'd gone too far (she was always going too far) and if he was asking for the check. But instead he asked Lorraine if they had hash browns. "The patty kind, not the chunky ones."

"Chunky ones is home fries. Hash browns *is* the patties. We got both," Lorraine said, exasperated, though Sophie was beginning to suspect she enjoyed being exasperated by Russell.

"Okay. Hash browns. With a side of apple sauce, and sour cream." Russell looked at Sophie. "Right?"

"Right," Sophie managed to say. Barely. Because of the sudden lump in her throat. Hash browns, basically latkes, with applesauce and sour cream? This was Hanukkah food.

"How did you know?" Sophie asked when she'd recovered.

"Genius thing, called a calendar," he said. "It's got all kinds of intel."

"The dates, maybe, but latkes are insider knowledge. Where are you *really* from?"

His grin was a little bit wicked. "You suggesting a brother from Texas can't know about latkes?"

"I'll bet it's a violation of several state statutes, actually," Sophie said.

Russell laughed. "Probably right. I used to date a Jewish girl."

Well then. "So they have Jews in Texas?"

"This wasn't Texas."

"Oh." Now that she thought about it, he didn't sound like he was from Texas. But she didn't sound like she was from New York, either. People on campus were surprised by that. She guessed her accent, at least, wasn't so big city. "So where are you really from then?"

"*Really* from? Not sure I'm *really* from anywhere."

"Now you're just trying to be mysterious."

"How'm I doing?"

"You're James Bond. But even he's from somewhere."

His face seemed to flatten out a bit. "Haven't lived anywhere long enough to be from there." Then he listed a roster of places he *had* lived: Dubai, Seoul, Amman, Mexico City, and, stateside, North Dakota, Colorado, and most recently, Houston, Texas. "My father's in the oil business," Russell added.

"Oh, I thought . . ." Sophie began as her brain fully digested yet another thing that should've been obvious. Russell was rich. Why had she had thought he was on scholarship, when all evidence pointed to the contrary?

"Thought what? That I was big city?" Then he looked up at her and something in her expression must've given her away. "Oh," he said. "You thought I was a jock on scholarship." His tone was still light, but a little guarded now. His version of a *just kidding.*

"Sorry," she said. And she was. More than that. A bit devastated. Somehow Sophie had gotten it into her head that she and this guy had something in common. The optimism that had been speeding along all night crashed into a brick wall.

"Nothing doing," Russell said, his expression saying otherwise. "Lemme guess. Basketball."

Sophie had lost the thread of conversation. "What?" she asked. "Oh, right, I guess."

Russell made a sound, kind of like a cough. Sophie snapped to, looking up at him. She expected anger or derision but it was worse than that. He was like a Christmas tree after you unplugged the lights. Sophie had joined the ranks of dumb commenters. She had let him down. Part of her wanted to explain why she'd thought that, and how she really hadn't, and to tell him about her black best friend and growing up in Brooklyn and all her big-city (urban) bona fides. But she didn't. Because somehow, he had let her down, too.

Just as the evening spectacularly stalled, Lorraine arrived with all the food stacked up her arms. Pie with cheese. Pie à la mode. Hash browns with applesauce. Only instead of sour cream, she brought cottage cheese. *Figures,* Sophie thought.

The food just sat there, cooling on the table between them. Sophie was desolate, miserable, and terribly homesick all of a sudden. This had to be the worst *What the Hell Have You Done, Sophie Roth?* moment so far.

She'd come here for knowledge but Sophie felt herself growing dumber by the minute. Case in point, what had just happened. It wasn't as if she was unaccustomed to being around rich people, all kinds of rich people. Though her neighborhood had been gritty and cheap when her mother leased their rent-stabilized apartment before Sophie was born, over the years it had gentrified. When Sophie was ten, a family bought one of the nearby brownstones and gutted it before moving in. They had a daughter, a girl Sophie's age named Ava, who quickly became one of Sophie's close friends. Over the years, Ava always offered to pay for Sophie, for her movies, for her dinners, for weekends away. At first the gestures—*BFF subsidies,* Ava called them—had been sweet, but then they had stopped feeling sweet and had only made Sophie hyperaware of what she lacked. She started declining the subsidies. Ava carried on offering. Sophie started resenting her for it. Sophomore year they'd had a huge falling out. "I'm not a Neediest Cases," Sophie had screamed. The offers stopped. And the friendship died soon after. Sophie felt bad about it, but was never sure how to repair things.

She wasn't sure how to repair things now, either, but as the food sat there untouched, a glaring reproach, she knew she had to. Russell had already rescued the first half of the evening. Not just by making her laugh and getting her away from a possible sweater orgy, but by giving her some space to be herself again. She hadn't realized how much she needed that. Of all the things and people she missed lately, it was odd to find herself at the top of the list.

She took a deep breath and out of the silence said: "What I was going to say before was that I thought you were like me."

He looked at her again, which was something, but it was clear from his foggy expression he didn't get what she meant.

So Sophie told him what she hadn't told anyone else here, though she knew it was nothing to be ashamed of. It was something to be proud of.

"*I'm* on scholarship. I guess I thought—hoped—that if you were too, it meant you might be like me."

The silence between them stretched. Sophie wasn't sure her admission had done anything to save the night, though it had righted something in her. But then Russell said, "Who says I'm not?"

He slid the cheesy pie across the table toward her. She was unsure if this was a challenge or an olive branch. Either way, she picked up her fork, and though the pie looked profoundly unappetizing—the cheese had bubbled into a blister—she took a small, tentative bite.

And. Oh. My. God.

The sharp tang of the cheddar brought out the hint of savory in the crust, and contrasted with the sweetness of the apples. And then there was the collage of consistencies: gooey, crumbly, juicy, all of it warm.

She took another forkful, larger this time. Russell watched her. He seemed amused. She took a third bite. Now he was smiling, a sort of shit-eating grin.

"What?" Sophie asked.

"Thinking I won that bet," Russell said.

They demolished the pie and most of the hash browns. They weren't too bad with the cottage cheese, after all. Pretty soon all that was left was a sad lump of ice cream. When the check came, Sophie reached for her bag. Russell shook his head.

"I was planning on paying when I thought you were rich, so wouldn't it be patronizing to let you split it now?"

Sophie laughed at that. "Wait, you thought *I* was rich?"

Russell quirked an eyebrow and attempted to look bashful.

"So, does that make us even?" she asked.

"Not really keeping score," Russell said. "But it does make things interesting." He laid a pair of twenties on the table.

"Thank you," Sophie said. "For everything. But especially for the latkes. Those will probably be my only ones this year."

"Why's that?"

"Tonight is the last night of Hanukkah. The latke window is closing."

"Aren't you going home for the holidays?"

"I'll be home for Christmas and New Years but no, not Hanukkah this year."

"Why not?"

Sophie paused, wondering which way to answer that. "Two hundred and sixty-seven dollars," she said finally.

She told him that this was how much the price of tickets dropped if she left next week. Sophie had fought with her mother about this, which was unusual. She was accustomed to frugality. It had always been that way, a matter of necessity with just the two of them and her mother's slender income. But also because any surplus had gone to Sophie's college fund. Then last winter, right as Sophie was filling out her applications, Luba had a stroke. She'd lingered in a sort of twilight and neither Sophie nor her mother could bear to put her in one of those public nursing homes (they were so Soviet). When she died, five months later, Sophie's college savings was history. NYU had said yes, but Sophie's dream school was suddenly exorbitant, even with a financial aid package. Then U of B came along with its generous offer.

Sophie's mom hadn't been able to fly her home for Thanksgiving. And now, this latest postponement. These were the first holidays with Luba gone. Sophie wondered if that wasn't the real reason for the delay. Maybe her mom wanted to skip the holidays this year. Maybe Sophie did, too.

Thinking about all this, Sophie started to cry. Oh, for Christ's sake. *This* most certainly qualified as a *What the Hell Have You Done, Sophie Roth?* moment.

"You okay?" Russell asked.

"Holiday stuff," Sophie said, wiping her nose. "I don't even know why I'm crying. Hanukkah's lame. Who cares if I miss it?"

Russell was looking at her. Curiously. Softly. Knowingly.

"Who says you're missing it?"

Since they'd started this Hanukkah thing, Sophie and Russell decided to see it through, by lighting the menorah she had buried somewhere in her closet. It was Luba's. The last time they'd used it was a year ago, just before the stroke. Hanukkah had come crazy early, colliding with Thanksgiving, so they'd had a huge feast: turkey and brisket and latkes and potatoes and donuts and pie for desert. But Sophie could only allow herself to think about that for a second. Summoning those memories was like touching a burning pot. She could do it only briefly before she had to pull away.

As they drove back to campus, Sophie realized that though she had a menorah, she didn't have candles. They drove to the grocery store on the outskirts of town. It was empty, the aisles small, the floors dingy and scuffed. Russell pushed Sophie around in a rickety cart as the tired stock boys watched them warily. Sophie whooped with laughter. Grocery-cart derby. Who knew that would make such an excellent dating activity? (And by now, she was pretty sure this *was* a date.)

The candle selection was unsurprisingly pathetic. A whole shelf of plug-ins, an odd assortment of birthday numbers (4 and 7 were disproportionately represented) and some glass emergency candles, meant for blackouts and other catastrophes. Nothing that would remotely fit a menorah.

Russell had his phone out, searching for stores that would be open this late. But Sophie was already reaching for the emergency candles. "This holiday is about being adaptable," she said. "My people are notoriously scrappy."

"I can see that," Russell said. "So how many we need?"

"Nine," said Sophie. "Eight for the eight nights of Hanukah, plus an extra lighter candle. If we're being official about it."

There were nine emergency candles on the shelf.

"Wow," said Sophie. "That's almost like the actual Hanukkah miracle." She explained the origins of the holiday, the oil in the menorah that should've lasted a single night lasting eight. "It's really only a minor miracle," she added.

Russell looked at her and cocked his head. "Not sure there is such a thing as a minor miracle."

They drove from the store back to campus. *Let It Bleed* was still playing, and they put "You Can't Always Get What You Want" on again. This time, Sophie sang along, quietly at first, then belting the words. If she was off-key, she didn't care.

Back on campus, after Russell parked his car, they walked through the quad toward Sophie's dorm. It was empty now, no sign of the reindeer orgy they'd escaped. That all felt like a million years ago.

"Why'd you talk to me earlier?" Sophie asked. "Was it really because of Ned Flanders?"

"Partly," Russell said, stretching the word out in a way that made Sophie want to scratch it.

"What's the other part?"

"You don't remember me then?"

Remember him? She would if there was a reason to. She was sure of it. Except he was looking at her like they had a history.

"Poetry Survey."

Sophie had only been in that class for a week. She'd *hated* it so much. It wasn't even taught by a professor, but a TA with a nasal twang who had insisted on very specific interpretations of the poems. She and Sophie had gotten into it about the Yeats poem "When You Are Old." It was yet another *What the Hell Have You Done, Sophie Roth?* moment, a big one. One that made her question coming here.

"I regretted not going to bat for you when you had your . . . disagreement."

Disagreement. More like a war of words. She and the TA had debated about one line from the poem—"How many loved your moments of glad grace"—and Sophie had found herself on the verge of tears. She'd had to leave the hall before the period ended. She'd dropped the class the next day.

"If it makes you feel better, after that, a bunch of us started challenging her," Russell said. "'Poetry isn't math' was our battle cry."

It was what Sophie had said to the TA. A sort of retroactive relief—or maybe vindication?—crept over her. She'd had defenders in that class. Wingmen. Even if she hadn't noticed them. Hadn't noticed *him*. The truth was, she didn't notice a lot of things at school. She kept her head down, wore blinders. It was a survival tactic. Only now did she wonder if it was a stupid survival tactic, like wearing a life jacket made of lead.

"I asked about you, after the class. Got some intel, about you being big city and all," he said with a teasing smile. "But I never spotted you for more than a blur. Until tonight . . . I was debating saying something. You were looking pretty fierce, not fit for company." He grinned again, but it was different, less oozy, more shy, and about a thousand times sexier. "But then you mentioned Ned Flanders, and I *had* to say something."

"What? Is Ned like your spirit guide?"

He laughed. That big, open-chested laugh. "We lived all over, sometimes moving every year. All the places I lived, *The Simpsons* was like this one constant. They had it everywhere, sometimes it'd be English, sometimes dubbed, didn't matter. It was my comfort food."

"You make it sound sad," Sophie said. "Living all those places sounds pretty great to me."

"Things are not always how they seem."

The look they exchanged was like a road map of the history they'd already traversed tonight. "So what was it *really* like?" Sophie asked.

"Ever see that movie *Lost In Translation*?" Sophie nodded. She loved that film. "Like that, over and over. But times a thousand because I'm black in places where they just don't get black. In Korea, they called me Obama." He sighed. "Before Obama's presidency, I was Michael Jordan."

"Is that why you came to school here?" Sophie asked. "Because you knew what to expect?"

Russell looked at her a while before answering. "Yeah. Some of that. Also, to piss off my parents. They thought I was crazy for coming here, but I thought I was making a grand statement. Like, hey, this is how it's always been for me so I'm just going to go back for more." He laughed, a little sadder this time. "Only problem is, they never got that and even if they did, being here isn't really punishing them. Beyond the expensive tuition." He threw up his hands. "Well, at least they've got a good journalism program."

"And an excellent liberal arts curriculum," Sophie added.

"And beautiful big-city girls who talk to themselves about Ned Flanders."

"Right. I read about them in the catalog," Sophie said, a little flustered by the *beautiful* comment. Also by the fact that they'd reached her dorm. "This is me."

Russell took her hand. It was warm. "Ready to get your Hanukkah on?"

"Okily dokily," Sophie said.

The suite was empty. Kaitlynn, Madison, and Cheryl had already left for the holidays, though they'd littered the suite with holiday cheer. Being in here alone with Russell, Sophie was suddenly knee-shakingly nervous, so she started talking in the same rapid-fire *bap-bap-bap* as Madison's blinking lights. "And here is our fake tree, threaded with the traditional offerings of popcorn and candy canes. And you'll notice the tinsel everywhere, not sure what that symbolizes, and that Santa balloon is made out of vintage Mylar. And if you breathe deep, you'll catch a whiff of pine-scented potpourri. Welcome to the land where Christmas threw up."

She was trying to carry on the joke of the Rudolph sweaters. But maybe it was a testament to how far they'd come tonight that the joke fell flat.

"Show me where you live," Russell said softly.

Sophie's quarter of the suite was like that thing on *Sesame Street*: One of these things is not like the other. No posters or corkboards with friendship collages. On her bookshelf she had a framed shot of Zora, an old shot of Luba looking glamorous and kind of mean, and a picture of her and her mother on a gondola in Venice. They'd had the same gondolier a bunch of times and he'd taken to calling her *Sophia*, crooning a song in Italian to her.

Russell was looking at the picture. "That was when my mom was in the Venice Biennale, a really big art show," Sophie explained. Growing up, there'd been so many times she'd wished her mom could be a lawyer or a banker or a producer, the kind of jobs some of her friends' parents had. But when her mother had been invited to show at the prestigious Biennale, and Luba had sold a ring so Sophie could accompany her, she'd been so proud of her mother, the artist. Glad that she'd stuck to her guns. It didn't hurt that the trip had been magical: the gondola rides, the tiny zigzag of canals and alleys, the packed art galleries, and more than any of that, the feeling of some kind of portal of possibility opening. She hadn't felt that way in a long time. She was feeling that way tonight.

"What kind of art does your mom make?" Russell asked.

"Sculptures. Though not the traditional kind with clay or marble. She works in abstract forms." She reached to her top shelf and pulled down a small cube, all tangled wires and glass fragments. "Most of her work is on a much larger scale," Sophie explained. "Like one piece could fill this room. Alas, my roommate Cheryl said she needed a bed so we couldn't keep one here."

For a second, she imagined Cheryl's horrified expression if she *had* brought one of her mother's larger, stranger installations. But then she remembered that Cheryl had seemed to admire her mom's smaller piece. She'd held it a long time the first time she'd seen it, much as Russell was doing now. "Your mom makes sculptures," she'd said. "My mom organizes bake sales." Sophie had taken it as a veiled big-city comment, yet another sign of her otherness, but only now did she wonder if perhaps she hadn't missed Cheryl's droll brand of sarcasm.

Russell turned the piece in his hand, seeing how the light played into the angles. "My grandmother used to make these things . . . not sure if you'd call them sculptures or what, out of wood and sea grass. On Saint Vincent. Ever heard of it?"

"It's an island in the Caribbean, right?" Sophie said.

"Yeah. It's where my mom's from. She came to the States for college, met my dad, and never went back. I used to go spend summers on the island with my grandmother. In this little house, painted in island colors, my grandma said, and there were always cousins running around, chickens and goats, too."

Russell was smiling at the memory. Sophie smiled along with him.

"Then my father started sending me to camp during the summers: tennis camp, sailing camp, golf camp. We only go to Saint Vincent for vacation now, every year for Christmas. Last few years, we've stayed at a fancy resort, like tourists. And people treat us different. Like tourists. Even my own people." He set down the sculpture, his expression wistful and yearning. "Except for my grandmother."

Sophie closed her eyes. She could picture his grandmother, a beautiful lined face, hands tough with years of solid work, a stern manner that masked a deep ferocious love. After a bit, the image of his grandmother merged with Luba, who she pictured last year, broom in hand, swatting the smoke alarm after it went haywire from all the latke frying. Instead of pushing the memory away, she let it wash over. She was surprised to find that it didn't burn. She could hold on to it. Then she opened her eyes. "Is your grandmother still alive?" she asked.

"Yeah." Russell smiled.

"Are you going to see her?" It suddenly felt very important to her that he was.

"Flying down Sunday," he said. "Looking forward to it." He paused. "And dreading it. You know? Holiday stuff."

"It'll be okay," she told him, but the words ricocheted back to her. *It'll be okay*. That's what people had been telling Sophie for a while now. After Luba died. It would be okay; time heals. After she started college. It would be okay; leaving home is an adjustment. Sophie hadn't believed it. You can't undo loss. You can't unmake a mistake.

But now she was wondering if a garden of memories might not grow over the hole of losing Luba. And if college wasn't a little like that first swim every summer—no matter how much Sophie looked forward to it, she still had to get used to the chilly water. Maybe *anywhere* Sophie had gone this year would've felt like a Bumfuck-ville.

Because *this* Bumfuckville had diners dropped from Oz. It had wingmen who had her back in poetry class. It had people like Cheryl, who, come to think of it, was pretty big-citily sarcastic herself. And it had guys like Russell.

What if the mistake wasn't coming here, but being blind to any of that?

What the Hell Have You Done, Sophie Roth? she thought to herself for the umpteenth time. But it felt different now. If she'd made a mistake, there was time to fix it. And more than that, she was looking forward to fixing it.

They unplugged all the Christmas lights and laid the candles out in a vaguely menorah-like shape on the ground. Sophie found Luba's menorah and put it out, too. They lit the candles. Where there was darkness, now, a warm glow of light.

"Normally you'd say a prayer in Hebrew," Sophie said. "But I kind of think we're doing our own thing, right? So I'm going to offer my thanks to that dumb caroling concert tonight."

"Okay then," Russell said. "I offer mine to reindeer sweaters."

Sophie chuckled. "To cars with butt warmers."

"And butts in butt warmers."

"To hash browns," Sophie said.

"Don't forget pie."

"Pie with *cheese*."

Russell pulled Sophie into his lap. He was tall and she could sit in the fold of his legs, her own legs crossed under her.

"To perfect fits," Russell murmured.

"And imperfect fits," Sophie said.

Sophie reached up to touch Russell's lips, and he grasped her fingers, kissing them, one by one: thumb, index, middle, ring, pinky, and back again.

"To Ned Flanders," Russell said.

"Oh, yes, a thousand times to Ned Flanders. We should devote the holiday to him," Sophie said.

Russell lifted up her hair and kissed her on the bony ridge of her neck. She shivered. "To the Rolling Stones," he murmured. At that moment, not even Mick Jagger could've sounded sexier.

"And not always getting what you want," Sophie said.

"But sometimes getting what you need," Russell said.

She kissed his lips then. They tasted of apples and cheese, of the revelation of things you never imagined going so well together. She tasted meting ice cream, too, melting defenses, herself melting into Russell.

She kissed him, not knowing if the kiss would go on for a minute, an hour, the whole night. She kissed him not knowing what would happen next semester, next year. But at the moment, none of that seemed to matter. The kiss was what mattered. Not just the kiss, but what the kiss said. What it unlocked. What the night unlocked. What they had unlocked.

Tomorrow would be different. Sophie understood this.

There really was no such thing as a minor miracle.

BEER BUCKETS
AND
BABY JESUS

MYRA McENTIRE

The whole mess started when I lit the church on fire.

To be precise, I didn't strike a match, and it wasn't the church proper, but the barn beside it. The one that Main Street Methodist used to store all the equipment for the annual Christmas pageant. Well, the barn they *used to* use.

Put this on your list of things to know: the combination of tinsel, baby angel wings, and manger hay burns like weed at a Miley Cyrus concert.

My questionable reputation was established in the first grade. Vaughn Hatcher, the boy who covered the class rabbit with paste and a liberal coat of glitter and set him loose in the faculty lounge. It turns out, teachers think of glitter as the herpes of the craft world—impossible to contain or exterminate. Hippity Hop was sent to a petting zoo, and I was sent to the principal's office. But it was too late. I'd already experienced the hijinks that could ensue when my creativity was put to good use. I was hooked.

I was the guy who taught the other kids how to egg houses, roll yards, and glue mailboxes shut. And the older I got, the more elaborate my pranks became. In middle school, I filled the clinic with Styrofoam peanuts. Last year, my junior year of high school, I decorated the town Christmas tree with neon thong underwear.

My list of achievements is quite impressive, if I do say so myself.

My failures equal one.

If I could justify casting off blame, it would belong to Shelby Baron. Shelby is a boy, by the way, and before I was kicked out of organized sports, he was the first-string quarterback. I was third. In basketball, he was starting center, and I cleaned up spilled Gatorade behind the bench. All of that, *and* he dated Gracie Robinson. He's just always been *better* than me, so therefore I don't like him. At least he's not better looking. He's Beefy Viking. I'm Tall, Dark, and Inappropriate.

On the day of the incident, I drove by the church and noticed that Shelby happened to park his Mini Cooper—seriously, a *dude* named *Shelby* who drives a *Mini Cooper*—underneath a tree. Said tree had a large flock of pigeons roosting on its branches, and there I was with a glove compartment filled with fireworks. I saw an opportunity, I predicted an outcome, and I had to see how it would all go down.

A lot of bird shit went down.

And, thanks to a wayward spark, I set the church on fire.

For the first time in my life, I was in *real* trouble. The juvenile system kind of trouble. But then something even more unexpected occurred—the pastor of Main Street Methodist swooped in and made a deal with the authorities. I was given a choice. If I'd agree to give up my Christmas break and help the church reboot the pageant, the incident would be expunged from my record.

For forty hours of community service.

I'd mowed a zillion lawns to save up for a winter-break trip to Miami. If I took the deal, I'd have to cancel it. No beaches. No nightlife. No bikinis. The most frustrating part was that I wouldn't be able to get out of celebrating Christmas with my family.

All two of us.

But my alternative was possible probation or worse. I had the grades to get into my top college choices, but way too many admissions counselors were concerned about my reputation, and I was concerned about getting any letters of recommendation. Setting a church on fire is the kind of news that gets around. College would get me out of this town. Away from my house. Away from my reputation. The judge said I had a choice, but it wasn't a real choice.

It had to be the pageant.

I couldn't stop staring at Gracie Robinson's pregnant belly. Well, not hers, exactly. Mary, mother of God's.

Gracie has dark hair, innocent blue eyes, and skin like butter. She's not yellow. I'm just sure if I ever got my hands on her skin, it would be soft. Not that I was planning on touching her or anything. Her father was the pastor of Main Street Methodist—the same pastor who was the reason why I was here, at the Rebel Yell, two days before Christmas.

The Rebel Yell was a dinner theater show that served fried chicken and beer in feed buckets. It featured a rodeo complete with clowns, tricks, and stunts, as well as rousing musical numbers. The theme pitted the Union against the Confederacy. Patrons picked sides and rooted for their favorite team—basically reducing the Civil War to a football rivalry. I hated generalizations about the South, but the Rebel Yell did make me embarrassed for my home state of Tennessee.

Though the church wouldn't be sharing a venue with these carpetbaggers in the first place if I hadn't destroyed their barn.

Twenty-nine hours down. Three pageant performances to execute. Opening night—tonight—and two tomorrow, for Christmas Eve. Eleven more hours, and I would be free from carrying wood, painting sets, sweeping floors, and climbing on catwalks to replace burned-out spotlights. The opening-night curtain would go up soon.

Yet somehow I'd found time to kill, just so I could be near Gracie. She'd always been nice to me—especially nice—but not the kind of nice that makes you wonder what percentage is actually pity. Since I started my community service, I've had exactly seven encounters with her. Not that I was counting. I caught her watching *me* a lot, but it was always while I was in the act of watching *her,* or while her boyfriend was around, so I tried not to obsess about it too much.

Her boyfriend wasn't around right now.

Even though I'd looked for opportunities to talk to her, when she'd sat down beside me on a bale of hay, my mind had gone completely blank. I believe that saying nothing at all is better than saying something stupid, so I waited for her to start the conversation.

And waited.

And waited.

I'd been fidgeting with a tangled string of fairy lights and giving her belly the side eye for at least five minutes when she reached into her fuzzy purple robe, pulled out a watermelon-shaped piece of foam, and handed it over. "Please," she said. "Inspect my womb."

"It's . . . nice. Plushy." I gave it a squeeze and handed it back to her. I wasn't up on faux-womb etiquette. I couldn't even believe she'd said the word *womb*.

"Thanks to you, I got upgraded to cooling-gel memory foam. I can't wait to see the rest of my costume." She smoothed down the lapels of her bathrobe. "Assuming they get it made in time."

I glanced around. Moms and dads were frantically putting the final touches on costumes that were replacing the ones that I'd turned to ashes. From what I could gather, robes and halos weren't too difficult, but angel wings were a real pain in the ass. Possibly because of the glitter, but I didn't offer up the herpes analogy. 'Cause you know. Church.

"I'm sorry." I stared at the lights in my hands. The past week had been enlightening. Main Street Methodist had been presenting the nativity play for twenty years, and I'd wrecked it in one minute. "I keep waiting for the thunderbolt."

"Stop looking over your shoulder. I didn't say that to make you feel bad." Gracie touched my knee for a split second before pulling away and tucking her hand into her robe pocket. "If my dad's forgiven you, the Lord certainly has."

I stared at my knee. "If the Lord and I started talking forgiveness, I'd be in a confessional for the rest of my life."

She grinned. "Methodists don't have confessionals."

"Your father did more than forgive me," I blurted out. "He kept me from going to jail. On Christmas."

So, so awkward.

"Good thing, right? I don't know if Santa visits juvie."

"He wouldn't come for me anyway. I'm on the naughty list."

She should have been furious with me. Her acceptance rendered me as impotent as a vice president.

Gracie Robinson was simply *nice*.

Her reputation was the exact opposite of mine. She was captain of the safety patrol in elementary school, a student council rep in middle school, and, most recently, homecoming queen. She was currently in line for valedictorian of our senior class. She always had an extra pencil, and it was always sharp. Girls like that and guys like me don't mix. Except when there's a pending court order.

"It's too bad we couldn't get the barn repaired in time," she said. "We tried."

A pang of guilt, somewhere below my left rib. Maybe I could work in some public self-flagellation. I doubted it would help. I gestured to the confederate flag and the mini-cannon, which were shoved into a corner. "How exactly did you guys end up . . . here?"

I didn't say Rebel Yell, because I couldn't without wincing at the Civil War–as-entertainment reference.

Gracie pursed her lips. "We ended up here thanks to Richard Baron."

Father of Shelby.

"He owns this franchise," she said, not meeting my eyes.

Right. Of course he did. He bought his son a Mini Cooper. Obviously, sound judgment climbed high in that family tree.

She continued, "When we figured out we wouldn't get things running in time, he offered us the venue for the two nights of the pageant. It's the only place around here that's big enough."

"I'd say." It had stadium seating and a huge, dirt-floor arena.

"Even so, claiming our own territory has been hard." She shook her head. "But I guess you'd know about that."

The job parameters of my community service ran the gamut. I'd done everything from helping the church move in the remaining props that I hadn't set ablaze to serving as a stagehand for the actual production. Sorting out what belonged to whom involved pawing through an eclectic mix of Confederate memorabilia, oversized scrolls, and shepherd's staffs. I still didn't know if the trumpets belonged to the Civil War buglers or a heavenly host of angels.

"I'm surprised your father didn't cancel it," I said.

"It would've been easier, but this is the pageant's twentieth anniversary. So many people were looking forward to it that Dad didn't feel like he could turn down Mr. Baron, especially after he offered to pay for all the new materials we needed."

Put another jewel in the Baron family crown. "Why did he offer?"

"Shelby is playing Joseph."

"Gotcha."

Just then, Gracie's father rushed to the center of the stage, holding a clipboard and an enormous cup of coffee. He looked too young to head up a congregation of five hundred people. Like, boy-reporter young. Gracie shared his dark hair but not his eyes. They looked older than the rest of him.

He waved to get the attention of the people arranging the set. "Okay, let's finish blocking these scenes so we can do a run through. I'm sorry, but that horse—when it's replaced by a donkey—will have to take a left, behind the Wise Men, after they approach the Holy Family. Can you move that bale of hay to make it easier? Donkeys don't jump."

As adept as I am at predicting outcomes, I had to ask the obvious question. "What happens if that horse poops?"

As if it had been cued, the horse lifted his tail and took his evening constitutional.

"Wow," Gracie said.

Pastor Robinson's coffee sloshed onto the ground as he tucked the clipboard under one arm. I waited for the anger—for him to yell at someone to clean it up, to throw the clipboard, or to slam down his coffee cup. I'd never seen him show anger, but that's what would happen if someone screwed with *my* dad when he was conducting business.

I heard Pastor Robinson's reaction before I saw it. It didn't register because it was illogical, to me at least. When he lifted his face, it was wet with tears.

A horse dropped a dump in the middle of his rehearsal, and the man was laughing.

"Not . . . what I expected," I said. Humor wasn't a typical emotion at my house even when my dad lived with us. Especially when he lived with us.

"If you don't do bathroom humor, we can't be friends." She elbowed me in the side. When I didn't respond, she said, "It's funny, so he's laughing. People do, you know." Like she knew what I was thinking. Like she understood the differences in the ways we were raised.

Pastor Robinson's hand rested on his shaking, Christmas-plaid-covered stomach. His wedding ring shone on his finger. It surprised me. Gracie's mom had died when we were in the second grade.

"Vaughn?" She touched the top of my hand. "You can laugh, too."

"Right."

I pulled away and grabbed a shovel.

My family didn't react to calamity with laughter.

My dad left when I was eight, and my mom never recovered. I'd tried to convince myself that it wasn't my fault he left, but I never succeeded. I was hell at eight, in trouble all the time, and I'd always wondered what kind of strain my behavior put on their marriage. I had a distinct feeling that my dad didn't like me, but he'd always been the one to handle the teacher's conferences and suspensions. He made sure I had food and money, but that's where penance for leaving his family stopped.

On the medication wagon, my mom could handle things like balanced meals and clean clothes. When she was down, she could barely take care of herself, much less her kid, and when she was up, she was a lightning strike—beautiful and unpredictable. I worked hard to keep her condition private, which is not a thing a kid should have to do. Fodder for country ballads, but also the reality of my life.

Shame leads to secrets, and secrets lead to lies, and lies ruin everything. Especially friendships. No kid wants to explain that his mom can't bring snacks to class because she ran out of Xanax before the pharmacy would refill the prescription. Other parents stop inviting you to birthday parties, because you don't reciprocate. No one asks you to join sports teams, because you never meet the registration deadlines, and if you do, no one ever remembers to pay your league fees. Soon enough, people forget you altogether.

So you do things that *make* them remember.

I kept my head down as I scooped the horse's early holiday gift into a rusty wheelbarrow. It had seen its fair share of manure. The wheels squeaked, but it rolled just fine. The wooden handles were worn and sturdy. I shook the contents into the compost pile, turned the wheelbarrow up against the wall, and washed my hands in the utility sink backstage. I jumped when Gracie's fingertips grazed my shoulder.

She was a toucher. I hadn't noticed before.

"Why did you do it?" Gracie asked.

"Um, the displeasing aroma?" I yanked on the paper towels too hard, fifteen came off in my hand, and the roll detached from the holder. "Because all the church robes drag the ground? Because somebody had to?"

"You know what I mean. The firecrackers."

I studied the paper towels, lining up the edges as I rolled them back onto the cardboard. "I do lots of things without a specific reason. I was bored. I wanted to see what would happen."

"Experiments are why you take a chemistry class, not why you blow up a bunch of pigeons."

"I wasn't trying to blow them up." I faced her. "I don't abuse animals."

"Hippity." She raised one eyebrow. "Hop."

"That wasn't abuse. That was art. Unfortunate, six-year-old art. As for the birds, I just wanted to scare them out of the tree."

"It worked."

"And they all lived."

Gracie took the roll of paper towels from my hands and hung it back up. "You still haven't told me why you did it."

Pointed questions were not part of my plan. My plan was to make it through the next two days and get a pass from the judge, not to reveal my longstanding crush or expose my deviously jealous ways. My mind raced, desperate for another way out besides the truth. "Okay. So have you ever seen *Sherlock Holmes*?"

Her eyes narrowed at what she assumed was a subject change. "Television or movies?"

"Either," I said.

"Both," she answered.

"You know how Sherlock sees things that shouldn't go together on the surface, but once he makes all the connections, the answers become obvious to him? The camera always shows it as a fast pan from one subject to another." I gestured for her to follow me back to the tangled lights.

"Ugh. That kind of camerawork makes me nauseated." But she smiled and crossed her arms over her womb. "So, what you're saying is that your mind works faster than everyone else's."

"I'm just saying . . . I'm good at seeing connections that could cause trouble." I sat down on a wooden crate and took stock of our surroundings. "For example, lighting. I could change the directions of all the spotlights. Or I could switch up the tape on the stage that marks the places for the actors. Rearrange the props table or just hide it all together. Mixing up the angels' wires could cause all kinds of interesting problems—not for the baby angels, of course, but for a free-swinging adult in wings? That sounds like a party." And a little dirty.

"So, chaos. Is that your ultimate goal?"

"Those were examples, not intentions. Is it *your* goal to play Mary for the rest of your life?"

"Definitely not." She stood. "But when your dad is a pastor . . . well, people have expectations."

"I assume the flawless skin and baby blues kick it over the edge?"

Her nose crinkled at *flawless*. It was an expression I'd seen before, usually when someone paid her a compliment. "Maybe. But the real Mary was Middle Eastern. And closer to twelve. The real Joseph was probably thirty."

"Gross."

"The Wise Men were astronomers, and they didn't show up until Jesus was around two, and no one knows how many there were. The manger was likely a cave."

Gracie was getting fired up, speaking faster and gesturing with her whole body. "And I'm pretty sure Jesus cried," she said. "He was a *baby*. It's ridiculous that we have to keep perpetuating these myths because of people's commercialized expectations." She thumped back down on the wooden crate beside me.

"Then why do you participate?" I looked at her. "Because of your father?"

"You'd think it's because he makes me. But he doesn't." She dropped her face into her hands, and then she peeked at me through splayed fingers. "You're going to think I'm terrible."

I paused, waiting for the middle school choir to pass. Once they were through, I said, "It's impossible to think badly of you, Gracie Robinson."

She sat up straighter. Maybe she blushed a little. I'd paid the compliment with too much admiration in my voice. "It's just . . . sometimes it's nice to be the one everyone pays attention to."

I tilted my head to the side, all cocker spaniel. "You were *homecoming queen*."

"That was a fluke. If Ashley Stewart and Hannah Gale hadn't been suspended for breaking into the principal's office and e-mailing all the teachers to tell them they were fired, I never would've won. They were the shoo-ins for the homecoming court."

I took a moment to check out my cuticles.

Her eyes widened. *"Vaughn."*

"I made a suggestion. Flippantly. And, possibly, handed over a skeleton key." Sometimes it's nice *not* to be the one everyone pays attention to.

She punched my arm. "Did you do that for me?"

I rubbed my bicep. "It wasn't entirely coincidental."

Her mouth dropped open, and her expression told me she was trying to figure out if she should yell at me or thank me. "I don't need to be front and center. I know I'm loved, and that I shouldn't seek out approval. But secretly?" She sighed and lowered her voice. "I suspect I tell myself that so I'm not sad when I don't get noticed."

"Do you want to be noticed or not? Because it sounds like you're talking out of both sides of your mouth." I dared to nudge her shoulder. "I'm not criticizing."

Gracie didn't move away. "When you're a pastor's daughter, guys tend to put you in the 'untouchable' category and never look at you again. I just like to feel special every now and then. You know?"

"Anytime you need to feel special, you come find me." The words were out before I could stop them—a cartoon bubble over my head that wouldn't burst.

Her brows pulled together in a frown. "Are you flirting with me?"

"I'm sorry." I felt my face getting red. My face never got red. "Did I take it too far?"

"No. You took it exactly far enough." The frown slipped into a grin. "I'm just trying to figure out the most effective way to flirt with you."

A rush of adrenaline shot through my body. I didn't know how to volley back, so I changed the subject. Because I was a chicken. "Speaking of flirting, where's your husband?"

She blinked.

"Your fictional husband. Your real-life boyfriend."

"My . . . you mean Shelby?" Gracie groaned. She slid her hands into her hair, clutching her head like it ached. "He is *not* my boyfriend."

"Oh, really?" I crossed my arms and sat back to listen to this one.

"Have you ever seen us holding hands? On a date? A real, official date that wasn't church-sanctioned or a school event? No, you haven't. Because we've never been on one."

"Then what's the deal?"

"I'm a cover for Shelby's real girlfriend."

I almost fell out of my seat. "His *real* girlfriend?"

"She's a very nice, liberal, feminist Christian named Ellie from New Jersey. They met at Bible camp two summers ago."

"Do they *make* liberal feminist Christians?"

Gracie rolled her eyes. "They make all kinds."

I understood why Shelby would need to use Gracie as an alibi. The father of a good old Southern boy would lose his mind if his son dated someone from New Jersey, let alone a liberal feminist from New Jersey.

"If you're just a cover, why is he so protective? Protective to the point of being an ass"—I quickly corrected myself—"*mean* to anyone who looks at you?"

"He feels *brotherly* toward me, and my dad takes advantage." She paused, watching a volunteer bedazzle the gift box that held the myrrh for baby Jesus. "What's Shelby ever done to you, anyway? I know he's a football player, but he's not a stereotype. He's not cornering you in the bathroom and giving you wedgies, is he?"

I shook my head.

"Does he stuff you in lockers? Duct tape you to flagpoles? Put Bengay in your jock . . . er . . . yeah. That kind of thing?"

I grinned. "You're cute when you blush."

"Don't change the subject." She was forcing herself to keep her eyes on mine. "Why don't you like Shelby?"

The conversation had come this far, might as well see it through to the end. "The fact that he had you seemed like reason enough."

"Oh."

I stared at her foam belly. Unbelievably, it was the least embarrassing thing in the room. "I'm guessing if I asked you out, your father wouldn't exactly be okay with that. I'm not a liberal feminist from New Jersey, but I can't rate much higher."

"Have you forgotten that Dad went to court for you?"

Look at the womb. Concentrate on the womb. "I haven't forgotten. But there's a big difference between bailing someone out of trouble and then letting your daughter date the troublemaker."

"Give him some credit. He's not like Shelby's dad. I mean, I'm sure Dad and I would have a serious talk beforehand, but I'm smart enough to know right from wrong. Dad knows that, and he trusts me. As far as you go, he believes in what he does, and in second chances. He loves people. I'd go so far as to say he loves you."

Loved me? "Why? I don't follow the rules. Aren't religious people into rules?"

"Rules make people feel safe. But they can turn into judgments.

Condemnation is easy, Vaughn. The harder choice is love, and it's one my dad makes every day."

"He still wouldn't let you spend time with someone like me," I argued, mostly because I wanted her to convince me.

"You act like what I want doesn't matter." She didn't sound pouty, she sounded strong. Certain.

My adrenaline was pulsing now. "Would you?" I stopped. Considered. Continued. "Ever want someone like me?"

Gracie leaned in. She smelled like . . . wood smoke. And fabric softener. "If you pulled fewer pranks and paid more attention, you'd know the answer to that."

If she meant what I hoped she did, I'd never pull a prank again.

Probably.

The backstage door opened and closed with a *bang*. A cold wind rushed through the curtains, catching the pages of the director's playbook. It held the prompts for every scene, the diagrams for all the stage markings, and possibly the location of the Holy Grail. We sprang to our feet to chase them down.

Gracie shivered, pulling the bathrobe tighter as she caught another flying page. "We'll never find them all."

"Sure we will. Then it'll be as easy as putting them back in order."

"I don't think so." She showed me the papers she'd grabbed. "No numbers. Mrs. Armstrong is going to freak out when she has to reorder them. It'll disrupt her precious schedule."

Mrs. Armstrong was proud of her director gig, and she made that clear with the laminated ID badge she wore around her neck. "Why wouldn't she number her playbook?"

Gracie laughed. "Job security. If no one else knows exactly how the scenes are supposed to go, or where everyone is supposed to stand, or where the tape is placed on the stage, she's necessary."

I was on my knees, checking under the table of fabric. "Why would you need job security for a volunteer position?"

"To place yourself on the highest possible rung of the social ladder."

"Church people are weird." The moment I said it, I felt like a jerk. "Sorry. I have this blurt circuit that can't be tamed. You might have noticed. Can we go back to when I wasn't insulting?"

"That far?" she asked.

"How far?" I stood.

"Third grade."

"What happened in third grade?" I pushed a box of halos aside to retrieve another wayward page.

"You broke all the pencils in your pencil box, and then told the teacher I did it. I had to write 'Abraham Lincoln is on the penny' five hundred times."

I laughed. "I'm sorry."

Gracie's eyes sparkled. "So was I."

The door opened again, and playbook sheets flew back into the air. Gracie ran to the right, lurching between the Dixie flag and a pile of scrolls. I ran to the left, onto the stage, dodging between hoop skirts and the trough that served as the manger. A horse—Confederate cap nestled between his ears—stood in the middle of the arena. He was flanked by General Robert E. Lee, who was in full Confederate regalia, down to his Smith & Wesson. There were five soldiers behind him, and they were in deep conversation with General Grant.

Pastor Robinson joined them with a smile. It melted like Frosty in the hothouse.

"Uh-oh," I said.

"Uh-oh, what?" Gracie peeked around me, putting her hand on the small of my back. I focused on standing up straight and wondered where putting my arm around her would fall on the awkward scale.

"Why are they here?" she asked.

"I don't know." I leaned forward, trying to catch the tone of their conversation.

After a brief and heated discussion—during which Gracie's delicate hand never left my back—her father climbed the stage steps. He was smiling, but it wasn't a real smile. I sensed panic.

"The Rebel Yell has a show tonight," he said.

Gracie handed me her pages and stepped into his line of vision. "*We* have a show tonight," she disagreed.

"Mr. Baron never removed tonight's Rebel Yell performance from the website, so people were still buying tickets online." Pastor Robinson gestured for us to follow him, and we made a beeline for the box office. After a brief discussion with the attendant, he turned around. "Not only are we double booked, but the Rebel Yell is sold out. And every single ticket for the nativity was distributed last Sunday. I . . . I don't know what to do. The show is supposed to start in *two hours*. What a catastrophe." Pastor Robinson ran his hand over his face. He looked so defeated and only twenty minutes ago, he'd been laughing.

Guilt swallowed me whole. But it was followed by a chaser of hope.

"Sir?" I stepped closer to him, clutching the playbook in both hands. My voice was the pitch of a tiny, wide-eyed Disney mammal. "I think I can help."

"Really?" he asked. "How?"

"Catastrophes are my specialty."

"I can't believe you did that." Gracie's awe could have powered me through a triathlon. "What now? You're just gonna throw stuff out there and hope something takes?"

"Pretty much. It's like that spaghetti thing—throwing it at the wall to see if it sticks."

"I wonder if that's real," she mused, tapping her finger against her chin. "Like, do you think the Olive Garden has a spaghetti wall? Do you think the wait staff has to draw straws to see who has to peel it off at the end of the night?"

I grinned. "Get to work."

Gracie made a list of the traditional media outlets, and I drafted an announcement for the social ones. "I'll call the radio stations first," she said. "HOTT FM is playing Christmas carols, so I'll start with them." She winked at me before she turned away.

They'd played *nothing but* Christmas carols since the day after Halloween, and I predicted most of the population had retreated to gangster rap to escape the merriment. But I didn't contradict her. She looked so hopeful.

A voice interrupted my thoughts. "We can manage the crowd, but the parking is another story."

Pastor Robinson was beside me, and I hadn't even noticed. I was thankful Gracie was still wearing the purple bathrobe, or he'd have caught me checking out her departure.

"We'll have to round up someone to direct traffic," he said. "Maybe there are some orange cones . . . we could make signs for entrance and exits . . ." He trailed off as his eyes scoured the junk backstage, seeking solutions.

"You work all the time, don't you, Pastor Robinson?" I asked.

"Dan. You can call me Dan," he said.

No, I couldn't.

Then he frowned. "I don't have office hours on Friday or Saturday."

"I mean . . . you're always on. Things don't filter through your brain by going in one ear and out the other. There's always something to process."

I could see him doing some processing right now. After a moment, he nodded thoughtfully. And then he gave me the kind of answer that adults usually avoid. An honest one. "I do quite a bit of reading, studying, counseling. Lots of speaking. I can put those things out of my mind, especially when it comes to Gracie. But you're right. There are always people who need caring for, and I can never turn that off."

I wanted to thank him for leaving it on for me, but I didn't know how. "Gracie said you believe in what you do."

"Yes, that's true."

"That's . . . cool." We looked at each other like we didn't know where to take the conversation next.

I had questions, but I couldn't drum up the nerve to ask them. Why had he chosen to be so kind to me after I'd screwed up his whole December? What made him arrange my second chance? Why did he have such an amazing daughter?

"Pastor Robinson!" The voice carried over the mayhem of the crowd. Rebel Yell versus Main Street Methodist. What were the odds? A woman holding three sets of angel wings and a fake golden brick waggled her foot in front of him to draw his attention. "We have a situation. It's bad news/bad news."

"Can we just pretend I know?" He rubbed his temples and closed his eyes. "Do you *have* to tell me?"

"Yep. Even though you can't do anything about it. This one will need to be handled divinely."

He opened his eyes. "Go ahead."

"It's snowing."

There was a flurry of activity by the stage door, and it opened wide. Our town looked like a snow globe being shaken by a toddler. The flakes whirled in circles and spirals, but they were making solid landings. A layer of sparkling, icy white covered everything, including the road, and it was growing deeper by the second.

Winter had come early this year, and it had been unseasonably cold, but no one in our town had expected snow. The only time anyone worried about that kind of weather was if they were traveling. If this kept up, no one would move for days.

There wasn't even time to hoard bread and milk. Or toilet paper.

"Hopefully . . . it will stop . . . soon," Pastor Robinson said. He looked like he might face-plant at any moment.

"I don't think so." Gracie entered, sans womb, with her bathrobe open over her street clothes. "One hundred percent chance. Some sort of vortex situation. The meteorologists are ecstatic—you know how they love weather drama—and the kids are all mad since they're already out of school."

I felt a little giddy myself. As rare as it was, snow definitely created drama.

Kids in our town spent their childhoods perpetually frustrated by the pink radar line on weather forecasts that never dipped far enough south to bring snow, yet always included us in tornado warnings. I wasn't far enough away from "kid" to subdue all my excitement, but I tried, thanks to the current situation.

"That's not all." Gracie approached her father and gently laid a hand on his arm. "The interstate north of us is already locked up, and the camels are stuck."

"The camels." His voice was dull, as if he'd just awoken from a nap. "Are stuck?"

"Yes, the camels," Gracie continued. "And the sheep."

"The . . . sheep?"

She broke the rest of the news quickly. "And the donkey and the ox. The traffic isn't moving and neither are they. PETA will jump our ass—our literal ass—if we push for transport in this kind of weather."

Everyone in Gracie's general vicinity dropped chin. I didn't know the church's stance on alcohol, but Pastor Robinson looked like he could use a margarita. He took a deep breath, the kind that every teenager recognizes and fears. "Grace Elizabeth Robinson. I know that was a play on words, and your attempt at levity is noted, as is the time and the place you chose to attempt it. Now you owe the swear jar a dollar."

Before she could reply, his phone rang. He answered, and the crowd around us broke up.

I stared at Gracie. "You just said *ass*."

She shrugged. A grin followed. "I can usually get away with that one, since it's in the Bible."

"*You* said ass."

"I'm aware of this."

"You guys have a *swear jar*."

She slid out her arms from the bathrobe, revealing a blue sweater that fit so well it deserved a vacation home in the Bahamas. "It's an old pickle jar we keep on our kitchen counter. My mom made it mandatory for my dad when he was in seminary, and he made it mandatory for me."

"Your father swears, too?"

"Not anymore. Last year, he emptied it to fund a trip to the Harry Potter theme park in Florida." Her grin went full blown. I wanted to kiss it right off her face.

"You wicked girl. You're not at all who I imagined you'd be."

"Ditto." She hung her robe on a wall hook. "How many days has it been since you pulled a prank? I had no idea you could behave for such an extended period of time."

"Maybe I'm trying to change. I've managed a streak of good behavoir before." I glanced at Pastor Robinson, who was pacing while he talked. "Remember the Good Citizenship Award in fourth grade? And how every single kid was supposed to get it?"

She nodded and leaned against the wall.

"I tried so hard. Everyone had been giving me crap, saying I'd never be good long enough to get it, but during the last month of school, I earned it. I proved that I could handle myself. And then Mr. Weekly passed me over at assembly. I *know* my name was on the list, but he said every name but mine. No one would believe me. That's when I realized everyone had already made up their minds about me. Why disappoint them?"

"Why not work harder?"

"I was nine," I said drily. "'Work harder' sounds like parental advice, and I didn't have the kind of guidance that you did."

"I'm of the opinion," she said, tucking her arm around mine, "that if you let a single life event define you, then all you need to change things—if you *want* them to change—is another."

I stared at her arm on mine. And then, when I looked up, she was staring at me.

A loud commotion erupted around Pastor Robinson.

Gracie turned her attention to him. "What now?"

Mrs. Armstrong had slipped on a set of icy stairs, and she was on her way to the hospital with a broken foot. The pageant had lost its director.

"How about that," Gracie murmured. "Double-booked venue, freak snowstorm, trapped animals. And now no director. Things are getting worse by the second." She clucked her tongue. "It would be easy to give up. No one would blame us. Or . . ."

"Or . . . ?"

She let go of my arm, practically bouncing. "You know how to make things go wrong. You excel at it." From anyone else, I'd have taken that personally. "Tell me you can't figure out how to make tonight happen."

"Are you trying to find a way to make your father accept me or something?" I didn't think so, but I had to ask. "Are you trying to fix me?"

"Why? Are you broken?"

Gracie tilted her head.

Parts of me were. I felt like Gracie could see every single torn-up edge. I shrugged.

"You said you were trying to change," she reminded me.

"I said *maybe*."

222 ★ MYRA McENTIRE

I was glad she wasn't holding my hand. My palms were a rain forest.

"You're so blinded by negative expectations that you can't see the truth. Pranks, jokes—they don't make you bad." She angled her body toward me. "They make you *you*. You have a lot to offer, Vaughn. And Christmas is about new beginnings."

"What about you, Gracie? Since I have so much to offer, would you be willing to start something with me? Or are you afraid I'll ruin your reputation?"

"What makes you think that I won't ruin yours?"

I choked on my own spit.

Gracie gestured toward the chaos onstage. "So?"

I counted the people backstage, the props. Thought about the possibilities "Let's make it happen."

"Hell, yeah!"

"Another dollar," Pastor Robinson hollered, before returning to his phone call.

I laughed. "Isn't that one in the Bible, too?"

"He's not been very forgiving lately," she said through her smile, as she gave her father the thumbs-up. "I think he's aiming for Hawaii next summer."

I had a flash of Gracie in a bikini, followed by one of Pastor Robinson in Speedos. I shook my head in a reflex action to push both pictures out of my brain. "You should get into costume. Where's your foam child?"

"One of the baby angels is using it for a pillow." She grabbed my hand and pulled me toward her father. "Hey, Dad! Vaughn has an idea."

Pastor Robinson agreed to go forward.

The traffic reports from the north of town were growing worse by the second. Things to the south weren't much better, but the traffic was moving. Pastor Robinson's phone lit up with calls from stranded cast members. Gracie and her dad were trying to figure out exactly which cast members were missing.

I was listening, but I was also thinking. Crazy-Sherlock thinking. Looking from the Civil War soldiers to the nativity costumes, from the arena to the stage.

Gracie watched me. "You're doing it again, aren't you? You're doing your brain thing. Right now."

I ignored her. "If the pageant is going to be short of players, and the Rebel Yell is, too, we could make a hybrid."

Pastor Robinson frowned. "You mean like General Grant and General Lee and Santa should give the presents to the Christ child?"

I hadn't meant that at all, but I stopped for a moment to picture it.

"No, Dad, the Wise Men costumes are here," Gracie explained. "We could just get someone from the Rebel Yell to put them on."

"That could work," he said.

"And," I was rolling now, "if both casts are down by half, maybe the audiences will be, too. We could combine the shows. And since your congregation can't barrel race"—I looked to him for confirmation, and he shook his head—"then maybe we can get the Rebel Yell employees to volunteer for us."

"I like that idea. I like it a lot. Let me feel them out."

I didn't mention that I was pretty sure I'd have to recruit waitresses to fill in for the missing angels. The *baby* angels. The waitresses would look more like prostitutes in their costumes.

At least we had shepherd's hooks. If things got too scandalous, we could always pull them off the stage.

Gracie didn't say I had to make a classy pageant happen. Just a pageant.

"Okay, what else?" She had a clipboard and a pencil. It was nice to see her taking my success so seriously, but the clipboard reminded me of a bigger problem.

"The playbook." It still sat on the director's stool, in complete disarray, pages sticking out everywhere. "We don't know what order to put things in. The Rebel Yell people will need markers to know where to go."

"I can help with that."

The voice was deep, and it could only come from one person.

Shelby's blond hair had grown out since his football season buzz cut, and it was sticking up everywhere. His face was unshaven, he had dark circles under his eyes, and his shirt wasn't buttoned right. I'd never seen him look unkempt before.

"I'm sorry," I said. In truth, I blurted it. I felt a little more kindly toward Shelby than usual.

"Excuse me?"

"I'm sorry I made those birds crap on your car." I'd never apologized, and it felt right to do it now. "It wasn't cool, and I didn't have a reason. Not a valid one anyway."

Gracie dropped the clipboard and stepped in front of me. "I told him about your girlfriend."

"Did you tell him about the Mini Cooper?" Shelby asked, urgently.

Gracie shook her head. "That's your issue."

"Dude." Shelby stepped around her and grabbed me, looking intently into my eyes. "I only drive the Mini Cooper because I have to. My dad gets weird ideas about things"—he jerked his head toward the lassos and clown wigs that were hanging on a nearby Peg-Board— "and that car is one of them. He surprised me with it, and he was so happy . . . I just wish you'd set *it* on fire instead of the church."

"Relax, big boy. I didn't mean to set anything on fire."

Gracie stepped in front of me again and knocked off Shelby's giant, sweaty hands from my shoulders. "But you forgive him, right?"

Shelby's body was large, but his brain was quick. He looked from me to Gracie. "Seriously? You two?"

"Can you help with the book or not?" Her hands were on her hips. "Because I'm not having this conversation right now, but I will remind you that you *owe* me."

"Very true." Shelby dropped his head. "Fine, hand it over. I know I can put those stage markings in the right place. They've always looked like football plays to me."

Gracie gave it to him, and he sat on the stool, heavily, as if he were exhausted. It creaked under his weight. "I'll let you know when I'm done," he called out. "And Gracie? We'll be having a talk later."

She waved him off and pulled me to the side of the stage. "That was an impressive apology from you. Unexpected."

We were right beside a corner. A small, dark corner. A corner that wasn't in her father's line of vision. And she was impressed with me.

"Was it reward worthy?" I asked, looking from her to the corner and back again.

"You *are* cheeky."

"I acknowledge advantageous situations."

"Cheeky. And smart, too." She grabbed the front of my shirt and pulled me into the darkness.

I was glad she hadn't put her costume back on. It's not like I had her pressed up against the wall or anything, but I was closer to her than I'd ever been. It exceeded expectations. Her hair smelled girly, like spring.

She still had my shirt wrapped around her fist.

"I know I'm trying to make better life choices," I said, "but I'd commit a crime every day if it meant I got to do this."

"That's not logical." She let go of my shirt. "If you committed daily crimes, the only time we'd have together would be an hour on Sundays."

I wanted to make a conjugal visit joke, but I didn't think we were there yet. "So you're saying you want to spend time with me?"

She answered with a giggle. Gracie wasn't a giggler.

"You're nervous."

"I'm . . . I've never . . . the only kiss I've ever had was with Milo Crutcher in sixth grade, and he stuck his whole tongue in my mouth. I understand his intentions *now,* but I didn't then. So, I've just . . . sort of . . . ." She gestured awkwardly with her hands. It was adorable. "I've avoided trying it again."

She thought I was going to kiss her, and she wasn't running away.

"That's a shame." I touched her face, ran my thumb along her cheekbone. "Although I'm glad he ruined it for you. I'll be happy to be the one to set things right."

"I b-bet you would."

I removed my hand from her cheek. "Your teeth are chattering. I'm sorry—"

"Hey." She grabbed my wrist. "I'm the one who made the move."

"And I appreciate it." I tipped up her chin with one finger. "But this probably isn't the time or place for this, and maybe I want to buy you a steak first."

"I'm a vegetarian," she said, but she'd stopped shaking.

I smiled. "I'll buy you a salad."

Then I gave her a peck on the forehead and stepped into the light.

I'd behaved for thirty-one hours, shown restraint with Gracie, and had an intelligent conversation with her father. I'd found tablecloths to cover the legs of the waitresses-now-angels, persuaded Lee and Grant to put on wigs and robes (two of the Wise Men were stuck in traffic), and attached cotton balls to sawhorses to create sheep.

I'd wielded a glue gun to finish hemming Gracie's costume—with no hit to my masculinity at all—and borrowed an eighth-grade gamer from the middle school choir to run lights. I'd untucked the robe from the back of an unaware shepherd's pants, removed the Confederate caps from the horses-now-donkeys, and located Benadryl for a nervous stage mother.

Talk about your Christmas miracles. There was only one problem.

No Joseph.

"Did we make him mad?" I asked Gracie. We'd found the playbook, perfectly organized, but Shelby had disappeared. "Is this my fault, too?"

"No, he's not that kind of guy." She threw her hands up into the air. "We never dated, not even once. Something's wrong."

We didn't have any extra bodies to stand in as Joseph. Gracie's father was outside handling the tickets and the traffic, and . . . that would be gross, anyway. I couldn't even pull an overgrown middle-schooler from the choir, because he was their only tenor.

I was at the end of my alternatives when Pastor Robinson reappeared. "We found Shelby," he said. "Passed out under a pile of burlap. He's running a high fever, and he's delirious. Keeps talking about Democrats and New Jersey and kissing."

"So we don't have a Joseph." Gracie kept her eyes on her father, but her hand moved to mine.

"No, we don't." He was very obviously not looking at me, either.

Oh, no.

"Come on." I took a step back. "No way. No one in this town will buy me as Joseph. They'll boo at the nativity. You can't have people booing at the nativity. And I might be a troublemaker, but what I do is underhanded. Sneaky. I don't like people looking at me. And people would *have* to look at me." I was babbling, but the last thing I wanted to do was put on a robe and a fake beard and pretend to be the father of Jesus.

"It's okay, Vaughn. You don't have to do it." Gracie squeezed my hand. "We have time to figure something out."

"Ten minutes!" It was the eighth-grade gamer on the earpiece.

"We could use one of the Wise Men," Gracie suggested. "Pull some-one out of the crowd to take his place. All he has to do is stand there."

Pastor Robinson nodded. "That could work. We might have to open the curtain a few minutes late—"

"I'll do it." *Was that coming from me?* It was. "I'll be Joseph."

"Son, you don't have to. I promise," Pastor Robinson said. He meant it, and not because he'd be ashamed for me to take the role. I could tell that he was thinking about me, my feelings. And he'd called me *son*. "Performing wasn't a part of your deal."

I looked from Gracie to her father, and all I saw on their faces was concern. Not judgment, not disappointment, not expectation. Nothing.

Just love.

"Directing the pageant wasn't part of the deal, either," I said.

"This is different," Gracie said. "No one wants you to be uncom-fortable—"

"I want to." I held up my hand when Gracie started to argue. "No. I really want to." I turned to her father. "The least I can do is put on a fake beard and stand up for what you believe in."

Gracie was biting her lip. I might have seen tears in her eyes.

"Thank you," Pastor Robinson said. And then he hugged me.

"Right." I swallowed the lump in my throat. "So where's the beard?"

Gracie and I were alone on the stage, waiting for the curtain to rise, just a young couple from Nazareth on our way to Bethlehem to be counted in the census. Minus a donkey, but some things couldn't be helped. Gracie told me the donkey thing wasn't in the Bible anyway.

I was sweaty and nervous, but Gracie was smiling from ear to ear. It made the whole thing worth it.

"I'd say good luck." I fiddled with a glue strip and slapped on the mustache. "But it's 'break a leg,' right?" My beard flipped over. "Crap."

Gracie laughed and reached out to fix it. Or so I thought.

"There are other things you can do for luck." She stood on her tiptoes, lifted her chin, and placed a kiss on my lips. It was soft and sweet.

My knees went weak. Like, so weak I had to lean on her. "That was a surprise. Don't get me wrong, a welcome surprise. But still."

"I'm sorry. Did I take it too far?" she asked softly.

"No," I said. The curtain began to rise. "You took it exactly far enough."

KIERSTEN
WHITE

Welcome to Christmas, CA

If you do a search for "US cities named Christmas" (which, get a life, weirdo), you'll get five main results. Arizona, Florida, Kentucky, Michigan, and Mississippi each had someone who decided, "Hey, let's name our city after Christmas, because then it'll be Christmas all year round!"

If you ever stumble across one of their graves, you are obligated to spit on it, because *honestly*.

However, on the I-15, between the glittering cityscape of Barstow and the stunning metropolis of Baker, there's a crumbling freeway exit that's so small and depressing, even Google doesn't know about it. And here, cradled in the bosom of the ugly brown desert, is my home: Christmas, California.

Technically, it's not a city. It's not even a town. It's a "census-designated place."

"Where are you from, Maria?" I'll be asked someday, and I'll be able to say with utter accuracy, "Just some place."

Christmas is slipping into a pit of obsolescence. That pit would be the local boron mine, where fifty workers literally squeeze their living from rocks. Someday the boron will run out, and our census-designated place will finally be allowed to die.

As I sit in the passenger side of my mom's boyfriend's eighteen-year-old Chevy Nova, the December sunshine coldly brilliant, I pray that day comes soon. It's a forty-five-minute drive from the nearest high school, which means I get an hour and a half of quality time with Rick every day.

Our script:

Maria enters the car. Rick removes a tape from the deck, then puts in one of two cassette tapes, Johnny Cash or Hank Williams.

"How was your day?" Rick asks.

"Fine," Maria answers.

"Homework?"

"Doing it now."

Repeat every day for the last three and a half years.

Today, as we pull off the highway and onto the bustling main strip (a car repair shop, a gas station, a series of slumping duplexes, and the Christmas Café), Rick breaks script.

"Paloma found a new cook."

I narrow my eyes suspiciously at the dull brick exterior of the Christmas Café, which isn't a café at all. It's a diner. But the *Christmas Diner* isn't alliterative, and saints forbid anything about the place not be ridiculous.

Ted, the last cook, died last week. He'd worked here since it was opened thirty years ago by Rick's mom. Dottie lives in a retirement home in Florida. Even though my mom has been with Rick for eight years, Dottie still refers to her as "that nice Mexican." That nice Mexican runs the diner—covers the ordering, keeps track of the accounting, forces her daughter to work for tips alone—basically does everything Dottie is too busy being retired to bother with. She also works full-time at the mine with Rick.

I keep trying to feel sad about Ted, but we barely knew each other, even after three years of working together. Still, it'll be strange not having him there. He was more of a fixture than a person. Like if I walked in and the freezer was just . . . gone. Another reason I need to get out of here, before I become stuck like Ted, stuck like Rick, stuck like my mom. Everyone here is miserable, and we're all just punching our time cards until we die.

Or, in my case, until May, when I graduate and leave Christmas forever.

Rick drops me off in front of the duplex, then heads straight for the late shift at the mine. They actually let me take the car when I turned sixteen, but I got in two accidents (both my fault), so it's still cheaper for Rick to drive me than for them to insure me. Cheaper trumps all.

I unlock the door and enter the dim, chilly stairwell. My mom doesn't believe in heating. It's a belief strongly supported by Rick. During the winter, it's colder inside than it is outside. I shrug into the jacket that I leave by the door, check the mail—always neatly divided into the Sanchez and the Miller piles—and climb upstairs to the kitchen. The fridge is plastered with so many years of my report cards, they've formed a sort of wallpaper. I push past the milk labeled "Rick," the yogurt labeled "Rick," the eggs labeled "Rick," and find a small container of unlabeled leftover turkey. It has the flavor and consistency of cardboard. I scoop it into the trash, still hungry.

Usually our fridge is packed with castoffs from the diner, but with it out of commission since Ted died, actual food has been scarce. My mom hasn't cooked a meal in years. Never thought I'd miss Ted "Moderately Edible" Dickson's culinary stylings.

My mom used to cook. Before Christmas, we hopped around. Sometimes living with relatives, sometimes on our own. No matter how small our kitchen, though, she made it work. She'd spend hours putting together tamales, dancing and spinning stories in musical Spanish. She's different in Spanish than she is in English. Warmer. Happier. Funnier. *Mine.*

English mom began when we came to Christmas. She got a job here as the site administrator—a fancy name for a secretary who has

232 ★ KIERSTEN WHITE

to do everything. We lived in a little trailer right at the mine site. Then she got a second job managing the diner, and she and Rick started dating. And it wasn't just the two of us anymore. One of these days, she'll show up with her own "Rick" label, right across her forehead.

Fridge possibilities exhausted, I head over to the diner to make sure our schedules haven't changed and to get something to eat. There's a dented minivan in the parking lot. Several car seats inside. Luggage strapped to the top. Bad news.

The door opens with a rusted jingle, and an animatronic Santa insults my moral virtue three times. Ho, ho, ho. A train track overhead circles the entire room, a dusty Polar Express forever stalled on the verge of reaching the North Pole. Every surface not reserved for eating is covered in holiday kitsch. Glittery Styrofoam snowflakes, empty boxes covered in sun-bleached wrapping, twinkle lights with one strand always blinking out of sync, stockings with hot-glue stains revealing where pom-poms used to be, and a stuffed deer head, red-bulb nose long dead and antlers strung with limp tinsel. As if that weren't freak show enough, from the ledge above the kitchen door, a sinister elf gazes malevolently down, its head cocked at a horror-movie angle.

A year ago, I stuck a tiny knife in its hand. No one has noticed.

I look for the other waitress, Candy—she covers mornings and early afternoon, while I do late afternoon and evening. But she's not here, and I was right about the minivan. The corner booth is a pending full-mop situation. A harried-looking woman wears a pair of sunglasses with only one lens. She's bouncing a screaming infant on her lap. A toddler climbs on top of the table in spite of the mother's cautions, while a middling-sized one whines and a bigger one pouts.

She sees me, a combination of hopelessness and annoyance warring on her tired face. "Good luck. We've been here five minutes with no sign of a waitress."

I freeze. If I back out now, I can leave. I'm not scheduled to work.

The bell at the window rings. Ted was short, like me, so he never used the order window. We always had to go into the kitchen to get it. "Order up!" a cheery tenor calls.

The woman sees my reaction and narrows her eyes.

"I—uh—I work here." *You* had *to admit it, didn't you, Maria.* "Be right back with some menus."

"Thanks." Her voice is tight.

I approach the window to find a miniature box of Cheerios, three kids' cups of chocolate milk, one large Coke, and a deep dish filled with—baked macaroni? I lean forward, breathing in, and . . . *wow*. I'm not huge on pasta, but this smells like comfort smothered in cheese. There's a bread-crumb layer on top that's baked a perfect golden brown. The whole thing is still steaming.

I get on my tiptoes, but my view into the kitchen is limited. "Hey? I work here? Who is this order for?"

"Table two," the voice calls. I look out to double check. There's no one else in the restaurant. Just the crazy family.

"She said no one has taken her order yet. Is Candy back there?"

"It's for table two."

Frowning, I walk the tray over. "Here's your food."

The woman huffs in exasperation, prying her hair out of the baby's fist. "No, we haven't even ordered. Can we—wait, what is that?"

I'm already swinging the tray away, but I pause mid-action. "I think it's baked macaroni. Do you at least want the drinks? No charge."

The woman pushes her glasses up on her head, finally noticing the missing lens. Her laugh surprises me. It rings through the room. "Well, that's embarrassing. And shows you what kind of birthday I'm having. You know, it's the oddest thing, but this macaroni looks and smells exactly like what my mom used to make us on our birthdays."

"Gramma?" the oldest child asks, perking up.

The mom's face softens. "Yeah." She touches the edge of the pale yellow dish. "This even looks like one of her baking dishes. That's so strange! You know what, we want this."

"Yeah?" I ask, confused.

"Yes. If we could get some plates?"

"Of course!" I rush behind the counter and grab four plates and silverware sets. The mom is in the middle of telling some story about a birthday treasure hunt. Everyone has calmed down—the older ones have stopped whining, the baby is eating the Cheerios, and the toddler is satisfied with his chocolate milk. The mom looks about ten years younger than she did when I walked in here.

"Can I get you anything else?"

She gives me a happy shake of her head. "This is perfect, thanks."

I retreat, relieved but puzzled. Why did the new cook make that? Maybe someone else was here? I push through the door to ask what's going on. And then I'm grateful my mouth is already open, otherwise I couldn't have covered my jaw-drop.

Because the new cook is not some paunched, sixty-something, chain-smoking deadbeat.

He's tall, a ridiculous chef's hat making him even taller. Lean, with shoulders slanting inward so he seems to take up less space than he really does. Thick, dark eyebrows. There's a single line between them that should make him look like a worrier, but there's something inherently *pleasant* about his face. Maybe it's the way his nose has the slightest off-center curve, like it was broken into a sideways smile.

Oh, and he's not old. Maybe twenty, tops.

Oh, and he's *not* unattractive.

"Hi!" He looks up from something boiling on the range. And there— when he smiles, his whole face lights up. It's like his other expressions are placeholders.

I realize I'm beaming back. I tame my own mouth so I don't look like a total idiot. "Hey. So. You're the new cook?" Oof, yes, ask the guy *cooking* if he's the new cook.

"Yeah! Isn't this place amazing?"

"There . . . was no sarcasm in that statement. I'm confused."

He laughs. "I couldn't believe my luck when they hired me."

Maybe I don't know him well enough to understand when he's joking. Surely he's not sincere. He removes the pot from the stove, wipes his hands dry, and then holds one out to me. "I'm Ben."

"Maria."

His hand is big, but not in a meaty sort of way. I let go before he does, self-conscious. I don't know what I look like right now. I didn't bother checking myself in a mirror before coming over, because again: this is *not* what I expected to find.

There must be something wrong with him. Like, seriously wrong. It's the only explanation for why he would consider himself lucky for getting this job.

The front door jingles as Santa insults another customer. Ben returns to whatever he's making—for no one, apparently—and I walk out and scan the restaurant. It's still empty except for the family, who seem to be having a great time. After checking to make sure their drinks are filled, I go back to Ben. I lean as casually as I can manage against the counter, but the kitchen is weird now. No comforting sameness. Ben has transformed it into an unknown quantity.

"So, who ordered the macaroni?" I ask.

"Table two needed it."

"Right. But she didn't order it."

He shrugs, as though he, too, is unaware of how this all worked out. But there's a sly pull at one corner of his lips. "They like it, though." It's not a question.

"They're thrilled. Have you looked at the menu? We don't offer baked macaroni. Probably because Dottie couldn't think of a way to make it Christmassy." Her signature dish is the Rudolph's Delight Salad—iceberg lettuce, ranch dressing, and one token cherry tomato.

He shrugs again, and this time both corners of his lips follow the upward movement. "First day. I'll figure things out."

"Maybe it's better if you don't. That looked way yummier than anything we make." Since it looks like Candy isn't here, I reluctantly grab my uniform from its peg. It's a red polyester dress that never sits right, with a red-and-white-striped apron. We also have to wear sequined reindeer-antler headbands.

Year. Round.

The door to the women's bathroom always sticks, so I shove it open with my shoulder. It nearly slams into Candy, who's leaning over the sink.

"Oh, sorry! I thought the bathroom was empty." I turn to go, when I realize her shoulders are shaking. "Candy? You okay?"

Her reflection is drained of color by the fluorescent lights. She has dark circles under her eyes, but that's nothing new. At least they aren't bruises this week. Two years ago, when she first moved in with her boyfriend, Jerry, she was bubbly and bright. We used to hang out sometimes after work, if Jerry was still on a shift at the mine. She wanted to be a hair stylist, someday open up her own salon. She even had plans to go to business school so she could run it. But little by little, she stopped talking about school. Jerry didn't like it. Then she stopped talking about doing hair. Then she pretty much stopped talking at all. I see her every single day, but I miss her.

She holds up a white stick, expression blank. "I'm pregnant."

I close the door behind me. "Congratulations?"

"I had to sneak out from my shift to buy the test. I'm sorry. I couldn't go any other time, because then he'd know."

Jerry always picks her up. I see him sometimes, on the front sidewalk, counting her tips. And on payday he holds out his hand for her check without even asking.

She leans over the sink. Her spine curves, her head droops. "How am I ever gonna get away now?"

I make Candy stay in the bathroom. It's not like it's busy. When the family leaves, I trudge toward their table, dreading the mess. Instead, I find everything neatly stacked, no spilled drinks, no overturned plates. And—gloriously, impossibly—a *twenty-dollar* tip.

I squeal so loudly that Ben sticks his head out of the window. "Everything okay?"

"Better than okay! Best tip I've ever gotten! Thank you, Benjamin!"

"You're welcome. But Ben isn't short for Benjamin."

The door jingles, announcing my mom . . . and *Rick*? Rick always says, "Why would I pay for someone else to make my food?" as he boils a scoop of rice or beans or whatever else he got in the bargain bin.

"What are you doing here?" I ask.

My mom glances around. She works in the back and rarely visits the actual dining area. She never can get over the diner's shock-and-awe decorating tactics. A penguin nativity, complete with little baby penguin Jesus, snags her attention. "Our shift was halted. Machine failure. We thought you'd be home. We wanted to make sure you were okay."

"Candy's . . . sick. So I'm covering."

Rick's hands are jammed in the pockets of his Wranglers. "Your homework done?"

"Yes." My voice is flat.

He nods. It's the same motion he makes every evening when he asks me the same question and gets the same answer. Usually it happens at home, though, when we all get in from our various shifts. Then I pass him the remote so he can watch old episodes of *Bonanza*. A few years ago, I went through a bout of insomnia, and without fail he'd be out on the couch. We'd sit there, silent hours passing, the boring black-and-white cowboy adventures filling in the space between us.

Okay, fine, there were a few good episodes. But still.

The order bell dings, and I frown. Ben has placed three to-go containers on the shelf. "No one ordered anything!" I shout. My mom looks disapproving, so I stomp over to the window. "Ben! No one is here. No one called in an order."

He leans his head over. "Oh, right! Well, it's embarrassing, but I messed up. Instead of throwing it out, I thought you could give it to your parents." He *says* it's embarrassing, but his expression is wrinkled with delight.

"Rick is not my dad."

"Cool. Well. Ask if they want it."

I glare. It's harder than it should be, like his sweet, smiley face is contagious. "Quit making food before people order anything."

"Right." He grins even bigger and then straightens so I can't see his face anymore.

I shove the containers at my mom and Rick. "I guess he messed up an order. Want some free food?"

Rick doesn't even ask what it is. Free is the only part that matters. He turns toward the door. "Are we going, Paloma?"

My mom frowns. "Tell Ben to note what he's using. We have an ordering system that doesn't allow for waste."

When they're gone, I check the women's bathroom and find Candy curled up asleep in the corner, an apron under her head. I hang an "Out of Order" sign and take the rest of her shift. As a small act of rebellion, I don't change into my uniform. It has nothing to do with Ben.

Well. Maybe a little.

It's busier than normal, a handful of locals sauntering in to check out the new chef. Ben doesn't talk much—he smiles and waves out the window, too busy to come out. I stick my head through to find him pulling cookies out of the oven. The telltale scent of gingerbread hangs in the air like the promise of holiday cheer. He even has flour on his crooked smile of a nose. It's adorable.

"You are a terrible cook," I say.

He looks up, gentle features set in alarm. "Have there been complaints?"

"You haven't followed any of the standard recipes. I've worked here long enough—I can tell." The mashed potatoes are creamier. The fries are crispier. And his rolls are golden, buttery-topped miracles instead of the straight-from-the-bag variety we normally serve.

For a moment, he looks distressed. And then the agitation melts away as his eyebrows lift, disappearing beneath his mop of brown hair. He is the definition of merry. "But has anyone *complained*?"

I blow my bangs away from my eyes. "No. They're just being nice because you're new."

That's not true. The regulars like their familiar terrible food, and if anything is ever different, I get yelled at. They're not nice.

Except . . . tonight, they are. Steve and Bernie, who always get a steak after their shifts and don't say a word to anyone, are laughing and swapping stories at the counter. Lorna, who after my entire life of never ever stealing anything still follows me suspiciously around her gas station, complimented me on her way out. And I swear, Angel, the mine's two-hundred-fifty-pound truck driver, he of the aura of constant menace, he of the incredibly inaccurate name—Angel actually smiled at me.

I think. It might have been indigestion.

But then he tipped me. Ten whole percent, which is a one hundred percent increase over his previous tips.

Ben hums as he dusts the cookies with powdered sugar. "I had to make them circles. What kind of Christmas-themed diner doesn't have cookie cutters?"

"The kind that doesn't offer gingerbread on the menu."

"Right, which, again: how does that make any sense?"

"None of this makes any—oh, no, what time is it?" I dart to the bathroom and shake Candy awake. "Ten minutes until your shift is over."

She sits with a start, the blood draining from her face.

"It's okay. You have time. Get cleaned up."

I clear the tables, and Candy emerges right as Jerry walks in. His eyes, gray and dull as sharkskin, take in the abnormally busy diner. I can see him calculating.

Candy lifts a trembling hand. "Hi, I—there's a reason—"

"You dropped your pad." I stand in front of her. "Here." I dig out my tips from my jeans and shove them into her apron pocket. She can't even look at me, but she squeezes my arm as she passes. And then I watch, Frank Sinatra crooning at me to have myself a merry little Christmas, as my tips go directly from her pocket into Jerry's hand.

Merry effing Christmas yourself, Frank.

I make it through the next hour until closing time. Everyone wants to linger, huddling around the old television playing a repeating loop of a log-burning fireplace. They're laughing, talking, acting like friends. Like people who are happy to be in Christmas.

"Feliz Navidad" stabs into my ears from the speakers, and I can't handle it anymore. I took a shift that wasn't mine, and I didn't even get my stupid tips. Ben emerges just as I'm about to scream for everyone to leave.

He's carrying a tray of gingerbread cookies. There's a near-visible trail of scent, which reaches out and tugs the customers after him. He holds the door open and gives each person a soft, warm cookie, and an even softer, warmer smile as they leave. And then they're gone. I flip the sign from "Merry and Bright" to "Closed for the Night" and deadbolt the door.

I turn, fists on hips, and direct my anger at the only person left.

"I'm not sharing my tips with you."

Ben holds out a cookie. "Okay."

"Usually we share tips with the cook. But I'm not sharing mine with you tonight."

"That's fine." He pushes the cookie at me, but I swat it away.

"That's all you're gonna say? That's fine?"

He looks down at the cookie like I've hurt its feelings. "Yeah, I mean, they're your tips. You can decide what to do with them."

"Of course I can. But we're supposed to cut you in."

"If you don't think that's fair, I understand."

I throw my hands in the air. "You're supposed to get mad at me. Then I can yell at you and feel better about everything."

He laughs. "How would that make you feel better?"

"Because I want to yell at someone!" I slump into a booth and pick at a chipped spot in the Formica table. Ben slides in across from me, setting the cookies between us. Whether as an offering or a barrier, I can't say.

"Who do you really want to yell at?"

"Ugh. I don't know. Candy, maybe. Her dumb, creepy boyfriend, definitely. My mom and Rick, sometimes. And I'd share my tips with you, but I don't have any, which means I worked all afternoon for nothing." I rest my head on the tabletop.

"No one tipped you?" He finally sounds outraged.

"*Everyone* tipped me. But I gave it all to Candy."

"Well, you earned a cookie."

"I don't like gingerbread."

"That's because you've never had *my* gingerbread."

I narrow my eyes. "Is that some sort of chef pickup line?"

He blushes. The way the red blooms in his cheeks as he struggles for an answer is almost too sweet to handle, so I grab a cookie to let him off the hook.

"*Díos mío.* What did you put in these? Are they laced with crack? Gingerbread cookies are supposed to be hard and crunchy. Not good. These aren't normal." They're soft, not quite cakelike, more like the consistency of a perfect sugar cookie. The spices zing my taste buds without overwhelming them—a dusting of powdered sugar counteracts the fresh ginger—and the whole thing is warm and wonderful and tastes like Christmas used to feel. How did he *do* that?

"See?" he says. "Not a pickup line."

"Good, because that would've been super lame." I take another cookie and lean back into the cushioned booth. Usually at the end of a shift I feel heavy, leaden, and ready for bed. But right now I feel light and soft. Like these cookies.

So I take a third. And, feeling generous, I decide to be nice to Ben. It's not a hard decision. He's kind, and even if he weren't the only guy around my age in Christmas, he'd still probably be the prettiest one. "Everyone loved your food."

His voice is shyly delighted. "I'm glad."

I'm glad, too. He'll make the time until I get out of here far more bearable. Maybe even exciting. "So, where'd you learn to cook?"

"Juvie."

I sit up. "Juvie? As in juvenile detention?"

His face loses none of its pleasant openness as he nods.

"When were you in juvie? What for? Did my mom hire you straight out of their kitchen or something? I *knew* there was a reason why you were willing to work here."

He laughs. "I've been out for six months. I applied for this job because I love Christmas, and it felt like . . . fate. Or serendipity. Or something. And I don't like thinking about the person I used to be, so if it's okay, I'd rather not talk about it except to say that I wasn't violent."

I wilt under the weight of my curiosity. "Fine. But it's gonna kill me."

"It's not, and neither am I, because again, not violent."

I flick some crumbs at him. "I gotta get cleaning." I stand, stretching, and remove my apron. Ben is staring at me. I raise my eyebrows. He looks away quickly, embarrassed, but I'm more than a little glad I'm not wearing my uniform tonight.

I survey the damage. Not too bad. Mostly it'll be dishes, but I'll mop up and wipe down the tables first.

I switch off the sound system in the middle of "Baby, It's Cold Outside."

"Thank you!" Ben shouts from the kitchen. "That song is the worst."

"I know, right?"

"Also terrible? 'Santa Claus Is Coming to Town.'"

"Santa as Big Brother. Just imagine his posters, staring at you from every wall. SANTA IS WATCHING."

"I love Christmas, but Santa is creepy."

"Thank you, yes! No one understands. If someone is watching me sleep, it had better be a hot vampire, otherwise I'm calling the cops."

Ben laughs and dishes start clanging. He must be prepping some food for tomorrow. I put in my earbuds and clean, dancing along to Daft Punk. Candy introduced me to them back when she still liked music. When I finally finish, I wheel the yellow mop cart to the kitchen, bone-tired and not looking forward to the dishes.

But the kitchen is pristine. All the dishes are done, the counters wiped. Even the handles to the massive freezer have been sanitized. A few trays of dough are out to rise overnight, but there's nothing left for me to do. A sticky note is stuck to the door, with a big, sloppy happy face drawn on it.

I clamp a hand over my smile, try to wipe it away. Because I don't like Christmas, so I can't like anyone here. Not even talented cooks with crooked noses.

Normally I drag out my after-school routine—locker, bathroom, library—as long as possible before shuffling to the car. But on Monday I practically sprint there.

You're excited about the tips, I remind myself. *Not the cook.*

Rick jumps in surprise as I throw open the passenger-side door. I buckle my seat belt as he fumbles to remove the tape that's already in the deck. *"Quieras bailar conmigo?"* a woman asks in a soothing, slow tone. There's a pause, and then Rick manages to get it ejected.

"What was that?" I ask, reaching for it. "Are you . . . learning Spanish?"

"Nothing. No." Rick tucks the tape into the pocket of his button-down shirt, clears his throat, and puts the car into drive. I watch him suspiciously but he doesn't even look at me. Spanish is *my* territory—

the thing my mom and I share that he doesn't. Even if she won't speak it with me anymore. I don't want him there.

As we get close to Christmas, I lean forward, bouncing. This time Rick eyes me with suspicion. Embarrassed, I pack up my bag. I've never been so relieved to be out of that car. It's a long enough drive when we're pretending not to notice each other. But when we're both being strange, well, it was interminable.

I take a shower, then mess around with my makeup. I skip to work ten minutes early, whistling cheerily.

For the tips.

"Ho ho ho yourself, you old sicko." I pat the animatronic Santa on the head. This place is hopping, not its usual dead zone. Candy's taking orders. She's stayed the last two nights to help with the extra crowds, even though she had to keep running to the bathroom to puke. She looks hollow today.

Angel is sitting at the counter. He grins. "*Hola,* Maria!" I've never seen his teeth before, much less his smile. I didn't realize his scowl lines weren't permanently fixed.

"Can I get you anything?" I hope I don't look as confused-slash-unnerved as I feel.

"Take your time, *chica,* you just got here."

"Right. Thanks." I barrel into the kitchen. "What did you do to Angel?"

Ben shrugs, clapping his hands together once in a satisfied sort of way. "He needed a good meal."

"Right. The man who has spent the last three years growling orders at me is now calling me *chica* and smiling."

"Yup."

"Okay, be serious. Are you a drug dealer? Is that why you were in juvie?"

He laughs, stirring something on the stove range. "No. Not drugs."

"I'm pretty sure you spice your cookies with something illegal."

"Cinnamon is not a controlled substance."

"That should be the title of your memoir." I reluctantly button my uniform over my tank top and leggings. Candy comes back as I'm clocking in.

"Hey!" Ben's eyes are bright and hopeful. "I made you something."

She puts a hand over her stomach. "No, thanks."

"I think it'll help." He holds the to-go container while she removes her apron and hangs up her uniform.

She takes the container. "Okay. See you tomorrow." She shuffles out.

Ben goes to the window, bouncing on the balls of his feet. Then his shoulders stoop, his whole body turning down in disappointment.

"She gave it to Jerry, didn't she?" I ask.

"It wasn't for him. It was for her." He frowns. "Tomorrow I'll make her something at the start of her shift, instead."

Animatronic Santa ho-ho-hos at a customer, and I'm swept up for the next few hours. Ben more or less cooks what people ask for, and no one complains. My feet are sore from how busy we are, but my tip-collecting pockets are happy.

Angel has moved to the corner booth, leaning over the back to chat animatedly with Lorna, the gas-station owner. He's drawing pictures on her napkin. I've never seen them so much as glance at each other before. But the way they're acting, you'd think they were best friends. They've been in here every day. A lot of the locals have been coming more frequently than new-cook curiosity can account for.

"Bennett," I say.

"Not short for Bennett," Ben answers.

"Do you have Angel's order?"

He puts up a tray, and I frown. "This is not his."

"It's for him."

"He ordered chicken-fried steak. He always orders chicken-fried steak. This is . . . what is this? Fruit salad? Have you *seen* Angel?" I gesture toward him: hulking, tattooed, shaved head with several prominent scars. "He's not the fruit-salad type."

"It's beets, carrots, jicama, and fruit with a citrus dressing. Ensalada Navidad! And here." He presents a second plate.

"Tamales." A sort of pain, like a sore muscle, pulses through my whole body. I'm filled with an inexplicable need to hug my mom. "We don't serve those here." The sudden ache inside my heart makes me sad. I scowl at Ben. "Make him the stupid steak."

"Maria. Trust me. Take it to him."

"No."

He sighs. "How about this: if he doesn't like it, you don't have to share your tips with me for the rest of the week."

"And you tell me how you learned to cook in juvie." His eyebrows come together so I raise my hand. "Not *why* you were in juvie. Only the cooking part."

"Deal."

I take the plate, surly but certain of victory. Angel has ordered the same meal for as long as I've worked here. When I set down the food, he looks shocked.

"I didn't order this," he growls.

"I'm sorry, it's the new cook, he—"

"Are those tamales?"

I still have my hand on the plate, ready to whisk it away. "Yes?"

He leans forward. His eyes wrinkle upward in a smile. I swear his skin creaks, having to force decades of grim frown lines in that direction. *"Y ensalada navidad! Mi madre siempre . . ."* His hard black eyes soften, looking far past this dinner.

"So . . . you want the food? Because I can take it back!"

"No!" He leans over it protectively. "I want it."

"Great. Let me know if you need anything else." I scowl at the kitchen window, where Ben is giving me his full-wattage smile. I give him the finger down low, where Angel can't see it.

"Maria!" my mom says, aghast.

I shove my hands into my apron like that will erase the offending digit. "What are you doing here?"

"Kitchen. Now."

I follow her back, dragging my feet. She pushes straight through the back door into the alley between the diner and the gas station.

"What was that?"

"Just . . . goofing off."

She throws her hands up in the air. "We can't afford to goof off!"

I fold my arms, take a step back from her. "I'm not getting paid. So goofing off is about all I *can* afford."

"Ay, Maria, we've talked about this. We're a family. Everything we earn goes into the same account, so—"

"We haven't talked about it! We never talk about anything. What do you need all my money for? So you can live in a crappy, nowhere town, in a crappy, freezing duplex, with your crappy, tightwad boy-friend. Yeah, Mama, I get it." I turn away from her, slam into the kitchen and past Ben, who is leaning over the stove so intently I'm positive he heard every word.

My mom stuck around for a while, talking to Ben about his weird food supplies requests. He convinced her to go along with it. I guess *he* can afford to goof off. Meanwhile, she ignored me until she left for the mine. When I finish closing, I'm going home, straight to my room, to recount the tips I've managed to save. Angel left me fifteen bucks to-night, which still blows my mind. That puts me at exactly $2,792. Three years of working every day, and that's all I have to show for it.

I turn around to find Ben, yellow bucket filled with hot, soapy wa-ter. He squeezes the excess out of the mop.

"That's not your job," I snap.

But he shrugs and gets started without a word. With his help, the restaurant is clean in record time. Ben and I shove the cleaning sup-plies back into the closet.

I hang up my uniform. "I'm still mad at you. I should have won that bet."

He pulls out a tray of cookies. "Eggnog-chocolate-chip peace offering?"

"Follow me." I take him out back, where a rusting ladder is bolted to the side of the building. We climb up to the diner's flat roof. I show Ben where to step to avoid tripping on the peeling tarpaper as we make our way toward the two lawn chairs that Candy and I hauled up years ago. She hasn't been here with me in ages.

The last time I climbed up was Christmas Eve. My mom and Rick took an extra night shift for overtime. We "celebrated" early, but sit-ting by myself in Rick's duplex was too depressing. So I came here, alone, and glared at the junky buildings around me, hating Christmas and Christmas.

The night is cold. Our breath fogs out in front of us. During the day it's warm enough, but at night the desert temperature drops. We sit, and Ben passes me a cookie. It's obscenely good. Warm, bright bursts of chocolate, with the creamy comfort of eggnog.

"Show-off." I elbow him in the ribs. I keep finding excuses to touch him.

I need to stop that.

I lean back, looking up at the sky. That's the one benefit to living in a census-designated place. The stars don't have any light to compete with.

"Everyone had to help at my juvie center," Ben says, without preamble. "Laundry, cleaning, kitchen duty. I'd never cooked anything before, but I had a knack for it, and, before long, they put me on permanent kitchen rotation. The staff was great—they *want* the kids to get better and have good lives—so they let me play around. I loved it. I've never felt anything so right as I did when I was making food for other people."

I shiver deeper into my jacket. "How do you guess what people want to eat?"

He looks at me sideways, eyes hooded. "What do you mean?"

"The woman with the macaroni that first day—no one even took her order. Don't think I forgot. Angel and the random Mexican food. And this weekend, that horrible green Jell-O with whipped cream, pineapple, and shredded carrots no one in their right mind would ever order, but that you made special for Lorna. She *cried*. You made Lorna cry with Jell-O. None of this is normal, Ben."

He shifts uncomfortably. "You'll think I'm crazy."

"You willingly moved to Christmas, California, to work in our dump of a diner. I already think you're crazy."

"Fair enough. I figured it out while I was in juvie. Kind of like . . . a sixth sense? For what would make someone happy to eat. I see someone and I just sort of *know*."

"So you're a food psychic."

He cringes, his friendly face shifting into something defensive, shielded. I don't like that look on him, so I hurry on. "My mom's aunt could tell every disease or health problem someone had by looking at their eyes. I kid you not. She had a perfect track record."

"Really?"

"We lived with her for a while in Los Angeles when I was little. People were constantly dropping by to have her diagnose them. So. Having a food sense seems way more pleasant than her eyeball trick."

He relaxes, more at ease now that I haven't dismissed him. "I think if you can find the right food to connect yourself to a happier time, or a happier version of yourself, it can help you remember. Help you get back to who you were when you were happy. It can change everything. For example, when did you start liking me?"

I stammer, grasping for some response other than *The moment I saw your face*. Is it that obvious?

Ben answers for me. "When I made you the gingerbread cookies. That's when you decided to be my friend."

"Right! Exactly. Yes, gingerbread."

He gives me a look that makes me think maybe he was saying more. Maybe he wants *me* to. But I don't know what to say, so he turns away again. "I like using something I'm good at to help other people. Even if it's something silly like cooking."

"That's not silly. You know what you love, and you're good at it. I wish I had something like that." The moment stretches between us, too honest, and that sore-muscle feeling wells up in my heart again. I clear my throat. "Besides, as long as you keep making cookies, I don't care if it's magic or not."

He balances a cookie on the tips of his long fingers. His ring finger is bent at an odd angle. Like his nose, it's a testament of broken bones in his past. "If you were a food, you'd be a gingerbread cookie. Spicy enough to keep life interesting, but with just enough sweetness to balance it out."

I laugh. "I'm not sweet."

"You gave your tips to Candy."

I dig my shoe under a strip of tarpaper. I don't want to talk about her, so I say, "What would you be if you were a food? No, better! What food would you use your sixth sense to feed yourself?"

He puts a hand on the edge of his chair, holding it palm up, almost as an offering. It would be so easy to slip mine into his. I nearly do, but . . . it'd be an anchor. I can't be anchored.

"I haven't found it yet." He flexes his long fingers, opening his hand even more. "I like it here. I'm renting a room for almost nothing, so I save what I earn. And small towns are cozy. Familiar. You can slip into other people's routines, become a part of them. I'm staying here until I have enough money saved for culinary school."

"I'm getting out of here as fast as I possibly can," I blurt.

His fingers curl up. "Why?"

"Why not? There's nothing for me."

"But . . . it's your home."

"I live in my mom's boyfriend's duplex. Nothing here is mine. I hate it here. The minute I graduate I'm leaving."

"Where?"

"Don't know. Don't care. I'm hopping on a bus and going until I can't go any farther. Until I find a place that feels like home."

He's quiet for a long time. "How will you know what home feels like?"

It hangs in the air between us, as frozen as our breaths. I don't have an answer.

Ben pokes his head out of the kitchen window. "How were the waffles?"

Candy barely glances at him. "Fine. Thanks."

He looks lost as he stares at her untouched plate. The waffles were crisp on the outside, fluffy on the inside, with a Nutella filling and sliced strawberries on top. Unlike Candy's, mine are gone.

"They were fantastic," I offer, but he disappears, muttering to himself.

It's three days until Christmas. The diner has never been busier. Locals come in whenever they can now. We're also getting a holiday bump in freeway travelers, lured by the seasonal coincidence of our exit's name. For once in my career, I don't pity their optimism. The Christmas Café is—dare I say it—worth stopping for.

Ben whips out holiday-themed plate after plate. Every shift, he makes something new for Candy. And when she inevitably throws it up or rejects it in her zombie-like demeanor, he looks even more discouraged.

I grab Candy's plate and turn toward the kitchen, looking up at my elf out of habit. Only he's not holding a knife anymore. He's holding a tiny glass vial with a skull-and-crossbones symbol on it.

I cackle so loudly that Candy jumps. She's actually trembling.

"Sorry!" I say. She flees, straight to the bathroom.

I find Ben leaning over the counter, furiously crossing off items on a list. "Benedict! Are you the one who messed with my elf?"

He looks up, distracted, and then shakes his head as though clearing it. A smile crinkles his eyes as he pushes his hair away from his forehead. His goofy chef's hat sits on the counter next to the paper and pen. "Not short for Benedict. But yes. I thought he ought to mix things up a bit."

I laugh again, delighted. "Nobody even notices him except me."

"I notice everything." His eyes linger on my face before he blushes. He clears his throat a few times, toying with the pen. "This Christmas menu isn't working. I don't know what to do."

I nudge him with my shoulder. "You always know what to do."

A deep line has formed between his eyebrows. "I thought so, but nothing's working."

"Everything's working! People have never been so happy to eat here. It's like they actually enjoy living in Christmas."

He looks back down at his paper. "Not you."

I hover, torn between leaning into him and backing away. I can't commit to this place or anyone in it. I have to be able to leave.

"And not Candy." He drops the pen. "I haven't made a single thing she's liked."

"Well, she's puking all the time. Kinda throws things off."

"I should be able to help. What would she like?"

"I don't know. She used to be my friend, but then she stopped. She stopped being anything." Just like my mom. They stopped being the people I needed them to be. "Don't worry about it. She won't let you do anything. No one can help her."

Ben's brown eyes are so soft, but somehow pierce right through me. "Someone needs to."

Santa ho-ho-hos the arrival of a customer. Scowling, I head for the door. Ben crumples up his list and throws it in the trash.

Later that night I storm into the house, pulling on my house jacket with an annoyed huff.

"Maria? That you?"

"Yeah," I shout, answering my mom.

"How was work, *mija*?"

The rest of my shift was terrible. Ben was being all, I don't know, *normal*—he made people exactly what they ordered. I tried to complain to him about Paul McCartney simply having a wonderful Christmastime, and he just shrugged. Two people stiffed me on tips. And, to top it all off, Candy's creepy boyfriend showed up early, while she was puking in the bathroom. She still hasn't told him the news, so I had to lie and say it was food poisoning. His stare was even colder than this wretched duplex.

My mom's standing over the stove, stirring a pot of macaroni. It gives me a pang of loneliness for Ben. Which makes me angrier, because why should I miss a person who I only left five minutes ago?

"Maria, we need to talk." She points at a stack of envelopes on the table.

"Were you in my room?" The envelopes are college applications, mailed to me or forced on me by my school counselor. I tried to throw them away—so many times—because they're pointless. But it felt too depressing to get rid of them, and too depressing to stare at what I can't have, so I shoved them under my bed. Right next to the duffel bag I keep my tips in. "Did you take my stuff?"

"I was vacuuming. Why aren't any of them opened? Where have you applied?"

"Did you take my money?"

"I would never take your money. I want to—"

"You take my money every day! I work my butt off at that stupid restaurant and you don't even let me get my own checks."

She sets her spoon down, looking worried. "I didn't take any money from your room. I want to know which colleges you've applied to."

I bark out a bitter laugh. "None. Why would I apply to college?"

Her eyes go wide. "None? You're going to start missing deadlines!" She grabs at the envelopes, frantically searching through them. "What about this one? It's in Barstow. It looks nice. Or Cal State San Bernardino. It's not too far away."

"I *want* to go far away! And since when am I going to college? We can't afford that."

She shoves the applications at me. "You can't afford not to. You don't want to be like me. We work so hard, and so long. We don't want that for you. You deserve more." Her eyes are intense, pleading. *"Por favor, mija, necesitas aplicar. Para tu futuro."*

It's the most Spanish she's spoken to me in years. She always said we shouldn't leave Rick out by using a language he doesn't know. But hearing it now makes me feel like a kid again. So, like an obedient little girl, I grab the first application and start filling it out while she watches, holding her breath.

"Can you help me with a project?" I ask Ben, two days before Christmas. He's slammed, doing as much prep work as he can, but he immediately stops.

"What do you need?"

"I want to make something. For my mom. Something special. But I don't know how."

"What were you thinking?"

"She used to tell me about rice pudding. Her grandma made it for them every Christmas. And she tried to make it a few years ago, but then she got sad and dumped it all down the sink, said it wasn't right. She's never tried again. She works really hard. She deserves some of your magic."

Ben's smile is the powdered sugar on top of a cookie. "I think we can do that."

We work all morning. He shows me how to get the milk simmering at just the right rate. I scorch the first batch, and we have to throw it out. But Ben insists it'll be more magical if I make it myself. So I try again. This time I keep the temperature steady. I skim the surface like he shows me, so that the milk doesn't get a skin. We add the rice,

WELCOME TO CHRISTMAS, CA ★ 253

and I tend to it with feverish intensity. He takes over the stirring while I mix together eggs, sugar, vanilla, more milk.

"It needs . . ." I tap my finger against the counter, glancing at him for clues. "Nutmeg?" He smiles wider. I sprinkle some in and pour the mixture into the rice on the stove. His body is next to mine, and we both lean in, breathing the sweet steam as it rises up. I turn my face and breathe him in, too. "Keep stirring?" I whisper.

He nods. And doesn't move. So we stand, occupying the same space, watching as ordinary ingredients combine into something I hope will be magic.

"Mama?" I push the door shut with my foot, carefully holding the still-hot dish. Normally rice pudding is served cold, but when I sprinkled the cinnamon on top, it felt . . . right. Perfect. "Are you home?"

"We're up here."

I hurry upstairs. They're just off a super-early morning shift. My mom wears her weariness beneath her eyes and in the slope of her shoulders, but she manages a smile for me. "Sit down," I command. I put the pot on the stove as I get out two dishes. I hear Rick pop a disc into his DVD player. The familiar sounds of *Bonanza*'s opening theme trigger memories of insomnia-plagued nights.

"Does he still stay up watching that show until four every morning?" I stir the rice pudding one last time.

"Hmm? Oh, no. Why would he?"

"I thought he liked doing that."

"You know he only did that for you, right?"

I stop stirring. "What?"

"I can't stay awake for the life of me. Never been able to. But he didn't want you to be alone, so he'd come out and watch television with you until you fell asleep."

"He—but—I thought he didn't need much sleep?"

"He was exhausted. But when he was growing up, he had a few years where he had insomnia, too. He said being awake when everyone else is sleeping was so lonely it made him feel crazy. He didn't want you to feel that way."

"That's weird." All those nights, all that sleep he gave up. It doesn't make sense.

"How is it weird?"

"Well, I mean, he doesn't really like me."

"What are you talking about?"

"He never talks to me. And when he does, he talks about when I leave. Like he's counting down the days."

"Sweetheart, Rick doesn't talk much, period. And he *is* excited for you to leave. Who do you think tapes your report cards up on the fridge?"

I'm shocked. Rick? Plastering my name all over something that belongs to him?

"It was his idea to drive you to and from school. He didn't want you wasting your time waiting for city buses. He worried your grades would suffer and you wouldn't get into college."

"I can't afford college! And besides. The food. All the labels. The penny-pinching, refusing to turn up the heat. I'm an intruder in his space. He puts up with me because of you."

Tears fill my mom's eyes. "Oh, Maria. Why would you think that? You've felt like this all these years?"

My eyes are tearing up, too. I get out one more dish. One for Rick.

She takes my hand. "Do you remember your father at all?"

I shake my head.

"Good." Her voice is fierce. "It's one of the proudest points of my life that that man has no imprint on you. It wasn't easy leaving. I had to sneak and save money for years before I had enough to get somewhere far away and safe. I was terrified you'd remember what it used to be like."

"I don't. I remember moving around until we settled here."

She nods. "Rick can't show affection the way most people do, but he doesn't have a cruel bone in his body. And, after my life, he's exactly what I needed. What *we* needed. I know Rick is odd. He labels his food so he can make sure that he's not spending more on groceries than he needs to. We keep the heat off so that we can save more, the same reason we take overtime and holiday shifts. The same reason we put all your paychecks straight into savings. He's been putting away money since the day we moved in. He—oh, we were gonna surprise you, but—Rick? I think we need to give Maria her present now."

The television goes silent. Rick comes back in the kitchen, hands shoved deep into his Wranglers. "What about Christmas morning?"

My mom laughs, wiping away her tears. "It already smells like Christmas in here. Maria made rice pudding." She leans over her bowl, breathes in deeply. I cross my fingers, praying I got it right. "*Mí abuela* used to make this for us. Then we'd sing and later we'd get an orange. Rice pudding and oranges." She smiles, happy tears streaming down her face. "I'd actually forgotten what it was supposed to smell like. This is perfect."

She takes a bite, sighs happily, and leans her head on my shoulder. I don't know what it's supposed to taste like, but I like what I made. If asked to describe the flavor I could really only say this: It's warm. Perfectly warm. And with this in my mouth, I can understand a little of how my mom remembered Christmas feeling.

Rick has already eaten his whole bowl. He clears his throat, then says in an exaggeratedly careful accent, *"Muchas gracias. Esta comida es muy buena. Me gusta."*

My mom gasps. I gape. Rick looks terrified as he continues. *"Yo estoy aprendiendo español. Para hablar contigo. Por que . . . te amo."*

My mom fully bursts into tears, which makes poor Rick look even more horrified. "Did I do it wrong?" he asks.

"No!" I beam. Because now I understand he wasn't trying to take anything away from me. He was just trying to fit better into our lives.

"That was wonderful," my mom manages. *"Muy, muy bien."*

Rick sighs in relief. He's actually sweating. He must have been so nervous. It's adorable, which I honestly cannot believe I'm thinking about Rick.

I look at my mom, *really* look at her for the first time in years. She's beautiful. Sweet and soft and warm, too. I wonder how we went this long without talking about things that mattered. And why it took a pot of rice pudding for me to be able to see that—even though she's not aggressively affectionate—she's here. She's always been here for me. She's done the best she can.

"This is for you." Rick slides over a sheet of paper to me. My mom gets up and stands behind him, squeezing his shoulder. The paper is a list of numbers. No . . . it's a bank statement. For a savings account with forty thousand dollars in it.

Under my name.

"How—what—*where did this come from*?"

"I told you," my mom says. "Rick started saving the day we moved in. Every bonus, everything we didn't need to live on."

"But . . . I can't . . . what about you two? The mine won't last forever. You won't have any savings!" Here I was, hoarding every penny I made so that I could run away to my own empty future. And here they were, saving every penny they made so that my future was a better one than their families gave them.

I am the worst person in the world. I'm crying, both out of gratitude and guilt.

"We'll be fine," my mom says. "The mine has a few years left."

"We can find work anywhere." Rick's voice is soft and even. I always thought of it as monotonous, but it's more like the rice pudding. Gentle. "Wherever you end up, we can move and get jobs."

"But this is your home," I say.

Rick raises his eyebrows, surprised. "Wherever you two are is my home. *Tu . . . eres mi casa.* That probably wasn't right." He frowns.

I smash them both into a hug. Rick clears his throat, clearly uncomfortable, but I don't care.

I was wrong.

I've been wrong for years.

Being wrong feels amazing.

On Christmas Eve, I show up at work to find Ben drizzling white chocolate onto peppermint bark. He's muttering to himself again. It looks like he hasn't slept.

"You're incredible!" I throw my arms around him, hugging him from behind.

He startles. "What did I do?"

"The rice pudding! It was perfect!"

He puts his hands on top of mine, tentatively. "You did that, re-member?"

"Only because you let me borrow your magic." I've been hugging him for probably too long now. I don't want to let go, but I begrudgingly release him and point at the peppermint bark. "What's that for?"

"I thought maybe Candy might like it. I don't know. I can't—it's not working. Nothing's working with her." He hangs his head, and his laugh has a note of bitterness that stings my heart. "Maybe I was never magic to begin with. Maybe this whole thing is stupid."

"Ben, I need to tell you—"

The animatronic Santa announces an arrival. I go up on my tiptoes and see the top of Jerry's head. "Candy!" he shouts.

I push through the kitchen door with a scowl. "Are you here to apologize?"

Jerry looks at me. His gaze is even but his fists are clenched. "For what?"

"For your bratty girlfriend! If she was going to ditch her Christmas Eve shift and make me take it when I requested it off a *month* ago, the least she could have done is let me know. Ben had to call me in when she didn't show."

"She isn't here?"

I gesture at the empty diner. "If she were here, why would I be? Tell her if she's a no-show again, I'm calling Dottie."

He takes a step closer, looming over me. *Don't look scared, Maria. Look angry.*

"Any idea where she is?"

I roll my eyes. "She's not *my* girlfriend, dude."

His nostrils flare, and he leans even closer.

"Maria." Ben is leaning in the doorway, casually holding a thick rolling pin. "I need some help back here." He nods at Jerry. "Tell Candy to call the next time she's not coming in, okay?"

Jerry storms out. I collapse against the counter, my heart racing. "Thanks." I gesture at Ben's rolling pin.

"Where *is* Candy? What was that all about?"

"She's halfway to an Amtrak station, on her way to live with an old high school friend. Rick picked her up at four this morning, while

Jerry was still on the night shift." When I told my mom and Rick about my new tip-funded escape plan, this time featuring Candy, they didn't even hesitate. Thinking about it gives me a burst of affection for Rick—silent, strange, gentle Rick.

"She's leaving?"

"Not leaving. Already gone."

Ben follows me back into the kitchen. I dip my finger into the bowl of white chocolate and lick it. "You were wrong. You *are* magic. But people don't need to remember how it felt to be happy and safe in the past. They need to have hope that they can get there again in the future. And sometimes the only thing to make that happen is, say, enough money to get away."

His thick eyebrows lift. "You gave her your savings."

"Turns out I didn't need to leave so soon, after all."

His whole face—eyes, mouth, eyebrows, even his crooked nose—is one big smile as he says, "You're not leaving?"

"Not until this fall when I go to college. I guess I like Christmas, after all. Lately it's been feeling extra . . . magical."

He leans forward, and I tip my head up—waiting, waiting—when we're interrupted by Santa. Ho freaking ho.

I might be okay with Christmas, but Santa is still the worst.

The rest of the day flies by, with a bunch of road warriors and even more locals than normal. They all want to double check Ben's posted Christmas dinner menu, as though there's any doubt they'll be here. It used to be the most depressing day of the year to work, but tomorrow promises to be a party. My mom and Rick will be off in time to come to dinner. My mom is even making the tamales.

Ben and I don't have a chance to talk again. He's extra busy with today's orders, plus prep for tomorrow. But his eyes follow me everywhere, and we keep sharing smiles that feel like secrets. By the time the last customer leaves, we're both slaphappy and exhausted. "I have so much more work to do." He rubs his face, leaving a streak of flour on his cheek. I lean into him and wipe it away with my thumb.

He tips his head down, closer.

I put my fingers on his lips, squashing the moment. And his very soft lips. "I've got some work to do, too." I laugh as I dart away. I finish my cleaning in record time, and then sneak out the front door. The logistics of what I'm planning next will be tricky. The likelihood of second-degree burns is high.

Forty-five minutes later—and with only one minor scalding—I knock on the back door to the diner. Ben opens it, a rolling pin clutched over his head.

He lowers it sheepishly. "Thought maybe you were Candy's boy-friend."

"Ha! No. Follow me."

"Where are we—"

"Just follow me!" I climb up. When I'm safely on the roof, the ladder squeaks its metal protests against Ben's weight. Then his head—his adorable goofy smile of a face—pokes up over the edge. I hold out a hand and help him up.

I don't let go of it as we walk to the edge of the roof and stare down at Christmas. The beauty I always had to look up to the sky to see has transported itself down to this ramshackle town. As we watch, Angel and a few other guys from the mine finish setting up a huge Christmas tree in the middle of the gas-station parking lot. It gleams and twinkles in the night. Lorna comes out of the station and screams about trespassing—before breaking into peals of shockingly sweet laughter and handing out free beers. More people join them, and from up here, it doesn't look like a throwaway freeway exit. It looks like a warm, happy community. It looks like, well, Christmas.

I tug Ben away from the edge and over to a cardboard box that I've set up in front of the lawn chairs. The box is covered by a red-and-white-checkered tablecloth. On top of it are two mugs, two candy canes, a kettle, and a canister of whipped cream.

We sit. Still holding hands. "Christmas Eve is my favorite," I say. "I think the anticipation is more fun than anything else. I kind of lost that. The idea that something—food, traditions, an arbitrary date on the calendar—can be special because we decide it should be. Because we *make* it special. Not just for ourselves, but for others. I've had people around my whole life to make things special for me, even when I didn't notice it. And you've been working so hard to make life special for everyone who walks into this ridiculous diner. So . . . who is making it special for you?"

He looks down. The bashful sweep of his eyelashes against his cheek makes my heart burst with something that is probably not the Christmas spirit, but which feels every bit as Joy-to-the-World.

"What food would you make for yourself?" I nudge him with my elbow as an excuse to snuggle closer. All of those practice nudges are finally paying off.

"I don't know. I don't have a lot of happy memories to fall back on."

"Well. I'm *creating* a happy moment for you. Tonight. Right now. Keep in mind I'm not magic." I pour water into the mugs, already filled with hot cocoa mix.

He laughs as he unwraps his candy cane to stir with. I take the whipped cream and swirl it, towering, over the tops of both mugs.

"If I'm a gingerbread cookie, you're a mug of hot cocoa. Makes you glad for cold nights like tonight. We can call this drink a 'Hot Cocoa Benji.'"

"Not Benji."

"Tell me!"

He smiles, licking cream from the corner of his mouth. "It's a family name. There's this famous story? About someone who was mean in his past, but then woke up to the horrors he was creating for himself. And he vows to go forward, being kind and doing good, and keeping Christmas in his heart year round . . ."

"*Díos mío.* Ben is short for the *Grinch*?"

"No! It's Ebenezer. From the Dickens story? And . . . you knew what I was talking about all along, didn't you?"

I laugh, and he joins me. "Sometimes you're more spice than sugar," he says.

"You're a chef. You like spices. But I'll stick with calling you Ben, if that's okay. Otherwise you sound like an old man."

"By all means. Also, this cocoa is the best I've ever had."

"Liar."

"Are you sure you don't want to go to culinary school with me?"

I snort, raising my mug to toast him. "Totally sure. But maybe we can find a college and a culinary school close by each other." I smile into my mug and take a deep drink to quell my nerves. "Because, you know, once a girl has had your gingerbread, how can she ever accept anything else?"

"Is that some sort of waitress pickup line?"

"Yes. Absolutely."

And then, as Christmas Eve turns into Christmas, anticipation becomes reality. We share a cocoa-and-whipped-cream kiss. It's hopeful and happy and exciting. Exactly how kissing Ben should be, our mouths smiling together.

If you do a search for "US cities named Christmas" (which, fine, everyone needs hobbies), you won't find my home. It's not a city. It's barely a freeway exit.

You won't find Angel, grinning and bursting with pride, showing off his new paintings—the only non-Christmas-themed decorations hanging on the diner walls. You won't find Lorna, organizing the Christmas book club and asking Ben's opinion on what to serve for snacks. You won't find Rick and my mom and me, sitting on the couch, watching the *Bonanza* DVDs dubbed in Spanish we got him for his birthday.

You won't find Candy. Neither will Jerry, for that matter.

And you won't find Ben and me, sitting on the roof, talking and laughing and planning in our warm, friendly, hopeful census-designated place.

But it doesn't matter anymore if you can't find my home.

I found it for myself.

STAR OF BETHLEHEM

ALLY CARTER

As Christmas stories go, this one isn't as sad as it could be. I'm not Tiny Tim. There were no Ghosts of Christmas Past, Present, or Future. All told, it is a tale completely free of angels and elves, wise men and shepherds. Even Santa didn't make an appearance.

Nope. As it turns out, I was visited by Hulda.

"Yes. Yes." I heard her voice, high and clear, through the crowd of people who stood too close, wearing coats that were too heavy. Our collective breath clung to the windows, almost hiding the sight of the 747 that was waiting right outside. I shifted on my feet, wondering if there is any place on earth more chaotic than Chicago O'Hare Airport five days before Christmas.

Families ran for connections. Carols played over a scratchy PA system while people stood crowded together. Waiting. But for some reason I couldn't stop staring at the blond girl leaning against the counter at gate H18.

"New York," the girl said. "I will go there please. Now."

Her voice carried an accent that I couldn't quite place—the consonants too precise, like someone who is very worried she might not be understood.

She slid her ticket toward the gate agent then forced a smile, an afterthought. *"Please."*

The agent took one glance at the piece of paper and forced a smile of her own. "Oh, I'm sorry, but this isn't a ticket to New York."

The blond girl rolled her eyes. "Yes. That is why I stand in this line and talk to you. You can change it to New York, no? It is okay. I will wait."

The gate agent shook her head and punched a few keys on her computer. True to her word, the girl waited.

"No. I'm sorry," the agent said a moment later. "Your ticket is nonexchangeable and nonrefundable. Do you understand?"

"I am Icelandic. I am not moronic."

"Of course. Yes. It's just that . . ." The agent trailed off, looking for words. "I'm afraid that *this* ticket cannot be used on *this* flight. And even if it could, this flight is full."

"But I must go to New York! I thought I could fly to where this ticket takes me and then take a bus or a train to New York, but it is very far. In Iceland, the distances . . . they are not so far. And now I am going to a place I do not want to go, to see someone I do not wish to see, and—"

"I'm sorry." The gate agent shook her head. "You can purchase a ticket for New York. We have another flight leaving at six a.m. tomorrow. If you wish to go to New York you must buy a ticket for that flight."

"But I have a ticket!" the girl snapped and pushed her old ticket forward again.

Meanwhile, another gate agent was approaching the door, propping it open as she announced, "Hello, ladies and gentlemen, welcome to flight 479 with nonstop service to New York's LaGuardia Airport."

The lady behind the counter gave a desperate look to the even more desperate girl. "You will either need to buy a ticket for a later flight or go to your original destination."

"But my boyfriend is in New York! And if you would only change my ticket—"

"This flight is full."

"But I do not love him!"

The woman looked confused. "Your boyfriend in New York?"

"No." The girl shook her head and shrugged. "My other boy-friend."

"Oh," the woman said, her mouth forming a perfect circle. Then she leaned closer. A kindness filled her eyes. "Are your parents here?"

The girl shook her head. "I am alone."

And right then I totally knew the feeling.

I watched the girl push away from the desk and start through the crowd of people that swarmed, jockeying for position as the gate agent announced, "We would like to welcome our first-class passengers at this time."

En masse, the crowd took another step forward, jostling the girl, who dropped her bag and wiped her eyes. Her footsteps faltered.

And that was when I did it.

I don't know *why* I did it. It wasn't even a conscious thought, a decision. Instinct alone was driving me as I stepped forward and blurted, "You want to go to New York?"

The girl looked at me, confused, but before she could even answer, I thrust my own ticket toward her and said, "Here. Take it. You can have it if you give me yours."

"But that is your ticket."

"You can have it. We can trade. Here." I waved my ticket, but the girl glanced nervously at the gate agent standing by the door.

"It's okay. They don't check IDs during the boarding process," I told her. "If you want to go to New York, this is your chance. Just give me your ticket. Give me your ticket and go."

I could practically see what she was thinking. I was a teenage girl, too. We were about the same height, the same weight. To anyone in that heavily secured airport we might have even looked like sisters. It's not like I was a creepy dude asking her to get into my van, but the offer probably sounded too good to be true. Which meant it probably was.

She hesitated, then snatched the ticket from my hand, held hers out to me.

"Go ahead." I motioned toward the open door. "You're boarding."

She pointed to another open door a few gates away, another mass of crowding people. "So are you."

It really was that easy, believe it or not. I started toward the open doors. For the first time in my life I did not look back, not until I heard the girl call, "You don't even know where I was going."

I shrugged and shook my head and said the only thing that mattered: "If you just want to go *away* then any ticket will get you there."

"Miss?" the voice came through the blackness, and yet I did not move. "Miss!" The flight attendant seemed almost sorry. "It's time. We're here."

That's when I realized the plane was on the ground; all the other passengers were gone. The lights were down and the tarmac was dark. Wherever the girl was going, I was there.

Walking through the nearly deserted terminal, I made a list of what I had to do. I had enough cash for a hotel and a car, but they'd never rent one to a minor. Especially a minor traveling alone. I took the battery out of my phone, knowing I'd need to buy a burner. I would have to—

"Hulda!" someone yelled.

I looked at the crowd of people waiting just outside of security.

"Hulda!" the woman at the front of the crowd yelled again, a massive *Welcome (to your new) Home, Hulda!* banner unfurled in front of her. "We're so glad you're here!"

As she rushed forward, she must have crossed into a secure area because an alarm started sounding—both in my head and out of it.

This was dangerous.

This was wrong.

This woman was invading territory that was better left roped off.

Secured. Barricaded and impenetrable to intruders. But the breach had already happened, and I let myself give in to the hug.

It was, after all, a really nice hug.

"Well, look at you!" The woman held me at arm's length. "You changed your hair."

I thought back to the short blond locks on the girl in the airport. The girl with the accent. The girl from Iceland. The girl these people were evidently waiting for.

I felt myself starting to panic, needing to run . . .

"You look so different from your picture," the woman said, and I managed to breathe.

The girl these people had evidently only seen in pictures.

Maybe they wouldn't get suspicious, call security. The police. Maybe I could just bide my time and slip away quietly and . . .

"Well, what am I doing hogging all the hugging? Ethan!" the woman yelled. She looked around, and I followed her gaze to the boy who was walking around the corner.

He wore Wranglers and boots and a plaid shirt heavy with starch. Until then, I'd thought boys like him only existed on the covers of romance novels. He must have been shocked by the looks of me, too, because he stopped short, frozen in the process of sliding a phone back into his pocket. Hulda's words came back to me:

I don't love him.

My other boyfriend.

"Ethan!" the woman yelled. "She's here!"

I started to spin, but I was too late. He was already there. Looking at me. I could see the truth playing across his face, the realization that I was not an Icelandic girl name Hulda. I was not his girlfriend.

"It's . . ." The boy started, and, mentally, I filled in the blanks.

An imposter!

A liar!

A fraud.

He moved closer.

"So good to see you!" the boy said.

And then he kissed me.

So it turns out that if you swap tickets with a girl who doesn't want to go see her boyfriend, then there's a good chance said boyfriend will meet you at the airport.

Along with his entire family.

"This is Aunt Mary," the boy—Ethan—said, pointing to the woman with the really good hugs. "You'll be staying with her," he added before pointing to the others. "My mom, Susan. Dad, Clint."

Clint took my hand in his big, beefy, calloused one, but he gave me a warm smile.

"Welcome." His voice had a soft, southern twang. They all did.

"Oh, and that's Emily. She's my sister," Ethan said as Emily looked up at me with the biggest bluest eyes that I've ever seen. I'm pretty sure she could see right through me.

"I'm twelve," she said before I could ask. "I'm older than I look."

We were walking toward the baggage claim, past a nativity scene where all of the wise men were dressed like cowboys, when the boy's mom looked at me and asked, "So, is this your first trip to Oklahoma?"

Oklahoma.

Middle of the country. Middle of nowhere. Approximately a thousand miles from New York, another thousand from LA. It was . . . perfect.

"First time," I said.

There was a long pause while everyone waited for me to do something. I felt like an animal at the zoo, an exhibit called *Icelandic Girl in the Wild*. But I wasn't an Icelandic girl. And I couldn't let them know that.

"It's nice to meet you all," I tried.

"My goodness," Aunt Mary started, "Ethan said your English was good, but it's perfect. Just perfect."

"I watch a lot of American TV," I said, and they all nodded as if that made sense.

"Okay, let's get your bags." Clint clapped his hands together.

"Oh, I don't—" But before I could finish, a huge suitcase came around the conveyor belt, a giant sticker of the Icelandic flag plastered to the side. "I guess that's mine."

Clint went to grab the old-fashioned suitcase, lifting the giant thing as if it weighed nothing at all. I had to wonder how long Hulda was expected to stay.

But that didn't matter. I wasn't Hulda.

"So . . . Hulda?" Ethan asked, and it took an embarrassingly long time to realize he was talking to me.

"Yes, Evan?" I asked.

"Ethan," he whispered. "My name is *Ethan*. You might want to remember that since you just flew halfway around the world because you are so in love with me." I studied his profile in the dim light of the backseat of his parents' SUV as it pulled away from the airport. His jaw was strong, and he kept his gaze straight ahead, as if trying to stare down the horizon. "You're never going to get away with this, you know? Pretending to be Hulda."

"Hulda is fine," I told him. "I didn't gag her and shove her in a closet if that's what you're thinking."

"Oh, I know. She called to tell me that she didn't get on the plane. She asked me to look out for you, and that is the only reason I'm going along with this crazy stunt. Hulda is a good person. You did her a favor, so I'm doing you a favor because . . ." He trailed off, then looked at me anew. "Are you in some kind of trouble?"

"No."

"Because if you are . . . if there's something about you that brings trouble to my family—"

"I'm not in any trouble."

"Because girls always trade plane tickets with strangers in airports. They're always flying off to meet some stranger's boyfriend."

"That's funny. According to the people in this car, *you're* Hulda's boyfriend. But Hulda didn't think so."

"What's your point?"

"We all have secrets."

He turned and stared straight ahead again. "I went on a foreign-exchange trip to Iceland last summer."

"And . . ."

The corners of Ethan's mouth turned up in something not quite resembling a smile. "What happens in Iceland stays in Iceland."

"I'll keep that in mind."

He glanced back at me. "So, what's in it for you?"

"I didn't want to go to New York."

"What's in New York?"

Aunt Mary was leaning between the front seats, talking to Ethan's mother and father. Emily was wearing headphones—I could hear faint traces of music as she closed her eyes, fading in and out of sleep. Ethan and I were alone in the last row, but the SUV was too quiet. Someone might overhear. Get suspicious. Find out.

I swore right then that no one would ever find out.

"I needed to get away, okay? I saw my chance, and I took it. I'll be out of your hair, and you can start mending your broken heart or whatever just as soon as we stop. I will disappear, and you will never have to see me again."

I expected him to protest, to complain that I was putting him in an impossible position. I didn't expect him to actually say, "You can't just run away."

But I was not in the mood to hear what I couldn't do. The list had been too extensive for too long.

You can't eat that.

You can't go there.

You can't be this.

Ethan didn't know that I was in that SUV-bound-to-nowhere because I had solemnly sworn to never let anyone tell me what I could or could not do ever again, so I leaned closer. *"Watch me."*

But he only laughed. "No. You don't understand. I know my father, and there is no way this vehicle stops until we get home."

"So I'll split as soon as we get there."

But that must have been hilarious, because Ethan just laughed harder.

"What's so funny?" I asked, but he sank lower in his seat, closed his eyes and whispered, "You'll see, *Not Hulda*. You will soon see."

In case you were wondering, by "soon" Ethan meant four hours later.

That's how long I sat squeezed into the backseat, listening to Hulda's fake boyfriend snore. He kept his cap pulled low over his eyes, so I sat alone in the dark vehicle, staring out over the lights of the towns in the distance and the red glow of the taillights of the trucks that passed us by.

When Clint finally pulled off the interstate and onto a small highway I thought we must be almost there, but it was another hour before we turned onto a narrow gravel road that wound and curved through the darkness. The lights of the city were long gone. There were only stars. Millions of stars. Honestly, it was like we were the only people on earth when Clint stopped beside a small white house with a wraparound porch and said, "We're here."

"This is your house?" I asked Ethan as we crawled out of the backseat.

"No." Ethan yawned, and I realized it must be after midnight. "Aunt Mary lives here. We're next door."

I turned to look, but saw only dark hills beneath that blanket of stars—a moon so large that it felt like I could touch it.

"With next door being . . ."

"About a half mile on the other side of that ridge." Ethan pointed to the darkness.

A cold wind blew my hair into my face, jolting me awake. I watched as Clint carried Hulda's huge suitcase up the stairs and through a door that opened without a key. That's when I realized I was literally in a place where people didn't lock their doors at night and the distance to the nearest neighbor was measured in miles.

If all I wanted was to go away then I'd done it. But Aunt Mary was beaming at me. Ethan's parents were giving me hugs and wishing me good night. And Ethan kept looking at me as if he expected me to bolt off into the darkness at any moment.

I had to congratulate myself on finding the perfect place to hide.

It was a shame I couldn't stay.

"You got everything you need, sweetie?"

Aunt Mary knocked on the bedroom door and it swung open. If she thought it was weird that I was still sitting on the bed with my backpack on my lap, she didn't say so.

"Do you need some help unpacking?" She pointed to Hulda's huge suitcase, but I shook my head.

"No, thank you."

"That's okay." She crossed her arms and leaned against the doorframe. "You've got five months to settle in."

Five months. A whole semester. I tried to imagine living in a tiny white farmhouse in the middle of nowhere for almost half a year. I had one bar on my cell phone (I'd checked before removing the battery again), and there was no cable TV. Could a person even live like this? Then I thought about the unlocked door, the big Christmas tree, and the handmade stocking already hanging on the mantel, the name *Hulda* sewn on in green sequins. And I knew that, for some people, the answer was absolutely yes.

"Your house is nice," I told her.

"It's old. Like me." Aunt Mary laughed. "And it's empty now that my husband and little girl aren't here. But it's mine. I was born here, you know." She glanced at the old building as if expecting it to finish her story. "This was my room when I was your age. And then it was my daughter's room. And now it's yours." She gave me a wide smile. "We're glad you're here, Hulda."

"I'm very glad to be here," I said because it was the first lie that came to mind.

For a second, though, I thought it must not have been the right lie, because Aunt Mary looked as if she knew there was something wrong with Hulda. Wrong with me.

Then she shook her head. "I just can't get over how good your English is."

"Thank you," I said, and remembered what Ethan had told me on the drive. "Ethan helped me with it when he was in Iceland last summer."

"Of course. He's a good boy," Aunt Mary said, but then something in the woman's countenance grew serious. She studied me anew. "I would hate for him to get hurt."

I looked into her big brown eyes. "I would hate that, too."

And at that moment I meant it.

I swear, I really did.

"She's so quiet." I could make out the words, but I couldn't place the voice. Or the room. Or the house. Or the overwhelming stillness that seemed to permeate everything around me. There were no honking horns, no dinging elevators or room-service carts being pushed down anonymous, never-ending hallways. That was when I told myself that I was still sleeping, that it had to be a dream.

"It's a long flight. She must have been exhausted," someone else said, and I remembered: Aunt Mary. The little white farmhouse with the big Christmas tree.

Ethan. Iceland. Hulda.

I threw off the covers and bolted upright in bed. The sun was too bright, burning through the white lace curtains that covered the windows. It felt like a spotlight, and I knew I had to get away—to get out of there before someone looked too closely, asked too many questions. By now, it would be obvious that I hadn't shown up in New York, and people would be looking for me. If they found Hulda, they could find Ethan. And if they found Ethan, they'd find me.

"Hulda!" Aunt Mary called from the door. "Good. You're awake. Come on downstairs, hon. Everyone's waiting."

"Okay . . . I . . . Everyone?"

Turns out I just *thought* I'd met all of Ethan's family.

Clint and Mary had a younger sister who had a set of identical twin girls a year behind Emily in school. They stared at me in stereo. It felt like something from a horror movie as they tilted their heads in unison and asked, "Do we know you?"

"Nope. Sorry. One of those faces," I said, and moved on through the crowd.

Clint's older brother had three daughters, two of whom were already married, one of whom had a baby boy of her own. The names and faces all ran together. The kitchen was a blur of smiles and hugs and plates full of eggs and biscuits and gravy. So much gravy. I started to shake.

"Hulda, why don't you tell us about your family?"

I heard the question, but I didn't know who'd asked it.

"How was your flight, Hulda?" someone else asked.

"What do you like to do?"

"How do you like Oklahoma?"

"Have you ever been on a ranch?"

The questions swirled around me so fast that I was almost dizzy.

Aunt Mary's hand was on my arm. "Honey, have you called home? Does your momma know you made it?"

"My mom is . . ." I started but couldn't finish. "I . . . I need to go to the bathroom," I blurted and ran for the tiny room and locked the door.

There was a narrow window, and before I even had time to think, I pushed open the glass and threw a leg over the edge. I was halfway down when I heard a deep voice say, "Good morning."

The voice made me freeze. I dangled from the window. My feet didn't touch the ground, but I didn't have the upper body strength to pull myself back up again, so I just hung there, listening to Ethan laugh until I finally gave up and asked, "How far is it?"

Two hands gripped my waist.

"Drop," Ethan said, and I did.

"Well, thank you." I tried to sound as cool as possible as I pushed my hair out of my eyes. It had snowed overnight, and I shivered without a coat, but Ethan was in his boots and jeans, a heavy jacket, and very worn gloves.

He looked at me, eyes mocking. "Does your room not have a door? It wasn't nice of Aunt Mary to put you in a room without a door. . . ."

"I . . ."

"You thought you'd run away this morning," he said. "Better than running away last night at least, I'll give you that. But if I know Aunt Mary, there's gravy inside. A person should never run away from Aunt Mary's gravy."

I'm not allowed to eat gravy, I wanted to say, but instead I asked, "How far is it to the nearest town?"

"Define *town*?"

I glared at him. "I thought I was the one who was supposed to have English as a second language."

"Bethlehem is three miles that way." He pointed to the east.

"Bethlehem?" I practically rolled my eyes. "At Christmas. Perfect."

"It's not much of a town, though. Just a post office and a Baptist church. If you mean town with a grocery store and a school, you'll have to go forty miles that way." This time he pointed due north. "If you need a movie theater, Walmart, or hospital, well, then that is sixty miles that way." This time he pointed to the south. "And, as you saw last night, the nearest airport is in Oklahoma City, which is literally *hours* away, so tell me, *Not Hulda,* what kind of town exactly are you needing?"

I walked away from him, toward the fence. Sunlight bounced off the smooth white hills, and I squinted against the glare. I needed a cab. A hotel. A different life.

I would have given anything for a different life.

"Real Hulda texted me, by the way," Ethan yelled after me. "She made it to New York."

I spun on him. "Did she . . ." I trailed off as I realized I couldn't exactly ask *Did she see anyone waiting for me? Did they find her? Do they know where I am?* So I didn't say anything at all.

But something shifted in Ethan's eyes. Like the wind, he was growing colder. His heart was freezing over, and this wasn't the adventure it had been the night before. Now, in the light of morning, Ethan was worried, and I couldn't blame him.

"Who are you?" He covered the distance between us in three long strides. "What are you doing here? Who are you running from?"

"No one. Nothing." The cold metal of the fence pressed through my shirt as I stepped back.

"Then tell me why I shouldn't march in there right now and have my parents call the police or the FBI or whoever you're supposed to call when there's a stray teenage girl who needs to be taken back to her parents."

"Is that what you think?" I didn't mean to shout, but I couldn't help it. My nerves had been fraying for days. Weeks. Years. And right then

I felt them starting to snap. "Well, you're wrong, Mr. I've-Got-a-Whole-House-Full-of-People-Who-Love-Me. My parents are not looking for me. There is absolutely no one who loves me who is worried about me at this moment. On that you have my word."

"Okay." Ethan took off his hat and ran his hand through his wavy brown hair. "Tell me your name at least. Please. Just tell me your name."

Even that question wasn't as simple as it should be.

"Lydia," I said after a moment. "You can call me Lydia."

"Okay. Hi, Lydia."

"Hi." I smiled. "So what happens now?"

"Now I've got to go feed."

I looked back at the house full of strangers and questions and gravy. Then I looked at the wide-open sky and the really cute boy. "Want some company?"

The tires of the old, beat-up truck rattled in and out of the deep ruts in the ground. Ethan pushed the clutch and shifted gears, and I thought that it was maybe the single sexiest thing I'd ever seen. He was so confident, so at home and at ease. This was his domain, the cab of this old truck with its big bale of hay and long line of black, hairy cows trailing behind us. They would have followed him to the ends of the earth, I could tell.

But Ethan and I stayed quiet in the cab of the truck that, even with the heater blowing at full blast, was still cold. I could see my breath. I put my hands between my knees. Ethan pulled off his gloves and handed them to me.

Finally, the silence must have been too much because he flipped on the radio and, instantly, music filled the cab. It was supposed to be "O Holy Night" but there were too many backup singers and the tempo was too fast. It made me want to be sick.

"Sorry about the station," he said. "Emily or the twins must have been in here. They love that teenybopper stuff."

He turned off the radio and I pulled on his gloves. They were still warm inside. "That's okay."

"Do you like music?" he asked.

"I used to. When I was a kid."

"And now that you're so old you're over it?" he asked with a grin.

"Yeah," I said. "Something like that. How long have you lived here?" Suddenly, I was desperate to change the conversation.

"Well, I'm seventeen now, so . . . seventeen years."

"Has your family always lived here?"

"I'm generation number five," he said, but the words sounded strange—not like Ethan had roots tying him to that place. It was more like he had chains.

"It's nice that you have a big family. That you all get to live together and work together."

"Yeah. I guess."

"Why did you go to Iceland?"

I don't know where the question came from, but I could also tell that it was the right question—that somehow the answer mattered.

Ethan shifted gears again and started over a ridge. The ranch spread out before us, white and clean and stretching for miles. It was the kind of place most people only see in movies and out of airplane windows.

"I was born here. I'm going to live here and work here for the rest of my life. And, someday—if I'm lucky, a long, long time from now—I'm going to die here. And . . . well, I guess I just wanted one little part of my life to be *not here*. And Iceland seemed about as *not here* as a place could possibly be."

I looked around at the rolling hills, the distant dots of cattle. "Here doesn't seem that bad to me."

"Yeah." Ethan shifted gears again. He didn't face me. "What about you? Where is your home? Or is that secret, too?"

"No secret," I told him. "I don't have a home."

"Hey, honey," Aunt Mary said when I finally returned to the house. She was kneeling on the living room rug while Emily stood on an ottoman with her arms outstretched, dressed like an angel. "We missed you at breakfast."

"I'm sorry I left without telling you. I—"

"You had to choose between running off with a handsome cowboy you haven't seen in months or staying in a house full of rowdy strangers . . ."

"And gravy," I told her. "I also ran away from the gravy. Which might have been a mistake."

"Then tomorrow I'll teach you how to make it. Would you like that, Hulda?" She looked as if she expected me to protest. Or maybe confess. I was officially paranoid.

"I'd probably burn down your house."

"It takes a lot more than you to turn this place to ash."

"Aunt Mary, are you done yet?" Emily shifted from foot to foot.

"Stop fidgeting," Aunt Mary commanded, then pulled a straight pin from the puffy band on her wrist and studied Emily's too-long costume.

"I'm tired," Emily complained, but Aunt Mary just cut her eyes up at her.

"You're not being very angelic," Aunt Mary said. "So, Hulda, do you have everything you need?"

"Yes."

"And are you settling in okay?"

"I guess so."

"And you know you can come to me, right? If there's anything you want to talk about. Anything at all."

"Of course." I smiled. I lied.

If it's possible for real life to turn into a montage from a movie, that's what happened next.

Every morning Ethan knocked on Aunt Mary's door and I went to help him feed. (My job was opening the gates. According to Ethan, it was a *very important job*.)

Every afternoon I helped Aunt Mary cook and deliver food to the older people in the community who couldn't get out in the snow. "Here," she said the first day, handing me the keys. "I don't drive much anymore."

Emily and the twins tried to teach me how to two-step.

Clint grilled steaks and we had big, noisy dinners at Ethan's house with everybody taking turns holding Ethan's cousin's baby.

Aunt Mary put me in charge of wrapping presents and the twins let me hold a baby pig.

And through it all, Ethan was there, teaching me how to drive a stick shift in the chore truck, teasing me when my boots got so bogged down in mud that I actually stepped out of them and had to walk back to Aunt Mary's on bare feet.

He didn't talk about Hulda.

He didn't ask me where I was from or why I was running.

He didn't look at me like I was a liar or a fraud or a cheat.

And, for a few days there, I wasn't really Hulda and I wasn't really me. For a few days, I was just . . . happy.

Because, for a few days, I had a family.

"You've got to keep stirring," Aunt Mary told me. It was the day before Christmas Eve, and even though it was below freezing outside, Aunt Mary's kitchen was hot. Steam collected on the windows while the brown concoction on the stove boiled and popped like something in a witch's cauldron.

"Are you stirring?" Aunt Mary asked.

"Yes," I said.

She eyed the boiling caramel. "Stir harder."

When the caramel began to splatter, Aunt Mary said, "Oh, hon, you're gonna get that all over your pretty top. Go grab an apron."

There was a hook full of aprons in the laundry room and I grabbed one that was pink and covered with white flowers. But as soon as Aunt Mary saw me, something in her eyes made me stop.

"What?" I asked, then looked down and saw the name embroidered on the pocket. Daisy. "Oh, I'm sorry. Is this your daughter's?"

"Yes, it is. But . . . you wear it," Aunt Mary said. "She'd want you to wear it."

When I started pulling my hair up into a ponytail Aunt Mary asked, "Did anyone ever tell you your hair looks nice away from your face?"

I swallowed hard and nodded. "My mom.".

"Do you miss her, sweetie? We can call her, or—"

"No," I said too quickly. "I mean, that's okay. The time difference, you know. It can wait."

The back door slammed open as Emily yelled, "Aunt Mary!"

"Boots!" Aunt Mary said, but Emily was already pulling off her muddy boots and leaving them by the back door.

"Aunt Mary, do you have any potatoes?" she asked.

"Why?" Aunt Mary sounded skeptical, but Emily cut her eyes at me.

"You'll see."

"Surprise!" Emily and Susan yelled in unison when we arrived at Ethan's house that night.

There was another sign. This one hung in the dining room, announcing *Happy Þorláksmessa, Hulda!*

"What is all this?" I asked.

"Well, we know it must be hard for you to be away from your family at Christmas," Aunt Mary said. "The holidays are *always* hard without your family."

Maybe I was imagining things, but it felt like the room changed as she said it. For a second, no one could meet anyone else's gaze.

"So . . ." Mary went on, "we thought we'd bring a little of Iceland to you!"

"Oh. Yay!" I tried. Only then did I really look around the room.

There were shoes sitting in all the windows. Yes, *shoes*. Sinister looking Santas lined the center of the table, and a pile of potatoes was arranged on a serving tray like some kind of strangely festive centerpiece.

"Wow. Someone went to a lot of trouble."

"Well, of course we did, silly. It's Saint Thorlakur's Day!" Ethan's mom said. Then she grew serious. "Am I saying that correctly?"

"Yeah, Hulda," Ethan said. "*Is* she saying that correctly?"

"Yes. Very good," I told her, and Susan beamed. Ethan smiled like he was about to choke on the canary he'd just eaten.

"Sit, sit." Aunt Mary ushered us all into chairs. "Part of the fun of hosting an exchange student is learning about their home culture. So we thought we'd have you teach us all about Christmas in Iceland!"

"Hulda is an *expert* on Christmas in Iceland," Ethan said, moving away before I could kick him under the table.

"We did a little research online," Susan said. "But we still have so many questions."

"Yeah," Emily said. "Like what's the deal with all the shoes?"

"Yes, Hulda." Ethan leaned back in his chair. "*Tell us all about the shoes!*"

"Oh, well . . ." I started slowly. "The shoes are really fascinating."

I looked back to the windows, the shoes that sat on every ledge. "We put them in the windows, you see . . ."

"Oh, we do see." Ethan nodded. "But why, Hulda? Why are the shoes in the windows?"

"Um . . . well . . . that's because in olden times . . . people would forget their shoes and . . . people left extra shoes in windows and that way travelers could find shoes when they needed them. Because Iceland is a hard place to live without . . . you know . . . shoes. *Land of Ice,*" I added seriously.

"I thought Greenland was the one covered by ice," Clint said.

"That too," I said.

"Why does Santa look so scary?" One of the twins was eyeing the little red-clad man who sat right in front of her, staring at her like he might be an axe murderer.

"That's a great question," Ethan said. "Tell us, Hulda, *why does Santa look so scary?*"

"That's not Santa," Emily said. "He's one of the Yule Lads."

"Yule Lads!" I blurted, as if I'd come up with the answer all on my own. "That's who that is. I guess they're kind of like our Santa?"

"How many are there?" Clint asked.

"Nine," I said, but Emily was already crinkling her brow.

"I thought there were twelve?" she asked.

"Well, maybe it varies in different parts of the country," Ethan said. "Right, Hulda?"

"Right!" I agreed. "Some places there are twelve, but where I live there are nine because . . . the other three died because they forgot their shoes."

Everyone at the table nodded as if that made perfect sense.

"Isn't that exciting? We have our own traditions, you know," Aunt Mary said. "Nothing fancy, but you can't live in a community called Bethlehem and not have a few Christmas traditions." She laughed. "We all meet at the church on Christmas Eve. There's a live nativity."

"That means real goats, and lots of small children dressed like wise men," Ethan clarified as his aunt talked on.

"And we sing carols and read the Christmas story. And everyone gets a sack of candy."

"That sounds nice," I said. But something about it made me feel sick. Like I was going to contaminate them all with my presence. With my lies.

"I . . ." I pushed away from the table. I had to get out of there. I had to get away. "I have a headache. I'm so sorry. I just . . ."

"Ethan," Clint said, "take her home."

Outside, the cold air burned my lungs. The sky was so clear and bright—too bright for three hours after sundown. No matter how long I stayed there, I would never get used to seeing so many stars.

"You okay?" Ethan asked, but I couldn't breathe, much less speak.

"I've got to tell them," I finally choked out. "They're so nice. They're going to hate me. They're going to hate *you*! I have to tell them. Right now. Tonight. I'll—"

"No." Ethan shook his head, firm in his resolve. "Tell them now and you'll break Aunt Mary's heart right before Christmas."

"She won't care about that. Her husband and daughter will be home soon and—"

But the look in Ethan's eyes cut me off. It wasn't shock. It was absolute sorrow.

"Gosh, Lydia. I thought you knew."

"Knew what?"

"They died," he said. "About a year and a half ago. Car accident."

I heard Aunt Mary's words: *I don't drive much anymore.*

"This is only her second Christmas without them," Ethan finished, and I felt like someone hit me in the gut. I thought of Aunt Mary's hugs, her empty house. Of the tree and Hulda's handmade stocking.

"It was one of the reasons why I thought Hulda coming was such a good idea," Ethan told me. "Aunt Mary doesn't like to be alone, and the holidays are so hard. . . ."

"Yeah. Of course. I wish I'd realized. I would have—"

"No! Don't change anything, okay? She gets enough sympathy from everybody else. It's nice having someone who doesn't treat her like she's fragile. She hasn't been this happy since the accident. If you tell her now . . . it'll crush her."

"She's going to find out eventually, Ethan. It's not like I can stay here. Eventually, I'm gonna have to leave."

"We don't want you to leave, okay?" He ran his hand through his hair again. "*I* don't want you to leave."

I didn't realize how close we were standing or how warm his hands were on my arms. I didn't see the way our breath mingled in the cold air. I didn't realize I was falling until it was too late, probably because I never hit the ground. It was a fall of faith, of hope, of . . . if you want to be technical about it, love. Or something like it.

And then Ethan's lips were on mine and I pressed against the warmth of his strong chest, his arms around me, holding me tight. And I wasn't running away anymore. I was running *toward*. This moment. This place. This boy.

"Just wait until after Christmas, okay?" Ethan pulled away and stared into my eyes. "Everything will look different after Christmas."

And I nodded, perfectly content to go on living with the lie.

On Christmas Eve, Ethan picked me up to take me to the church that sat between a wheat field and a pasture. It was tiny and white with a steeple climbing up into the sky. By the time Ethan parked the truck, the church bells were already chiming.

"Come on." He took my hand. "We're late."

Together we ran laughing toward the doors, but as soon as we stepped inside I straightened and stopped. Ethan's hand was still in mine, though, as we stood at the back of the crowded room.

"Hulda! Ethan!" Ethan's mom whispered, motioning to where the family was saving us a pair of seats.

"Good evening, everyone!" I looked up and, for the first time, noticed Aunt Mary standing behind the pulpit, a hymnal in her hands. "Merry Christmas," she said.

The entire congregation echoed her. "Merry Christmas!"

The room was lit entirely by candles and the white twinkle lights of a half dozen Christmas trees. Mistletoe hung on the end of every one of the old-fashioned pews. It wasn't like walking into a church. It was like walking back in time. The people of Bethlehem had been celebrating Christmas Eve in that way for a hundred years. There was a comfort in knowing they would probably celebrate it that way for a hundred more.

"You okay?" Ethan whispered, and I nodded. At the front of the room, a pianist began to play.

"Let's begin with hymn number 101," Aunt Mary said as Ethan and I sat down on the end of his family's pew.

There was a fluttering of noise as people picked up songbooks and turned to the page, but I didn't need to see the music. I knew every word. Every note. And yet, when Aunt Mary sang "O Holy Night," there was no way I could join in.

"The stars are brightly shining . . ."

Suddenly, I wasn't in that little church in the middle of nowhere. I was in a hospital room singing for the small, frail woman on the bed. I was picking out the song on my keyboard. I was watching her eyes fill with tears as she asked me to sing it again.

"It is the night of the dear Savior's birth . . ."

I was glad for the dim lights and crowded room. No one was watching me. No one noticed how my eyes began to water and my hands began to shake. And, most of all, no one looked at me and expected me to dance or sing. No one in that room cared if I ever sang again.

"Long lay the world, in sin and—" Aunt Mary's voice cracked. The words faltered. She moved her lips, but no sound came out as her face turned white and she seemed lost, frozen.

"This was Daisy's favorite," she said after awhile, her voice so soft it was barely a whisper. It was like Aunt Mary was lost in a fog of memory and regret and the realization that she would never again share that hymn with her daughter. The pianist kept playing, but no one sang. No one moved.

Ethan's mother wiped her eyes, and I felt the overwhelming wave of emotion that was rushing through the room. It was about to overtake us. And when the pianist reached the chorus, I felt it overtake *me*.

It was like when I offered Hulda my ticket; I didn't make the decision to stand. I didn't will myself to sing. But before I knew it, I *was* standing, walking to the front of the room.

"Fall on your knees . . ." The words came pouring out of me, my voice filling the tiny church as I stared into Aunt Mary's eyes and realized she was no longer crying. She held out her hand, and I took it and sang louder.

"Oh hear the angel voices!" I sang like I hadn't sung in years.

And I kept singing. I sang just for the joy of it. For the moment and the music and for me. I sang for Aunt Mary and Daisy and for all the people who couldn't sing anymore. I sang because *not singing* would never bring them back but singing might make us all remember.

I sang because that is what I do when I am happy and when I'm sad. I sang because it is who I am when I am being the best possible version of me. I sang because I wasn't alone as I held Aunt Mary's hand.

I sang because it was Christmas.

When the song was over, I went back to sit by Ethan, who had his phone out. He was looking between it and me as if something didn't quite make sense.

"It's you!" One of the twins spun around and looked at me from the next pew, her voice was almost vibrating. "We knew it was you. We knew—"

"Hulda." Ethan's voice was cold, and I could tell he wasn't calling me by my fake name. He wasn't acting along. Instead, he held out his phone so I could read the message on the screen.

From: Hulda
Tell Liddy they're coming!

"What are you doing here?" the other twin asked. "How did you meet Ethan? Where—"

But I couldn't make out the words. The packed room was suddenly freezing. I swear I felt a chill. And when I looked up, I saw someone standing by the back door of the church. His hair had been blown askew by the strong wind. He wore a dark overcoat and a red scarf, Italian loafers that were perfectly polished. He didn't belong in that place. In that world. But I also knew that there was no way he was leaving.

"Who's Liddy?" Ethan's voice sounded a thousand miles away. "Look at me." He took my arm. "*Who is Liddy?*"

"I am," I had to admit.

"You said your name was Lydia."

"It is. I mean, it was. My mother called me Liddy." I met his gaze. "Ethan, I'm Liddy Chambers."

I waited for the words to sink in—for the name to mean something. But Ethan just asked, "Who?" and I could have kissed him. He didn't scream my name or roll his eyes. I was neither adored nor abhorred by that boy in that moment, and I think I might have loved him for it. Just a little.

"What does Hulda mean, *they're coming*?" he asked.

"She's wrong." I shook my head and looked at the man who stood by the doors, glaring at me. "They're here."

I wasn't looking as Emily walked down the center aisle, moving to the front of the church, but she sounded like an angel as she began to read the Christmas story from the Book of Mark. The lights dimmed even further. Little boys dressed like shepherds were carrying baby goats and taking their place at the front of the room, but it felt like I was in a trance as I eased away from Ethan and his family, clinging to the shadows before I slipped outside.

The man who followed didn't offer me a hug. He didn't ask if I was okay or tell me how worried he had been. No. The first words out of his mouth were, "Did you know you had a show tonight?"

"Didn't you see? I just did one," I shot back.

He grabbed my arm and pulled me toward the helicopter that was sitting in a nearby field, waiting for us.

"A helicopter, Derek?" I rolled my eyes. "Really? Subtle."

"Come on. We're leaving."

"No," I shouted. "I have to say good-bye. I have to—"

"Lydia!" Ethan's voice sliced through the clear night air. "Wait."

It was all I could do to pull away from Derek long enough to look back.

"Who are you?" Aunt Mary was half a step behind Ethan and closing the gap between us quickly. "Where are you taking her? That child is my responsibility!"

Aunt Mary looked and sounded like a force of nature, and Derek might have recoiled a little if there hadn't been so much riding on that moment. Riding on me.

He puffed out his chest and spat, "No. She's not. And she's leaving this place. Now."

"Hulda, what's going on here?" Clint had appeared at his sister's side. "Is this man bothering you?"

"Clint, he's trying to take her away," Aunt Mary explained.

"Are you her father?" Clint asked, and Derek laughed.

"I'm her legal guardian." Derek eyed Clint in his starched Wranglers and Carhartt coat. "And you, sir, are going to get out of our way before I have you arrested for kidnapping."

"Kidnapping!" Clint shouted.

"They didn't know!" I wedged myself in between Clint and Derek. "I ran away. I pretended to be an exchange student named Hulda. I lied, and they took me in."

The church was quickly emptying, and it seemed as if all of Bethlehem now gathered around us. I kept waiting for someone to make a

"What Child Is This?" joke, but no one said a thing. We had all said too much already.

"My name is Lydia," I told them. "Liddy. Liddy Chambers."

The night was clear and cold, and my breath fogged as I struggled to make sense of all that had happened.

And that was when I heard the singing.

It was my own voice, but not the song they play on the radio. It was the version of "O Holy Night" I'd recorded in Mom's hospital room three years before. It was the song that was played ten million times on YouTube. It was the reason Derek and the record company came calling.

And when Mom got really sick—when we could no longer ignore the fact that she wouldn't be around to raise me—that song was a big reason why she made Derek my guardian, why she thought she was giving me my dream.

"It's her!" One of the twins held up her phone, playing the video for everyone to see. "See. It's really her. It's Liddy Chambers!"

"No." Ethan shook his head. "It's Lydia."

Derek made a motion in the air and, in the pasture beside the church, the helicopter turned on its blades. Snow began to spin, filling the night sky with a swirling white. Derek started toward the chopper, but I was staring at Ethan and his family.

"Liddy!" Derek yelled. "Now!"

I took a few steps, then looked back. I was glad for the spinning snow and dark night. I didn't want them to see the tears that filled my eyes as I said, "I'm sorry. I'm so sorry I lied and—"

"Oh, honey," Aunt Mary said. "You think we didn't figure out that you weren't an Icelandic girl named Hulda? You think we weren't on to you ages ago?"

"You were?" I didn't know whether to feel hurt or relieved. "Why didn't you say anything? Why didn't you send me away?"

"Sweetheart, when you lose someone, you lose a little bit of yourself, too." I wasn't sure if Aunt Mary was talking about what happened to her or what happened to me, but it didn't matter. It was true in any case. "And that missing piece? Sometimes you have to lose the rest of yourself to find it. Besides"—she cut her eyes at Derek—"I'm pretty sure I would have run away, too."

Derek buttoned his coat and gathered his scarf as it blew wildly in the air. "I'm her guardian. And she's coming with me."

Derek reached for me again, but I jerked away.

"You're not my guardian—you're my *manager,*" I yelled, as if that could make any of them see the difference. "I'm an act to you. A property. I sing and I dance and . . . my mom was dying. She was sick and scared, and we were broke. That's why she granted you custody." Even though it hurt to admit it—not to the people of Bethlehem, but to myself—I had to say, "My mom didn't know what was best for me."

"Liddy, get in the chopper. Now! Before I call the authorities," Derek warned.

"You mean the sheriff?" Aunt Mary asked. Then she pointed to a man in the crowd. "That's him right there. Let's ask him. Hi, Ben."

"Hey, Mary. You need some help?" the sheriff asked.

"No, thanks. I've got this."

"That's corruption," Derek said.

"Yeah. Let's ask the county judge." Aunt Mary turned to the woman who had been playing the piano. "Your honor?"

The judge gathered her hands together and studied me. "I see no reason to remove this child from your care, Mary. I'm certainly not letting her leave with some man we don't know. And since the courts are adjourned for the holidays, I see no choice but to allow her to remain with you at least through Christmas."

"This is ridiculous," Derek scoffed. "She's Liddy Chambers and I'm her legal guardian! When the press hears about this—"

"When the press hears what, Derek?" I snapped. "That I ran away from you? That you had no idea where I was for almost a week and never notified the authorities? That my mother was under the influence of so many painkillers when she gave you custody that she couldn't even remember her own name? Huh? Tell me *exactly* what you're going to tell the press. Because there are a few things I'd like to tell them, too."

"Liddy." Derek lowered his voice, pleading. "Come with me. Come with me now and we'll forget this ever happened."

"Do you want to go with him?" Aunt Mary asked, but it was Ethan who found my gaze and kept it.

"Do you?" he asked, and I couldn't deny the truth, the reason why I never could stop running.

"If I don't go, he'll come back." I thought about what Ethan had asked me the night we met. "I'm worth a lot of money to them."

"Oh, honey," Aunt Mary said, "don't you know you're worth more than money to us?"

"You had your little break, Liddy. Now, stop kidding yourself. You want to be a star. You can't give that up," Derek said. It was almost like a dare.

"You're right. I used to love music. I used to love singing and playing and making people happy—that made *me* happy. But . . . but I didn't know what happy was then."

"And you do now?" Derek sounded like he would have laughed if he hadn't been so inconvenienced.

He didn't know what I know. About the way Aunt Mary's house smells when she cooks bacon, or how the cold wind feels on your face when you do chores at six in the morning, slapping you awake as if, until then, you had been sleepwalking your whole life. If he'd only looked up, he could have seen how big the sky really is and how easy it was to get lost there.

"Now I know what real stars look like," I told him. "I'm sick of the imitations."

I felt the townspeople gathering around me, but it wasn't an angry mob. It was a blanket, a shelter. And, slowly, Derek backed away.

"Enjoy your Christmas, Liddy. I'll be back," he called. "I'll be back to get you."

The helicopter rose and disappeared in the blackness as I stood, surrounded by the entire town of Bethlehem. The stars were so bright overhead that a part of me couldn't help but wonder if they'd led me there, guided me to that place and time.

"So, Liddy," Aunt Mary said, "I was thinking that—if you wanted—you could stay with me permanently. The judge thinks we can get your custody situation changed. If you want that. You don't have to decide right now, of course. It's just that—"

"Yes!" I felt tears sting my eyes again. This time for entirely different reasons. "Yes, please."

Aunt Mary pulled me into a tight hug, but I couldn't stop looking at the boy standing just over her shoulder.

When Aunt Mary released me, he said, "You're staying." It wasn't a question.

"I'm staying," I said.

"No more running." Ethan shook his head and stepped closer.

"No more running," I said, and then he kissed me. And then he held me close and I looked up at the stars over Bethlehem, knowing I'd come home.

The Girl Who Woke the Dreamer

Laini Taylor

I t is the custom on the Isle of Feathers for young men to leave small gifts for their sweethearts on each of the twenty-four days of Advent.

Having no sweetheart and desiring none, Neve Ellaquin woke on the first of December without expectations. Well, that's not strictly true. She expected rain, because rain was as sure a feature of a December day as hungry foxes. And she expected quiet, because that's what she'd had in abundance since the twins died together in late summer, leaving her alone in this benighted place. She expected, roundly, a heaping spoonful of the same dolorous drear that November had served up, only colder. That was the way of things as Neve knew them: there were no good surprises, only bad. In the evening, when she took her single, cherished book out of the chest to read by the fire, it would hold the same stories it always had, and so would her days, until they ended.

Her feet fell off the bed's edge like lead weights, and the morning's first sitting-up breath was a sigh.

"It's too early in the day for sighs," she said aloud. She talked to herself all the time now; she used her voice to slice the heavy air into strips so it wouldn't smother her. "If I spend all my disappointment before breakfast, what will I go on for the rest of the day?" And she smiled at herself for being such a sour thing. She thought of Dame Somnolence at the factory, whose advice to the girls was to "live bitter, so the crows will have no taste for you when you're dead."

"And why should I deprive them of nourishment?" Neve had countered, because before this summer she'd still had it in her to be saucy. "Don't they deserve a treat, too?"

"And you want to be that treat?"

"Why not?" Neve had asked. "What do I care for my carcass once I'm done with it?" And ever since, Dame Somnolence had called her Crow Food instead of her name. Never mind that it no longer suited her. Neve thought she had to be the bitterest snack of flesh on the island these days—especially now, with Christmas coming and the twins gone and gone.

The twins. Ivan and Jathry. With Neve, they'd been part of the batch of kids brought here twelve years back: plague orphans from the Failed Colony, bought cheap and worked hard, the boys in the field, the girls in the factory, their food thin and their beds thinner, out in the wind-taunted sheds behind Graveyard Farm. The light at the end of the tunnel for the lot of them: they were free once they reached Age. "Age," they all called it, that simple, like it was the only one that mattered. Age was eighteen, and as for "free," what does *free* mean to work orphans turned loose with their pockets full of air, on an island in the middle of the blasted great Gliding? Ship's passage cost more than their lives were worth, and some boys chose to pay that price, just to get away. Signing themselves over to a crew on a contract they'd be lucky to pay off before they saw fifty—and what sailor on the Gliding ever saw fifty?

So most of the boys stayed on the Isle of Feathers, and all the girls did, because though a ship would have been happy to take them, it was on a different kind of contract, and no girl—none—could ever hate the island enough to make that choice. So "freedom" for a girl meant one thing only: freedom to marry, and so that's what they did. The lucky ones caught the eye of a boy from a First Settlement family—or perhaps not a boy but a man (there being no shortage of widowers on the Isle of Feathers)—and the less lucky, one of the late-come tradesmen who'd hung up shingles in the harbor town. The least lucky of all? One of Neve's own caste, a "plague boy" with nothing to his name but a pair of work-rough hands.

The First Settlement families owned all the good land, so those girls got real houses whose walls didn't moan and sway, and gardens that grabbed the best sun, and maybe even a ribbon of clear water slipping across their plot, as aglint with green-gold fish as the mosaics of the church floor. And some of the tradesmen did well enough and some didn't, so those girls might end up in one of the skinny, gabled row houses on the pitched streets of the harbor town, or else in a flat above a shop, or the cellar beneath a pub, or some place like that. And the orphans' brides? Well, there were parcels of land to be had for free in Fog Cup—the valley in the middle of the isle so named because it was little more than a cup for fog—and no one would call it *good* land, but most years it was enough to make a life on. Most years. If you didn't have too many mouths to feed, and you didn't mind the damp.

I ask you, who doesn't mind the damp?

Still, that had been Neve's plan: Fog Cup, with the twins. They'd thought, once upon a time, that they'd be married all three together. Why not? Back then, to them, marriage just looked like grownups living in their own house and making up their own rules, and what else had they wanted since setting foot off the stinking ship that brought them here? Later on, though, Bill Childbreaker told them—in more detail than was necessary or decent—what went on betwixt husbands and wives, and they'd stared at each other, red-faced, their innocence dissolving like scoops of beached sea foam.

Not marriage, then.

If Ivan and Jathry had been one boy instead of two, then Neve

296 ★ LAINI TAYLOR

guessed she would have married him, but choosing between them was never an option. When they walked down a road, Neve walked in the middle. That's just how it was. And when they grew up enough that the carnal secrets of marriage no longer shocked them, well. If either Ivan or Jathry felt husbandly toward her, Neve never knew it, and she had no wifely stirrings herself. They were strong boys with good faces, and they'd been part of her heart since home—true home, long lost—but it wasn't like that between them. There were no glimmering moments where their looks hooked on to each other and grew hot, and no catching sight of one of the boys in a ray of sun and thinking, *I wonder what his skin tastes like.* There was never a hint of a blush, nary a tingle, never any of the things the other girls talked of at the factory, breathless and blushing and purring with longing.

Oh, and today would be rife with blushing and purring, Neve knew, and with crowing and gloating from girls who got the best gifts, and weeping and sulking from those who got none, or worse: a gift from the wrong fellow, some drunk or lecher, or maybe that shameless nose-picker "Three-Knuckle" Mickle-Jon Herring, perish the thought.

And then there was Reverend Spear, a category of threat all his own.

A cold weight settled in Neve at the thought of the island's tall, handsome preacher. He was fire and brimstone, a man possessed, and his sermons were like travelogues of Hell. This lake of fire, this pit of the damned, these gnawing serpents, and all the ingenious implements in the hands of demons who would spend an eternity peeling you like fruit and slowly devouring you, only then to begin afresh, and savor you for another thousand years. If children didn't wake screaming on Sabbath nights, he considered the sermon a failure and the next week's was worse. Once, when a farm boy was caught with a potato in his pocket, the reverend convinced Bill Childbreaker to lash him as an example, and when a clatch of girls were found swimming by moonlight at Song Beach—in their petticoats, not even their birthday suits!—he had them shut in their houses for the whole rest of the summer, with signs on all their doors that said INDECENCY IS AN AFFRONT TO GOD.

He'd lost his third wife this year—to the same fever that took Ivan and Jathry—and he made it no secret that he'd be choosing another for Advent. Why pay a charwoman for work a wife would do for free? And besides, wives were more than just unpaid charwomen, weren't they? Neve saw him looking the girls over in church like they were his own box of chocolates—*eeny meeny, who am I in the mood for next?*—and she'd felt his gimlet eye settle on herself a few too many times for comfort.

His pupils always looked tiny to her, like painted-on dots.

She told herself she didn't have to worry. Spear liked to claim that pretty girls made troublesome wives, he'd learned it from experience, and had even said once, for all to hear, "Beauty is free to the eye to enjoy, and the bedroom is dark, after all. But just try pretending your dinner unburned, or your house clean and your children tended."

In essence, wasn't their good man of God saying to close your eyes and picture some other man's wife while you grunt atop the poor homely slave who's your own?

Neve hated him, and she was honestly sorry for whoever got his gift this morning, but she didn't think it would be herself. She knew she was pretty, and if she'd never had cause to be grateful for it before, here was proof that there's a first time for everything. Maybe she'd be the one he pictured in the dark, and that was a notion vile enough to choke on, but she wouldn't be the one he courted.

She just wouldn't.

She dressed herself. The shed was frigid; dressing quick was an art learned early. Washing quick was harder; you had to really care to even bother. Neve cared, Lord knows why. At least her basin wasn't skimmed with ice yet. That would come by January and last through April. Still, this water was kissing cousins to ice, and she was shaking with chill when she yanked on her stockings and slip, her dress and kirtle, her many-pocketed apron, her old, dull boots. Even numb-fingered, it was the work of a minute to bind up her hair, honeysuckle bright, and cover it with a kerchief the color of mud.

And then what? She glanced at the door. On a normal morning, she'd tromp out to the henhouse first thing—not that her sad hen Potpie had been laying of late, but she still checked as a matter of course—but she found herself hesitating and knew well enough why. She was wondering at the state of her porch.

Was it as empty as she'd left it the night before?

"Please God," she whispered, and right away it struck her as the wrong plea. If there *was* a god, then Neve's whole life was a crime He had committed against her, and she dared attract no more of his attention.

She looked to the milking stool that served her for a bed stand and drew some strength from what lay upon it.

A dead flower.

How many girls on the Isle of Feathers had a dead flower ready this morning? And then, how many knew there was no courtship so bad that she could afford to reject it?

That was how it worked: You woke on the first of December to find—or not find—a token of affection on the porch. A paper cone of sweets or a whittled bird or a posey, maybe. To reject the suit, you left a dead flower in the spot for the fellow to find the next night. Acceptance was tacit. You did nothing, just rose each morning to see what your future husband had left for you, twenty-four days in a row until the Christmas Eve gather in Scarman's Hall. That's where the couples came together under a lacework of paper snowflakes and frosted lamps and sealed their fates with a dance. You set your hand in his and that was it: contract sealed with the clamminess of a girl's despairing sweat.

How romantic.

Neve had no expectations, but she had a dead flower ready, just in case. It was a thorn lily, left over from summer.

From before the fever.

She lifted it gently. It was crisp as paper, light as nothing. When this flower was alive, Ivan and Jathry were too. Neve had picked it on a Sunday when the three of them climbed up to Fog Cup to inspect the land the boys were going to take. They'd been closing in on Age, though Neve still had nine months to go; the three of them were the youngest and last of the plague orphans, she herself the very youngest, the very last. She'd always known she'd be alone here at the

Graveyard sheds for a time before they set her "free" too, but that would have been a different kind of alone: just waiting, just biding time before she could claim her own plot up by the boys'.

She was still going to take the plot, even if it didn't make sense anymore. The boys had been the farmers. What was she good for? Needlework. That was what they did at the factory. They embroidered lace tablecloths for ships to carry to rich folk on every shore of the Gliding, and Neve was better than passing fair; she was better than good. She was an artist. Even Dame Somnolence said so, calling her "Crow Food" with at least a hint of respect. But a great lot of good were needle and thread when it came to building a house in a drear damp valley and tilling stony soil without a mule, and all the other things she'd have to do to live.

If you could call it living.

Neve was scared clear down to a deep place inside where a part of herself was caged like a creature, mute and huddled and numb. She'd been numb since the heat of August mingled with the heat of fevers, but even so she knew that as long as she kept breathing, life would keep coming at her—like the swarms of beetles when you're harried enough to take the shortcut through Nasty Gully in springtime. They come flying in your face, loud and buzzing, and get tangled in your hair and in your skirts. They even push their way into your *mouth*.

Life would do the same. Neve couldn't pretend otherwise. In truth, she dreaded the lonely penury of Fog Cup almost as much as she dreaded the breathing weight of a man she couldn't love, and if there *was* a token on her porch, she knew in her secret heart she'd be a fool not to consider it. But she didn't *want* to consider it. She wanted to be free, and if she could never be free, at least she wanted to be brave— brave enough not to sell herself, no matter what the payment, or the cost of refusing.

Holding the dead flower, she squared her shoulders. *Brave,* she thought, and went to the door. *Brave,* she thought as she opened it.

But brave she was not when she saw what was sitting there, incongruously fine against the buckled boards of her rotting, charity-shed porch.

It was a Bible bound in red leather and stenciled all over in gold.

Only one man would leave such a gift. One man had done so, in fact, three times before—three times for three wives whose graves now stood in a row, and with plenty of space at the end for that row to grow and keep adding to its collection. *Who's next?* called the cemetery earth. *Why, the last of the orphans, the artist, the girl with the honeysuckle hair.*

Neve clutched her frail lily and stared at the Bible whose pages had been thumbed by dead women. So Spear wanted her after all. In that place inside where her fear was caged like a creature, something stirred and rose, and she spoke a new plea without pausing to think. Not to God, Spear's coconspirator. God was a newcomer here, carried over on the same stinking ships as the orphans and livestock.

There were older powers in the world than Him.

"Please, Wisha," whispered Neve, and she felt the forbidden word part the air like the wings of a bird and go forth from her. *Wisha. Dreamer,* it meant in the old tongue. It was an execration to speak it, but it didn't feel like one. It felt like power, like the birth of a small wind. Neve imagined it skirring its way into the world, new-alive and wild with her own desperate thrum, kicking up eddies of air that might grow, some day, into thunderheads and sink a fleet of ships half a world away. But what good was that to her? Much nearer and in that instant, at the threshold of her freezing shed while rain hissed at the roof and the heavy air pressed down, dense with its absence of voices, she saw something happen. The red leather cover of that unwanted Bible flapped open in a violent gust. Pages riffled and came loose, rising into the air like a flock of something freed. First the pages, then the rest.

All of it rising, swirling, gone.

"Please," Neve whispered in its wake. "I am alone." If her fear were a creature, this would be its bones. *Alone. Alone.* This was the fear that wore all other fears like skin. Her next words sounded like a bastard version of the catechisms she'd been forced to recite for twelve long years, but they felt truer. Cleaner. "To your protection I commend myself, soul of this land. Wisha."

And there came a change in the atmosphere, a . . . tautening, as though the land itself were baring its teeth. Neve felt it.

She welcomed it.

Wisha.

When the first ship made landfall here two hundred years ago, its crew found no sign of folk—nary a chopped tree nor a circle of stones to hint that men had ever walked here. The land was fertile and primal and deepest green, untilled, ungroomed, and as wild as the Gliding itself. But for one thing.

The black hill.

It was perfectly symmetrical, wider than it was tall, and taller by ten than a haystack. It looked, at a distance, like a miniature volcano, and its true curiosity was its covering. It was dressed all over in strange plumage: feathers, oil-black and overlapping as neat as fish scales. Far too large for crows, each plume was as long as a man's arm, and some said that only a bird as big as a man could have plumes so very long. Of course, no such bird existed, and because of that—and because of what was *inside* the hill, *under* the plumes—the sailors set fire to it.

And died.

It was the smoke, said the survivors. Oil-black as the feathers themselves, it . . . writhed.

It *hunted.*

The sailors who were upwind of the fire saw what it did, and ran for their ship.

Some of them made it.

It was a full twenty years before another ship came, and this one came ready, armed with God and shovels, and they didn't burn the feathers this time but buried them, and they built a church on the hill and filled it with saints' bones and imprecations against evil. They divvied the dark green land among themselves, taming the place with prayer as they shaped it with labor, and the long black feathers became a thing of myth. Children might play at "quicksmoke," chasing each other with burning crow feathers and acting out gruesome deaths, but the true accursed plumes had not been seen for near two centuries.

No one was afraid anymore, not really.

On this first morning of Advent, though, as the isle folk stirred awake and girls darted barefoot onto porches to find what was left for them, the isle stirred too. Only a little, and only Neve felt it. The old hill—long since defeathered—was a lonesome spot, far from any farms, and its bare stone church saw visitors but rarely. It would be Christmas day before the damage was discovered—the floor caved in, a pocket of deep, dark air opened underneath—and by then the events of this Advent would be done and known.

By then, everyone would know that the Dreamer had awakened.

In the harbor town, the folk were decorating. Swags of limp tinsel wove down both sides of the high street, and dames were up ladders, skirts tucked tween their knees as they stretched to hang up fishing floats and old baubles of scratched mirror glass. Every door wore a wreath and red ribbon, and hunchback Scoot Finster was making his way from shop to shop with stencils and a bucket, dabbing scenes onto glass with his own recipe of fake snow.

The harbor folk loved their Christmas, and it was no secret that they loved it like pagans. They wanted to dance and drink, put on their oversize saints' masks and caper about frightening babies. Unlike the First Settlers, who were of Charis stock and came into the world, so they said, with their hands folded in prayer, these latecomers were mostly descended from Jhessians, those sharp-eyed folk of old tongue and older gods, and they wore their civility as light as summer shawls. But life was hard here and the myths were dark, and the Church kept them proper, most days.

"Mornin', maidy," Scoot called to Neve as she passed him on her way to the factory. "Find ought on your porch this drizzle-blasted morning?"

His smile seemed genuine, so Neve guessed he didn't know. The fishwife behind him, though, sucked in one cheek to chew and looked caught between pity and envy, and that's how Neve knew the word was out.

She didn't answer. She couldn't very well lie and say no, but neither could she bring herself to admit it, at least not without making clear how she felt about it, which would simply not do. Girls were supposed to be happy that someone wanted them, as though they were kittens in a basket, and any left by day's end would be drowned in the pond.

Scoot misread her silence. "Well, maybe the ghosts of your boys haunted off all your suitors," he said kindly. "It's the only explanation, a sip of honey like you."

Neve murmured some response, though she couldn't have afterward said what. She cast down her eyes and kept going, glancing back at the turning of the lane to see the fishwife talking in the hunchback's ear, and him looking rueful after her, like she was a kitten already sinking beneath the water.

Was she?

No.

Because she was going to refuse.

"You're going to *what*?" demanded Keillegh Baker when Neve told her.

It was midmorning, and they were at their hoops in the longroom, needles busy. All down the row girls blushed and purred and crowed and gloated and wept and sulked, just as Neve had known they would. Irene had a length of lace from her sweetheart, Camilla a comb from hers. May's too-straight back told her tale of woe, while Daisy Darrow had gifts from three boys, and the delicious drama of a tussle on her porch, too, when they bumped into each other at midnight, all surly fists and mayhem.

"I thought Caleb would *kill* Harry," said Daisy, eyes shining with the thrill of it. "But then Davis broke a pot over his head. Oh, Mam was mad. It was her strawberry pot from Cayn."

Neve did not join in, but only whispered her news to Keillegh, the baker's daughter, who was the closest she had to a friend anymore, and not quite a friend at that. The thing about having friends who are as close as blood, as true as your own heart—as the twins had been to her—is you don't bother much with other people. And if you've the misfortune to get left behind, well, you've made yourself a lonely nest to sit in.

"I'm going to refuse him," Neve repeated.

Keillegh was shocked, and Neve in turn was shocked by her shock. "Do you really think I could say yes?" she asked, incredulous. "To *him*?"

"Yes, I think you could say yes! What else will you do? You're not still thinking of killing yourself at Fog Cup."

"Not killing myself, no."

"Not outright maybe. Just a slow death by mildew, if you don't starve first. Ilona Blackstripe lost the rest of her toes, did you know that? And have you ever seen sicklier babies?"

"Well, I won't be having babies, so it's not my main worry."

"No babies." Keillegh shook her head, fingering the little silver chain that was her gift from her own boy. "I'll never understand you, Neve. It's like you're another species. You had those two strapping boys out there and you never even kept warm with them, and you don't want babies either? What *do* you want, may I ask?"

What did Neve *want*? Oh, wings and a hatful of jewels, why not? Her own ship, with sails of spider silk. Her own *country,* with a castle in it and horses to ride and beehives in the trees, dripping honey. What use was wanting when a full belly was as remote as a hatful of jewels? And she did want babies, truth be told, but in the same way as she wanted wings: in a fairy-tale version of life, where they wouldn't look like those poor Blackstripe sicklings, and she wouldn't be digging tiny graves every couple of years and pretending life went on.

And what about love? Did she want that, too? It seemed an even wilder fairy wish than wings. "Nothing I can have," she replied, before the sparkle of senseless wanting could grow too bright.

Keillegh was blunt. "So take Spear and count your blessings. He may be a misery of a man, but his house is warm, and I happen to know he eats meat every week."

Meat every week. As though Neve would sell herself for that! The rumble of her tummy just then was happenstance—a result of forgetting breakfast in all her nerves that morning, not to mention that her hen had dried up, poor Potpie, destined soon to fulfill the promise of her name.

The reverend, Neve knew, had a dozen hens and a strutting rooster to rule them.

The reverend had *a cow.*

Butter, thought Neve. *Cheese.* "That's all lovely," she said, settling her grumblesome tummy with a firm press of her palm. "But there *is* the matter of that row of graves. How many wives should a man get to put in the ground before someone tells him to get a new hobby?"

"So suppose *you* put *him* in the ground."

"Keillegh!"

"What? I don't mean by murdering him. Only outlasting him. It has to be easier than Fog Cup."

Maybe so. Easier didn't mean better, though. Some kinds of misery make you hate the world, but some kinds make you hate yourself, and—butter and cheese notwithstanding—Neve had no question that Spear was the latter.

But what if... what if... there was some other future lying up ahead for her—one without any misery in it at all—and even now it was trailing its way backward in time to meet her, and take her hand, and show her how to find it? It was funny. In life as perpetrated against Neve, there were only bad surprises, never good, but as the day wore on, she had a fancy that the queer small wind of the morning—kidnapper of Bibles—was circling round to check on her. Sure she was imagining it, but it didn't feel like the usual longroom drafts. Those were errant shivers, chaotic, like little boys darting up to slip an icicle down your back.

This circling gust, this curious breeze... it wasn't even cold.

The Dreamer could not have said how long he'd slept. He opened his eyes from dream to darkness, and to stillness—stillness like death, but he was not dead. The air around him was, and the earth that wrapped around that was, too, and something was wrong. He should have felt the pulse of life in it, in soil and roots, and seen the memories pulled down through grass and seeping water and burrowing beast. It should have been a symphony of whispers in his chamber, echoing and glorious with life. But all was silent.

Except for the call.

The language was strange to him; the words were just sounds, but they pierced him with such an urgency that he sat up on his catafalque—too quickly. Head spinning, he slid to his knees, and he knew a moment of panic so profound that his shock painted the darkness white. Behind his eyelids, inside his head: trembling, blinding white.

Something was wrong.

He had slept too long. On his knees in the dead dark, he knew—he *knew*—that the world was dead and he had failed it. Above him, around him, the veins of the earth had ceased to pulse. If he emerged he would find a vast waste, the gray dead hull of a dried-up world.

His heart that had beat so slow for so long: now quickened. His lungs that had lain airless for time indeterminate now wanted to gasp. Asleep, the Dreamer could abide inside this hill of earth. Awake, he could not.

But he dreaded what he would find if he emerged. Failure and death and *ending*. He felt it. It oppressed him with a heaviness he had never known.

In the end, it was the call that gave him courage. It had pierced him awake, and now it drew him up. He didn't know the language, but this was a plea deeper than words, and his soul strained to answer it. Summoning all his strength, he burst upward. The hill should have opened for him like a flower, but it resisted. Something *weighed* on it. On him. He couldn't breathe. With a savage effort, he broke through.

And discovered that the world was not dead. He stumbled out into it, drunk with gratitude, blinded by even the dim winter sun, and fell to his knees in the grass. He sank long fingers in and felt the pulse and drank the memories, so many, so deep—how long? As his senses grew accustomed to the outside world, he saw and smelled many things that had not been here before.

The stone building that squatted on his hill, for one.

People, for another. When he had made ready his place of rest, humans had dwelt along the green coasts of southern lands, but these islands had been wild, the province of petrels and seals. Now he scented smoke on the wind, the warm odor of manure, the sharper reek of cesspits. The wildness had been broken.

Had *he*? What had they done to him, these folk?

They had stolen his feathers and smothered him under some blunt sorcery of their own. They had broken, for a time—how long?—his connection with the earth.

But . . .

He turned in a new direction. There stood a fringe of trees so green they looked black in the soft light, but beyond them, rolling away, where once had been forest, now all was plucked, carved into corners, scraped into furrows. Wisps of hearth smoke rose at intervals, and the Dreamer sensed the coursing of many lives. But one most brightly.

The one who had awakened him.

T wo things, at the end of the day, in case Neve hadn't made up her mind.

First, Dame Somnolence held her back when the other girls left. "Here," she said, thrusting a flower at Neve. "In case you don't already have one."

Fumbling to take it, Neve saw that it was dead. She looked up, right in the old woman's globe-round eyes—too large, too unveiled, the lids never quite seeming up to their job.

"You think I should refuse him, then," she said.

Dame Somnolence gave a snort. "I think he's due a nice long tour of that Hell he loves to preach about, that's what I think. Or maybe he's been there already, to know so much about it. Take this, Crow Food. Put it on your porch. There's not a bird in the world that would eat his brides. You think you know bitter now? You'll taste like ash before he drops you in a grave."

Neve already had a dead flower. She tried to return the dame's, but she wouldn't have it. "Take it," she said. "I killed it special for whoever got his gift."

And so Neve did take it, and she was glad to have it when she found the man himself waiting for her just outside of town.

This was the second thing.

He smiled when he saw her coming. His teeth were so white and square they looked chiseled out of walrus ivory. "Good evening, Neve," he said. This was a liberty. He ought to have called her Miss Ellaquin.

"Sir," was all she managed, and it was the best she could do to keep her feet moving forward.

Right past him.

He fell into step beside her. "I hope you liked the Bible," he said. "Which passage did you read first? I always like to know."

As though she'd sat down on the spot, keen to know more of the Lord's rules and punishments? "I didn't read any," she replied. "The wind carried it off before I even stepped onto the porch."

Between them, silence twisted, and Neve did not look up to see his eyes with their painted-dot pupils. His shadow, cast ahead, was so much larger than her own. "Excuse me?" he finally said, as though he might have misunderstood her.

"The wind," she repeated. "I'm sorry. The Bible's gone."

He stopped walking, and when she did not stop with him, he reached for her arm and made her. His big fingers splayed from her elbow to her shoulder, and his grip was not gentle. "That was a family heirloom," he said, and she had no choice but to look at his eyes now. Glassy, she thought, and imagined flames reflecting in them as he scouted the geographies of Hell. "It was precious to me."

"Then maybe you shouldn't have left it on a porch," she said, trying to pull her arm free. "It wasn't my doing."

When he still didn't release her, she panicked and thrust Dame Somnolence's flower at him. A rose, and red, it made a more striking display than her dainty thorn lily would have. "Here," she said, voice shaking. "You honor me, but I don't mean to marry. My answer is no."

He didn't take the flower, and he didn't let go of her arm, and when Neve met his eyes again, growing more panicked by the second, his look spoke. Some looks do, the way she remembered her mother's eyes telling her as plain as happiness, in the time before grief, "I love you more than life, my sweet girl." Or how Ivan's dying eyes had said his greatest desperation was in leaving her alone.

Spear's look was eloquent. "I will have you, and I will hold you. I will learn a thousand ways to make you weep. Your tears will be the sugar in my tea, your misery my delight," he promised, while his lips said, "I wasn't asking, Neve. I've made my choice." His fist closed on the dry-dead rose and ground it to a dark red dust.

He finally released her arm, and his parting words, before he turned back toward town, were, "When I greet you tomorrow I expect a smile. A blush if you can manage it."

Neve walked home stumbling-fast, the mud sucking at her boots. Coming into the yard, she spotted Spear's bootprints among the usual fox tracks, and saw with fresh eyes what a poor sanctuary was this row of shanties. In her shed, she was like a nut meat to cracking teeth. Spear could eat her for breakfast if he wanted. Worse, he could have her for a midnight snack.

This midnight. Any midnight. Who would come if she screamed?

She shivered and barred her meager door. She built a meager fire and cooked a meager meal. Her ears were tuned to the night outside, but she only heard the rain. There was nothing for her fretting but to get out her book, her treasure, her one thing from home: true home, long lost, the Failed Colony. It had had a real name, once, but all those decades of striving and living and building and planting and loving had been reduced in a single season to that wretched word: *failed*.

The book had eighteen stories in it, and when she read them—aloud, always—it was with her mother's cadence, which was imprinted on her heart. She turned to the one that suited this night: a maiden, pursued by an ogre, transforms herself into a doe rather than become his wife. Her eyes were tired from a long day squinting at stitches, so she let them flutter shut. But she knew the story by heart and it kept going, into the woods on fleet deer feet and down a mossy slope.

And all of a sudden she was in Nasty Gully. She knew she was dreaming, because her book had nothing to do with Nasty Gully. The spring beetles were there, all glint and shimmer in the ferny half light, but they weren't flying at her face. They weren't flying at all. They were motionless in their hundreds, and when Neve stepped in close, she saw that they were jewels. They were beetles made of jewels, and when she took one up it was a ring for her finger. Another, it was a brooch. The gully was quiet and the light was soft, and she sensed that she was not alone.

"Hello?" she whispered, and woke in her chair, no sound besides rain and the pop of the dying fire, but a whisper seemed to follow her out of sleep. It wasn't that she heard it so much as felt it.

It felt like a breeze through a forests' worth of leaves.

"I will free you, and I will lift you. I will learn a thousand ways to make you laugh. Your smiles will be the honey in my mead, your enchantment my delight."

And in her shed by the dying fire, Neve sensed, as she had in the dream, that she was not alone. But it wasn't a lurking feeling, as a figure in the night. It was the sense that she wasn't alone in the world, and that was a very different thing.

She slept. She dreamed. There was music such as she had never heard, and singing in a language as far from her own as the spitting rain was from the roar of the sea. Dancing, too. A hand held hers, and she couldn't see whose it was but only felt herself spinning spinning spinning, safe in a circle made by strong, dark arms.

But in the morning, the yard held a fresh set of preacher tracks and another gift on the porch—a framed miniature of the man's own smug face—so Neve knew it had been all and only dreams, all and only her own fool hopes, coaxed up out of hiding and tricked into dancing, dancing all alone.

"Stupid," she whispered, and gave the portrait a nudge with her toe. She wanted to kick it out into the mud but didn't dare. Tricked by a dream into hoping, and hoping for what, dancing and a pair of strong arms? "Stupid," she said again, with more venom. You'd think she was new to despair and just learning its tricks. She stumped into her boots and made for the hen house. The axe was in the chopping block, and she thought maybe today she'd do it. What good is a hen that won't lay?

About as much good as a girl who won't marry, said a voice inside her, and she roused Potpie, who gave a sleepy blink. "What do you say, old girl? Did you make me any breakfast today?"

There would be no egg. Neve knew it. It was pathetic that she still checked—proof that hope had its hooks in her, whatever she might think—

She let out a chuff of surprise. There *was* an egg. "Well done, you," she said to Potpie, unreasonably pleased for such a small thing as an egg. She reached for it. Took it. She picked it up and held it and knew that it was not an egg.

It looked like an egg.

But it wasn't an egg.

An egg feels like nothing but what it is. This was too light. It was air and shell and something, but that something was not yolk and fluid, and Neve should have wanted to drop it—not even *wanted* to but just done it instantly, instinctively, as a reaction to a wrongness. But she didn't drop it. She did not, in fact, sense a wrongness. She held the egg, and it was warm and smooth, and it fit her palm like a rightness.

Breakfast forgotten for the second day running, she carried it back across the yard, and once she was inside she looked at it some more and weighed it gently, hand to hand. Something shifted in it when she moved it, and she wondered what to do. She could leave it as it was, intact. But eggs aren't meant to remain intact, are they? They're meant to open. To disclose.

So she cracked it, gingerly, and the sound it made knocking at the rim of her old clay bowl was like a note of music. The eggshell split and opened and the something inside it . . . sparkled. Neve spilled it into the cup of her palm and couldn't believe her eyes.

It was a beetle.

From her dream of Nasty Gully. Here was one of the jewel beetles, and it had a diamond for a body—as big as her thumbnail, and as dazzling as a star encased in crystal—and two half moons of milky jade for wings. They were set on cunning hinges and opened at her touch, and its head was an emerald with cabochon eyes of some stone she couldn't name, soft pearl pink and flecked with gold. Like in her dream, it was set on a ring and fit her finger just right, as though faeries had measured her for it in her sleep.

At first there was only wonderment, her staring at it and opening and shutting its jade wings in slow, astonished delight. Then the questions crept in.

How?

And, of course . . . *who*?

So the world was not dead, but it was so altered as to seem a new place—and not a better one. It was dirtier, paler, tarnished with sadness, and the Dreamer felt himself lost in it. He still didn't know how much time had passed, but he understood that it was *too* much.

That the Dreamers had, by their absence . . . forfeited.

But how had it come to pass? Where were the others, and why had none of his brothers or sisters come to wake him? Did they sleep too, in their own far-flung hills? Had their feathers been stolen as his had, their wits and senses dulled? He would have to find them and draw them out of the earth, but first, something bound him here.

Some*one* bound him.

She had asked for his protection. No. She had done more than that. She had *summoned* him, even through the barriers of the colorless, choking sorcery that had held him in its stupor. He owed her for that. When he went to find her, it was to settle a debt.

And then he saw her.

He saw her, and the clamors and stinks of this new world fell away, as murmurs overcome by a bright surge of song. He saw her on her lonesome road, her brightness ill-concealed by the dun disguise of such dull clothes, her grace scarcely hindered by the mud-caked weight of boots, and his panic died away. His was the panic, you understand, of one who has overslept and is late for work . . . when the work in question is the making and keeping of the world. It would return, and all the world-clamor with it, but for now, it was silenced by the sight of a girl.

She was so alone, so brave and so afraid, and so beautiful. His heart—that had beat with the earth's slowest pull since it first tested its turning—slipped into a new register, as sweet to his blood as birdsong to his ears, and it liked it there.

She was not his subject. He had conjured green in its every varia-tion and carried it with him out of dreams. He had given storms to the world, and riverbanks, and bees. But the shape of this girl, the fierce gloss of her eyes, and the layers and treasures of soul and mind that were in her to discover, that was none of his doing. The Dreamers were the gods of all things *but* mankind. All the rest they had made, but not these striving things, that had made themselves.

For better or worse.

He was the god of tide-lap and wingbeat, talon and pearl. She was the goddess of . . . *herself.* And he could not look away from her.

Neve went through all the paces of an ordinary day: the walk to and through town, the row of girls at their hoops, and tiny stitches on an altar cloth for some far-off cathedral she couldn't even imagine. Nothing was different, but *something was different.* She had put Spear's miniature into a pocket of her apron, and the jewel beetle into another. Into one pocket—can you guess which?—her hand slipped again and again, and, each time, her cheeks flushed with the confirmation that she hadn't dreamed the first good surprise to ever come her way.

She tried to stop herself from wondering what it meant, to take it like a story from her book, where logic could find no firm footing. It wasn't easy.

Who?

All day long, that one word lurked behind every other that she spoke, and when she wasn't speaking—which was most of the time—she was wondering, dreamily, *Who?*

"Well?" Dame Somnolence wanted to know. "Did you give him the flower?"

Neve nodded. "He ground it in his fist and came again last night." She took out the miniature and let it dangle from its chain.

Seeing that she was not distraught, the old woman misunderstood the reason. "Well, won't the coffin maker be pleased," she sniffed, her big, doleful eyes going narrow with the affront of advice ignored. "Don't say I didn't warn you."

Neve didn't try to explain. What could she say? That she'd called for protection and been answered? When she even dared to think it, she saw how preposterous it sounded, doubted it all anew, and had to slip her hand into her pocket and cup the beetle in her palm.

She was so preoccupied that when, walking home that evening, she passed Reverend Spear on the high street, she unthinkingly did as he had bid her the day before. Half of it anyway.

She smiled.

Oh, the smile wasn't for him. It was on her face already when she chanced to turn his way—it was slight, and quizzical, and dreamy, but certainly a smile—and with difficulty she kept it from sliding off. She didn't blush, as requested, but the smile seemed to suffice. He stood in a company of men—leering, knowing looks from all of them—and didn't stop her but only nodded, gentlemanly, though his eyes burned at her, hot with something that was not anger. That was worse than anger.

Never mind. It was best not to draw his ire.

I'm not for you, Neve thought. She had twenty-three days till the Christmas Eve gather, and the understanding had come to her slowly through her wonder that the beetle in her pocket—worth such a fortune, she didn't doubt, as had never been seen on this island before—meant her freedom from both Spear and Fog Cup, even if it meant nothing else. She could take ship any time she wanted and set sail toward any life she wished, and that was a reason for smiling, certainly, but it wasn't the best reason.

Someone had given it to her. Someone was out there. She felt him. *I will free you, and I will lift you.* Those were his words from her dream. He had freed her already.

What now?

What now?

A chain of mornings, and the Dreamer made the world anew, in miniature, for her. On the third morning he gave her a bottle that held every birdsong in the world. Each time it was opened, a new one floated out, and her favorites could be called upon at will.

A spider next, that would weave her wonders: gloves of gossamer enchanted against chill, and such lace as human craft could never equal.

On the fifth morning it was flowers. That is to say, she opened her door to find her mud yard in bloom: an impossible winter garden, blossoms from all the world's array. His favorites were here, dreamed in another age and so extravagant and improbable that beside the isle's hardy vegetation, they were like dragons among donkeys.

It thrilled him to see her wade through them, vivid with delight and lost to her waist in a bay of color, dressed half in petals over her usual drab. She cut a bucketful of stems and took them in to brighten her poor room, and so the next day he gave her a tapestry to hang: a scene in vibrant colors that would change day by day, and show the world to her in glimpses.

On the seventh day—it shamed him to the roots of his teeth that it took him so long to think of it—he gave her food to eat.

She was hungry. This bright and wondrous girl. The Dreamer had no words for his dismay.

He made her a basket that replenished itself whenever its lid was unlatched, and which yielded something new each time. Like the jar of birdsong, her favorites could be called upon, and within a few days she *had* favorites—a luxury she'd all but forgotten.

And every day that passed, he found it harder to keep a distance between them, but he did keep it, and watched as wonder brought new light to her face. Her eyes had been brilliant the first time he saw her, but that had been the sheen of unshed tears.

This was happiness.

She spoke to him—from the porch, or on her walks to and from town, as though she knew he could hear her. Soft *thank-yous* at first, and then words strung together, her shyness wearing off until, a few days in, it was natural to her to speak to the air, to the wind that escorted her, warmer than the isle's salt breezes.

As the Dreamer's heartbeat had slipped into its new rhythm, so did he slip into this ritual of courting. What did he know of humans? Here was time to learn: twenty-four days until the cycle came to its end, and what then? He had decided. He would stand before Neve and hold out his hand, in the way of her people, for all to see.

So would the other man, who walked in such arrogance and pride that he didn't guess he wasn't Neve's only suitor—let alone that her other suitor was a god.

The Dreamer watched him come each night and leave his dry and useful tokens on her porch. A wooden spoon, a bottlebrush, an apron of sturdy gray. He watched him pause, every time, and stand in the yard, staring at the door as though he could see through it.

Considering. Considering.

Considering too long before finally going away. On the eighteenth night, it was raining hard, and the Dreamer watched him stand in the downpour, jaw clenched and water coursing down his face as he struggled with himself . . . and lost. He turned his head slowly, first one way and then the other. To be certain he was alone before he stepped onto the porch.

He was not alone.

He didn't reach the door.

The Dreamer didn't kill him, though it would have been so terribly easy. Fragile flesh, fragile spirit. *Where is your god now? Will he come to protect you, or is that not his way? Does he only appear when it's time to punish, or is it simply that that's when you summon him?*

He contented himself with spinning the reverend toward home and planting a fear in his gut like a canker: from this day on, whenever he sought to master a woman, whether by threat or strength or even with a look, the fear would flare and overtake him—so wild and sudden it would drop him to his knees to cower in terror, gibbering for solace from his distant, punishing god.

One supposed his life would be quite different now, and his parishioners', too.

And then it was the Dreamer's turn to stare at Neve's door, rain coursing down his face, the feel of her radiating outward as though she were a sun and he a flower. He understood temptation, but not the weakness that would succumb to it. He turned his back to the shed and stayed there through the night, standing guard in the rain, which, though it was his own creation, he'd never felt in quite this way before.

Six more days, he thought, and wondered what Neve would make of his final Advent gift to her.

And wondered, with a frisson of nerves, what she would make of *him*.

Scarman's Hall was the grandest structure on the Isle of Feathers, and never grander than on Christmas Eve. The gather was the social event of the year, and the betrothals were its heart. Every marriageable girl had been planning her gown for months, and every suitor his final gift: a ring.

Neve had a ring already. It had been her first gift from the Dreamer—the jewel beetle—and she'd carried it in her pocket ever since.

Tonight she would wear it on her finger.

She would also wear the dress she'd made of fabric he had given her. It was blue as the sky and as cunning as all his gifts: it wasn't one blue but *every* blue—all the hours and moods of the sky. From minute to minute, it changed its hue, deepening from cobalt to midnight and setting out stars. And when she smiled—she discovered, looking at herself in the mirror that had also been a gift—it flushed to sunset orange, as bright as flame.

Imagine: the last of the plague orphans turning up at the gather in such a gown! It was like the story from Neve's book, about the cinder maid and the fairy godmother. She didn't have a pumpkin coach, though, or slippers made of glass—only of spider silk, with a sheen like dew on a petal—but she had her old cloak and boots for the long walk, and when had she ever had qualms about mud on her hem?

She looked in the mirror and wondered if it were true or enchanted. How could she know if this was herself reflected or some dream version. Did it matter? She smiled, and watched her dress again flame from midnight to sunset. Her heart felt like an ember in her chest, ready to catch fire and throw sparks.

What would happen tonight? She didn't know. Spear's hand would never hold hers. She knew that much, and Fog Cup would never be her home. A mere twenty-four days ago, those had been her only two choices. Now miracles were her daily fare and her pulse still beat its one simple question: *Who?*

She understood that he was the Dreamer, whom she'd called upon in her despair. But how could she know what that meant? What was he? She'd felt his presence in her dreams but had never seen him, and he didn't leave tracks in her yard as the reverend did (or as the reverend *had,* anyway, until six nights ago, when his gifts abruptly ceased).

Once, she'd dreamed she embraced a hill of black feathers and felt the pulse of a heartbeat deep within.

And then last night, a miracle unlooked for: she'd opened her book to read a story and found in it not the eighteen that there had always been, but nineteen, and the last was called "The Dreamers."

He was one of ten, born before time, who had, through the millennia, taken it in turn to sleep, and dream. It was they who conducted the symphonies of growth and death that turned the world. They were gods from before there were men to invent the word *god,* and they cared nothing for worship or thanks. Only for the act itself: creating.

Sometimes destroying.

And so she knew who he was, but not what form he might take. There had been no illustration to accompany the tale, and no description, either. It didn't matter; by now she loved him in any skin. In her book there was another tale—one of the original eighteen—of a dragon who had a human wife, and Neve had never understood it before, at least from the wife's point of view. But she did now. Love was love.

But she hoped that he was not a dragon.

She stepped onto her porch, ready to walk to town, and found there was a creature in her yard.

It gave her a start, considering her train of thought, but then she had to laugh at herself, because this was only a mount to carry her. It was a buck, a splendid beast, all white, its antlers festooned with ribbons, and its tack and bridle glittering silver. It dropped a knee for her to mount, and Neve laughed again at the wonder of it. Would she become numb to wonder, if this kept up, as she once had been to misery?

Never.

She rode and it was like gliding, down the long sodden lane from

Graveyard Farm into town. Either the drizzle stopped or an unseen bubble curved above her, but not a drop fell on her the whole way. The beast carried her to Scarman's Hall, right up the broad stone steps to deliver her to the door, and it was as though the scene froze around her and became a painting, and she the only moving figure in it.

As many candles flickered in the hall's hoisted lanterns on this one night as had burned in all the previous six months together. Mist diffused the light to haloes, overlapping by their dozens, and the pangs of a solitary cello wove among them, sweet and pure.

Neve dismounted. Everyone else just stood and stared. There was Keillegh Baker and her boy, both agog, and Bill Childbreaker, ill at ease in his cheap Sunday suit. There was a gaggle of First Settlement girls in matching crowns of holly berries—their shock held no wonder, only envy—and Dame Somnolence, whose eyes had never looked larger or less doom-struck.

And then there was Reverend Spear, as motionless as all the rest. He stared and stared, Neve's splendor diminishing his own. He seemed to shrink before her eyes like a shadow at the rising of the sun.

Neve faced them all and smiled, and beheld the deepening ripple of their shock when her dress flushed from blue to flame, and when she walked past them, she felt like she was floating.

Maybe she was. Nothing seemed impossible now.

The corridor was wide, its ceiling vaulted high, and at the end of it, the ballroom glowed with a light too bright for lanterns.

He was already there. She felt it even before she heard the singing— the language of her dreams, wind through a forests' worth of leaves— and she knew that the isle folk were crowding behind her as she drifted; she felt them, too, but with nothing like the pulse of radiance that drew her onward. They were the past, already receding.

In her spider-silk slippers, she came into the ballroom.

And there he was.

The senses have their limits, and we can never know how short they fall in revealing to us the truth of a vision, a scent, a sound. Gazing on the Dreamer, Neve felt herself career into the boundary of her human limitations . . . and push past it. The others were left behind. They saw him too, but only a mirage of him.

Perhaps they saw a man.

He was not a man. Had she really thought he would be?

She had never been able to imagine him, but when she'd pictured this moment, Neve had thought she would go to him, that he would hold out his hand and she would take it. But how could she go to him when he did not stand on the ground?

He drifted above their heads, up amid the glittering bowers of paper snowflakes, precious glass icicles, and lanterns whose copper chains swayed with the draft of his wingbeats. The Dreamer had wings.

Of course he did.

He had found his black feathers, wherever they'd been buried, and they were as glossy now as they had been the day ages past when he shook them off to lay down to his dreaming. His hair was black, and wasn't hair . . . not only. In one glimpse it was pelt, the next feathers, the next the bright obsidian of scales, and then again the long luxuriance of new-spun silk. He was dragon and bird and wolf and orchid and lightning bolt—and he was man, too. A thousand facets, he was like a jewel of infinite dimensions.

The facet he turned toward the gathering crowd was human, and so that was how Neve perceived him . . . mostly. He was darker than any person she had ever seen, his skin a deep umber, so rich with hue that the shadows cut by the planes of his face read as color to her artist's eyes, too: indigos and violets, shades she associated with rarity and riches, because the dyes were so precious that only the best of embroiderers were allowed near those threads. His eyes weren't color, though; they were black, in the way the sea is black under starlight, and she beheld the form and limbs of a man—though not clad and hidden as was "decent" and "proper" to human society as she knew it. She saw his body. His chest. The dip where muscles met to form a smooth channel to his navel.

His navel.

Looking up at the Dreamer, her head tilted back and every nerve alive, Neve became aware of her hands. The whole surface of them from palm to fingertips began to tingle, petitioning to discover the texture of those dark contours. This was a new sensation, and her lips were not immune to it.

Nor the tip of her tongue.

I wonder what his skin tastes like.

Neve's face grew hot. She had woken the Dreamer, and now it was her turn to wake. It was like hatching out of a small, dark life into a great, unfathomable one, and the man before her, the god before her—above her, adrift in a sphere of his own radiance—was waiting to take her hand.

But how could she reach him?

She needn't have worried. No sooner did she lift her own hand toward him than the rest of her began to rise—

I will lift you . . .

—and . . . to change. Her honeysuckle hair came unpinned, transforming, as it tumbled free, to a sheath of pale yellow feathers. For an instant, this concealed her other transformation, but only for an instant, because wings such as these could not be hidden.

A god of the old world took a girl into his arms, and she was no longer a girl. She was still herself, still flesh and blood, and still lovely—eye-bright, slender, smiling—but Neve was no longer human, not quite, and she was no longer bound to the earth. She beheld the sweep of her own new wings—the same pale yellow as her hair—and remembered when wanting had seemed futile. She reached for him.

Her hand, his hand—finally. The Dreamer drew Neve close and whispered his true name in her ear. Mystery flowed into her like music. The paper snowflakes detached themselves from the ceiling of Scarman's Hall, and by the time they fluttered down to the upheld hands of the isle folk, they weren't paper anymore.

All evening long, real snow would fall from the ceiling to glitter on the lashes of dancing girls and ardent boys, but Neve and the Dreamer didn't linger.

They had other things to do: *all* of them. All the things, dreamed and undreamed, in the depth and breadth of the whole spinning world.

Amen.